Raves for

THE BLUMHOUSE BOOK OF NIGHTMARES
The Haunted City

"Jason Blum has done it again with this collection of start-lingly imaginative and remarkably potent tales. Anyone who loves a brilliant story—scary or otherwise—should read this book."　　　　　—Ryan Murphy, co-creator of
American Horror Story

"Like the best horror movies, these stories begin in the real world, then slyly move you to a darker place, a nightmare world just beyond our reality. I enjoyed my visit to *The Haunted City*—but I am still shivering."
　　　　　　　　　　　　　　—R.L. Stine, author of
Goosebumps and *Fear Street*

"I found myself double-checking that my door was locked. This anthology is a compelling reminder that it does not take anything but a good story to terrify."
　　　　　　　—M. Night Shyamalan, writer and director of
The Sixth Sense and *Unbreakable*

"Great horror storytelling. Jason Blum has assembled the top twisted talents for this anthology."
　　　　　　　　　—James Wan, director of *Insidious*,
The Conjuring, and *Furious 7*

THE
BLUMHOUSE BOOK
OF NIGHTMARES

The Haunted City

THE
BLUMHOUSE BOOK
OF NIGHTMARES

The Haunted City

PRESENTED BY

JASON BLUM

BLUMHOUSE BOOKS | A DIVISION OF BLUMHOUSE PRODUCTIONS, LLC
VINTAGE BOOKS | A DIVISION OF PENGUIN RANDOM HOUSE LLC
New York

BLUM HOUSE
BOOKS

A BLUMHOUSE BOOKS / VINTAGE BOOKS ORIGINAL, JULY 2015

The Library of Congress has cataloged the Doubleday edition as follows:
The Blumhouse book of nightmares : the haunted city / presented by Jason Blum.
pages cm
1. Horror tales, American.   2. Fantasy fiction, American.
3. American fiction—21st century.   4. Cities and towns—Fiction.
I. Blum, Jason, editor.
PS648.H6B65 2015   813'.0873808—dc23   2015015090

Vintage Books Trade Paperback ISBN: 978-1-101-87391-5
eBook ISBN: 978-0-385-54000-1

Book design by Michael Collica

www.vintagebooks.com

Printed in the United States of America
10 9 8 7 6 5 4 3 2 1

Contents

Preface

There is an old saying in Hollywood: Those who can't write or direct, produce. Hence, producer Jason Blum. I knew at an early age that I wanted to work in the movie business, but writing and directing are not my thing. So I learned how to support writers and directors by building the right environment in which they can thrive. That is what we try to do at Blumhouse in film, television, and now books.

Whenever I am meeting with a new filmmaker, I always say the same thing: "I can't promise you a hit movie, but I can promise you that it will be *your* movie." At Blumhouse we call it relinquishing creative control.

To ensure directors get that freedom, we keep the budgets low. Sometimes, those compromises can be frustrating. But oftentimes, they inspire ingenuity and creativity, as when James Wan created a ghoul merely by putting a gas mask on a puppet in *Insidious*. Or when Scott Derrickson had a ghost in a paused video turn his head ever so slightly in *Sinister*. Or when Oren Peli attached a harness to Katie Featherstone and yanked her out of bed in *Paranormal Activity*.

In Hollywood people who make horror movies are outsiders. We operate, to a large degree, outside the traditional system. As a result, an incredible community has grown, filled with some of the most talented storytellers around. We all know one another and we all help one another out. We want one another to succeed simply for the love of all things scary.

This incredible sense of community is what we wanted to replicate and build on in the anthology you now hold in your hands. Growing up, I read all the classic horror stories and later many of the great horror novels. My current scary-reading obsession is true crime. So it was a thrill to fulfill a longtime dream and invite some of today's most powerful storytellers to contribute to *The Blumhouse Book of Nightmares: The Haunted City*.

They were given only two guidelines—let it take place in a city and enjoy no other creative constraints whatsoever. When I first started approaching the creators, I joked that this is the first project I've done where they didn't have to worry about going over budget. They could write as big or as small as they liked. And that is what they did.

I hope you enjoy their work as much as I have. But you just might want to avoid doing that at bedtime. They say movies are the shared dreams of the audience—that's why they have to be experienced in the dark. Well, when you turn off the light, these stories may cause nightmares. And there'll be no one with you in the audience to share it.

Sleep tight,
Jason Blum

THE
BLUMHOUSE BOOK
OF NIGHTMARES

The Haunted City

Hellhole

CHRISTOPHER DENHAM

"One point three million for a one-bedroom?"

Sam and Martha Rathbone stood still in the vacant apartment. As if any sudden movement would further reduce the square footage. "That's just the asking price," the Broker said. "Two bids came in at one point eight. Cash."

"It's one bedroom," Sam said. "And there are three of us. Three people."

"Technically, two people," the Broker said. "One child."

"Technically, the child is a person."

"A small person."

Martha said, "I think our son needs his own room."

Sam checked the stairwell, where their six-year-old son, Max, was coloring in his coloring book. Max made a funny face at his dad. Sam made the face back. It was their face.

"Everybody wants to be in Brooklyn," said the Broker. "At your price point, Williamsburg is out of the question. Williamsburg is for Alexander Wang models. Greenpoint is for trust funders. Carroll Gardens is colonized by shortlisted novelists. And Bushwick has been bought up by boys in bands. At your price point, you're going to have to go off the grid."

"Can you please stop saying 'price point'?" Sam turned to his wife. "Maybe we should just stay in Manhattan. Keep renting."

"Renting is just throwing our money away," Martha told him. "It's time to leave the Lower East Side. It's time to buy. Before the interest rates balloon. Everybody's buying."

"How can anybody afford this?"

The Broker broke up the domestic disturbance: "Brooklyn does go beyond the first three stops on the L train. Do you want to be followers? Or do you want to be pioneers? Stake your claim in terra incognita. This isn't just real estate, folks. This is manifest destiny."

"It's our destiny to raise our son in a studio," said Sam. "You've showed us ten places and every place is totally undersized and totally overpriced."

"Well," said the Broker, "I do have *one* more place to show you."

They shared a cab from Williamsburg. Sam, Martha, and Max in the backseat and the Broker up front. Looking out the window, Sam watched the pageant of epicene hipsters in genitally challenging pants drinking forties up and down Bedford Avenue. Sam and Martha used to spend more time in Brooklyn. Back when they used to get tattoos. Back when Sam used to have gallery shows and drink his weight (160 pounds) in foam Budweisers at Rosemary's Tavern. The drinking days were done. The days of skateboarding across the BQE with seven cans of Molotow and spray-painting rubyliths across the viaduct, pretending to be some gutterpunk Basquiat. Pretending he didn't have a BFA in painting from RISD. Sam didn't do street art. Not anymore. He repaired furniture. He refurbished divans. Hell, they had bills to pay. They had a child. And they were about to have a mortgage.

"Dad?" Max asked. "Where's that flag from?"

Max pointed at the faded blue, yellow, and red flag decal adhered to the taxi's Plexiglas partition. Sam said, "I don't know, Mad Max. I sucked at flags in school."

Martha said, "Honey, why don't you ask the driver?"

The taxi driver had a cleft-palate scar on his upper lip and was listening to very loud, very foreign music. The music, Sam thought, sounded weirdly pastoral. Incessant tambourine. Russian? Belarusian? Gypsy music.

Max asked for Martha's cell phone and googled national flags and found, on Wikipedia, the corresponding ensign that matched the peeling decal. "Romania," said Max. "The driver is from Romania." Max opened Google Translate. It was his favorite app and he would spend hours translating random languages. Sam and Martha thought it was a better heuristic hobby than all those books about boy witches. Max typed in a few words and an automaton voice translated into Romanian: *"Numele meu este Max! Sunt vechi de șase ani!"* (My name is Max! I'm six years old!) The driver spewed out a spate of foreign declamations and fist-bumped Max: *"Baiat bun!! Baiat bun!!"*

From the front seat, the Broker turned and said, "Welcome to your new neighborhood."

Crown Heights was not a neighborhood they had considered. Too dangerous. Too far for Martha's daily commute to Manhattan, where, as an advocacy lawyer, she made no profit working for a nonprofit. Sam, Martha, and Max bundled up against the winter wind and followed the Broker across Nostrand Avenue, whose concrete median segregated the Hasids on one side and the Caribbeans on the other. Kosher bakeries. Check-cashing joints. Family Dollar. "Trust me," said the Broker, "Crown Heights is a diamond in the rough. It's where everybody who is anybody will be in two years."

Just off Franklin Avenue, they passed a sketchy windowless bar/social club from which a man in a tracksuit emerged and mumbled Eastern bloc obscenities about Martha's ass.

"It's not exactly SoHo," said the Broker, "but there are plenty of places to eat and drink."

"My dad doesn't drink," Max told the Broker. "My dad went to rehab."

"Okay, Max," Sam said, taking his son's hand. "Thank you for sharing."

Sam locked eyes with the West Indian employees inside a bodega. They sold blunts and pirated DVDs. And, judging by their derisive faces, the locals didn't just see Sam and Martha as speculative homeowners. They saw Pilgrims on the shore proffering smallpox blankets, the harbingers of an impending invasion of craft beer and artisanal cheese.

The Broker also attracted his share of sideways glances at his coiffed fauxhawk, skinny tie, and androgynous gait. Impervious, he led the charge past the parkway, past Empire Boulevard, and down Midwood Street, a residential side street flanked by ill-maintained, boarded-up, turn-of-the-century row houses. "You'll notice the gabled roofs. Casement windows. Transoms. All the original mullions."

Martha said, "I bet this block used to be beautiful."

"Yeah," Sam muttered. "When it was built in the last century. Now it's just crack dens."

"What's a crack den, Dad?"

"It's a place where plumbers live and you see their butt cracks all the time."

"Are you ready?" said the Broker. "This is the place."

They stopped outside 223 Midwood. A decrepit brownstone. Sagging gutters. Graffiti sprayed across the plywood in the windows. A FORECLOSED sign staked into the moribund grass. Martha said, "It looks like it's seen better days."

"It looks like a monster, Mom."

The Broker unlocked a chain lock, pushed aside the plywood, and led them inside. Sam was stunned at the state of disrepair. The banisters were barely held in place by loose spindles. The high ceilings had water damage, wreaking havoc on the plaster moldings. Sam had his doubts about the structural integrity of the vaulted hallways. The bathrooms were shellacked with rust.

"You'll notice the fireplace," said the Broker.

Sam unlatched the flue and the fireplace rumbled an inchoate epithet.

"Santa might get killed coming down this."

Martha, on the other hand, saw potential in the mahogany floors. The dust-covered cast-iron stove. She fell in love at first sight with the copper claw-foot bathtub. She saw children's names and heights sketched onto the door frame: ciprian 4'11". dragos 5'7". rodica 5'4". This house had a history. This house had been a home. A place where a family lives. A place Martha, raised by a single mother in a series of single-bedroom apartments, had never had.

"Built in 1946," the Broker said. "Can't you just feel the history?"

"I can smell the asbestos," Sam said.

Martha asked, "Who used to live here?"

"It was a foreclosure, so it wasn't disclosed," the Broker said. "It's a great bargain."

"It's definitely a fixer-upper," Martha replied, "but my husband definitely loves power tools."

"That's right," the Broker said. "Remind me, Mr. Rathbone; you build stools or something?"

"Furniture. Not stools exclusively. But this might be a little above my pay grade."

"My mom makes more money than my dad," Max told the Broker.

"Thank you for sharing, Max."

The Broker led them into the dark basement.

"This is huge!" Martha gushed. "It's totally perfect for your studio, Sam."

"It's totally unfinished," Sam said. "We'd need to insulate. Plus, I bet we'll be sinking money into a sump pump. This place would need a lot of work."

"This place has a lot of potential," Martha said. "Did you see that claw-foot bathtub?"

"Do you hear that furnace? The radiant coils are rusted."

The Broker said, "For the square footage, you're not going to get anything close to this at your price point."

"What's the list price?"

"Two hundred and twenty-five thousand dollars," said the Broker. "It's a steal. I have ten other clients seeing this house. Someone will be buying it today. It should be *you*. C'mon, Max, I'll show you the backyard. You have a dog, right?"

The Broker led Max upstairs, leaving Sam and Martha alone in the basement.

"I think this might be it," Martha said.

"Uh. I think it's a *hellhole*," Sam said. "It's a money pit."

"It's the best our money can buy," Martha said. "It's exactly what we need. It's not just a place to live, Sam. It's a new start."

He knew she was right. She deserved a clean break. He *owed* it to her. To Max. After all the shit he had put them through. After what he had done. What he could not undo. "This will be a lot of labor," he said. "Like some Bob Vila–type shit."

"Bob Vila gets me hot and bothered," Martha said, kissing Sam. "I like men who know how to use their hands. All that elbow grease all over me. Why don't we go upstairs and test out that claw-foot bathtub?"

"Martha. Honey. You can't seduce me into buying real estate."

"You can't resist."

Her lips were warm on his neck. He said, "You make a good argument."

"I *am* a lawyer," she said.

"I guess we're buying a house."

"It's not a house," Martha said. "It's a home."

They kept kissing, illuminated by the single bulb in the mildewed basement.

On the front lawn, the Broker took a cell-phone picture of Sam, Martha, and Max posing for a family portrait in front of their new home.

"We'll take it," Sam said.

The renovations began. Sam put his own business on hold and did most of the carpentry. It was a full-time job. He fitted new pipes for the plumbing. He installed new fixtures, bringing in outside help only to replace the termite-ridden ceiling beams. Martha took a couple weeks off and did most of the painting (Sand Dollar subtle velvet from Restoration Hardware).

Their dog, Dave, was just happy to no longer be confined to a minuscule Manhattan apartment. The white German shepherd was content to spend his days in the backyard consuming mulch and, subsequently, his own feces.

Max loved having such a big house to explore. It was so big he skateboarded between rooms. Max's favorite room was a walk-in cupboard built beneath the staircase. His mom called it a broom closet. One day, Max snuck inside the tiny, spandrel-ceilinged room. He spun three times around and pronounced: *"Levitas vominos!"* like his favorite boy wizard. Dizzy, Max dropped his pencil/wand between the floorboards. Bending down, he noticed a small ring embedded in the wood and lifted up a hatch in the floor, revealing a small storage space.

Behind a wall of cobwebs and dusty canned goods, Max found a doll about his size. Its body was made of sticks tied together with twine and its head was a burlap bag filled with twigs. It didn't have hair and it didn't have clothes. Nothing cute about it. Which was fine by Max. He hated cute toys.

He pulled the doll out and asked, "What's your name?"

Max went down into the basement, where Sam was putting the final touches on his studio, using an electric belt sander on a sheet of Baltic birch. Max knew all the tools by name. Almost before he could walk, his dad had taught him the basics of furniture fabrication. Max knew about the mattock axe. The mallets. The C-clamps and tenon cutters. He even knew the dowel jig and spokeshave. He also knew that tools were not toys. Never play with power tools. Especially the DeWalt. Max thought DeWalt was a funny name. Was it short for DeWalter?

"Hey," Sam said. "What's going on, Mad Max?"

Max showed his dad the old doll.

"Wow, buddy. This is quite a relic. Must be fifty years old. I'm amazed the moths didn't destroy the burlap."

Max said, "His name is Mr. Sticks."

Sam turned the doll over. On the back of its burlap head, he saw a faded symbol. Hand drawn. A circle inside a circle. "Well," Sam told the boy, "this old piece of junk is probably besieged with bedbugs. We should probably get rid of it."

"But he's my friend."

"There's nothing friendly about bedbugs, Mad Max."

Martha appeared at the top of the stairs, holding groceries. "C'mon, boys, I need your help. DEFCON 3. We've got a party to prepare for."

The housewarming didn't feel like a party to Sam. Probably because he didn't feel drunk. Probably because he wasn't drinking. Those days were done. He drank coffee instead. He'd need heavy fuel to survive the

fusillade of facile insults: "Crown Heights is totally up-and-coming."
"The neighborhood is so diverse." "Does Crown Heights even have
Seamless?"

The house was filled with Sam's friends from RISD. Martha's friends
from law school. Friends of friends. Everybody had tattoos. Everybody
had beards. Dancing and debating the literary merits of Patricia Lock-
wood's tweets. Scream talking over the vinyl Gogol Bordello: "Franklin
Avenue is having a renaissance. You have to wait an hour to get into
Barboncino."

"I think I saw Colson Whitehead buying brie at Wedge."

"Doesn't Anthony Mackie own a nightclub next to Mayfield?"

"I'm telling you, man, Crown Heights is well on its way to becoming
Greenpoint. For God's sake, there's an organic Laundromat next to
Café Rue Dix!"

Sam stoked another Duraflame as people congregated around the
fireplace. Everybody drinking penicillin cocktails and/or PBR while
they dissected the recessed bookshelves filled with Sam's books from
art school (Bosch to Banksy) and ate the goat burgers Martha had
bought from Whole Foods.

"Is the goat too gamey?" Martha called out from the kitchen. Sam
swooped in behind and clutched her waist. "No, honey, the goat is not
too gamey."

"Do people like the house?" she asked.

"People love the house. They hate how much we paid."

"Manifest destiny, bitches. We're totally pioneers."

Sam kissed her. After all this time, after all their work, the house
did look amazing. So did Martha. With her vintage dress. With her
Veronica Lake hair. "You go socialize," he told her. "I'll man the meat."
Martha played with his facial hair, kissed him, and headed into the soi-
rée. Sam opened the Whole Foods bag and pulled out another package of ground goat tenderloin, formed a few dense patties, and tossed
them into the frying pan. The grease fomented the flames.

Martha made the rounds through the social circles. Dave, the white
German shepherd, somehow managed to fall asleep in the middle of
the party, in the middle of the living room. "Did someone roofie our
dog?" In the dining room, Martha intercepted Rachel, a good friend
from undergrad. "Great party," Rachel said, "great house. I love the

high ceilings. The fireplace. The reclaimed wood. When do you guys plan on flipping this shit?"

"Well, actually, the plan isn't to flip. The plan is to, you know, put down roots. It took like six months to refurbish and we're not even close to done."

"Settling down in Siberia, huh? Be careful. I know the crime rates are kind of crazy. How are the schools?" Rachel asked.

"The schools are good. And there's always charter when Max is older. He just started kindergarten. But enough about me. About us. How are things at Columbia?"

"Academia is a boy's club. I'm on the tenure track but they keep promoting penises. How's the not-for-profit world?"

"There's no profit," Martha said. "I'm still saddled with all these law school loans. And we just put all this money into the house."

"Go corporate, girlfriend. Fuck advocacy law. Do patent law. Make some bank."

"It makes me happy. It's such hippie bullshit, I know, but I'm basically fighting the good fight. I'm fighting for low income housing. Tenants' rights. Rent stabilization. Every day it's like I'm kicking inequality in the testicles."

"How are the neighbors? What does everybody on the block think?" Rachel asked.

"Think about what?"

"Think about you guys. Moving in."

Martha hesitated. Vaguely insulted. "People don't really talk to us. We don't really talk to them. Puerto Rican. Russian. You know, language barrier."

Martha turned and, in her periphery, saw Sam taking out the garbage.

"How is Sam adjusting?" Rachel asked.

"It's an adjustment for all of us. Crown Heights is a little quieter than the Lower East Side. Max has trouble sleeping without the sound of taxis honking. The drunk people coming out of bars."

"Not a lot of bars out here," Rachel said. "That's probably good. For Sam."

Martha paused and said, "It's good to see you, Rachel. I'll be right back."

"I'll be here, Martha. For you. If you ever need me again. If he ever—"

"He won't," Martha interrupted. "This is a new house. And Sam's a new man."

Up in his room, Max wore his dad's headphones. They were Bose noise-canceling, so he couldn't hear the party below. He couldn't hear anything. In fact, it was too quiet to sleep. So he took off the headphones and took out his notebook. He drew pictures of a place that was filled with fire. He drew pictures of bodies burning.

Max heard a noise outside and walked over to the window. It was dark outside. Past his bedtime. The streetlights made shadow puppets. Down below, Max saw his dad taking out the garbage. He was carrying a trash bag and he was carrying Mr. Sticks. His dad stuffed the old doll into the garbage can and slammed down the lid. His dad looked up and saw Max in the window. Max shut the curtains.

He didn't cry because crying was for little kids. Mr. Sticks was his only friend. The only one he could talk to. The only one who told him the truth. About his father. About the house.

Max heard a noise outside and peered through the curtains. His dad was gone. The street was empty.

From the shadows, Max saw an old woman emerge. Or an old man. Hard to tell. The hood of her winter coat slung over her head, her face hidden by long strands of greasy white hair. *White snakes,* thought Max. The old woman with the hood opened the garbage and started digging through the trash. From a Whole Foods bag, she pulled out an empty package. Goat meat. The meat was gone. But there was juice left in the plastic. The old woman pressed her face against the package and licked it dry. She took Mr. Sticks out of the trash. Touched his twig arms. Touched his burlap head. *It's not her toy,* Max thought, *it's mine. She can't just take my toy.*

Max pounded on the window. The old woman lifted her face and looked right at him. Through her hair, the hair that looked like white snakes, Max saw the old woman's eyes. They appeared to be black.

A hand grabbed Max's shoulder and he screamed. His dad was right behind him. "Past your bedtime, Mad Max."

"Th-there's a woman outside," Max stammered.

Sam looked out the window at the empty street. "There's nobody there," Sam said, tucking Max into bed.

"Dad. Why did you throw my toy away?"

"I told you. That thing was old and probably covered in mold. I don't want rat mites in our house."

"It's not our house," Max said. "It doesn't belong to us."

"Who does it belong to?"

"Mr. Sticks."

That night, after the party, Sam and Martha made love. The claw-foot bathtub presented some logistical challenges. But ten years into marriage, their bodies were maps and they both knew the cartography. They knew where they wanted to go and how they wanted to get there. What they didn't want was to be interrupted by the dog downstairs. "It's two a.m. What's he barking at?" Martha asked. "Stay here," Sam told her, toweling off and throwing on boxers.

Sam walked past Max's room, saw the boy was soundly asleep, and headed downstairs to the party detritus of beer cans and paper plates. Nothing suspicious. Except, of course, the front door, which was inexplicably open and swaying back and forth in the winter wind. Sam looked out at the street. Plastic bags blowing in the gale. He closed and locked the door.

More barking. He followed the noise and found Dave, hackles raised, baring his teeth at the basement door. "Easy, boy," Sam said as he clutched the closest weapon, a butter knife from a cheese plate, and descended the steps.

In the basement, Sam tentatively inched forward across the concrete floor. Scanning the darkness. Sam approached his workbench and switched the knife for the mattock axe. No one had stolen his tools. No one had touched a thing. At the top of the stairs, the dog was still barking his head off. "What's the matter, boy?"

Sam looked down and realized he was standing in the middle of a circle. A circle that had been drawn in blood.

"Probably just kids. We get lots of graffiti in the area."

Thirty minutes later, the cops were in the basement. Two beat officers. Young. Hispanic. Bewildered.

"This isn't graffiti," Martha said, visibly shaken, "and this isn't paint. This is *blood*."

Officer Rodriguez said, "Well, ma'am, this is probably just a case of drunk punks having a good time."

"No," Sam responded. "This is breaking and entering."

"The front lock wasn't broken, sir, and we have no proof anyone entered."

"Proof? This twenty-foot circle drawn in blood on my basement floor looks like proof to me!"

With the lights on, Sam saw it wasn't just one circle. It was several circles within a circle. Crudely but meticulously painted.

"Can't you trace the footprints? Do a DNA search? Follicle analysis?"

"We could," said Officer Diaz, "but we're *not*. This isn't *CSI: Crown Heights*. That's a waste of time and resources for vandalism."

"Does this look like vandalism to you?" Sam got on his hands and knees, inspecting the continuous loop of concentric rings "This is obviously some kind of Black Mass symbol. Devil worship."

"Don't devil worshippers do pentagrams?" Officer Rodriguez said. "This is more of a circle."

"This isn't a joke," Martha said. "We have a six-year-old boy sleeping upstairs."

"We will file a report. That's all we can do at this point. All *you* can do is call us with any more suspicious behavior. In my experience, Marilyn Manson fans are actually fairly harmless. We'll show ourselves out."

The officers headed upstairs. Sam started taking pictures of the circle on his cell phone. Martha, on the verge of a breakdown, said, "I don't want this scaring Max in the morning. Can you clean this up?"

"I'm not cleaning it up," Sam said, taking more pictures. "Not until I know what it is."

"Who cares what it *is*? The only thing I care about, Sam, is our son's safety. We should have never moved to this neighborhood."

"You're the one who wanted to leave Manhattan. You're the one who fell in love with this house."

"Yeah, and I'm the one supporting this family financially. Maybe if you had a real job we could have moved to a real neighborhood."

"And maybe you're a hypocrite who advocates for poor people all day but doesn't want to live on their block."

"I want to feel safe in my home! How can we feel *safe* here anymore?" she asked. "What if something had happened to Max?"

"I'm fine, Mommy."

They turned to find Max standing at the bottom of the stairs.

He was hugging Mr. Sticks.

The next day, Sam installed new locks on the doors. He dug up Max's old baby video monitor and installed the small camera in the basement. The camera streamed in real time and he could access the live feed on his laptop. Sam spent half the day on his laptop, uploading hundreds of cell-phone pictures he had taken of the circle. He sank into the morass of Google results for "satanic symbols." Clicking through ceremonial pentagrams and inverted crucifixes, he couldn't find a single match for the circle in his basement. It had no apparent ties to Satanism or paganism or any ostensible occultism. The symbol was as mysterious as its sudden appearance. Maybe it had no meaning. Maybe its only purpose was to taunt Sam. To remind him that his home had been invaded and his family was no longer safe. Sam barged into Max's room and grabbed Mr. Sticks. Cramming the doll inside the furnace, he watched the burlap burn. His son had plenty of other toys.

Sam started to spend all day every day in that basement. Simply staring at the circle. Unflinching. Two prizefighters taking the measure of their man. Somehow, in some way, Sam knew it was inevitable. Inexorable. Martha was wrong. A Brillo pad wouldn't do a damn thing. You couldn't just scrub the symbol off the concrete. That would not be the end of their problems. Their problems, Sam surmised, were just beginning.

It began with the heat. "Seems a little hot in here," Martha said over breakfast, gulping a glass of water. "These steam radiators really dry me out."

One by one, Sam turned off all the radiators in the house. It didn't matter. The dog kept panting. Max was eating pancakes in his underwear.

"Um. You need to see this," Martha said as the butter on Max's pancakes began to bubble up and boil.

Max and Martha opened the windows, despite the January air. It was unbearably hot—a cloying, adhesive heat. Sam went downstairs and shut down the furnace.

It just got hotter.

By midday, Sam and Martha had moved all the fans in the house into the bathroom. They took all the ice from the ice trays and filled the claw-foot bathtub with cubes. The Rathbones sat in bathing suits on the edge of the tub and stuck their feet inside the glacial watering hole. Martha said to Max, "Just pretend we're on vacation. In Alaska."

Sam leaned forward and turned on the faucet and a viscous black oil spurted out. Jumping up, Sam, Martha, and Max watched the gurgling sludge fill the tub. It sizzled against the ice and made a noxious steam. The smell of death itself. "What the hell?" Martha asked. Another geyser of black tar erupted from the faucet in the sink.

"I'm calling the plumber," Sam said, rushing to the various sinks throughout the house.

Tar was egesting out of every faucet. An invasion of creosote. Sam ran into the basement, where the washing machine was vibrating violently. He couldn't turn it off in time. The fluid slammed against the glass window, forcing open the latch. A deluge converged in rancid runnels.

The tar snaked forward and, inexplicably, formed a perfect ring outlining the large circle on the floor. Sam stopped in his tracks. Baf-

fled. A sudden eruption of flames as the tar ignited. Sam scrambled up
the stairs, only to find Martha holding the fire extinguisher.

"Fuck this house," she said, dousing the flames.

The plumber came an hour later.

"With those old houses, with those old galvanized pipes, what happens is you get rust."

"No way in hell that was *rust*," Sam said. "This was *tar*. Black tar. It
lit itself on fire."

"Could be sewage backup. Clog in the main line. Tree roots."

"I snaked the pipes when we moved in."

"Only one way to be sure," the plumber said, pulling up his pants.
"I'd recommended an overhaul. Lay down new lines. Remove the
rusted copper. Put in new PEX piping."

"How much would that cost?" Martha asked.

Too much, they determined. Way too much. They were already
hemorrhaging money on that house. The plumbing would have to
wait.

It took them twenty-four hours to clean and disinfect the house. They
did it as a team. With Max borrowing the mop handle as a de facto
broomstick. Finally, there was no olfactory reminder of the plumbing
malfunction. But the heat showed no signs of abating.

During dinner (organic chilled gazpacho), Max said, "Mommy. I
can't stop sweating."

"I know, honey." Martha put a cool rag on Max's head. "I know it's
hot. We'll go to a hotel if it doesn't cool off."

"For Christ's sake, we're not *leaving*," Sam said. "A little heat won't
kill us. I'm going to figure this out."

"Don't be mad, Daddy," Max said.

Martha said, "Daddy is just sweaty and tired and being a jerk. It's
hotter than hell in here."

"What's hell, Mommy?"

"Hell's not a real place, honey. It's just imaginary."

"Hell is real," Sam said quietly. "Hell is here."

"Stop it, Sam. Can we change the subject?"

Sam heard a noise. An indistinct vibratory chatter. "Do you hear that?"

Sam and Martha followed the noise into the living room. The noise was closer now but still hard to source.

Max pointed at the wall. The wallpaper appeared to be moving. Sam stood on the couch and touched the edge of the already peeling wallpaper. He pulled down the sheet and revealed a wall covered in locusts. The insects buzzed in unison. An incantatory wall of sound.

Martha screamed and dragged Max upstairs to his bedroom. Sam went from room to room and pulled down pieces of wallpaper, revealing wall after wall of locusts, congealed in a gossamer of mucal larvae. Their strident dirge vibrated through the house.

The next morning, while they ate cage-free eggs and fair-trade pancakes at the diner down the block, the guys from Brooklyn Pest Control fumigated the house (using naturally derived pesticides). It cost them three thousand bucks, but Sam said it was worth tapping Martha's 401(k). The pest-control guys covered the house in plastic tarps and sprayed down the walls. Within an hour, the locusts were dead. "Don't usually see locusts in Brooklyn," the pest control guy said. "There might be more in the woodwork. Let's keep the plastic tarps up for a few days. In case we have to come back."

The locusts stayed away. At least at first. But Sam assumed they'd be back. That was just the opening salvo. War had been declared.

At nine p.m., Martha heard screaming in Max's room. Martha thought maybe it was the heat. She gathered three rotating fans around his bed and tried to blow in the cold air from the open window. "Shhh," Martha said. "It's just a bad dream."

"It's not a bad dream," Max said. "It's *him*."

Max pointed behind Martha. Mr. Sticks was sitting in the chair.

"I don't want to sleep with Mr. Sticks."

"Why not?" Martha asked. "I thought he was your friend."

"He's being mean to me."

"How is he being mean to you, honey?"

"He keeps saying mean things. He keeps saying this isn't our house. And . . . he said he's going to take me away. Take me somewhere bad."

"Where does Mr. Sticks want to take you?"

Max held up his notebook filled with crayon drawings of demons dripping with dark tar. "Hell," Max said.

Martha hugged him. "Mr. Sticks isn't going to take you to hell. Hell doesn't actually exist. You were just having a bad dream. Mommy will protect you. So will Dad."

"What if Dad goes away again? What if they take him back to the place where they put pillows on the wall?"

"Dad's not going anywhere. Daddy was . . . sick. But he's better now. He's not going away. But Mr. Sticks is."

Martha kissed Max good night and carried the doll down into the basement, where Sam was conducting his nightly ritual, kneeling in front of the symbol like some entranced penitent. The dog was sitting next to Sam, also watching the circle, on guard. Martha had to say Sam's name three times before he noticed.

"You spend too much time down here," she said.

"I'm protecting my family," Sam said.

He turned around. He was wearing a sleeveless shirt, and Martha noticed that his arms were covered in smeared marker. He had drawn the circle symbol again and again across his skin.

"You're scaring me. Snap out of it, Sam. You need to finish fixing this house so we can put it back on the goddamn market."

"It's our house. They're not going to scare us away."

"They? Who's they?" Martha asked.

"They . . . it . . . whatever it is. The plumbing, the heat, the locusts. All of it. It's not just a coincidence. It's evil."

Sam turned and saw that Martha was holding Mr. Sticks. The eyeholes in the burlap head seemed to taunt him.

"You seriously need to stop it with this evil stuff," Martha said. "Did you know your son was just having a nightmare about going to hell? He's six years old. He's drawing pictures of Dante's *Inferno*."

Martha threw down the notebook filled with demonic stick figures spreading black wings. Sam examined Mr. Sticks. "I destroyed this doll. This is impossible."

"Don't do this. Not again. This is how it started, remember? The delusions?"

"I'm not delusional, Martha."

"Spending seven hours googling 'satanic symbols' is not exactly normal. If you're having another nervous breakdown—"

"I never had a nervous breakdown," Sam said.

"The doctors had to *put* you someplace, didn't they? *Involuntarily?* For three weeks? I had to explain to my son why his dad had to go away. I had to explain to my friends that my husband was dealing with a little chemical dependency–slash–manic episode."

"I'm not having another manic episode," he said. "I'm not popping pain pills. I'm clean and sober and I'm trying to tell you there is something demonic going on here."

"The only demons in this house are *yours*," she said.

Sam picked up the mattock axe.

Martha took a step back.

Sam raised the axe.

Limb by limb, he dismembered Mr. Sticks, severing the doll into several dozen pieces. The dog stood vigilant guard.

When Sam had finished, Martha started up the stairs. Holding the banister to steady her nerves, she said, "We're going to put this house on the market."

"We're not going anywhere. Not without a fight."

After midnight, despite the heat, Sam grabbed a hot coffee from the kitchen and checked his laptop. The live feed of the baby monitor in the basement showed no movement.

Sam walked upstairs to the master bedroom and watched his wife sleep. Martha had never looked more alone. Sam wanted to be in that bed with his wife. But he had to protect her. He had to be vigilant. He was holding the axe, gripping it tight. Ready.

Fatigue crept in. For a split second, Sam allowed his eyes to close. Two sleepless nights catching up to him. When he opened his eyes, his wife's body was covered in snakes. A cocoon of black cobras. Sam blinked and the snakes were gone.

A noise downstairs.

Sam rushed down to the living room and pushed through the maze of plastic tarps left by the exterminators. He caught a glimpse of something—a shadow—darting behind the translucent material. He turned. No hint of what he had just seen. Maybe it was just exhaustion. Retinal fatigue.

From behind the tarp, a figure pressed itself against the plastic. Impossibly tall. Several rows of serrated teeth. An apex predator. Sam couldn't see any real detail, but he saw enough. *The beast was in his house.* Sam clutched the axe in his hands and took a swing. The tarp ripped. The beast was gone.

Sam ran through every room in the house, scanning the darkness with the light from his cell phone. All he saw were dead locusts clinging to the plastic tarps.

Sam turned the corner and noticed footprints in the foyer. Rather hoofprints, forged in tar still steaming. Sam knelt to inspect the prints, pulling back tendrils of tar with his fingertips.

Sam looked up and saw a goat standing in the hallway.

The goat was completely coated in black tar. Its eyes teemed with maggots. Sam choked up on the axe.

Barking came from the kitchen. Sam left the goat and ran to find Dave at the top of the stairs, baring his teeth at the basement. Suddenly, the dog was yanked into the darkness. The door slammed shut behind him.

Sam pulled on the door. It wouldn't budge. Sam swung the mattock axe against the thick oak, but the wood barely splintered.

Sam ran to his laptop and, in the baby monitor's feed, saw the dog growling at the circle symbol. The concrete inside the circle had become a smoldering cauldron of boiling oil, steaming froth rising from a subterranean crematorium. A black hand emerged from the bile. The obsidian fingers elongated and coiled three times around the dog, then constricted. Once the animal was motionless, the tensile fingers dragged the dog down into the stygian abyss.

Sam screamed as tar seeped out of his laptop's USB ports. Locusts crawled out of his keyboard. The screen itself became a black hole. His MacBook Pro was now a portal to perdition.

Sam extended his hands and reached inside the screen, his fingers breaking the barrier, penetrating the birth canal of death. His probing arms disappeared completely into the wall of tar.

Sam was inside the laptop.

Pulling out, his palms scalded by the mucilage, he held a charred dog collar. His laptop burst into flame.

Sam threw it into the dishwasher and turned it on cold wash. He ran outside, into the backyard, and pulled open the storm door. Running down the stairs, Sam discovered that the basement was empty.

The dog was gone.

Sam spent the dawn hours ripping apart his books from art school, tearing out hundreds of images of hell. From the fiery landscapes of Hieronymus Bosch to Gustave Doré's illustrations for *The Divine Comedy*. Orpheus and Eurydice. The Hydra. The great pit of Tartarus. The tiers of infinite torture. Sam used duct tape to hang the illustrations until every square inch of the basement walls was covered in his tarnation collage. Front and center were Max's crayon sketches of eternal damnation—the stick-figure portraits of demons with hooves. Demons with wings. His son had talent. There was no doubt. Maybe he'd be an artist someday, like his father had tried and failed to be. For once in his life, Sam was grateful for his fallback profession. When your house is being invaded by the forces of evil, it helps to have a basement filled with power tools.

Using the table saw and spokeshave, Sam crafted dozens of wooden crosses and hung them throughout the house. He was a disciple of Christopher Hitchens but desperate times called for desperate measures. It was better to believe in God than to believe he was going insane.

Sam turned on the television and found C-SPAN broadcasting a congressional hearing. Some senator from somewhere ranting and raving: "Abortion and homosexuality are paving the road to hell! What happened to one nation under God?" Sam cranked the volume. A sonic exorcism.

Martha and Max came down the basement stairs to find Sam at the table saw, fabricating a life-size cross. Six feet tall.

"They took Dave," Sam said. "They're going to take us next. We have to be prepared to fight."

Martha stared at the crosses and paintings of hell.

"Max, go to your bedroom. Pack your backpack with clothes."

"Are we going to hell?" Max asked.

"No," Martha said, "we're going to Aunt Sharon's."

Max ran upstairs. Martha asked, "What did you do to the dog?"

"They *took* him," Sam said. "The circle isn't just a circle. It's a gateway. Last night it opened. But now it's closed. You have to believe me."

"I believe you're having a psychotic break. I love you, Sam, but you have to get out of this basement. We all have to get out of this house. Now. Go over to my sister's."

"*You* go. You'll be safer. I need to stay."

"You need help, Sam. You need to talk to Dr. Cronenberg."

"Doctors can't help me, Martha. Only God can help us now."

Martha came closer to Sam. Restraining tears. She touched Sam's face and ran her hand along his beard.

"Please," she said. "I'm begging. Come with us. Let's leave this place."

"I can't leave," Sam said. "This is our house. This is our home."

Martha and Max packed their bags. Sam helped carry the luggage down the stairs. "Why do we have to leave?" Max asked.

"Because, bud," Sam said, "it's not safe here anymore."

"I don't want to go, Daddy."

"Don't worry, Mad Max. Wherever you go, I'm always going to find you."

"Let's go," Martha said, picking up Max, who was now crying. Sam walked them to the front door. Martha turned and kissed him.

"I love you," she said. "Good-bye, Sam."

Martha turned the handle and opened the front door.

Instead of broad daylight, a wall of tar cascaded from the doorway. An avalanche of toxic asphalt swept them away and filled the house, sloshing against the walls and rising above the windows.

Sam struggled to grab Martha and Max as they swept past him on the wave of black fluid. The house was engulfed in a typhoon of tar. Locusts broke through the windows. A cacophony of insecticidal screaming.

The flood carried Martha and Max toward the basement door, which shattered, and the undercurrent dragged them down the stairs. Sam trudged through the mire, clinging to the railing on the basement stairs, fighting the squall.

Below him, the tide funneled into the circular hole in the basement. A sinkhole. Swallowing the flotsam of floating power tools. Martha and Max were drifting toward the hole. Helpless.

Sam kicked the railing, frantically, until it broke off the wall. He lunged forward with the pole and Martha just made contact. "Don't let go!" he screamed, straining to be heard over the gushing waterfall of black tar.

Martha reached out. Sam grabbed her wrist.

"I GOT YOU!"

Drenched in dark turpentine and a newborn's veneer of vernix, a demon emerged from the sinkhole. In its mouth, rows and rows of fingers extended and grasped for their prey. The infantry of teeth-hands grabbed hold of Martha and Max, pulling them inside a marsupial pouch. Sam saw their limbs thrashing inside the beast's folds.

He jumped into the lagoon and grabbed the mattock axe. He took a futile swing as the demon spread its venous wings and dropped into the hole.

The hole closed. The flood was over. The house was quiet and the locusts were gone. So were Martha and Max.

Sam raised the axe and hit the concrete floor. Again and again. Until his body buckled. He dropped the tool and realized his family wasn't coming back.

Apparently the neighbors called the cops. "Domestic disturbance," Officer Rodriguez told him. "Disturbing the peace."

Sam had to admit it looked suspicious. His house and his clothes covered in tar. His verbalization bordering on catatonia.

"Where's your wife, sir? Where's your son?" asked Officer Diaz. All that Sam could muster was to feebly point his finger in a downward motion.

"Your family is in the ground? Is that what you're telling us?"

"Can you explain this black shit everywhere, huh? Is it asphalt? Did you bury the bodies?"

Near the front door, Officer Rodriguez noticed the luggage. "Let me guess. Your wife wanted to leave. She wanted to take your son. And you wouldn't let 'em go?"

"We ran your name through the system," Diaz said. "Couple priors. Drug offenses. Brief stint at Bellevue psychiatric. You run out of happy pills?"

"You're coming to the precinct."

Officer Rodriguez took his eyes off Sam to take out his handcuffs. He didn't notice Sam reach for his belt loop and pull out the mallet.

Sam connected with the cop's face, breaking his nose. Diaz went for his gun, but Sam was already out the door. Diaz called for backup and hauled ass down the block, trying to catch the crazy man covered in tar.

The chase continued all the way down Nostrand Avenue. Sam finally lost him by ducking behind a bodega dumpster. Once the sound of the police radio receded, Sam found the nearest hiding spot.

He needed to lay low. He needed a drink.

Sam took out three hundred bucks from the bodega ATM and scurried toward the windowless bar on the corner. The unmarked metal door was locked, but he heard a television blaring inside. He knocked. Loudly. A large man wearing a tracksuit unlocked the door.

"This is not bar," the guy said in a thick accent. "This is private social club."

Sam held up the wad of cash. The large man let him in.

The joint was empty and dark and reeked of stogies and spiced meat. There was an old bar in the front room with a few stools and booths off to the side. A Romanian flag on the wall. A high-definition television gave the only semblance of modernity. The large man in the tracksuit (apparently the bartender) was watching Romania versus Greece. "Piţurcă kill us!" he screamed. "Couldn't coach a fucking potato!"

Without prompting, the guy poured Sam a double whiskey neat while continuing his rant: "The 1994 World Cup. Round of sixteen we beat Argentina but Sweden kicked us in anus."

Instead of taking a drink, Sam took out his iPhone. Found the

Instagram photo of his family hugging outside their house on the day they made their offer. They smiled auspicious smiles. Six months later, their dreams had disappeared into a hole in the ground. Sam Rathbone had lost everything, including, probably, his mind. *Did he kill his dog? Did he kill his family and bury their bodies in asphalt (which would explain the tar on his clothes)?* He didn't care if they put him back in Bellevue. The only place he wanted to be, the only place he deserved to be, was hell itself.

Sam raised his whiskey to the mirror behind the bar. His hair and beard congealed with tar. Just before he could take a drink, an accented voice interrupted him.

"You look like hell."

An old man sat at the end of the bar. He was in a wheelchair, with tubes in his nose running to an oxygen tank.

"Don't mind him," the bartender said, in his broken English. "He always here. He never have cashmoney."

Sam picked up his whiskey. Walked over to the guy. Placed the drink down in front of him. "This one's on me, old-timer."

"I am not old," he said. "I am *cursed*. The same could be said for *you*." The man nursed the whiskey. Savored it. "*Mulțumesc,* young man. Kindness begets kindness. You have helped me. Now I help you."

"Only God can help me," Sam said.

"God doesn't visit Brooklyn." The old man swished the whiskey around his dentures.

"The *devil* does," Sam said.

"You made a mistake." The old man pointed at Sam's iPhone resting on the bar. The picture of their brownstone was visible. "You shouldn't have bought that house."

The old man pushed away from the bar and rolled his wheelchair through a curtain of beads across the hallway. Sam gave a glance at the bartender, who was all consumed with the soccer: "*Kick the ball, you fucking lama!*"

Sam pushed through the beads, walked down the wood-paneled hallway, and found himself in a dilapidated banquet room. Parquet floors. Upholstered booths. A small altar of some kind in the corner. The walls were filled with framed photos of immigrant families from different eras. The old man in the wheelchair was occluded by shadow.

"What do you know about my house?" Sam asked, inching toward him.

"It's not *your* house," the old man said. "You didn't build it. *They* did; 1946."

The old man pointed at the pictures on the wall. A Polaroid from the 1970s of a Romanian wedding. A birthday party. A wake. And there, amidst the sea of Kodak moments: a faded black-and-white photo dated 1946. A dark-haired family of three (husband, wife, young daughter) posed in front of a brownstone: 223 Midwood Avenue. The house looked immaculate. The masonry just completed. The shingles in perfect condition.

"The Minka family," the old man said. "They got off the boat from Bucharest in 1944. They were rounding our people up. Sending us to Dachau or Treblinka."

"Jews?"

"Romany. The Roma. Gypsies."

"You're a Gypsy?"

"I'm not a unicorn. Don't sound so surprised. Lots of Gypsies settled in Brooklyn. The diaspora washed us ashore. The Ustaša wanted to wipe us off the face of the earth. The Einsatzgruppen were skinning us alive in the streets. The Gypsies almost went extinct in the Porajmos. Almost. The Jews were considered enemies of the state. The Romany were witches."

"Witches don't really exist."

"We don't really fly on fucking broomsticks. In America, witches are bedtime stories. In Romania, witches are taxed by the government. They are very real. And very powerful. They poured mandrake in the Danube to curse President Băsescu. And they have cursed you, young man."

"Are you telling me my house was built by witches?"

"*Vrajitoares.* The house was inherited by their daughter, Rodica, who lived there until last year. Until the bank foreclosed."

Sam looked at the photo. The little girl, with dark hair and dark skin, was wearing an amulet necklace. A pointed obelisk. She was holding a doll with a burlap head. A doll that Sam immediately recognized.

"My son found that doll in the house."

"That is no doll. That is a poppet from Ulmeni."

"A voodoo doll?"

"Voodoo is for Haitians. But the same principle applies."

"Like you stick pins in it?"

"Like you break every bone in somebody's body," the old man said. "How do you think I ended up in this wheelchair?"

"That little girl did this to you?"

"Rodica. I was the little boy next door. We grew up together. Rodica wanted to get married. I didn't. Let's just say she doesn't handle rejection well. She ruined my body. Ruined my life."

"My life is just about over too, old-timer. The cops think I'm criminally insane, and I'm starting to think they're right. I mean, here I am. Talking to *you*—a geriatric Gypsy in a wheelchair. I can't believe you expect me to believe this shit. I have to go."

"It doesn't matter where you go. She will hunt you down."

Sam stopped and said, "Why is she doing this, huh? What does she even *want*?"

"What our people have wanted for centuries. *A home.* You took it from her. She is taking it back."

"She took my wife. My child. Can I save them?"

The old man rolled his wheelchair over to a small wooden altar. Votive candles encircled a deck of ancient tarot cards. The old man picked up a card that featured a faded illustration of a round symbol. Circles within a circle.

"That's it!" Sam said, showing him a cell-phone picture of the symbol. "That's the mark she made in my basement."

"This symbol is called a *naibu*. This is the infernal curse." The old man flipped the card over, revealing a stanza in Romanian. The curse itself. "She has opened a hole to hell. A door into the darkness."

"Is there any way to get my family back?"

"The only way to reverse the curse"—the old man hesitated—"is to put the curse on her."

"Tell me what to do," Sam said. "Tell me how to find Rodica."

"First things first. Do you happen to have a goat?"

———

Sam pulled the hoodie over his head and snuck around the corner of Third Street in Gowanus and hurried inside Whole Foods. On the streets, he was a wanted man. In Whole Foods, he was just another customer, blending in with the bearded clientele.

He ordered ten pounds of organic goat meat and waited as the tattooed butcher wrapped the loins in wax paper.

"Sam!" Sam turned to see Rachel, Martha's friend from undergrad. "I didn't get to tell you at the party, but your house is so amazing. Please put me on the list if you guys decide to flip it."

"It's our house. We're not leaving."

"I don't mean to throw you into the middle of the scrum, but is Martha mad at me? I've texted her like two hundred times. She's not texting me back."

"She's gone," Sam said blankly.

"Where did she go? Astoria? She mentioned she might go see her sister . . ."

Sam felt Rachel inspecting his appearance. He looked like shit. Like a homeless man on methamphetamine. A man possessed.

"Where did she go, Sam?"

"Martha and Max went to hell," he said. "But I'm going to bring them back."

Rachel stared in abject befuddlement as Sam grabbed his goat meat from the butcher's counter and walked away.

By the time Rachel took out her phone and called the cops, Sam was running out the door.

Sam took the 3 train to Brownsville in the eastern ambit of Brooklyn. The subway car was crowded with Sunday passengers. A couple of Sikhs, some Jamaican nurses, and a Ghanaian woman wearing kente. Sam tried to blend in. It wasn't working.

Maybe it was the fact that his clothes were caked in black. Maybe it was the smell of the goat meat. Everybody was staring.

Nobody saw what Sam saw. Locusts on the light fixtures.

Sam started to sweat. Panic.

He pushed his way between people when he saw a homeless man in the adjoining subway car holding a cardboard sign: REVELATION 20:14. HELL IS HERE.

Sam reversed direction. Elbowing the crowd. Looking through the glass door, Sam saw that the subway car on the opposing side was empty. There were no people.

There was just a goat.

The goat was covered horns to hoof in black tar, as if it had been christened in motor oil. No one else paid any mind. The goat started shaking. Convulsing. An epileptic seizure.

The goat opened its mouth. A snake emerged, slick with lipids. Then another. Another. The snakes coiled themselves on the subway poles. Hissing.

The goat's mouth cracked open even wider. A hand emerged. Then a forearm. The hand was wearing a wedding ring. A face emerged, pushing through the dilating trachea. Plastered with placental fluid. It was Martha.

Sam screamed her name and kicked the door. It wouldn't open.

He felt a hand grab his shoulder, and a hipster with a mullet yanked him around. "Calm down, man. You're scaring people." Sam frantically looked back at the opposing subway car. Nothing but commuters. *The goat was gone.* So was Martha.

The train stopped. Suddenly. The hipster lost his balance and staggered back. Sam pushed him and exited the train, wedging himself through the closing doors. A narrow escape.

Lugging the goat meat, Sam ran all the way from the Rockaway station, down Dumont, until he ran out of breath in Brownsville. The old man had written her address on the back of the old black-and-white picture of young Rodica Minka and her parents: BROWNSVILLE HOUSING AUTHORITY, 307 BLAKE AVENUE.

The projects weren't hard to find. There had to be more than twenty run-down buildings crammed into twenty run-down city blocks. The barred windows and fenced-in basketball courts made Sam think more of a penitentiary than subsidized housing. Someone had spray-painted a graffiti mural of Satan. This wasn't just squalor. This was hell on earth. Sam was in the right place. Somewhere inside this labyrinthine slum, a Romanian witch was about to be deported to the under-world. First he had to find her.

Sam slung the hood over his head and approached the stoop of the first tenement building. A couple of black teens were playing on their PSPs. They made no effort to conceal the guns bulging in their waistbands. Sam decided to risk it and muttered "Eight ball" under his breath. Surprisingly, they let him pass. He did resemble a crack fiend.

He wandered the graffiti-lined hallways of the projects, reverberat-ing with the sound of subwoofer bass and crying babies. He passed a few open doors, catching glimpses of infinitesimally small living quar-ters. This wasn't a place you lived. It was a place you waited to die. Just pick your cause of death: Bullets in the stairwell? Rats in the ventila-tion? Exposed wires dangling from the fluorescents? Sam saw a family of six crammed in one room. The toddlers huddled on a box mattress eating microwave mac and cheese. The smallest boy was wearing a paper-plate mask. Sam kept on walking.

At the end of the hallway, past a web of police tape, Sam saw double doors that led outside, where he could hear music. Flourishes of pas-toral guitar. Tambourine. Gypsy music.

Sam followed the cadence outside into a courtyard. It was lightly snowing. There was some kind of event he couldn't quite see through the clotheslines of laundry. A celebration around an improvised fire pit. About fifty people dressed in old-fashioned raiment of blouses and head scarves. A hirsute man banged a hand drum. A flaxen child ran around with incense. A small man with scoliosis released a chicken from a cage. A drunk guy pushed past Sam, carrying a flask.

"Happy wedding!" the guy said with a Romanian accent. "The *lăutari* are playing the fuck out of that flute!"

The drunk guy had a cleft-palate scar. The taxi driver who had driven them to Crown Heights. The guy dragged Sam into the wed-ding festivities and then darted off to dance with a trio of corpulent ladies who were missing several important teeth.

Through the throng of dancing peasants, past the pyretic flames of the fire pit, Sam saw a woman in white. She stared right at Sam. His body tensed. Despite the distance, Sam could see the pointed amulet she wore around her neck. Sam checked the black-and-white photograph. It was the same necklace young Rodica was wearing in 1946. That was her. The witch was here.

The witch was holding Mr. Sticks. Clothes on the line moved in the wind, blocking her momentarily. When she was revealed again, the old woman was holding Max. Max turned and smiled at his dad and locusts came out of his mouth. Sam tried to scream. He could not.

Another gust of wind moved the clothesline again. When the old woman reappeared, Max was gone and the witch was again holding Mr. Sticks.

Rodica had aged well. Even without makeup. She had an ageless, timeless sort of beauty. High cheekbones. Cerulean eyes. The faintest palimpsest of wrinkles. Her shock-white hair was more magisterial than matriarchal.

Sam's eyes were playing tricks on him. Because, when the clothesline swayed again, Rodica now appeared to be fifty years younger. She was a virginal woman. Barely twenty years old. Wearing a wedding dress. Rodica smiled at Sam and removed her dress.

Against his will, Sam advanced toward her. Polarities of a magnet. She was drawing him in. Blocked by the linens, he could catch only glimpses of her pale skin exposed in the January snow. The outline of her curves silhouetted through the sheets. When the sheets parted again, the woman had become Martha. Sam's wife was standing naked in the courtyard of a Brooklyn tenement. A circle of blood drawn on her stomach. Martha opened her eyes and two snakes came out of the sockets.

The witch was in his head. Controlling his mind. He had to break the spell. *He had a job to do.* Sam stuck his hand in the fire pit and screamed. Before anyone could stop him, Sam ran around the corner, between buildings, where they kept the Housing Authority dumpsters.

Making sure the coast was clear, Sam unwrapped the Whole Foods goat meat and smeared the goat blood into a circle on the pavement. He removed the tarot card from his pocket—the tarot card the old man had given him—and made sure the symbols matched. He flipped over the card and stared at the curse written in Romanian. He attempted to enunciate the words and ineffectually repeated the curse. His Romanian accent was wrong. The curse was not working.

At that moment, the taxi driver with the cleft-palate scar came around the bend to take a piss against the dumpsters. Sam had to hurry. He had to invoke the curse before he was lynched by Gypsies.

Sam took out his iPhone and opened Max's favorite app, Google Translate. One by one, Sam typed the Romanian words from the tarot card into the interface. A male automaton spoke in stilted oratory and Sam repeated the words. Quickly. Quietly.

"*Va merge în Iad. Diavolvu va inghiti. Osanda vesnica.*"

The taxi driver zipped up and poked his head around the dumpster. Seeing Sam and the blood circle, the man smashed his beer bottle and charged, but not before Sam said the final word: "*VESNICA!*"

The circle opened. The concrete caved in and an ascendant geyser of tar arose. The guy was ready to slice open Sam's jugular, but now he stared down, terrified, into the churning whirlpool. He had no time to react as ductile arms protruded from the magma and dragged him down into eternal servitude as Lucifer's chattel.

Sam dove into the dumpster. He knew what he had wrought. He knew what was about to be unleashed.

A battalion of beasts crawled out of the hellhole, curled into balls of fetal fluid. When they stood, arising on cloven feet, they had to measure eight feet tall. They spread their wings of darkest sable and, opening their mouths in a hyenic war cry, charged.

It wasn't a battle. It was a crime against humanity. Peering over the edge of the dumpster, Sam caught only fractions of the rampage. The hellion assault was unleashed. One by one, demons dragged people down into the hole. *It wasn't supposed to happen like this,* Sam thought. He wanted revenge only on Rodica. Not on innocent bystanders. He didn't want to depopulate the projects of the Brownsville Housing Authority.

Banshees stormed the tenements and hauled the apartment dwellers into the pit. The gun-toting teenagers stopped playing their PSPs and started taking cell-phone videos of the apocalyptic killing spree. Grainy images of Sodom and Gomorrah in mid-decimation. One boy ran and hopped the fence, but he did not notice the black-winged fowl circling above as it plucked him up and tossed him into the molten gullet.

Sam didn't see the witch anywhere. He hoped she had met her fate. Sam started to climb out of the dumpster when a bottle of vodka fractured his face. He fell backward, clutching his bloody nose.

The witch hopped into the dumpster with surprising agility. Eyes rabid with rage, Rodica stood over Sam's helpless body and howled. She raised the broken vodka bottle (sustainably sourced). She was ready to kill Sam.

Sam wasn't ready to die.

He ripped the amulet from Rodica's neck and buried the conical talisman into her trachea. Stunned, Rodica dropped the bottle. Blood seeped from her windpipe. She locked eyes with Sam. She didn't seem afraid. Given where she was about to go, maybe she should have been.

"Go to hell," Sam said.

A demon swept down and wrapped Rodica in his wings, stuffing her body inside his marsupial skin pouch. Together they plummeted into the fulminating and fathomless hole. The hole closed. The asphalt was restored. The residual tar receded into the drainpipes.

Sam climbed out of the dumpster and surveyed the damage. A swing set creaking in the wind. A basketball bouncing across midcourt. Bloodstained laundry hanging on the clotheslines. The Brownsville Housing Projects had become a ghost town. This wasn't Brooklyn. This was Chernobyl. Mass extinction.

Back in Crown Heights, Sam opened the front door. The house was back to normal, the way it had been before the curse.

"Martha?" he called out. "Max?"

Not hearing a response, Sam walked from room to room before heading downstairs.

On the concrete, inside the circle symbol, Martha and Max lay on the basement floor. They appeared to be sleeping. Sam knelt down and gently woke them. They stirred, bleary and light blind.

"I had a bad dream," Max said.

"It's all done, Mad Max," Sam said. "The nightmare's over."

Dave the dog emerged from behind the washing machine and ran over to Sam, tail wagging, and licked his master's face.

Martha sat up. "Where are we?"

"*Home,*" Sam said, embracing his wife and son. "We're home."

At that moment, a dozen NYPD officers stormed the basement and surrounded the Rathbone family. Their guns pointed at Sam. Martha held on tight to Max.

Sam just smiled. "Don't worry, Mad Max, they're taking me away. But I'll be back before you know it."

"Where are they taking you, Dad?"

"The place where they put pillows on the walls."

The Broker gave a tour for two real estate developers in bespoke suits.

"The premises are vacated. All these abandoned buildings are just waiting to be torn down."

The Brownsville Housing Projects had all been boarded up. The city wanted to rezone after the public safety violations.

"This neighborhood is a war zone," one prospective developer said. "Wasn't there just a mass murder here? Gang related? Nobody's going to invest in this ghetto."

"Sir, while *you* see a ghetto of subsidized housing, *I* see the future site of luxury condominiums."

"Brownsville is too far east."

"Brooklyn does go beyond the first three stops on the L train," the Broker said. "Do you want to be followers? Or do you want to be pioneers? Stake your claim in terra incognita. This isn't just real estate." The Broker gestured toward the housing projects and a spray-painted mural of Satan. "*This is manifest destiny.*"

Valdivia

ELI ROTH

I had always wanted to attempt a "year-long summer," chasing the good weather around the world. This was probably a result of having grown up in the suburbs of Boston, where you spend a good part of the year in a deep freeze and most summer days are too hot, too humid, or too gnat-ridden to spend outdoors. Occasionally you would get a perfect summer day where you could enjoy a sloshball game (beer at each base) until nine in the evening, when it got too dark to catch fly balls. Then you'd stretch the perfect day into a night of hanging out at the movies or taking out your adolescent rage on a golf ball. It was those long, endless summer days that seemed to evaporate once I hit my thirties.

Summer in your mid-thirties meant working in an office, hoping to finish early enough to get in a workout or a bike ride. I missed summer—my Massachusetts *childhood* summer. I missed it desperately. I even missed working as a camp counselor wrangling screaming ten-year-olds, getting them ready for swimming or arts and crafts. I always got deeply depressed at the end of summer; there was nothing worse than that dreaded September Monday when you went back to school and the countdown began all over again. Just the name "September" still makes me feel like I'm in a cold, dark classroom stuck to a freezing metal chair attached to a plastic desk. I'd sit there half asleep, looking out at the early morning darkness, replaying my warm summer like a song on repeat.

This longing for summer was probably the reason I convinced myself I needed to live in Southern California, where it snows only in the mountains and kids skateboard to school in January. This, of course, was my fantasy, fed to me by a steady digest of cable television. The reality is that California is still a desert, and in the morning and at night you can freeze your ass off year-round. California felt like being in a lukewarm hot tub year-round.

I was getting bored with my life there. I was tired of my job. I was bored with the girls I was sort of dating. I was even bored with the money. Nothing seemed to add up. I was so much happier as a kid, suffering through those endless winters for a few days of perfect summer. Nothing was wrong in my life beyond a mild knee injury from overtraining. I had everything I thought I was supposed to want, but I wanted something more, something I couldn't buy. I wanted to feel like a kid in summer again.

It was my friend Nico who finally convinced me to go to Chile. He grew up in Santiago with American movies and culture, so for all intents and purposes, he was American. But he wasn't. He was Chilean, and as I learned, they're a very particular type of South American. For years he had been telling me how Chileans go out until six in the morning and that Latin girls are way less uptight than Americans and don't take offense when you hit on them at the gym (his words, not mine). Twenty-year-old South American girls couldn't care less about a fifteen-year age difference. I told him that I preferred to date girls within seven years of my age, and even that was pushing it. He just shook his head and said, "You're so gringo. It's so sad." I tried to convince him that technically Jews weren't gringos, and that with my swarthy complexion I could easily pass for South American, but he didn't buy it. "You can't see it. Get your ass down here and have some fun. Your winter is our summer. Come in December; it's the best time of the year."

I had spent my previous summer traveling the Amalfi coast, and in September I decided I didn't want my vacation to end. I quit my job and enjoyed the last breath of California summer in October and then in November flew to Argentina and Uruguay, finally working my way to Chile. I wanted to save the best for last, and Nico was determined to make sure his country delivered on his promises.

When I first arrived in Santiago, what struck me most was how much it looked like Los Angeles. A W hotel, Starbucks—there's even Applebee's if you're really feeling homesick. It all felt like a cleaner, safer Los Angeles.

"San-*hattan*," Nico boasted, waving his arms, proudly showing me the Santiago skyline from the rooftop bar at the W.

Nico had a number of businesses, the main one being club promoting and events. It all seemed kind of shady to me, even though it probably wasn't. We had met years earlier in San Diego through a friend, and over the years that friend became less important because I realized that more than anything, Nico and I shared an identical sense of humor. Taking me from the airport to a rooftop welcome party filled with young models and telling them I was a photographer was his idea of a good joke.

This event was his attempt to show me how much better Chile was than America. It was working. The crowd was more international than I'd imagined: Spaniards, Germans, Brazilians, Argentines, and a few older gringo Americans who mostly stuck to themselves in the corner, gawking at the crowd surrounding our booth.

"Everyone's coming to Chile, dude. Everyone. Europe's falling apart and they're all moving here. You know what they used to call us? Sudacas."

I told him it sounded like *tsadakkah*. He had no idea what I was talking about. His friend Igal laughed. Igal was a Chilean Jew, one of the eighteen thousand living there. He got my lame pun.

"Sudaca. That's what people from Europe used to call anyone from South America."

"Is it an insult?" I asked.

"It's like saying someone is black," he explained. "Depends how you use it."

A waiter handed me a pisco sour. "Our national drink," Nico said proudly, and toasted me. "But now we have a term for all the Europeans whose countries fell apart and are now here begging for work. 'Nordacas.' And they fucking hate it." Chile survived a tough dictatorship but had never lived irresponsibly and spent beyond its means, like

Argentina. (Again, Nico's economic assessment; I don't claim to know anything about Argentina's economic troubles.) "The Argentines think they're in Europe," Nico explained. "It's fucking crazy. Do you know that to get an iPhone in Argentina it's cheaper to fly to New York, spend two nights in a hotel, buy one there, and fly back? That's fucking insane, dude. That country's falling apart. We don't even get our beef from there anymore."

The warm December breeze felt nice. It was the beginning of summer, and everyone was throwing Christmas parties to celebrate. We spent the next two weeks going out almost every night to a different party, usually sponsored by a brand or company, on the rooftop of some hotel. My idea of Christmas mainly consisted of Chinese food, movies, hot chocolate, and ski lodges. In Chile they talk about who's going to host the Christmas pool party that year. They celebrate on the twenty-fourth, open all their gifts at midnight, and then spend the twenty-fifth at the pool or the beach. We would probably do the same if we had ninety-degree weather in December.

After what seemed like our tenth night of consecutive partying (five a.m. was considered an early night), Nico and Igal took me to a club called Amanda. Tuesday night at Amanda was where all of Santiago was headed. Nico gleefully explained that the colleges had just let out for the summer and that tonight would be "packed with hot girls getting extremely drunk." I told him that maybe at my age it wasn't the best idea to be chasing college girls, which he took as yet another opportunity to make fun of me for being "super-gringo about everything," and he reiterated that in South America the rules are different. "Nobody gives a fuck. Girls like older guys." Not wanting to flout a local custom, I of course went.

Amanda was a mosh pit of sweaty teenagers, or at least they looked teenaged to me. I had gotten past the point where I could really tell whether a girl was fifteen or twenty-five. It all was starting to look the same. I had tried going out with girls in their twenties but found it mostly boring because I like going to bed at a reasonable hour. But now was time to get out of my comfort zone, to push myself to stay

out as late as I could every night and take advantage of whatever stupidity came my way. The parties we had been to were fun but mostly
variations on the same theme. Amanda, somehow, had a different
vibe. Everyone in the club danced, celebrating the end of school and
the beginning of summer. I had forgotten the fun of that first night
of summer. Of knowing you had no real responsibilities for the next
ten weeks. I didn't know most of the music, but it didn't matter: girls
would lip-synch lyrics to my face on the dance floor, making sure I
got whatever it was Calle 13 was singing about. I don't know what
kicked in that night, but I finally started to let go. I didn't feel judged,
no co-workers' eyes on me, no phones recording my every move. Just
dancing with lots and lots of girls. In Chile you kiss on the cheek when
you meet someone of the opposite sex. At my old job you could barely
shake hands with a member of the opposite sex without a lawsuit.
Here if you *didn't* kiss them they got offended. So every girl I said hi
to I kissed, and they'd kiss me back, warmly. I had no idea how old
they were, and I didn't care, and neither did they. It was summer. I was
drunk, having fun, dancing. That's when I noticed her.

She was blond, tall, with blue-green eyes. She towered over the
other girls. She wore a white T-shirt with a gold cross necklace, cutoff
jean shorts, and brown boots. She had lots of bracelets on her arm and
a beautiful golden tan. She saw me looking (gawking) and smiled. I
wound up near her at the bar and ordered another piscola (pisco and
Coke). She heard my order and turned to me.

"Your first time in Santiago?" she asked, in English, much to my
surprise.

"That obvious?"

She laughed. "It's not hard to tell."

"Well, look at you," I said. "You look way more gringo than me."

She shook her head no, waving her finger. "I'm Chilean."

"What's your name?" I asked, hoping for an excuse to do the lean-in
kiss on the cheek.

"Sophie."

"Nice to meet you." I leaned in and kissed her on the cheek. She
kissed back. "I'm not used to seeing blond Chileans."

"I'm from Valdivia," she replied. "That's where all the blondes are
from."

Nico suddenly appeared, cutting between us and talking to her in Spanish. She was a model he had invited to a few of his events. I listened closely, understanding about a quarter of what they were saying but missing a lot due to the fact I don't really speak much Spanish, and even if I did the music was too loud to hear anything. Nico was the greatest wingman a single guy could ask for. He knew every girl, he could break the ice with anyone, and he could tell instinctively that I was culturally out of my depth and had swooped in to save me. I heard Nico tell Sophie something about me maybe investing in clubs with him in Chile, which was total bullshit, but his stories seemed to be working. Sophie kept looking at me and laughing at his jokes. Nico ordered us more piscolas and handed us the drinks. He shook his head at me—"Valdivia, dude. All the fucking hot blondes come from there"—before disappearing back into the crowd.

I talked with Sophie awhile longer before she told me she had to go back to her friends. One of her girlfriends had broken up with her boyfriend that night, so they were out to cheer her up. But before she left I did manage to get her number and WhatsApped her.

"Nice to meet you" was all I could come up with.

"You too," she replied, with a smiley-face emoji, and then a little face with a kiss.

Igal and Nico could not believe I didn't hook up with her. "Dude, that girl is fucking hot," Nico declared, as if I didn't know.

"I know, but her friend was all sad. I got her number."

"You're such a fucking gringo! Why do you think she was talking to you? Get her back to your hotel room."

Igal agreed. "It's every Jew's secret fantasy to fuck a hot Nazi."

I laughed. "What do you mean, 'Nazi'?"

"She's from Valdivia, dude. Why do you think they're all blond?" Nico said this as if it was the most obvious thing in the world, and Igal laughed. I couldn't tell if they were joking or not.

Nico suddenly got serious. "Valdivia's a weird place. Like, for real."

Igal nodded in agreement. They had been there once for the film festival, and he said everyone was looking at him like he was a Jew.

"Even with all those hot girls, it was still weird?" I asked.

"The signs are in German. Like you're in Germany," Nico explained. Nico had tried to visit Villa Baviera, a village where only German is spoken, which has its own Octoberfest. "The menus weren't even in Spanish," he said, shaking his head. "Fucked up."

I had always assumed the Nazis who fled to South America assimilated into the culture in some way, but Nico and Igal told me it was the opposite. An ex-Nazi named Paul Schaefer came to Chile and built a complete German town, going so far as to import the same German products he loved. He called it the Colony. Schaefer even went so far as to build a concentration camp–type compound, with barbed wire, attack dogs, and underground tunnels to use for torture. It was shut down in the 1990s and turned into a tourist village, but it left a lasting influence in the area. The remaining Nazis had moved into Valdivia.

"That's why their Chilean supermarkets are packed with foods imported from Germany," Igal said.

"Is it still like that?" I asked. They nodded. They claimed there were still sections in Valdivia where people spoke only German, and they know right away when you're an outsider. Especially a Jewish outsider.

I didn't believe it. I had to see this for myself, but they had no interest in taking me. Nico was promoting a music festival that weekend and dismissed it as just another city that's pretty but not that exciting; Santiago would be way more fun. I'd had enough with partying and drinking and chasing after twenty-one-year-olds who weren't really that interested in me anyway. I wanted to find the Nazi town. Did it still exist? Was it filled with old Nazis, or had their Nazi traditions gotten passed down to the next generation? What happened to the people who lived in that compound after it was closed? Would they really know I was a Jew just from looking at me? Every Jew has the fantasy of going back in time into Nazi Germany and killing everyone in sight. What if that town really existed—*today*? What if there was a secret Nazi community of actual World War II Nazis hidden at the end of the world and I could go there and expose it? I had spent time in Berlin—they seemed to have far fewer Nazis than South America did. I felt safer as a Jew in Berlin than I had anywhere else in Europe; the Germans couldn't have been nicer to me. This was different. These were people who not only didn't hide their past, they proudly kept it alive. Nico told me some strange stories about people who went near the Colony and disappeared. They had their own rules, their own police—the German descendants controlled it all. Nico even alluded to Schaefer having dungeons in the underground tunnels, where he raped children. It was stuff only the Nazis could come up with. Nico just shook his head. "There are fucking Nazis there, dude, I'm telling you. It's hard-core." I had to see for myself.

The next day I took the train to Valdivia. I looked up a few hotels online and found one that seemed halfway decent and booked a room. The whole ride I tried to imagine what it was going to be like when I got there. I step off the platform and am greeted by German shepherds, then moved to a crowd for selection. I dive for a Nazi, grabbing his gun, killing as many as I can before they sic the dogs on me . . . Or it would basically be just another city filled with Chileans, some of whom happen to be blond.

It turned out to be the latter. I don't know why I was disappointed that I didn't get off the train at a concentration camp with German shepherds barking. I was probably the first Jew ever to feel that way. That said, Valdivia was a lovely city. I took a taxi out to Villa Baviera, which turned out to be nothing more than a few German restaurants, a hotel, and a tourist shop. I walked around the old section of Valdivia, ate in a restaurant by the water (Peruvian, not German), posted some photos, and by late afternoon I was already bored and regretting having booked the room. The next train out was at 12:40 at night, but I decided to sleep there anyway since I had already paid for the hotel, and I found myself wandering around the town square. It was a warm summer night—a beautiful, bug-free evening, the kind I would have spent at the driving range drinking ice-cream sodas when I was seventeen years old. I found a pub that looked vaguely Germanic and was surprised to see that although the menu was in Spanish it offered a large number of German beers. I was sitting at a table, by myself, when my phone buzzed with a new message:

Look up.

I did, and right in front of me, across the pub at another table, a pretty blond girl waved to me: Sophie. She sat next to a larger, heftier blonde, who looked about thirty. I smiled and gave her a surprised look, and she waved for me to come join them.

"What are you doing here?" she asked.

"Well, I wanted to see where all the blondes came from. I was looking for the factory."

I kissed her on the cheek, and she introduced me to the other girl, whose kiss was more polite than flirty. "This is my sister, Angela," Sophie said. Upon closer examination, Angela looked like a heavier, frumpier version of her younger sister.

"Nice to meet you, Angela," I said, putting on a calculated smile.

"She doesn't speak much English," Sophie explained. Angela went back to her phone. Sophie asked where Nico was, and I told her he was back in Santiago at some music festival. She nodded; a lot of her friends were there too.

"How come you're not going?" I asked, eating some pretzels from a basket on the table. Her sister looked up from her phone, annoyed that this was not going to be a brief encounter. Angela was clearly accustomed to being the third wheel in groups with her model sister.

"My grandfather's sick," she explained. "I try to come home whenever I can. I feel like every visit could be the last."

"I'm sorry," I replied, not really knowing how to parlay that information into something more flirtatious.

"It's okay, he's very old, and he's not really there mentally. It's more for my mom." Her mother was taking care of her grandfather, who was living in their house. Or, rather, she was living in the grandfather's house, the house she had grown up in. Just then a few more guys arrived—*cuicos*, Nico would call them. These were the Chilean version of preppies, the handsome, athletic assholes from the high school movies I grew up on.

"My friends are here," Sophie said, getting up, waving to them. The guys didn't enter the pub. They looked over at me, nodding, lighting cigarettes, texting. In a flash I could see that the night wasn't going to end next to Sophie.

"We're going to a party at a friend's house if you want to join us," she invited.

"That's okay. I don't . . . really want to crash your friend's party. But thank you." I think she appreciated that I didn't make up a story that I had something else to do, given that she'd found me sitting alone in a pub in a city I had never heard of twenty-four hours ago.

"Okay. Well, when are you leaving?" she asked.

"I have a train tomorrow, but I can go anytime."

"Come for dinner at my mother's house. She makes an amazing Sunday dinner. It's worth the trip for the food." Her sister nodded in agreement.

"That sounds great," I said. She said she'd WhatsApp me the address, and I told her I'd see her there. Then she left with her friends. She looked back once more and smiled with a little wave. The guys also looked back, and the big one gave me a nod, the international gesture for "Nice try."

I spent the next morning jogging and then walking around town. I wanted to see more of the city but in a strange way didn't want to run into Sophie, as if that would give her some excuse to wiggle out of our plans. But she didn't. She just texted me around two: "Still coming?"

"Of course. I want my Sunday dinner!" I said, adding an angry-face emoji. She responded with a winking smile.

Sophie's house was small and unassuming and looked as if it had been built in the 1940s. She told me to be there at 7:30, so I arrived at 7:40 out of fear that she wouldn't be ready and I'd be stuck in a living room with her mother, pretending that I knew her daughter better than I actually did. In fact, when I arrived, they were already seated and eating, and I felt embarrassed. Sophie had told me not to bring anything, but of course I brought a bottle of wine, chalking it up to the nice Jewish boy manners my mother had hammered into me. Sophie's whole family was blond. Her mother, Katia; her uncle Karl; and some cousins, whose names I can't remember. "We started early because of the kids,"

Sophie explained, kissing me hello, making it clear that I hadn't done anything wrong by showing up a little late. I said hi to Angela, who seemed to be in a much friendlier mood. The mother, an even larger version of Angela, gestured for me to sit down and then heaped salad, rice, and fish on the same plate and put it in front of me. There was no mention, nor sign, of a father, so I didn't ask. Sophie made sure I sat next to her, and when I finally settled she gave my leg a little squeeze to let me know she was glad I'd made it. I felt the same.

The family didn't speak much English —the kids knew a bit more than the parents, and Sophie acted as a translator for the table. I tried my best to explain why I was in Chile. At first I started continuing the Nico lie about opening a club with him in Chile, but I soon dropped the act and said that I had sold a business for a lot of money and honestly had no idea what I wanted to do next. Sophie was still in school; she modeled on occasion to pay her bills but she really wanted to go into design. I saw some of her childhood drawings around the house and realized that her entire childhood had taken place when I was already an adult. They asked how old I was, and I joked my way out of it by saying I was seventy-five but that I looked very good for my age.

I noticed one empty seat at the table. There wasn't even a place setting. Sophie caught this.

"Grandpa's upstairs. He stays in bed mostly. We'll go say hi after we eat."

"Is that weird? You bringing some random American?" I asked. I don't know why I said "random." I felt stupid as soon as the world left my mouth.

"No, he's used to me bringing home strange men week after week," she teased, keeping a straight face.

"Oh, perfect," I added. And then we ate dessert.

I had no idea I was making a social faux pas when I stood up to clear my dishes. The entire table jumped, commanding me to sit down. I assumed it was because I was a guest, but then I learned that it's because I was a man, and that men don't do dishes in Chile. The women do. My mother raised me that you always help—always—but they were telling me to sit my ass down and let them take care of it. I was more than happy to oblige. I'd had about three glasses of wine at that point and was starting to feel it a bit. "Okay, okay, I had to offer. My mom raised me that way." Sophie took my empty plates with a smile, winking at me. "Just sit. Enjoy your wine." And so I did.

After dinner the mother went upstairs and then called down to Sophie. "Come," she said, leading me up the stairs. I passed by the pictures in the stairwell, watching Sophie and her family grow before my eyes as I walked by. At the top of the stairs, at the end of the hallway, I could see an old man sitting up in bed, the door wide open so he could see everything going on. We walked into his room and I noticed a distinct smell of old man. I wondered if that's what I was going to smell like if I ever made it to that age. The mother was standing over some kind of oxygen regulator, a very high-tech version of a scuba tank, next to an IV drip. She was trying to get the old man to eat the last little bit of food, but he wasn't having any of it, weakly waving her away.

I stood behind Sophie, following her cues. She got very quiet.

"*Hallo Opa*," she said in German.

"*Mein Kind*," he said weakly.

She looked at me. "He always calls me that. It means 'my child.'" His age shocked me. This wasn't an eighty-year-old grandpa. He looked like he was over a hundred. I couldn't tell if this was some illness, or if he was just really fucking old, but this man looked more like a great-great-great-grandfather than a grandpa. Sophie introduced me to him in German.

"Hello," I said. I looked at Sophie, asking if I should shake his hand, and she waved that it was okay, I didn't need to.

"This is my grandfather, Hans."

"Nice to meet you, Hans. *Guten Abend*." It was about all I could muster. He nodded.

"Where's your grandfather from?" I asked, knowing the answer.

"Austria. His family moved here when he was young." That was all she would say. I nodded, looking around the room. There were some books, old photos, a painting of a European countryside with people bathing in natural springs. Something from the motherland, I assumed.

Sophie's mother then asked her in Spanish to help her with something in the kitchen. I started to follow them out, but Sophie looked back and said, "It's okay, I'll be right back. Keep him company. Don't worry, he won't bite or anything."

And with that, she left me alone with the old man in the bed.

I stood there looking at Hans, who looked back with steel-blue eyes. It seemed far more awkward for me than for him. He was too old, too sick, and too tired to care what was happening. He nodded and smiled.

I looked around the room and noticed an antique wooden dresser with a picture on it of a young man in a military uniform. It was an old, faded photograph of a soldier. I looked closer. The soldier's uniform looked like something from the war. I couldn't tell what it was.

I pointed to the photo, and I don't know why, but I just asked him, "Austria?"

He looked at me, silent, as if he pretended not to hear me, but I know he saw me ask him.

I pointed to him. "Austria?" I repeated.

He nodded slightly, just a tiny head gesture. Maybe this was all he could communicate.

"Not German?" I asked, pretending I misunderstood. The old man didn't respond, so I pointed again.

"German?"

The man then mouthed a little, as if he was trying to say something, but all I could faintly hear was a sound that resembled air slowly escaping a bicycle tire. It took too much effort to speak, and he just closed his eyes. I was almost standing over him, watching him breathe. I looked at his night table. There were lots of medications, a carafe of water, a plate with some crumbs. A notepad. A pen. *A Sharpie.*

I don't know what possessed me, but I picked up the marker. I turned my back to the old man, so I was facing the doorway. I heard Sophie and her mother in the kitchen, the dishes still clanging, furniture moving. I rolled up my sleeve.

I stood directly over the old man. His eyes were still closed. When he opened them, I held out my arm in front of him, showing the number I had just written on my forearm:

A-15598

He looked up at me, then at the number again. His breathing started to increase, just slightly. I couldn't tell if he was angry or scared, and I pointed to the number again. Then I spoke the second word of German I had learned that morning on the train ride, specifically anticipating this moment:

"*Geist.*"

It meant "ghost." I pointed to myself, then to my tattoo, and repeated the word, this time more strongly, inches from his face.

"*Geist.*"

He began to shake, reaching his hand to the side for a call button. I moved it just enough so he couldn't reach it. I took a tissue from his night table and covered the underside of my hand with it. I then reached over to the knob on his oxygen tank and opened the valve with a turn. The sound of hissing oxygen filled the room, or at least I think it was oxygen—whatever it was flowing to the tubes running into his nose. He coughed a little, which turned into a spasm. I shoved my tattoo right in his face. He coughed louder, his eyes tearing. He looked up at me, begging with his eyes, his hand trying to touch mine. I then turned the nozzle fully open—the room now filled with the sound of hissing gas. I leaned over him, putting my eyes inches from his shaking head.

"*Brausebad,*" I breathed. He knew the meaning of that word. *Shower.*

His eyes locked with mine. They shook, welling with tears, until they rolled back into his head. His hand trembled and, after a moment, stopped. Completely. I leaned back. He wasn't moving anymore. I kicked the bed slightly to be sure. Nothing. I turned the knob back to where it had been, rolled down my sleeve, crumpled the tissue into my pocket, and left the room.

Sophie was helping with her mother in the kitchen when I came in. I told her that I had just gotten a text from Nico, that he had me on the list for some cool VIP party for the music festival, and that I had to catch the next train back to Santiago. I thanked her for dinner and told her I'd love to see her again that week. I kissed her on the cheek and turned to her mother, who gave me a very sweet hug and a kiss. She hugged me with just her arms, as her hands were wet, and looked at Sophie, smiling in approval. Sophie saw me to the door.

"She likes you."

"I like her. Thank you again for inviting me. It was really nice." I
kissed her on the cheek again and walked outside.

I inhaled a long, deep breath of the warm summer night air. It felt
spectacular. I could hear the sound of crickets, the same ones I used to
hear at overnight camp in Maine. I started walking, slowly at first, then
picked up the pace into a light jog. Soon I was running, arms wide
open, sucking in every delicious drop of the wind. And as the smile
grew across my open mouth, I erupted in the most joyous laugh I'd felt
since I was a teenager. It was summertime. I had no responsibilities. I
could do whatever I wanted. I felt *alive*.

Golden Hour

JEREMY SLATER

Batman is getting ready to puke.

He's been in a foul mood all morning. Picking fights with the other performers, edging his way into group shots, chasing down any tourist foolish enough to snap a picture without paying. That was before the wind died, before midday hit and the temperature spiked into the low nineties. Now Batman is slumped against the brick wall, with jagged slashes of black mascara running down his fat cheeks. The rest of us give him a wide berth. We've all had heatstroke. We all know what's coming next.

I sit cross-legged by the escalator, drumming my hands against the pavement. No signs or tip jars, not today, but that hasn't stopped a few people from pausing long enough to drop a few crumpled dollars on the ground. I smile politely and leave the bills where they fall. Sooner or later, some kid will come along and scoop them up. That's fine. I'm not here for the money.

I've staked out a shaded alcove at the far end of the Hollywood and Highland shopping complex. Here tourists crowd the forecourt of the Chinese Theatre, taking pictures of the sidewalk tiles or squatting to press their palms against the celebrity handprints in the concrete. Their children trail behind, bored out of their minds. They've never heard of James Mason or Clark Gable.

A few yards away, Oscar the Grouch is posing with four heavyset teenagers. He has his arms around their shoulders, and the girls are all shrieking with laughter. Just beyond that, Captain Jack Sparrow has stepped to the curb to bum a smoke off some cartoon badger that I don't recognize. The badger's head rests at the curb by his feet, its big plastic googly eyes staring right at me.

I'm wearing a costume too, but of a different kind: saggy-assed jeans, a stained tee, and a denim jacket that's split neatly down the back. There's a thin band of cloth to keep the sun out of my eyes and a rubber band holding my beard in check. An old pair of Jordans, swiped from the backseat of some gym rat's Grand Cherokee. Green socks, a few sizes too large, which keep slipping down and bunching around my ankles. Nothing that would make you look twice. Just another cautionary tale.

Okay, that's not entirely true. There is one misplaced detail, one element that doesn't quite belong. A faded red-and-white checkerboard scarf is bound securely around my left wrist. The fabric is delicate, gossamer, nearly transparent. It's my only keepsake from my previous life. I bury my face in the scarf and inhale deeply. On good days I like to imagine that I can still pick out lingering traces of her shampoo: one of those cheap brands in a green plastic bottle, some coconut-infused attempt at tropical flavor. Today I can't smell anything at all.

Another dollar lands at my feet. "God bless," I murmur automatically. Wondering if it's safe to risk another look. Knowing that I don't have a choice, not really. I need to know if it's still there.

I raise my head, slowly, casually, and scan the crowded street.

I feel a bright flare of panic when I don't immediately see the thing . . . but that's the point, isn't it? The harder you look, the better they hide. I force myself to relax, to take a deep, calming breath. Letting my eyes gradually lose focus, like a child trying to puzzle out a Magic Eye illusion. The world blurs, all the sharp edges dropping away.

And I see the creature.

You figure out which neighborhoods are safe. They rarely come over the hill, and never farther than Toluca Lake or North Hollywood. They tend to avoid the beach cities, and they hate the desert.

Stay away from Disneyland. It's crawling with them.

West Hollywood is usually safe, as long as you don't go near the bars on Sunset. Be careful near the reservoir. Beverly Hills is a death trap.

I try to avoid downtown altogether. That's where the big ones hide. As a general rule, I don't fuck with anything that's large enough to use a skyscraper as camouflage.

"Son of a *bitch*."

Batman takes a lurching step away from the wall. Jack Sparrow sees it coming and mutters something to the cartoon badger. They watch impassively as Batman leans over the trash can and heaves up his lunch. A few of the tourists look repulsed, but most seem delighted. They stand in a rough circle, phones out, recording the vomiting crime fighter. Here at last is the authentic Hollywood they came to experience.

I reach inside the folds of my jacket and absently run my fingers along the blade. The sporting-goods store called it a "parang," but that's just another fancy word for machete. Eight inches of curved steel attached to a textured neoprene grip. It's made for cutting firewood, but it should work for my purposes.

If I can lure that thing close enough.

I let my eyes flicker upward, just for a second. The creature is still across the street, balanced carefully on its hind legs. It's not the biggest one I've ever hunted, but it's damn close. At the moment, its entire head is jammed through one of the third-story windows of the Roosevelt Hotel. It has been rooting around in there for almost forty-five minutes now.

I can't imagine what's taking place inside that hotel room.

What would happen if I placed an anonymous call to the Roosevelt and told them one of their guests was being murdered? Most likely nothing. Even if I could somehow convince them, even if they sent up hotel security to kick down the door, what would they actually see? Probably some failed pop singer from Kentucky, sprawled across the hotel bed with a pill bottle in her hand and a throat clogged with white foam. Or maybe a lonely old man floating in a bathtub, both wrists opened, the water stained black with blood. Give the creatures this much credit: they're fanatical about cleaning up their messes. The bodies they leave behind rarely arouse suspicion.

One thing's for certain: the security guards wouldn't see the creature's wedge-shaped head, flat and ugly, protruding through the solid wall like some kind of demented hunting trophy.

You don't see them unless you know where to look.

I suppose anyone who undergoes a life-changing experience—call it an awakening, an epiphany, or just a nervous fucking breakdown, it's all the same to me—emerges on the other side with a story. You feel an overpowering need to explain to other people why your nice, orderly life suddenly jumped the tracks. Why a part of you simply left and never came back.

My story started with a girl. Isn't that always the way? Her name was Kimberly, but her friends called her Kimmy. We had been exchanging texts and e-mails for a few weeks. Nothing serious, not yet, but things felt like they were moving in the right direction. The potential was there.

This was back in the Time Before, back when I still had a name and a Social Security number and close to three quarters of a million dollars in the bank. I was a senior marketing manager for a company that supervised the postconversion process for 3-D movies. It sounds exciting, I know. In reality it was a bunch of bleary-eyed programmers sitting in dark offices, arguing about plate differentials and variable focal points. I spent most of my time smoking cigarettes on the balcony and taking online personality quizzes. Let the nerds do their thing. I was just there to sell the finished product.

It took some work, but Kimberly finally agreed to meet me for drinks, frozen strawberry margaritas at the El Coyote. The restaurant was booked solid, but we managed to claim a booth near the bar, both of us yelling to be heard. Kimberly got lit off her first drink and told me she was writing a novel. She bobbed her head when she talked, nervous and birdlike. At one point I told her that Sharon Tate ate her last meal on earth right here at the Coyote, just a few booths from where we were sitting. I tried to make a joke of it, but she recoiled like I had slapped her. Girls. You never know what's going to set them off.

I bought another round of margaritas, but when I returned to the table, Kimberly was already shrugging on her jacket. This was fun, she said. There was something crooked in her smile, something ugly and insincere. I felt a familiar prickling sensation just behind my eyes.

She kissed the air beside my cheek. She said, Let's do it again sometime.

That's when the headache came on in full, a roaring jet of white-hot pressure. I've always had what my mother used to call a "touchy" nervous system, prone to tension headaches and migraines, but I knew right away this was different.

The pain rolled over me in waves, each one stronger than the last. The room darkened, my field of vision constricting to a narrow pinprick of light. I gripped the sides of the table, my knuckles turning white, willing myself not to scream. From somewhere far away I heard Kimberly (Kimmy to her friends) asking if I was all right, if I needed any help.

After that, things got a little fuzzy.

I awoke on the floor, my body curled around the base of the table, one cheek flush against the cold metal surface. Several waiters loomed over me, their faces pale and frightened. My headache had mercifully faded to a dull background murmur. I tried saying I was fine, that I didn't need an ambulance, but the words came out wrong. There was a sour, coppery taste in my mouth. Blood. It was smeared across my teeth, running from the corner of my mouth. I had chewed away part of my cheek.

Kimberly's seat was empty.

I asked one of the waiters where she had gone, thinking she was probably in the lobby, explaining the situation to a manager. Or maybe she was already outside, waiting to flag down the ambulance when it arrived.

"I dunno, man." The waiter shrugged, embarrassed, not quite meeting my gaze. "You were saying some pretty weird stuff."

Stay awake long enough and you can straddle the line. One foot in our reality, the other in theirs. If you've ever gone without sleep for several days, you know what I'm talking about. You've probably caught glimpses of their world. It's the place where colors bleed, where light doesn't hold its shape.

I call it the Golden Hour. It's when I do my best hunting.

Somewhere along the way, they must have figured out that I was onto them. That I was closing in on the truth.

They came for me first.

Back then I had a nice little spot staked out in Tent City with all of the homeless. It was prime real estate too: a Chinese takeout joint on one side, an all-night Laundromat on the other. I wasn't stupid; I knew downtown could be dangerous, but in those days there were only a few of the truly big ones wandering around, and they were easy enough to avoid if you kept your eyes open. Besides, there were close to two hundred of us cordoned off in those two blocks, a crush of humanity, faded tents and makeshift campsites spilling across every sidewalk. I figured that had to count for something. That's how green I was: I still believed in concepts like safety in numbers.

And I had a partner. Dave Stacks, a nervous kid with sleeve tattoos and watery blue eyes. He couldn't have been more than nineteen. Dave had come from Grand Rapids in a cherry-red Datsun, bringing only two boxes of clothing and an electric guitar. But these were the streets of Jim Morrison and Brian Wilson, of Axl and Eddie, and no one here gave a shit about a perfectly serviceable bass player. It was an old, boring story. The Datsun was the first thing he sold, the guitar the last.

In those days, I would talk about the creatures to anyone who would listen. Most people ignored me, but not Dave. He was quick to understand and eager to believe. He would listen for hours, wide-eyed, bobbing his head in agreement. I taught him everything I knew about our enemy. Their hunting patterns, their preferred methods of camouflage. It turned out Dave had a knack for spotting them, and it wasn't long before he was seeing a creature on every corner.

We divided each night into shifts. One person sleeping, the other standing watch. It seemed to work well enough, and entire weeks passed without incident. My tension headaches went away. For the first time in a long time, I began to feel safe.

Then one night I woke up halfway down the throat of one of those fucking things.

I could feel its esophagus constricting as it worked me down, inch by inch. The creature was grunting happily, a gentle piggy sound, its eyes rolled back with pleasure. They looked like two dull white marbles.

I tried to scream, but the pressure around my chest was enormous, forcing the air from my lungs. I looked around wildly and saw Dave sitting cross-legged a few feet away, his back against the Laundromat wall, his brows furrowed in confusion. A shard of bright green glass was buried in his throat, part of a broken beer bottle. Dave's shirt was wet and glistening black in the moonlight. I felt a momentary flash of confusion. *How had the creature even held the weapon?* It had no arms or legs; it was little more than a long, serpentine neck, flowing down into the sidewalk. There was still so much I didn't understand about their kind.

Dave was staring right at me, unblinking. He must have screamed. I don't know why I didn't hear it.

The crushing pressure intensified. I could feel my rib cage shifting, the bones grinding together. The creature must have realized I was awake. It was trying to force me down. To swallow me whole.

I worked one of my arms free and clawed at the creature's snout. Its skin was surprisingly soft, almost velveteen, and cool to the touch. Cold-blooded, then. I filed that information away for future use. Farther down, at the junction where the creature's body fused with the sidewalk, its skin hardened and took on the dusty color and texture of dry cement.

The creature arched its neck, lifting me off the ground and slamming me back down. The back of my head cracked against the concrete, filling my vision with white-hot tracer rounds. My jaws clacked shut and I tasted blood. Its nubby little teeth dug against the small of my back.

Once more the creature lifted me and brought me crashing back down, but this time I was ready. I reached out, straining for Dave's body. My fingers closed around his shirt, sticky with blood, and I pulled him closer.

The creature snorted hungrily.

My hand closed around the shard of glass lodged in Dave's throat. It was stuck fast in the gristle. I worked it free, slowly, methodically, knowing I would get only one shot at this.

The shard popped free with a wet sucking noise, just as the creature lifted me skyward and slammed me sideways against the brick wall. I found myself staring into one of the monster's milky white eyes. It was watching me with an uninterested expression, almost bored. I drove the shard into its eyeball, as deep as it would go.

The creature let out a muffled roar, more surprise than pain. I mashed the shard deeper, the pupil running like jelly between my fingers. The creature's jaws relaxed, its tongue working desperately as it tried to expel me, to vomit me back onto the pavement.

I held on tight. I wasn't going anywhere.

Finding her address wasn't difficult. A house on Kirkwood, right at the mouth of Laurel Canyon, in a neighborhood filled with broke old hippies and rich young assholes. I got there a few minutes past midnight, but the driveway was empty and no one answered the door.

I decided to wait in my car.

It was crazy, I knew that, showing up unannounced in the middle of the night. Maybe it was crossing some kind of imaginary line. But what else was I supposed to do? Kimberly wouldn't answer my calls, wouldn't return my texts.

And all I wanted was a chance to explain myself. To show her I was a nice, normal guy. The kind of guy you bring home to meet your parents. And if I had said some weird stuff during my little (*not a seizure don't call it a seizure*) blackout period . . . well, who could blame me for that?

Besides, she was the one who left me in that restaurant, convulsing on the floor. The more I thought about it, the angrier I got. What kind of person does that? As far as I was concerned, *she* should be apologizing to *me*, not the other way around.

The hours ticked by. I killed the radio to conserve the battery. My breath frosted strange patterns on the glass. I'd left the house without grabbing a jacket. Stupid. I did find a bottle of Ketel One in the backseat, somehow already half empty. I didn't remember opening it, but that was the least of my worries. I drank deeply, letting the warmth radiate throughout my body, leaving my limbs heavy and useless. There was pressure behind my sinuses, but the pain was manageable.

I stared at her house, waiting for a car to pull into the driveway, for a light to appear in the upstairs window. The world was swimming in and out of focus, all shapes and suggestions. The white stucco façade became a wall of flashing static, the windows dead pixels. Every time a car passed on the street, its headlights left contrails of bleeding color.

My gaze drifted higher, toward the second-floor balcony. There wasn't much to see up there. A few Target lawn chairs, halfheartedly arranged beneath a faded sun umbrella. A ceramic ashtray overflowing with butts. A women's ten-speed chained to the railing. Nothing else.

Except that wasn't quite right, I began to realize. There *was* something else on the balcony. I had been staring at it this entire time.

Something *shifted*. That's the best way I can describe what happened. One moment it didn't exist, and the next it did. Its skin was pebbled, covered with bumpy little spines and ridges, perfectly camouflaged to match its surroundings, like some kind of overgrown chameleon. The creature solidified with an audible popping noise, its form snapping into focus. My first guess wasn't too far off: the thing actually looked like a goddamn lizard, with a long, flat head that tapered to a narrow point and sunken, diamond-shaped eyes. Its skin had split apart in places, revealing jagged bone protuberances, twisting outward from its brow like antlers. It stood pressed against the patio wall, balancing on its muscular hind legs, perhaps twelve feet long from tip to tail.

I held my breath, not even daring to blink. I was dimly aware of a spreading warmth between my legs, but I didn't care. I slowly set the bottle on the floorboard, careful to keep my gaze fixed on the creature. Somehow I knew that if I looked away, even for a second, I would lose it forever.

The creature swiveled its head around and, for a moment, held my gaze. Its eyes were muddy green, flecked with shooting streaks of gold. Its lips curled back in an exaggerated yawn. The inside of its mouth was an explosion of small, serrated teeth, all pointing in different directions, like headstones in a cartoon graveyard. Its gums were bone white, cankerous and diseased.

I blinked and the creature bolted.

Try to understand: these things move in the space between heartbeats. Faster than the human eye can follow. When they're in motion, the world judders and skips like an old movie projector. You have to try to anticipate their trajectories, to slide your eyes along a parallel line and hope for the best. If you're lucky, you might catch just a flicker, the barest suggestion of motion. I call them "pings," like the radar pings in some old submarine movie.

The creature vanished from the porch, blinking out of existence. I caught a lucky *ping* as it landed atop the recycling bin by the street corner, its skin instantly changing color to match the hard blue plastic. Then it flickered out of existence again, its body somehow shifting upward this time. There was one last fleeting *ping*, the spectral residue of the creature's serpentine body coiled around the top of the nearest telephone pole, and then it was gone, ghosting into the night.

Like it was never there at all.

I was lucky; I know that now. Once it realized it was being watched, the creature could have turned on me. It could have launched itself through my windshield, could have torn out my throat with a single, savage tug of its jaws. But instead it turned and fled.

Most of them don't.

The creature is still rooting around inside the Roosevelt, but now it's slowing down. Its neck jerks and bobs as it chews methodically. I'm not quite sure what their kind feeds on—human suffering? psychic trauma? snacks from the minibar?—but it's obvious this particular meal is just about over.

I have to act soon. A full belly means the creature will be lethargic, its reflexes dulled. I'll never get a better shot.

The old, familiar pressure begins to build, a freezing ice pick lodged just behind my sinus cavities. Another headache. I'm not surprised.

Every hunt begins the same way, with a dull, pounding roar between my ears. In some distant part of my mind, I feel an old memory trying to claw its way to the surface. It's an image, a snapshot of a kindly, round-faced doctor. *This is the hard part,* the doctor is telling me. He writes down the name of an online support group, encourages me to get a second opinion. He places one meaty hand on my shoulder. All the while watching me with a look of practiced sympathy.

I shove the memory aside. I can't afford to let anything break my concentration. Not when I'm so close.

I have to steady myself. Focus and control. I carefully unwrap the scarf from around my wrist. The gingham pattern dances across the fabric, marching columns of red and white. I hold the scarf against my face again and this time I can smell it: that familiar tropical breeze, warm and inviting, with just the faintest hint of coconut and spice. It's so unexpected that tears spring to my eyes. I had thought the scent was gone forever. I thought I had lost her.

Batman has finished throwing up, but he remains hunched over the trash can, hiccuping slightly as he struggles to catch his breath. His face is glossy with sweat, the skin waxy and swollen. It makes him look airbrushed, like a caricature portrait. Like he's not even real.

Pain flares between my eyes, the ice pick rotating a few more degrees, but I barely feel it. I climb to my feet and start toward him, binding the scarf around my wrist as I go.

"You all right, man?" I call out.

As I approach, Batman's legs buckle and he nearly pitches over. He braces himself against the wall and belches again. The muscles in his upper arm tremble. Up close, his costume is shockingly cheap, the sort of thing you'd buy the day before Halloween, when the racks are empty and all the best costumes are gone. There's a sour smell coming off him in waves, bourbon and sweat and whatever's left of his lunch.

I place a friendly hand on his back to steady him. "Whoa, easy there."

"Geddis fuggin thing off," he mumbles, tugging at the plastic cowl.

"You got it," I say cheerfully as I slide the machete into his side.

The blade goes in easily, slipping between his ribs with almost no resistance, almost to the hilt. He makes a low noise, halfway between a gasp and a sigh.

Across the street, the creature's head whips around. Staring right at me.

The hardest part is always getting their attention.

Once you start noticing them, you see them everywhere. Curled around the arches of a gas station on Western. Crawling along the walls of the Scientology Celebrity Centre, clustered like bloated ticks. Huddled beneath an overpass in Commerce, hundreds of them, their lidless eyes rolling madly in the shadows.

Do you understand what I'm trying to tell you? This isn't a warning, or a call to arms, or anything like that. The invasion is over. The war already happened, and our side didn't even bother to show up.

Jesus, is it any wonder that we lost?

I pull the machete free. The blade is wet, but there's no arterial fan of blood, no cartoon geyser of gore. Batman simply sinks to his knees, wheezing and holding his side. I hear someone scream, but the sound is muted, far away.

I run.

Now people begin to notice the dying man in their midst. A ripple of shock and panic passes through the crowd. Then it's pandemonium. Parents grab for their children. Tourists stumble blindly into the street. Tires scream and horns blare. I duck and weave down the sidewalk, cradling the machete to my chest, and the crowd parts before me.

Out of the corner of one eye, I spot the creature. It's still on the far side of Hollywood Boulevard, but it's matching my pace effortlessly, loping along on all fours. It cycles through objects and structures, becoming part of the buildings, the traffic light, the souvenir cart, the crosswalk. Changing form and shape faster than my eye can follow.

It's trying to head me off. To catch me out in the open.

I change direction and dive back into the crowd. There is a flash of motion in my peripheral vision, but it's only the scarf around my wrist, flapping in the wind, a vein of bright crimson trailing behind me.

A staircase materializes in my path, and I take the stairs two at a time. Orange helium balloons are tied to the railing, most of them partially deflated, sagging in the breeze. AUGUST IS FRIENDS AND FAMILY MONTH! Some distant part of my brain registers this with alarm; I had thought we were only halfway through June.

As I reach the double doors at the top of the stairs, a guy in baggy beach shorts emerges, adjusting the straps of his bicycle helmet. Without slowing down, I sink the machete into the fleshy part of his shoulder. It's nothing personal, but I have to be sure that thing is still following me. Mr. Bike Helmet is too surprised even to react. The muscles in his face sag all at once, his expression going slack, like he's somehow disappointed in me. He sits down with a grunt. I tug the blade free and stumble through the swinging doors.

It's a gym, one of the trendy upscale ones, with rows of stationary bikes overlooking a maze of Nautilus equipment. Two pretty young girls are perched behind the counter. One of them starts to smile at me, but then she sees the machete and her mouth twists.

I quickly scan the room, searching for the emergency exits. There has to be another way out of here, or I'm a dead man.

I feel a sudden drop in air pressure, a change in the room's equilibrium. Behind me, I hear a dry clacking noise, claws against cement, and realize it's already too late. I'm out of time.

I paid one more trip to the little white house on Kirkwood Drive. By that point I had been hunting long enough to understand the creatures' methodology. I knew if they were hanging around Kimberly's house, there was probably a good reason.

She was consorting with the goddamned things.

Communing with them.

She was Kimmy to her friends, but it was becoming obvious that she would always be Kimberly to me. I got to her house a little after two in the morning, and this time she was home.

She answered the door still half asleep, wearing yoga pants and an oversized Ohio State sweatshirt. Her hair was pulled back, tucked beneath a scarf with a red-and-white gingham pattern. She must have been expecting someone else—a boyfriend, perhaps, or possibly even one of *them*—because it took her a moment to recognize me. When she did, that dreamy little half smile disappeared. She tried to shut the door, but I was faster.

By the end, she confessed to everything, just like I knew she would. I clawed it out of her, the truth, the awful truth, piece by piece. And when I had heard enough, I wrapped the scarf around her neck and pulled both ends tight. Her heels drummed against the kitchen tiles, fluttering like an arrhythmic heart, beating out a message in a code meant just for me. She never blinked, never broke my gaze. Her damp hair spilled across the floor, spreading like a stain. She must have just washed it, because it still smelled like coconut oil.

I spot the creature, gliding forward on silent paws, and I feel another pinching sensation behind my sinuses, another white-hot starburst of pain. For an instant I'm somewhere far away, sitting in an antiseptic examination room, staring at cold blue X-rays, images of a hollowed-out skull flecked with malignant patches of white, while the friendly, round-faced doctor asks me if there's someone I can call. I push the memory aside and stumble forward, ignoring the shouts of alarm. A black man with a shaved head reaches for me, his expression concerned, almost gentle. I shove him aside, forgetting about the parang in my hand. He jerks away with a cry, cupping his left wrist, blood bubbling up between his fingers.

Ahead of me is a staircase leading to the second floor, where the free-weight equipment is located. There's a blond girl marching up and down the stairs, head bowed, her legs pumping like pistons. She's wearing earbuds, a lucky break. She doesn't hear me coming.

I feel another rush of air as the creature comes for me. I grab the girl's arm and spin her around. She's pretty, with wide-set hazel eyes and a mouth that forms a perfect circle of surprise. All at once I'm struck by her resemblance to Kimberly. They could be sisters. Then her gaze flickers up and to the right, focusing on something just over my shoulder, and she sees it too. Sees the creature scrambling toward us on all fours, thick and ungainly, slobber spilling from its cracked mouth, its eyes twin pits of burning coal.

I'm not crazy, I think, feeling a sudden, desperate surge of gratitude. *It's real. She sees it too.*

The creature flows up the steps behind us. It leaps into the staircase railing—*ping!*—then passes into the girl's hand—*ping!*—running along the length of her entire arm. For one brief instant, she is part of the creature, and it is part of her.

And in that instant, the creature is tangible.

Mortal.

Using both hands, I ram the blade through her chest, putting my full weight behind it. There is a moment of terrible resistance as the blade scrapes along her sternum, then it slips a few millimeters to the left and slides the rest of the way in. The girl's teeth snap shut and she arches her neck. In some distant corner of my mind, I can hear the creature shrieking, its voice reedy and childlike.

Got you, you fuck.

Got you good.

The girl's legs give out, and I gently lower her to the ground. All around me, people are trampling toward the exit. I know that I should be running too, but all I feel is a sense of peace. My skin is warm to the touch, and the pressure in my sinuses has vanished entirely. I always feel like this in the moments following a successful hunt. Like I'm floating in tropical waters.

Carefully, I wipe the blade on the girl's shirt. I hold the gingham scarf over her mouth for a moment, hoping to capture her last breath, perhaps even some small part of her essence. She's staring up at me, her eyes wide and puzzled. I hesitate, then reach down and slide her eyelids shut. I feel sorry for her, of course. It hardly seems fair that she had to die. But she was part of a larger war, whether she knew it or not, and wars demand sacrifice.

I leave her there, sprawled across the steps, one leg bent crooked beneath her body, and I head for the emergency exit. The front desk is deserted, but the music is still playing from somewhere high overhead. I push open the exit door and jog down the stairs. I realize I'm smiling, a great daffy grin plastered across my face, and I wonder if it has been there the whole time.

I can already hear sirens in the distance. They're headed this way, but I'm not worried. They won't catch me, not tonight. After all, I'm good at hiding.

I learned from the best.

A Clean White Room

SCOTT DERRICKSON AND C. ROBERT CARGILL

The Lobby

The *clack-clack-clack* of his wing-tip shoes rings out stark and steady against the polished marble floors, echoing with a tinny din through the cavernous old lobby. At one time this place was the height of luxury, but now the wallpaper is decades old, yellowed with water stains, peeling in places, the mahogany front desk chipped, abused, languishing just this side of total ruin. Yet somehow the browns, yellows, and whites blend together into something homey, comforting. In the right light it might even seem quaint.

But it never quite holds the right light. In fact, it is rare that this building has exactly the right light at all. *Quirky.* That's how the Landlord had put it. The wiring is *quirky.* Damned inconvenient is what it really is.

He's pacing again, counting his steps again, each stride just shy of covering the breadth of the black-and-white checkerboard pattern splayed from one dingy wall to the other. Eighty-seven and a half steps wide, 112 from door to desk. But it feels bigger. Sounds bigger. It seems to change shape in the night, the walls growing farther apart or contracting inches at a time. But it is always 87½ steps wide and 112 steps from door to desk. No matter how many times he counts, it is always the same.

He stops. He turns. And there are his groceries. Two large paper bags filled with the same items they held last week. And the week before that. And as many weeks back as he can remember.

He didn't hear a knock, or a key in the tumbler, and the delivery boy made no announcement. He'd always assumed the delivery boy was scared of the place, creeped out by the images on the carved ebony front doors, chased off by the eerie silence that always pervades this place. But he never saw him, never spoke to him, couldn't say with any certainty that such a delivery boy even existed. Groceries simply appeared, always when he wasn't looking. So he walks back 112 steps, picks up his groceries, and walks 43 steps back toward a large oak door with a small, slightly corroded brass plate that reads: SUPERINTENDENT.

The Superintendent fumbles in his jacket pocket and keys clatter into his hand, several dozen different cuts and shapes and metals all bound together on a single large brass ring. He thumbs through them, finding the right one by touch. The key goes in smooth and silent, the lock clicking only faintly, the knob whispering gently as it turns. It is the quietest door in the building. It has to be, for it hides its greatest secrets.

He opens the door, slides quickly in, and sniffs deeply at the air of the place.

The apartment beyond is opulent, almost ridiculous, both in size and architecture. While all of the rooms in the building are unusually large, the Superintendent's dwelling is second only to the penthouse in size. In any other building it would sell for millions, but in this one, nothing—a prize instead only for someone willing to hold the building together with spit, baling wire, and moxie alone. The ceilings are vaulted, ebony beams running across them, chandeliered lights dripping from the center of nearly every room. The floors are hardwood, dark, scuffed, the wood soft in places from the tread of a century's worth of traffic. The walls had once been white but are now a sort of eggshell from the smoke of five previous superintendents. The fireplace is massive, brought stone by stone across the sea from some ancient residence. And the kitchen is large, designed with servants in mind, updated just enough to be modern, but not so recently that everything worked properly.

Despite the opulence, the apartment on the whole is spartan. No art, no photos, no statues or sculptures, just a simple table with a single chair, one red crushed-velvet couch—well worn—a rocking chair by the fireplace, and a bed, a wardrobe, and a nightstand in the adjoining master bedroom. It is otherwise stone, wood, and wallpaper. Nothing more.

The Superintendent methodically puts his groceries away in the kitchen, each sundry finding its way to a very specific, well-rehearsed location. There is an order to it, almost a ceremony. The flour goes in a perfectly sized clean spot amid a dusting of scattered meal where all of the other bags of flour had rested before; the oil in a spot flush against the cabinet's back corner; the carton of milk immediately below the refrigerator's bulb. Each item in its exact place despite there being no lack of room for them to find another home. It is as he wanted and no other way.

THUMP.

He looks up, eyes narrowed at the room above him. Apartment 202. The one with the ironwood door. Another *THUMP.* Then a series of rumbles and rattles like an awkward tap dance by large, clumsy, untrained feet. The Superintendent sighs deeply.

It shouldn't be time yet, he mutters to himself.

He quickly puts the last remaining groceries away before adjourning to his bedroom to get changed. Strips out of his sweatpants, jacket, and T-shirt, opens the doors on the antique mahogany wardrobe. Inside, a single gray wool suit. Three-piece. Single-breasted. A narrow gray wool tie. And a cotton shirt with bone buttons. The Superintendent dresses quickly, leaving neither a hair nor fiber out of place.

He opens the bottom drawer, digging through a pile of T-shirts and pants, drawing out from beneath them a small fifteen-inch ebony lockbox, carved seemingly from the same wood as the front doors and almost identically decorated. Angels upon demons upon knights and knaves. The Superintendent takes a deep breath, cracks his neck from side to side, and leaves his apartment, grabbing his key ring on the way out, locking the door silently behind him, and making his way across the lobby to the elevator.

The Desert

He was swallowed by the moonless black so deep and far-reaching, the only way to tell the difference between the earth and the sky was by where the stars began. The sky was riddled with them. More than he'd ever seen at once. It was the type of sky one expected to see only in the still quiet of an uneventful night. But this was far from that.

There was shouting, screaming. And when a mortar exploded half a football field away, the *BOOM* rattled his bones and the landscape lit up with a flash of daylight. But just for a moment, a scant terrifying moment. He scanned the ground for shadows, for bodies, for the things that might be hiding, waiting for him in the black. His breaths were measured, controlled, desperate for calm, and he counted his paces—253 of them in total between the latrine he'd just left and his bunker.

He had to find his way back, had to get back to the concrete bed beneath which he could cower and cry to himself, more afraid of the things that might be lurking just outside the light than the explosives and shrapnel that might shred him into a puff of pink mist. *Only fifty more steps to go. Only forty-seven more steps to go. Only forty-three more steps to go. Only forty more steps . . .*

202. The Ironwood Door

The lift key turns and the tiny antiquated brass-and-iron elevator rattles to life. It jerks and sputters in fits on the way up, but it's better than taking the stairs. You never know how long the stairs will take. The insides are polished to a high shine and the Superintendent eyes his reflection, nervously adjusting his tie before brushing a bit of stray dandruff from his shoulder. It takes nearly a minute to get to the second floor, and when the doors open he quickly steps out, staring headlong into a mirror. He looks both ways down the hall, unsure where 202 is today. These halls are tricky. They coil around like snakes twisted up in themselves, the lengths seeming sometimes impossible, other times merely improbable.

To the right the overhead lights shine bright and steady, but to the left they dim ever so slightly every few seconds before brightening back up, an ever-present buzz oscillating along with them. The lights are always stranger near 201, so he turns to the right and begins a winding tour of the second floor. One hundred twenty-four steps. It is always 124 steps. Three turns and a long corridor later he finds it. Just as he remembers, 124 steps in. The ironwood door. Three small brass numbers. Two zero two. And a brass knocker, a small piece of note card slotted into it with the tenant's name: Mr. Fitzpatrick.

The Superintendent jangles his keys, searching for 202. He hasn't used it often yet, still hasn't memorized its shape, and tries three different keys, all black stainless steel. The first two get stuck halfway in; the third slides in like cutting through butter. The knob creaks a little as it turns but not too loud, and the hinges whine softly as the door swings open.

The inside of the apartment is even more spartan than his own. White walls. No table. No fireplace. Just three mirrors, each on a wall of its own. And a single wooden chair.

Tied to that chair with brown leather straps is Mr. Fitzpatrick.

Fitzpatrick is a nebbishy man. A small man. Wiry. Like a bundle of sticks pieced together beneath khaki pants and a polo shirt, each stick ready to snap under the slightest pressure. His hair buzzed close, balding around an ailing widow's peak. Skin pale, chin weak, eyes a little too close together. Trembling, he looks up at the Superintendent, lip quivering, a scream caught in his throat.

"Please, don't kill me."

"What did I tell you?" asks the Superintendent, his voice croaking, deep with bass.

"Please God. Don't kill me. Just let me go."

"What. Did. I. Tell. You."

Fitzpatrick looks shamefully down at his ragged tennis shoes. "Not to make a sound."

"So why am I up here?"

"I made a sound."

"You made several."

"You're just going to kill me anyway."

"I don't want to," says the Superintendent.

"But you will."

"I don't have a choice. Not now."

"You don't have to kill me."

"This is all on you and you know it."

"Please," begged Fitzpatrick. "I have a family."

"No, you don't," he says coldly. "Not anymore."

Fitzpatrick's eyes go wide, his mouth yawning in terror.

"What did you do?" he whispers.

The Superintendent slowly opens the ebony box, eyeing Fitzpatrick all the while. Inside is a twelve-inch wooden dagger, blackened by fire, sharpened from hilt to tip, decorated with symbols and scrawl, letters from a long-dead language. He grasps the hilt, squatting to set the box gently on the hardwood floor. Then he springs across the room, holding the blade against Fitzpatrick's neck, rage spilling out from calm waters. "Who are you?" he bellows.

"Jerry Fitzpatrick!"

"No! I didn't ask who you were. Who are you *now*?"

"Jerry!" Fitzpatrick bounces around in his chair, screaming. "I don't know what you want me to say! Tell me and I'll say it! I'll say anything! Please!"

"I want the truth."

"I told you the truth. You want me to lie."

"You're full of lies. Nothing but. Tell me who you are and this can all be over."

Fitzpatrick looks down at the knife. Wooden, but carbonized and razor sharp. He wets himself.

"Jerry Fitzpatrick," he says meekly, knowing full well what is coming.

The Superintendent clenches a tight fist, punches him square in the jaw, knocks the chair over onto its back. Fitzpatrick's head bangs against the floor, the sound like a hollow being hit by a hammer. Tears stream down the side of his face into his hair, piss turning half of his khakis a deep soaking brown.

The Superintendent looms over him, pointing the blade like a wand directly at his heart.

"Who are you?"

THUMP. THUMP. THUMP.

They both look up, Fitzpatrick's eyes wide with surprise, the Superintendent furrowing his brow, scowling at the ceiling. *Three oh one. Goddammit.* The Superintendent leans over, grabs the back of the chair with his free hand, flinging it upright in a single motion.

"Stay here," he says. "Stay quiet. Or this will all get worse. Much, much worse."

Slamming the door behind him, he stares down the hallway at his reflection in the mirror. He seethes, breathing heavy, teeth clenched, dagger clutched tight in a white-knuckled fist. Then he storms down the hallway, his shoes sounding a far brisker *clack-clack-clack* than before, his mind desperately retracing the steps back to the elevator in order to then find his way to 301—the one with the Spanish cedar door.

The Desert

The daylight was harsh, the heat unbearable, barren earth stretching as far as the eye could see, broken only by shacks and stone buildings. His team leaned back against the mud-brick wall, crowded around the door, M4 carbines held close against their chests. Their packs were heavy on their backs, sweat pouring down their brows, dripping onto their hard plate vests.

Miller nodded, his pale blue eyes revealing only confidence. Jackson nodded back, kicking in the door before he could even finish the nod. The wood was old, barely serviceable, and it shattered around the knob as the boot came crashing through. Splinters rained down as the team barreled in, shouting, rifles trained. Arms went into the air, white and black and cream-colored robes hitting the floor, begging in Arabic for mercy. Claims of innocence; accusations of a mistake.

It was shadowy inside. Some of the rooms didn't have lights. The Superintendent wasn't sure what he was more afraid of—some*one* dangerous lurking back there . . . or some*thing*. He remembered his training, fell back on instinct, tried to bury the images of claws and lithe oblong shapes back into their deepest recesses so he could focus on his job. His job was what mattered, it was all that mattered. Everything else was just fear. And fear is only in the mind. *Do the job, do the job, do the job.*

He crept slowly on unsure feet into waiting dark.

301. The Spanish Cedar Door

The key crowds into the lock like a drunk in a packed subway car, bumping and scraping against every tumbler along the way, trying to settle in, find its place. The door is plain, a polished sandy blond with only a handful of nicks. Everything about it seems as if it has seen very little use at all, as if it were either long neglected or a recent cheap replacement. It swings open slowly, a bit crooked on its hinges, squeaking rather than creaking.

The inside is as plain as the door, and every bit as plain as 202. Three full-length mirrors, one mounted on each of three walls, and a chair facing the doorway. Strapped to that chair, much like the one before it, is a woman: thin, pretty, with high cheekbones and hair almost as sandy blond as the door. Her eyes closed, lips drawn tight.

"You moved your chair," says the Superintendent, waving the dagger in one hand as he talks, closing the door behind him with the other.

She says nothing.

"We talked about this." He walks over, spins her chair 180 degrees so it faces the mirror on the opposite wall. "You're not to move. Not a muscle. Not an inch."

"I don't like looking at myself."

"You're not supposed to. That's the point."

"Just get it over with."

"Not yet. Not until you tell me. Not until you show me. Tell me the truth and it'll all be over."

"You think you know, but you don't. You don't know anything."

"Who are you?" he asks.

"Emma."

"Emma what?"

"Emma Goerte."

"When were you born, Emma?"

"What? What does that matter?"

"When were you born?"

"In 'eighty-seven."

The Superintendent sighs. "Which 'eighty-seven?"

"What?"

"You heard me. Which 'eighty—"

BZZZZZZZZZZZZZZZZZT! sounds the old intercom, cutting him off midsentence.

"You should get that," she says.

The Superintendent clenches his fist, punches her square in the back of the head. The force lifts the back legs of the chair off the ground, her head flopping around limply as if her neck was broken. She doesn't move.

BZZZZZZZZZZZZZZZZZZT!

He walks over to the old brass intercom, presses a well-worn button, leans in to the corroded old speaker. "Yes?" A soft, lingering silence hangs in the air, small pops crackling over a light static. In the background, just beneath it: wails, moans, tiny distant screams. "YES?"

Nothing. That could mean only one thing. The Landlord.

The Desert

"She was great, you know," said Burke. He smiled so wide that all thirty-two perfect teeth showed. His hair was black, cropped short but styled, his eyes always glassed over as if they didn't give a shit about anything they had seen. "Really fuckin' great."

"I don't want to hear about it," said Miller, his hand gripped tight on the wheel, the Humvee rattling with every bump on the bomb-blasted, rubble-strewn road.

"Well, what the fuck else do we got to talk about?"

"I want to hear it," said Jackson, who sat in back with Burke.

Miller swore beneath his breath, shook his head a little.

"We're talkin' tits out to here, beautiful big brown nipples—you know, like perfect slices of thick meaty cooked sausage—narrow waist, a stomach like she was doing Pilates, and one of those yoga asses. You know what I'm talking about? The yoga asses? With the pants?"

Jackson giggled like a thirteen-year-old boy. "Yeah, man. I love those." He did. He'd seen them online but never in person. Not out of the pants, at least.

"And she was tight. Hairy as fuck, but tight. I mean virgin tight. That pussy just gave and gave and gave like it had never felt a dick before. Gripped me like a fucking pro. It was like being in high school again. That's the thing about these fucking haji girls, man. No one knows what they've got hiding under those burqas. I was probably the first one there. Her face wasn't nothing to look at, but those tits, man. Just thinking of those perfect fucking nipples is getting me hard all over again. And the jiggle and bounce of those tits. It was like porn-star shit. And man do they train those girls right. They just lie there and let it happen. Wait for it to be over. Whisper haji talk in your ear. It sounds like they're begging for it."

"Burke! Goddammit!"

"I bet she was," said Jackson.

Burke's head bounced up and down like a dashboard bobble toy. "That's the thing, man. American girls. You've got to fucking *woo* them. Empty your wallet just to get them to lie there like a limp fish. But these girls, all you need is a firm hand and a gun. And they'll fucking writhe in all the right ways."

"You listening to this shit?" muttered Miller, glancing at the Superintendent. He wasn't, not really. He only pretended to. His eyes were out on the road, watching the setting sun, hoping they got back to base before the dark set in.

"Did you get her number?" asked Jackson.

Burke laughed. "Nah. I did the only thing you can do. Did her in with a rock and set her on fire. You know she has four or five angry brothers. When they find out Sis isn't a virgin they always go out and waste some poor sap in a uniform. Can't have that on my conscience. Waste of a perfect set of tits."

The Landlord

He wears a white cotton suit, a pair of horn-rimmed glasses, speaks with just the hint of a southern accent, all lilt and no twang; sits in the rocking chair, next to the fireplace, where a blaze now roars; pulls his glasses down from his face, steams them up with a breath, cleans them with a handkerchief. "How's occupancy?" he asks.

"Fine," says the Superintendent. "A little busier than usual, but nothing I can't handle."

"Anyone new?"

"Two oh two. Fitzpatrick. I don't know much about him yet."

"Right upstairs. That's cutting it a little close, don't you think? I don't want this building full."

"I'm taking care of it."

"Taking care of it?" he asks sharply.

The Superintendent nods nervously. "Yes."

"Do you want me to take you back? To where we found you?"

"No," says the Superintendent. "I don't."

"Why haven't you done it yet?"

"It's easier if I wait."

The Landlord finishes polishing his lenses, then slowly slides his glasses back onto his nose. "No. It's harder if you wait."

"It's trickier if I wait. But it's easier once I see who they really are. The longer they're here the more real they become, the more their true nature shows through. It's easier to kill someone when you know he's not innocent."

"No one is innocent, especially not them."

"But it's easier when I can see it for myself, see what they're willing to do, how far they are willing to go to get out."

"The more of them you have and the longer you wait, the more dangerous this all becomes."

"I know why I'm here. I know what I was hired to do."

"Because we put you right back where we found you. To a bus station, shivering, covered in your own piss, your last few worldly possessions clattering around in a tattered old pillowcase. I will drive you there now and this can all be over. You can beg in the streets and chase the light after sunset to hide from the things that call to you from the shadows, that tell you all of those horrible things, that *show you* all of those horrible things."

The Superintendent shudders.

"No."

"What is it you want?" asks the Landlord.

"I want to go home," says the Superintendent, his voice cracking with a childlike tenor.

"You don't want to go back there. Not after how they treated you, the way they cast you out, tossed you into the streets like garbage. Tell me what you *really* want."

"I want a clean white room. With a bed and a desk. A window would be nice, but I don't need one. A rec room with a good TV. My medicine. The kind that makes everything quiet, not the one that makes me tired all the time. I want the voices gone. I want the noises gone. I want the *things* gone. I just want to be left alone, in my room, my clean white room. And maybe watch a little TV." The Superintendent scratches his head, eyes cast down in shame.

"And we'll give you that room. That was the deal. We'll pay for that room for the rest of your life. But you have to do this for us first. You have to go upstairs. You have to kill them. You have to kill every last one of them."

"It's hard."

"If it were easy then everyone could have his own room, his own quiet. It takes a certain kind of person to do this job, a certain kind of person who doesn't come along every day. You're that certain kind of person. That's why we chose you."

The Superintendent purses his lips, nodding slowly.

"I'm your man."

"All right. Take that knife. Go upstairs. And do what you have to do. Do your job." The Landlord looks around the room, listening closely to the creak of the building, the pop of the embers in the fireplace. "Sometimes I think there's very little life left in this old building. I'd hate to have to start all over again. From scratch."

The Desert

The Humvee smoked, broken, tires flayed by shrapnel, fires crackling, moments away from exploding. Jackson hung half out of the window, body crushed, guts showing in places, eyes wide like he was still surprised—like he could still feel surprise. Miller hung upside down, still strapped in, chest blown open.

It was dark now and the smoke billowed, disappearing above them into the night.

The M4 jumped in the Superintendent's hand, gunfire popping. He wasn't aiming at anything in particular; he just wanted everyone away from him. He prayed silently for the choppers to arrive, to spirit them away, to take them back into the light.

Burke screamed, firing, laughing, the bullets tearing through two men as they ran. "Get them! Don't let them get away!" His rifle roared, his teeth clenched tight.

"We don't know they did this!" the Superintendent called back.

"Yes they did! Yes they fucking did! They all did! Ain't none of them innocent! Not a goddamned one of them! Get 'em! Fucking get 'em!"

And that was the last thing he said.

The sniper's bullet tore through his neck, almost taking his head clean off. He fell to the ground, knees buckling like jelly, legs bent backward beneath him, boots to ass, his arms wide like he was crucified into the dirt. His mouth hung open, gurgling, throat shredded.

The Superintendent dove for cover, not even bothering to scan for the sniper.

The night went quiet, only the Humvee making any sound. It would blow at any moment, he knew it. It was all over.

Then it came. Shrieks. Howls. The bloodthirsty slavering of a gibbering beast. He'd heard it before. Cowered from it beneath his covers since he was a kid. It was a thing from the shadows. He knew what it looked like even before it crept out into the flickering firelight.

It was tall, terrible, impossibly thin. Mangled hands with razor claws as long as its fingers. Bulbous eyes like black glass set in umbral, pallid flesh. Wings three times the size of its body. Once out of the shadow, its gray skin seemed to glow even in the slightest illumination. The thing pounced on Burke, tore his chest open through his vest, pulled his screaming soul out through a shattered rib cage. Its head splayed, a mouth that wrapped around from cheek to cheek growing wide, rows of razor-sharp needle teeth glinting.

And it shrieked again, long and loud.

Then it leapt into the air—straight up twenty feet—diving right back down into the shadows behind the Humvee, Burke's soul grasped tight in its arms.

The Superintendent wrapped himself into a ball, tears streaming, begging quietly into his radio for help as he waited, desperate for the choppers to arrive. He whimpered, he cried. But he couldn't hear the choppers. Not yet.

202. The Ironwood Door

The door flies open and the Superintendent bursts through, his right hand tight on the dagger. "When were you born?"

Fitzpatrick startles in his chair, wriggling against his leather restraints. His skin cold and clammy, the smell of his piss hanging stale in the air. Narrow-set eyes look up at the Superintendent, pleading.

The Superintendent puts a firm hand on Fitzpatrick's shoulder, holds the blade inches from his chest. "When were you born?"

"I don't know!"

"What do you remember?"

"About what?"

"Don't be an asshole. Before you got here. What do you remember from before you got here?"

"Pain," he whimpers.

"What kind of pain?"

"The worst kind."

"Fire?" asks the Superintendent. "Burning?"

Fitzpatrick nods. "And cold. Terrible cold."

"Why were you there?"

"I don't remember. Please. Please don't—"

"Stop begging. You're only making me angrier. Why were you there? There must have been a good reason."

"No. I didn't do anything. I swear. I . . ."

The Superintendent's eyes squint, his countenance darkening. "Now I know you're lying."

"No! Please—"

The knife goes straight through his sternum, deep into his heart. Black, frothing blood spurts out, foaming around the edges of the wound, spraying the Superintendent from face to stomach, soaking his gray wool suit. Fitzpatrick bounces in his chair, the last few seconds of life spent wrestling against the restraints, black blood gurgling in his throat. The Superintendent knows that sound, remembers that sound. He shivers, memories washing over him, the grip of the knife loosening in his hand. Then he falls to the ground, listening silently to Fitzpatrick's last gasping breaths, knife still deep in the man's chest.

For a moment he listens past the gurgles and the breath, past the convulsions and the death rattle, listening close. Expecting, if only for a moment, the sound of choppers.

301. The Spanish Cedar Door

He stands in the doorway, gray suit stained black, blade dripping. She was facing his way again, sandy-blond hair limp and greasy on her shoulders, eyes trained on him, seething. For a moment they just look at each other, each waiting for the other to say something.

"Eighteen eighty-seven," she finally says.

"What?"

"I was born in eighteen eighty-seven. But that doesn't matter now, does it?"

"No. Not anymore."

"I heard what you did. I heard the screams. Then the quiet. It's my turn now, isn't it?"

"Yes."

"You didn't eat him, did you?"

"What does that matter?"

She laughs. "That's all that matters. He'll be back, you know. He'll be stronger."

"What do you know of it?"

Her eyes go black, glassy black like the things that creep in the dark and the shadows. Then her hair blows back, as if caught in a gale-force wind, and she croaks, long and loud, like steel being dragged across concrete. Her chair begins to rattle, each leg jumping an inch off the ground, and the mirrors shake on the walls and the room itself quivers from some unseen force.

"*Meshalok beluh kommorah! Betak mek anshorti!*" she cries out.

The room echoes with the voice of Hell, growing at once cold, and the lights flicker as the whole building stirs, seeming to settle in on its own bones, threatening to topple over, crumble to dust.

The cabin melts in around him, the air crisp, almost frozen, a weak fire struggling against it, failing. Shadows flicker in the light. Everything wood, iron, rustic. A baby cries atop a table, its mother in tears above it.

She's angry. Angry at the man who left them. Angry that the last scraps of food were gone days ago. Angry that her baby WILL NOT SHUT UP!

She grabs it, throttles its throat, choking it hard, fingers so tight they crush the windpipe; shaking it so hard that she snaps its little neck. BANG! BANG! BANG! goes its skull against the tabletop. BANG! BANG! BANG! until the crying stops.

And it does stop.

And the silence wails instead.

It's cold. Frozen. A wooden shack in an icy wasteland, miles from town. Miles from anything. From anyone.

And the woman with sandy-blond hair strips off her clothes, her milky white skin pulled tight over visible bones, her breasts raw from feeding. She opens the door, wind howling in, three feet of snow piled up outside.

Then she steps out, staggering into the night, half dead before the door swings shut in the wind behind her.

And the apartment melts back into place, the cabin gone, the dead struggling in her seat.

She pushes against her restraints, the leather giving way, stretching, about to burst.

The Superintendent braces himself against the door frame, grabs the door, slamming it shut.

"Hell is waiting for you, sin eater!" she shouts in a second voice, the first one still shaking the world apart. "There isn't a sin eater born who finds his way to any other place!" Her restraints snap. She bolts upright.

But the Superintendent is quicker, if by only a fraction of a second. The blade sinks deep into her belly and the voice stops, her eyes melting back into a pale brown rimmed by a bloodshot white. "Not today," he says. "Not ever." He jerks up on the knife, slicing her open from stomach to sternum. The black blood gushes like a geyser, hosing him down in a sticky ichor, its smell like stinking carcasses, her sins too numerous to pick out from the scent alone. Entrails slop on the floor, rancid and foul, maggots writhing in black like twinkling stars.

"See you soon," she gasps. And the world falls quiet again, the building once more at rest, once more at peace. It's a cold, eerie silence, like standing in the middle of an empty freeway at midnight.

The Superintendent pushes her off the blade and her body collapses to the floor, her eyes staring lifelessly into the darkest corner of the room.

The Chopper

The blades whirled overhead with a *WHUPWHUPWHUP* that shut out the rest of the world. Beside him in the belly of the aircraft lay the rest of his unit, each torn apart or crushed, covered in silver blankets so he couldn't look at their faces and see soulless eyes staring up at the roof. He was the last one left. His skin was pale, his stomach roiled, and he would have thrown up had he not already vomited everything left in his system.

He looked down out the window at the darkness below, knowing that they were there, creeping, jumping on anything they could find—he could almost feel them, skulking, braying, waiting for him. Screeching at the stars, wondering where he was. They were down there claiming the dead, dragging their souls headlong into Hell. And he was next. He knew it. They wouldn't wait forever.

There had to be some reason he could see them, hear them, smell them. He just didn't know why. And he didn't want to.

The Superintendent took a deep breath, counting silently to himself, wondering how much longer it would be until they made it back to base, made it back to the light. There was a comfort in the light, even the cheap fluorescents that lit up the plywood and sheet metal structures. Even those lights were strong enough to chase the things away. Even those lights could be trusted to let him sleep. That's all he wanted to do now. Sleep.

The Stoop

The Superintendent sits out on the front stoop, drinking in the afternoon light, smoking a cigarette. He normally hates it outside. There is too much commotion, too many people. It is too easy to get confused, find himself screaming again at some poor fool who has gotten too close, find himself swinging angry fists at a mother just trying to soothe a crying child. Loud noises mess with him, bring too much back. He likes it quiet, likes being alone, likes the night when it isn't so dark.

The air has a comfortable chill to it, the trees holding tight their last bursts of autumnal color. He sits in his suit, still soaking in sticky black. No one would bother asking about it, no one was likely even to care. After all, he has the kind of face that makes people uncomfortable. Something about the way he never smiles, or his eyes wandering nervously looking for roadside bombs or beasts with snarling maws. It probably just looks like a sewer backup anyway, like he was some unlucky sap who had been standing in the wrong place at the wrong time.

That's how he always feels anyway. He might as well play the part.

He takes a moment and drinks in the building, its stone a rough-hewn onyx, its glass gleaming, polished and almost as black: an ancient, crumbling, broken monolith with rusty wrought-iron fire escapes and two massive doors made of solid ebony. It is an eyesore to be sure, the sort of building no one pays any mind to when they pass, as if something primal inside of them whispers in the back of their brains to *just keep walking*. Maybe they can't see it for what it is, or maybe they can and just can't admit it to themselves.

He stares at the doors, each intricately carved with figures and scenes like a Rodin sculpture he'd once seen. They appear at first glance to be art deco re-creations, but the wood somehow hints at them being far older than that. One door has finely polished angels, cherubs, and seraphim; the other crudely carved demons, devils, and despots. Between them, along the inside edges, stand knights and knaves fighting for both sides. It is a war between Heaven and Hell, but if you look closely, examine the expressions worn into the wood, count the bodies piled on the ground, one could see that Hell is clearly winning.

The Superintendent smokes the last few puffs of his cigarette, enjoys his last few moments of daylight. He still has two bodies to drag down to the incinerator in the basement. They can't be up there when the

Landlord returns. He can't do what the Landlord wants. He just can't. Not anymore.

201. The Knotty Alder Door

He hears the bump, smells cheap cologne, musk, and beer in the air. The smells of the previous tenants linger in the hallways, but he can always smell when something new is coming through. What he doesn't understand is what it is doing so far down the building. These things keep creeping closer to the ground. They are supposed to stay up high, as far away from the crack as they can, but now the lower rooms are filling up instead. This isn't a good sign. Apartment 201 was the last one left that wasn't his own. And they can't manifest in his own room, can they?

The door is made of knotty alder, a rich, vibrant, expensive-looking wood. He fumbles through the keys, trying to find its match. He still doesn't know what half the keys do, if they even do anything at all. Maybe they are for old doors; maybe they are for doors yet to be put in. He tries half a dozen keys until the seventh, a small copper one with only two teeth, fits like a glove.

He turns the key and the lock sounds out like a small-caliber gunshot. *Shit!*

He doesn't have much time. If that thing is standing already, it might make a run for the door. He hasn't brought the knife, hadn't even thought to. Those things never know that he is coming.

The Superintendent swings wide the door, jumps through, slamming it loud and angry behind him.

The thing lies on the floor, trying weakly to stand, still coming to its senses.

The Superintendent grabs the chair from the corner of the room and some leather straps tucked into his waist. He places the chair in the center, facing a mirror, and hoists the thing on the ground up into it. It wears fatigues and a hard plate vest. It has a holster but no pistol for it. Its hair is black, cropped short, but styled. It looks familiar. Very familiar. And then the Superintendent freezes, jaw dropping, eyes wide with shock. He can't even bring himself to finish tying the straps.

"I know you," Burke says, still groggy, eyes struggling to give his face a name.

The Superintendent quickly regains his senses, tying the straps so tight that it might cut the circulation of a living man off entirely. "We served together."

"We don't anymore?"

The Superintendent steps back, giving himself a wide berth. "Not for a while now, no. I got out. So did you."

"I don't remember that."

"You will. It'll come. With time."

"With time? What the fuck does that mean?"

"It always comes. It just takes a while."

Burke looks around the room. "What's with the mirrors?" he asks, eyes avoiding them.

"The dead hate mirrors. It confuses them, angers them, reminds them of what they really are."

"I ain't dead."

"Yeah. You are. You have been for a long time."

Burke eyes him suspiciously. "What the fuck is going on here? Where are we?"

"Just a building. A very old one."

"What kind of building?"

"The kind you build on top of a crack in the world. The kind meant to keep things in."

"I don't . . . I don't understand."

"You will. You'll remember. You'll remember everything. Iraq. The girl. The thing that came out of the darkness. Everything. And then you'll remember what came after."

"*What* came after?"

"Hell."

"No." Burke squirms against his restraints. "What the fuck is going on here? WHAT THE FUCK IS GOING ON HERE?"

"You came back. You found the crack. And I have to send you back to where you came from."

"No. No. No! Fuck no! That ain't right. That ain't fucking right!"

"Nothing about this is."

The Superintendent withdraws, opening the door, slipping quickly, quietly into the hallway.

The door closes behind him, his heart pounding, head swimming. He can hear the chopper—the blades right above him. He can see the bodies, smell the bodies. Remembers them looking right at him. Remembers the bullet that tore out his throat, the thing that tore out his soul, the smell of his corpse on the chopper. The war comes rushing back. He punches the wall, his vision red . . . screaming, wailing.

Then black.

The Desert

"Get a load of this little shit," said the brutish ox. He was big—easily six four— and ugly, his body a layer of thick fat laid over well-hidden muscle. His speech was slow and slightly affected, making him sound as beef-witted as he looked. Everything about him pointed to him having no other choice but to go to war—it was that or move heavy things around all day under strict supervision, lest he hurt himself. Nodding, he laughed as he pointed at the Superintendent. "What's wrong with your eyes, little shit?"

His voice bellowed through the canteen, its deep bass resonating through the prefabricated fixtures meant to give the boys a little taste of home.

The ox's friends laughed with him. Another piped in. "Yeah. He's like one of those shaking little rat dogs."

"Chihuahuas," said another.

"*Yo quiero Taco Bell?*"

The Superintendent ignored them. It wasn't the first time he'd been treated like that; it wouldn't be the last.

"Hey! Chihuahua!" said the ox. "You hear me? You fucking listening, boy?"

"He hears you," said Burke, standing up from his chair. "I hear you too. And if I keep hearing you, I'm going to put so many of those nasty, twisted backwoods teeth down your throat you'll be shitting dentures."

He cracked his neck to both sides. "Now. Do you hear me, you sorry shit-for-brains piece of shit?"

The ox stood up. "You said shit twice."

"Only because I didn't think you could count that high."

The ox swung hard, but Burke was faster. Burke ducked low, threw a wicked uppercut to the ox's balls, then followed it with a haymaker to his jaw just as he doubled over in pain. The ox spun around, hit the ground with a loud crash, dazed.

An officer poked his head through the canteen door. "What the happy fuck is going on in here?"

"He fell," said the ox's friends.

"Yeah," said Burke. "I was just getting up to help him to his feet."

The officer nodded, knowing better but not really giving a shit. "All right. Carry on."

Burke helped the dazed ox to his feet. The ox flinched but accepted the help.

"Don't fuck with my squad," said Burke, "and you and I will get along just fine."

The ox nodded, returning to his chair slow and easy, his bell thoroughly rung. Burke sat back down next to the Superintendent.

"Thank you," said the Superintendent.

"No worries, brother. With all the hajis out here trying to kill us, no reason for us to be shitting on each other like that."

The Landlord

The Superintendent lies faceup on the red crushed-velvet sofa next to a roaring fire in the peaceful quiet of his apartment. The last thing he remembers is standing in the hall, assuming he might wake up to find himself lost in the maze of the second floor. But he isn't. He is here. Across from him, once more in the rocking chair, sits the Landlord. And he doesn't look happy.

"Did you really think I wouldn't know?"

The Superintendent sits up, gathering his wits about him. "No, I . . . I mean—"

"The job was simple. Kill the things that come through and consume them so they can't come back."

"They haven't come back."

"When was the last time you went up to the fourth floor? Or the penthouse?"

He couldn't remember. It had been weeks. Months, maybe.

"The building can only keep them for so long. They'll work out the mazes, find their way down the stairs. They'll find the door. They'll find a way to open it. And then they're out in the world. We work very hard to make sure that doesn't happen. We keep Hell where it belongs. That's the job."

The Superintendent nods. "I know, I just . . . I didn't know how hard it would be."

"That's what you get for associating with the hellbound. Why would you even know someone like that?"

"I went to war."

"Fair enough." The Landlord leans over, picks up a wooden box, slightly larger than the one that holds the knife, sets it in his lap.

"If you thought this was hard before, it's about to get much, much harder."

He opens the box. Inside is a revolver—an old-style single-action Peacemaker with fancy inlay and a metal grip—a leather holster, and several rows of wood-tipped bullets.

"I thought bullets couldn't kill them. That's the point of the knife, right?"

"The dead can only be affected by the dead. It's the reason for the doors, the wood floors, the chairs, the leather, all of it."

"If you had this all along, why have I . . . why did you make me do it with a knife?"

"You said it yourself. This is a hard job. Some superintendents can't handle it. It just becomes too much for them. We found that leaving a gun lying around, well . . . it's easier to pull a trigger."

The Superintendent nods. "I understand."

"You know what you have to do?"

"Yes."

"You know how hard this is going to be?"

"Harder than anything else."

"Right." The Landlord stands up, hands the box to the Superintendent. "It's going to get harder the higher you go. Those things have been here far too long. I'd start with your friend."

"I didn't say—"

"You didn't have to." He pauses, standing to his feet, straightening his jacket. "Go put on your suit."

201. The Knotty Alder Door

The Superintendent drags his dining room chair into the room behind him with one hand, the other resting on the grip of the pistol on his hip. Burke still faces the other way, eyes closed, head turned to the side. The Superintendent was right: Burke can't stand to see himself in the mirrors.

"So this is it, then?" asks Burke.

The Superintendent spins Burke's chair around toward his own and takes a seat, the two sitting face-to-face, though several feet apart. "It is."

"Why are you doing this?"

"I didn't have anywhere else to go."

"You could have found something better than this."

"I was born to do this."

"Who told you that?"

"Not everyone can see you, you know. Almost no one can. You're the thing that goes bump in the night. You're the thing that slams doors and crawls inside little girls and makes them swear and spit and do awful things."

"That's bullshit," says Burke. "I'm not any of those things."

"Not yet. You aren't strong enough. You're still coming through. Once you're all the way in, you'll be nothing but hate and anger and pain."

"So why don't you just get it over with? Shoot me and be done with it. That's all you have to do, right?"

The Superintendent doesn't answer.

"What the hell else is there?"

"The things that come through—"

"Stop calling us things."

"The *things* that come through. I have to eat them."

"What the actual fuck?"

"I have to eat them. Swallow their sin. Purify them."

"You fucking do that?"

"I used to. But I haven't in a while."

"Why not?"

"It's hard. Hardest thing I've ever had to do."

"Why the fuck do you have to eat them?"

"Limited transubstantiation. Or at least that's the word they used. It's supposed to cleanse them. Send them back clean so they don't have enough power to come back through. I don't really understand it. I still get confused sometimes and the words get jumbled. I just do what I'm told. What I can, at least."

"Like Iraq," says Burke.

"Like Iraq."

Burke leans forward, genuinely curious, speaking softer than before. "What's it like? The taste, I mean."

"Sweet at first. Savory. Like good pork." The Superintendent pauses, mind swelling with unpleasant memories. "But then you can taste them. The things they did. The things that rotted them from the inside out. All the evil little things pile up and it's like eating stink. Raw, rancid, meaty stink. You can taste the piss, the shit, the cheating, the hurt, the murder. All of it. And then you're sick for days. Puking, diarrhea. It's about the most awful thing in the world."

"So you're gonna eat me?"

"I don't want to. I know what you've done. I remember. I don't want to taste that. I don't want to know what it's like. Not that."

"But you will."

The Superintendent nods. "I have to."

"So why haven't you done it yet?"

"I've been alone here a long time. Alone in general even longer than that. It's been a while since—"

"Since you've had a friend."

"Yeah."

"But now you have to kill me."

"Yes."

"And then you're going to eat me."

"Yes."

"And you don't think that's a little fucked up? You don't think that they might be lying to you? Maybe they didn't choose you because you were born special. Maybe they chose you because they knew you might believe them, that you might do all of these fucked-up things without asking questions. Like Iraq."

The Superintendent shakes his head. "No, I—"

"How do you know we escaped? How do you know we weren't let go—maybe we did our penance and got lost somewhere along the way. Maybe you're the bad guy. Maybe you're the one doing all the awful things. Just think about what you're saying, what you're doing. This ain't right. This shit ain't right. They're playing you for a sap."

"That's not what's happening."

"Then just fucking do it! Get it over with. Eat me and send me back to the great beyond. You're right. All of this is real. Every last bit of it. Hell. Demons. Mirrors that can scare spirits. Hallways that move and change to keep us lost. All of it."

The Superintendent narrows his eyes.

"I didn't say anything about the hallways."

Burke smiles, his shit-eating grin crawling all the way up to the wrinkles around his eyes. "You didn't?"

The Superintendent stands up, his hand on the pistol. "No. I didn't."

"Well, shit," Burke sighs. "So this is it, then."

"Afraid so."

"Not like this, though."

"There's no other way."

"Not sitting down. Not shot in the face like that. Don't let this be an execution. Let me stand."

"I can't."

"I won't struggle. I won't fight. Let me die on my feet, that's all I ask. Pay me that kindness. Let me die like a man."

"No," says the Superintendent firmly.

"I thought we were friends."

"I was friends with Burke. You aren't him. You're something . . . else."

Burke smiles.

"You're right. I am."

The walls quiver, mirrors vibrating. Burke's eyes become a solid, glassy black, and his smile shifts into something sinister without his muscles moving at all. The entire building buckles under the strain, groaning against the evil taking hold of it. Everything shakes. Everything except the Superintendent. He stands firm, raises the revolver, points it right at Burke's heart.

"I've seen this show already. And it didn't turn out so well for her."

Burke struggles against the restraints. They stretch, threatening to burst. Still, he smiles. "Sure. But was there an extra chair last time?"

"What?"

201. The Knotty Alder Door

He awakens facedown on the floor, head splitting, ears ringing, covered in the battered remnants of the dining room chair. The Superintendent isn't sure how long he's been out, but the swollen puddle of drool creeping away from his face suggests it has been more than just a few minutes.

He shoots upright, looks around. The door is wide open. All the mirrors are shattered, glass scattered across the floor in wide arcs. Burke is gone. The Superintendent pats himself down. *The keys!* Gone. He fumbles for his revolver, finding it a few feet away, and says a silent prayer for small miracles. But this is bad. Really bad. There is no telling how long ago Burke escaped, no telling how far he's gotten.

The Superintendent wipes the splinters of the chair from his suit and cradles the knot on the back of his head. He checks his hand for blood. Not enough to worry him. He shakes off what he can of the blow and races into the hallway.

The elevator is 133 steps away, but he has no idea in which direction. The halls could have moved while he was unconscious and probably have. Time is running out. Burke has the keys and could open the front doors, could get out into the world, never to be seen again. Not by him anyway, not by the Landlord. There won't be any clean white room waiting in his future. All of this for nothing. All of it. He can't let that happen. He can't let Burke out. Burke was a monster in life; there is no telling how bad he could be now that he'd brought some of Hell back with him.

He takes a left—as good a choice as any—and starts counting steps. The lights flicker overhead, the ever-present buzz like a swarm of gnats further aggravating his headache. He moves slowly, carefully, gripping the gun tight, unsure if Burke has even managed his way off this floor. Step. Step. Step.

Nothing but the buzz.

Step. Step.

The building groans again, creaking, shifting. *No, no, no!* If he wasn't entirely lost before, he's lost for sure now. He runs, bolting around one corner, barreling down the hallway beyond. Ahead of him, the hallway twists, rolling over itself, and snaps into place with a slight wobble like waves rippling across the surface of a pond.

He turns the corner, looks down the hall, and sees Burke's knotty alder door, still open. It was on the exact same side of the wall as he'd left it. Somehow he was now on the other side.

No turning back now.

He presses on, sprinting in the same direction as he had when he'd started. He rounds the corner and races down another hall. Another corner. Another. Another. And another.

And then the elevator.

He reaches for his keys before remembering that he doesn't have them. He will have to take the stairs. *Fuck.* He hates the stairs.

He looks up at the small brass arrow above the elevator doors. It points at 3 and doesn't move. *Why the hell would he want to go up?* Then the answer hits him hard and his heart sinks so deep in his chest that he could poke it through his navel. He isn't ready to leave. Not yet. Not alone.

The Superintendent steps to the side, grabs hold of the stairwell door handle, summons all of the courage he has left, and pulls it open, his eyes shut as tight as he can manage.

The House with the Red Front Door

It was a white house, the kind with two pillars out front, a green, well-manicured lawn, and a bright red door dead center like a beacon. Eight Thirty-Seven Briar Street. It had a long driveway and a two-car garage, but there was only one car there, and had been for quite some time.

He was seven years old and this was the first time he had seen them. Not the cars. The *things*.

Every child hides under the covers from the noises he hears in the dark. And until this night, so too had the Superintendent. It was late, he was thirsty, and now that Mommy had gone to live with Daddy's friend, he had to get up and get his own damned water. That's what Daddy said. *Be a fucking man.* Be a fucking man. It became a mantra. *Be a fucking man and get your own damned water.* He always stank when he said it, so the Superintendent became accustomed to sniffing out how angry Daddy would be that night. Some nights he didn't get angry at all. Some nights he just cried. But not tonight. Not at first.

He was angry as all hell that night. He'd punched walls. Screamed about the bike in the driveway. Drank everything in the house. Kept saying *that bitch* and *that literal motherfucker*. The Superintendent went to bed early that night. It was all he could do not to get hit again.

So he crept down the hallway on his tippy toes, every muscle tense, trying desperately not to squeak the hardwood floor. Some of the boards were loose, but he knew where each one was. He took five steps, counting silently in his head, then turned, took two steps more, and turned again. Seven steps. One step. Two steps.

And then he smelled it. It didn't smell like anger. It smelled like fear. It smelled rotten. It smelled like old death. It was something the Superintendent wouldn't understand for a long, long time.

The therapist would tell him that he imagined it, that it was a memory created after the fact. But he knew better. He knew what it really was. And when he saw it for the very first time he knew nothing would ever be the same. Tall, lithe, impossibly thin. Claws. Glinting teeth. Cold and sickly. Corpse-pale gray. All of it. It slunk from the shadows, swelling large and terrifying out of the dark, hulking over his tiny seven-year-old frame.

It leaned in, growling low and mean, sniffing him up and down, vacuuming up every scent.

Then came the *POP* from Daddy's room. It was like fireworks, but sadder. Lonelier.

And the thing grew excited, forgetting the young boy in front of him, darting for Daddy's room like a dog racing for fresh meat. Teeth bared, snorting, leathery wings knocking pictures off the walls of the hall. Daddy's door flew open, the light of a nearby lamp enough to reveal the remaining half of Daddy's head, with just enough light left over to see the rest of it dripping red and viscous from the ceiling.

The thing pounced, reached in through the wide hole atop Daddy's head, and pulled his soul out screaming into the night.

It knew. It knew before it happened. It was waiting for him to do it.

That's what they were. They were the things that knew. Death didn't follow them and they didn't bring it. But you never saw them without death nearby. Seeing them meant death. Seeing them meant Hell.

No. This wasn't some memory he created after the fact. That was therapist bullshit. This happened. He knew it. And it kept happening. Time and again. This was real. It was all real. It had to be.

The Stairs

The Superintendent spends a lot of time with his memories. He clings to them like a group of friends he can't quite stand anymore but knows deep down he can't live without. Sometimes they hang in the air like a stench; sometimes they are as real as anything else. But he always knows the difference between a memory and the present.

The stairs don't.

Even with his eyes shut he sees it. Clear as day. Iraq. The dark. The stars a full half of the world. The flashes of the mortars around him. He is halfway between his bunker and the latrine. He tries to remember how many steps he has left. But he can't. He doesn't know where he is.

And then he remembers that he isn't there at all. Not now. This isn't Iraq. These are the stairs. He tries to ignore the screams and the whistling and the explosions. But the stairs will not relent. They keep screaming. They keep whistling. They keep exploding around him.

He has to keep walking. He has to count the steps from the door, not the latrine. *This isn't real. This isn't real. This is not real.*

One. Two. Three. Four. Only fifty-nine more steps to go. *Five. Six.*

An explosion. Red mist. Winthrop. This is the night Winthrop died. He never knew Winthrop, but everyone will speak about him in the morning as if they had.

Seventeen. Eighteen. Nineteen.

He hears the soul torn from its mooring, but he can't see the thing. Not tonight. *Not that night.* He has to remind himself. He isn't there. None of this is real. Not this time.

Thirty-three. Thirty-four. Thirty-five. Turn.

He hopes he is counting right. Hopes Burke won't be waiting for him at the top of the stairs. Hopes that this is the last time he has to take the stairs.

Fifty-eight. Fifty-nine. Another flash, but no mist. No more screams. No more souls being dragged off to hell. But snarls. He hears the snarls. He hears them waiting. They know death is coming. It might even be his own.

Sixty-three.

He reaches out into the dark. Grasps for a handle he can't see. Prays silently that he hasn't lost count.

302. The Brazilian Rosewood Door

The door opens and Iraq fades away, only the darkness of the unlit stairwell enveloping him now. Concrete stairs and wrought-iron railing trail behind him into the gloom before vanishing entirely in the murk—a distance he doesn't remember traversing. Not for a moment. Just outside, past the door, the third floor beckons—less frightening than the stairs, but no safer. He thinks back to how recently he'd been here, wondering just how long ago that really was. The Superintendent isn't good with time anymore. When he's hungry, he eats; when he is thirsty he drinks; and when he has to piss, he does. Time doesn't otherwise seem to matter in the building, doesn't seem to make much sense. *Was it this morning that I was here? Yesterday? Last week?*

He honestly can't remember.

And it doesn't really matter.

He steps out into the hallway, scanning for Burke, not seeing a damn thing but tacky wallpaper and shadows from a handful of burnt-out lights. The large brass arrow on the elevator points sternly to 4. *Fuck.* In the time it took him to make it up the stairs, Burke has moved on. The Superintendent has to move quickly, has to make sure this floor's last remaining occupant is still in his room.

The shadows on the wall flutter just enough to look like a trick of the eyes. His heart skips a beat. But nothing comes of it. *Room 302. One hundred forty-five steps.* He turns and starts counting, takes a right where there should be a left, walks fifteen paces before another sharp turn.

Down the hall he sees it: apartment 302. The one with the Brazilian rosewood door, the grain of its wood dark and wavy, its finish a deep crimson—almost blood red from his distance. Wide open. A gaping maw having loosed its terrible tenant into the halls. *Or has it?*

The Superintendent slowly reaches for his gun, drawing it silently as he takes several careful steps down the hall. His training kicks in, heart pounding, adrenaline surging through his veins. He's kicked in a lot of doors in his life. Shot a lot of people on the other side. Of all the things he has to do as superintendent, this comes the most naturally.

He breathes in through his nose, out through his mouth. In through his nose, out through his mouth. In through his nose, out through his mouth. His heart slows, his head clears.

The tenant in 302 is a problem for him. A tough case. The first he'd chosen not to eat. He couldn't bring himself to do it. The creature is foul, to be sure, but it understands the nature of what it is and how it came to appear. And the Superintendent just couldn't eat it. It was the first—the genesis of all this trouble.

And now it has to die.

He spins around the door, gun trained, finger on the trigger.

Nothing. Nothing but a chair in the corner and three shattered mirrors. There is no telling how long it's been in there, how hard he's focused to stay quiet, or how powerful he's grown in the subsequent weeks. All that is certain is that it is loose, either prowling these halls or upstairs with Burke. *But which?*

It takes only three breaths to get his answer.

The hallway grows ice cold, the lights dimming, a sloppy, congealed mess of blood slithering across the walls like creeping moss. The blood has a texture to it as if it's been drying in the sun but is still wet and sticky to the touch. Black masses of curdled blood and tumors form static waves as fresh blood oozes onto every inch of wall.

Then comes a sudden skittering across the ceiling—like a thing with more limbs than it should have, all of them made of claw and bone.

The Superintendent spins around, trains his gun at the sound, breath coming out in pillars of steam.

Nothing.

Then a hellish giggle from behind him.

He spins. And he sees it. Standing on the ceiling.

Four feet tall.

Overalls stained in blood.

Blond bowl cut falling on his face as if he were standing upright.

Little Jamie Osmunt. Eight years old. Fresh from the second grade. Eyes glassy black, mouth wide in a hellish scream, shark's teeth lining his mouth in numerous rows.

He wasn't eight when he died, but he was eight when he damned himself. And that's how Hell spits you back out—the way you looked the first time you dipped your toe into its fires. For a moment the Superintendent recoils at the flood of memories from the first time he killed Jamie. The image of Jamie's five-year-old brother at the bottom of a ravine, skull crushed beneath a large rock, made to look like an accident. That was how the Superintendent had envisioned the girl Burke raped—pieces of skull in pooling blood with a small boulder mashing in a pulp of gray matter.

But the images don't stop there. He remembers Jamie's years of cats and dogs. The first girl Jamie drugged at a bar and left in the woods. The seventeen girls who followed. The feel of the cop's bullet as it tore through Jamie's chest, snuffing him out. All of that races in and out again in the span of a hot, steamy breath.

And he regrets, more than ever, never having eaten the small boy.

He fires and the child leaps out of the way, falling sideways to land flush on the left wall.

Jamie runs, barreling at him, 102 demon teeth bared and snarling.

He fires again, winging it in the shoulder.

The beast flips, bellowing, landing on its feet, still sprinting without missing a step. Clawed hands reach out, grasping, paces away.

He fires once more. The bullet strikes true, tearing a hole between Jamie's eyes, blowing out the back of his skull like smashed melon.

The child falls limp and broken at the Superintendent's feet, still reaching, claws inches away from his toes.

There is no time to drag the body back into the room. He has to get to the fourth floor. Has to stop Burke before he unleashes any more of these monstrosities into the building. But that means he has to take the stairs. Again.

The Stairs

The desert. But not like last time. It's still dark and there are howls in the distance. Behind him the Humvee crackles, upturned, tires shredded, bodies hanging out of it just as he remembered. And on the ground, Burke, gurgling his last breaths.

He needs to wait for the choppers. He needs to hide from enemy fire. But he can't. He has to walk. He has to walk sixty-three steps. These are the stairs. The desert is an illusion. It's all in his head. He knows that now. It doesn't make the fear any less real, doesn't make his heart beat any softer, doesn't make the staccato of gunfire any quieter. But it makes it easy to ignore Burke as he reaches out to him, gasping for him to stay, and it makes it easy knowing the thing bounding out from the dark doesn't want him. Not yet. It's not his time.

One. Two. Three. Four.

401. The Black Oak Door

The Superintendent skulks out from behind the door, shaking off the last shivers of his memories. He glances up at the elevator's arrow and sees it still pointing at 4.

Burke is here, somewhere in the halls. Somewhere waiting to ambush him. His fingers squeeze the grip of the gun.

He rounds a corner. Rounds another. Winds through a sharp, abnormal series of twists and turns. Finds himself staring down another long hallway. At the end, Burke.

Unlike any of the other doors that open off the sides of a hallway, the black oak door sits at a dead end.

Burke is fumbling for the right key to open it. But there are too many keys, too little time.

He tries this key, then another. Then he stops. He knows he's being watched. Knows the Superintendent has the drop on him.

"Did you find our friend on the third floor?" Burke asks over his shoulder, not turning around.

"Yep."

"So you brought the gun."

"I did."

"And have you figured it all out?"

"What do you mean?" asks the Superintendent.

Burke turns around slowly, hands held open, up just above his shoulders, key ring dangling from around a single finger.

"This," he says, motioning to the building. "Have you figured it all out? What it means? What is really going on?"

"I know what's going on."

"You *think* you know what's going on. But do you really? Or are you still accepting everything at face value?" He looks around. "This *place* isn't what you think it is. It isn't a building atop a crack in the world. Those aren't magical wooden bullets and hallways don't re-arrange themselves of their own volition. And you, you're not who you think you are. Do you even remember your name?"

"Yes. Yes I do."

"No you don't. You know how I know?"

"How?"

"You keep calling me Burke."

The Superintendent narrows his eyes.

"Because your name is Burke."

"You were right when you said I wasn't Burke. That I was something else. I am something else. A shadow. A reflection. Of you. You're Burke."

"No. Fuck you."

"You said it yourself—you get confused sometimes. Things don't make sense. The logic of this whole place vexes you, twists you around so you can't tell day from night or remember when you last ate. How long has it been since you last saw me? A few minutes? A few hours? Days, maybe? Does anything about this place make sense to you? It's all phantoms. This is Hell and you think yourself some punisher of the damned, condemned to consume the sins of others because you refuse to face up to your own sins. Acknowledge that it was you in the desert who died in the dirt. Who raped that girl and caved in her skull with a rock. Who did oh so many terrible things that you don't even want to think that it was you who did them. All that. Have you figured all that out yet?"

The Superintendent stares down the hallway at the shade glaring at him, gun trained, sights set. His finger twitches on the trigger, confusion and regret setting in.

"No," he says.

"What a sad and lonely Hell you've created for yourself."

He thinks back, back to the desert, back to his father in the chair, back to things in the darkness and the Landlord by the fireplace. And he tries to picture the girl, see her face. He can see her breasts, her brown sausage nipples, the sweat on her body as she pushes into him, crying. But he can't see her face. Because none of it is real.

It's conjured. Fragments put together from other memories as told by Burke. He remembers the desert all too well. The smell, the stink, the howls. It is real. All of it. None of what Burke said is true. This is no Hell. He is not Burke. This is something else. He is something else.

"Bullshit," he says. "The dead lie even more often than the living. You only tell enough truth to keep yourselves from being predictable liars. I'm not Burke. I never was. Nice try."

Burke raises his hands a little higher in the air, smirking.

"I had to try. You gotta give me that."

The Superintendent pulls the trigger.

Burke's back explodes, showering thick, black hellspit over the walls and door. He slumps slowly to the ground, bleeding out.

The Superintendent advances slowly, gun at the ready to fire again. Burke clutches his wound, his smile eroding quickly.

"Fuck you," says Burke, tears welling in his eyes, a bit of black spittle spraying out with every *F*. "Fffffuck you." He coughs. "You don't know what Hell is like."

"No. But I have an idea. And I know you have it coming."

Burke raises his hand from the wound, sees his own rancid ichor clinging to it. "Why'd you go?"

"Why'd I go where?"

"To war, asshole. I know why I went. But you. What? Did you think you'd find the courage to fight your boogeymen or some shit? Is that what it was?"

The Superintendent nods. "That's exactly what it was."

"Did you find it?"

"Not there." He pulls the trigger, sending Burke back to where he belongs.

He breathes a sigh of relief, says a silent prayer for the part he liked of his friend, then stares at the black oak door. He stares long and hard, thinking about what to do next, thinking about Burke.

Then the Superintendent rears back, kicks the door in with a single vicious blow, firing wantonly. He doesn't hesitate. He doesn't fear what might be waiting. This is what he has to do, and it is best just to get it over with. It is going to be a long day . . . or night—he isn't sure which. But he has two more doors to kick in after this, two more souls that need purging.

And sometimes the old methods work best.

The Superintendent's Quarters

He eats. He hates every moment of it, but he eats.

The bodies are stacked awkwardly in an awful pile, one atop another, flesh and oozing black spilling across the hardwood floor, maggots wriggling out of their wounds. The corpses gaze out, eyes lifeless, seemingly begging for mercy. For freedom. But there's no life left in them. Only sin. Disgusting, filthy, rotten, sour sin.

The Superintendent sits at the table, fork in one hand, carving knife in the other, slicing pieces of them off and jabbing them angrily into his mouth. He chews, his teeth grinding against fatty tissue, the taste getting worse with every bite.

He's lost track of how many times he's thrown up, stopped bothering trying to make it to the bathroom. Black, fleshy vomit covers the floor beneath his feet, dribbles down his chin and onto his suit. There's almost no gray left to the suit at all—just black. Blood and puke covering almost every square inch of him.

He chews. He tastes the sin. Remembers the details. Sees the horrors. And he grows sicker with every passing minute.

He thinks that maybe, if he had more time, he could eat them one by one, taking the time to regain his strength and see out his term as Superintendent. Take the time to digest all that sin and seek penance for it. But that ship has sailed. He had that chance. It's exactly what the Landlord offered. And he had to go and fuck the whole thing up.

It is on him now. All his fault. Every bite is killing him. Damning it. All the color draining from flesh. There is no other way around it.

In the corner he can hear it. Scuttling, scurrying, waiting for the right moment to pounce, its pallid skin catching hints of the light, even as deep as it is in the shadow. The Superintendent just waves his knife at it.

"I'm not done yet. You can't have me until I'm done."

The thing waits. The Superintendent is doomed. It knows it. He knows it.

So the Superintendent keeps eating, slicing his way through body after body, doing the job he was hired to do. Whether he likes it or not, whether he understands it or not, whether it means anything to anyone else or not. That's not the point. These things can't come back. Not again. That's all that matters now.

And as he takes his last few bites—hours, days, maybe even weeks after he started—his body failing, eyes bloodshot, arm so weak it can barely lift the fork, he waves his knife at the thing in the corner, the thing waiting for him. He knows what's next. What's coming for him.

He waves at the thing, waving it over, whispering, "All right. It's your turn. Do what you've got to do."

He doesn't scream. Doesn't whimper. Not even a little. There just doesn't seem much point to it anymore.

The Landlord

The oak door swings open and the Landlord slides the key out of the lock. He offers a carnival barker's arm to the room, presenting its space and grandeur to a nervous young man. The young man looks around carefully, taking it all in, unsure what to make of it. The hardwood floors have been recently cleaned, but the walls are still stained from years of smoke.

"So that's it, then?" asks the new superintendent.

"I'd hardly say 'that's it' about the job," says the Landlord. "It's a hard job. An important one. Not a lot of people can do what you do. Most of them, well, they can't serve out their term."

"They leave?"

"Sometimes."

"But if I stay? And fulfill the terms of the deal, I mean."

"Then we'll fulfill our end as well."

"A bed with a roof over it. Three meals a day."

"For the rest of your life."

"And the voices. The . . . things."

"The doctors will have pills for that."

"One year. That's it?" asks the new superintendent.

"One year. That's it," says the Landlord.

"I'm in. Sign me up." He puts out a firm hand.

The Landlord shakes his hand, nodding, mood darkening for a moment as he hands over the jangling ring of keys.

The Leap

DANA STEVENS

The phone call woke me up that morning. It was a Saturday. I didn't like answering the telephone on Saturdays. I needed peace. Most weekends I didn't even shave, or dress. I stayed in the apartment with the curtains drawn. But in my half-sleep confusion, I answered. Perhaps I was meant to answer. In hindsight I think that must be true. It was a booking. Her name was Alexa Mortimer, and it was her fortieth birthday. She apologized profusely but said it was an emergency. She had hired a psychic to do readings for her party, and the psychic was flaking. Was there any chance that I was available for the day? She lived nearby, in the fancy part of Brentwood. She had gotten my name from her friend Renee Schwartz, one of my regulars. A real piece of work. She would call at all hours of the day and night and expect me to tell her something over the phone. So I told her things. Don't buy the Porsche. Don't have an affair with your contractor. But the truth is, we can't establish a real connection over the phone. Or on Skype. We have to be in your presence. I hated parties. With all the people around we get bombarded with images. I hated large groups of any kind. Even the thought of it made my nerves start to buzz, forcing me back toward a childhood habit of tapping my fingers against my forehead.

"I'm not that kind of psychic," I said. "I don't read palms. I don't throw tarot cards. I don't predict the future."

"What do you do?" she asked. Tap tap tap. I don't like to explain. It sounds so phony when you say it out loud.

"I see auras. Color, emanating from people. From places," I said. "I get visions, from the past and maybe from the future, but I can never tell which. And . . . I see Entities."

She didn't respond. Some clients get frightened when I tell them that. I don't blame them. As a child I thought everybody saw the things I saw. One day, I think I was six, I asked my mother to tell my brother to stop talking all the time. She looked at me funny and started asking questions. Did I think I had a brother? The alarm on her face made me opt for silence. She took me to a therapist, who asked me about my brother, and what he said to me, and whether I "heard voices." I lied. I said no, I didn't. The therapist's concern, and my mother's, was disturbing, the weird shrinking of their auras, a yellow that seeped into their skin and the whites of their eyes as they looked at me. It didn't take me long to figure out that color was fear. That's why they call cowards "yellow." Fear is dangerous. Fear is an invitation. Dogs will more likely bite when they smell it . . . the Entities sense it too. They like it. They collect around a frightened person like ants on a discarded piece of candy. Living people are their treat. Their craving. And the Entities are everywhere. Watching us. Some of them are "confused." That's what psychics are supposed to say. We're not supposed to say "evil."

Alexa Mortimer didn't sound afraid. Her voice softened. I could feel her smiling through the phone as she said, "Please, Edward. I know it's probably painful for you, to put yourself on display, but it's my birthday."

She said my name. I'm not embarrassed to tell you, just that small gesture sent a pleasing chill coursing through me. The kindness in her voice was something I rarely heard in my day-to-day. She told me that Renee said I was very good. That I was "the real deal." Then she laughed, a warm laugh. A sexy laugh, if I can say that.

I said I would be there and hung up the phone.

As you can imagine, I've never been normal. I've never had a girlfriend. I was going bald. The hair I still had was dark and lank and long in the back. My palms sweat. My skin was pale. I always wore a cheap dark suit with a dark shirt and no tie. I was never comfortable. Anywhere, even in my apartment. Even in bed. But you play the cards you've been dealt. Weird paid the bills. Especially the undeniable strangeness I possessed. People have an innate radar for authenticity.

The Normals. They were literally taken aback when they met me, and though mind reading was not one of my gifts, I knew they were thinking, *This guy's a freak. Maybe he knows something.*

Unfortunately for me, I did.

The Mortimer house was on a tree-lined street, a humble one-story in a neighborhood of McMansions. It was probably built in the 1940s for a well-off doctor who smoked in the operating room. As I turned off my car and sat looking at it, I could hear laughter and music from the backyard party floating over the trees. The inflated dinosaur head of a bouncy castle was just visible over the roofline, gyrating gently from the happy, unseen children inside it. Another brownie point for Alexa Mortimer. She invited her guests to bring their children to her fortieth birthday party. I anticipated a pleasant afternoon of attractive Brentwood mothers, fit, toned ladies who would smile and blush at my knowledge of them. But as I walked up the brick path to the front door, I was hit with a feeling of dread. The air between me and the house shimmered and warped like a force field. If I reached out my hand to touch it, it would wobble like gelatin. The blank windows of the house stared back at me. I was already getting things, images appearing on the other side of the strange wall of air: a woman running from the house, terrified; a man on the roof, tipping off it and falling; numbers floating by, two sevens and two nines; and then one last vision, crime scene tape across the porch, a body on a gurney, a dead body covered with a sheet.

I tried to breathe. My heart pounded. New places did this, flooded me all at once. The images seemed like they might be historical, based on what the people wore. I looked up into the big tree that spanned across the yard, trying to land, to plant my feet firmly on the ground of the now. It was an old tree, a sycamore, its gnarled white arms stretching out toward the house. The big leaves rustled. I wiped my palms on my pants. My brother was talking. It would sound like babble to you, like a radio through a wall, but I knew him. I knew what he was saying.

"Don't go in. Turn around. This is not for you."

He did this to me a lot. I never knew if he had my best interests at heart. Sometimes I think he wanted me to fail. To end up on the street in a cardboard box, with no one but him for company for the rest of my life. I told him I need money to live, just like the Normals. Life in a body has logistical requirements. This woman had agreed to pay me five hundred dollars for two hours. Didn't he understand? Didn't he trust me? As I stood there, muttering and sweating, the big red front door opened, and Alexa Mortimer herself stood there, gazing out at me, a smile on her face. All the voices and strange visions dissipated, and I was just there, with her. Like magic.

"Are you Edward?" she said, as she came out onto the brick porch.

I knew her. I mean, I had seen her before. At the Whole Foods and at the little muffin shop by the gas station. I had noticed her aura. It was the most beautiful saturated violet aura I had ever seen. Violet is rare, reserved for the most evolved people. Alexa Mortimer was dazzling. She was tall and slender, wearing a halter dress that stretched to the ground, her long blond hair swept casually up. She had searching, intelligent eyes that drew me. My brother's words rang in my ears as I stepped up to the porch: "This is not for you." I put my hand in hers, just to feel the velvety violet seep from her skin to mine. It was heavenly.

"Everyone's so excited to meet you. I put out a sign-up sheet, is that stupid? I didn't know how else to do it." She made a sweet, funny face as she led me inside, past some stacked-up cartons in the foyer. "Don't mind those boxes. We just moved in a month ago. This is our first party in the new house."

I nodded, relieved. The images I had seen—the crime scene tape, the dead body—must belong to an old family. Another time. My heartbeat grew calm as she chattered on.

"The sign-up is completely full, people are actually fighting over the spots! I may have to ask you to stay another half hour, but I'm glad to pay. You only turn forty once, right? Just don't tell my husband," and she touched me again, leaning in. I said something, I don't remember what. Her aura was like a drug, like a pulse waving through my brain, temporarily shutting down all systems.

She set me up in the cool, dark dining room, which was, of course, the perfect place to read. Everything she did seemed perfect. She gave me a glass with some ice and a bottle of Coke. Her adorable sign-up sheet was resting on the table. She had given people fifteen-minute intervals, and that was more than enough for her shallow party guests. Renee came in before I started and scolded me for neglecting to bring a stack of business cards. I found about ten in the pocket of my jacket . . . a little dirty around the edges, but I put them out. They were simple; my name, Edward Jennings, my cell phone number, and my e-mail. I asked Alexa to tell people that I would not be touching them or reading their palms. They would write down one question on a piece of paper and hand it to me. The questions give their fifteen minutes a focus. But truthfully, all they had to do is walk into the room. With very little concentration, information would start coming. I would use the paper, rub it back and forth on the surface of the table, to keep myself from tapping my forehead, especially if the reading became frightening. Most clients want the psychic to look deeply into their eyes, to be parental. If a psychic treats you like that, he is a fake. We are not parental. We are wary. People gave me their questions, and they wanted to feel seen, they wanted someone to know them. They wanted to touch an ancient human energy that, if they weren't assholes, sent shivers across their arms. If I read them right, it was like sex to them. Like sucking their mother's milk and looking into her eyes. Talking to a psychic, they felt both daring and safe. Even though no one is safe. Safety is a pipe dream.

I took a moment to walk into the backyard and survey the group. Alexa had a few interesting friends, but none of them even approached her violet aura. I wondered how she ended up here, and why. Violet-aura people usually cluster together. But they also tend to have a purpose. I had no sense of hers yet. It certainly wasn't the husband, Tom, a big athletic type whose aura was a muddy green. I'd never met somebody so tethered to the earth. He struck me as a bully. Naturally, he did not want a reading. He just wanted to size up the charlatan who was taking his money to entertain the troops. When he shook my hand, images came to me: a young woman, dress bunched at her waist, bent over a sofa, his hands gripping her naked thighs and pounding into her, animal-like. The woman was not Alexa. I let go of his hand immediately, and he looked away. He murmured something about finding his son and wandered to where Alexa was.

"Honey, where's Lucas?" Tom said to her.

"He doesn't like the dinosaur." Alexa's eyes searched the yard. As I watched her, suddenly Renee was standing beside me.

"Their son is on the spectrum," she whispered. "Probably autistic, but they're in denial."

I hated Renee in that moment. It was time to get started, if only to get away from her. I wandered inside and through the empty house, surprised I had not encountered any Entities. Every house has at least one or two, but Alexa's seemed strangely clean. I would not need to take my usual precautions, smudging with sage, wearing a religious icon, sending out messages of love. They hide from love, the bad ones. I returned to the cool darkness of the dining room.

The party guests on the sign-up sheet came sheepishly, one by one: a panicked single girl who had lost her job, a middle-aged man whose question read: "Would I be happier as a woman?" There was a female Entity curled in his paunchy middle, hiding there, probably because he was strong and she was afraid. He may have invited her in, with his desire to be a woman. Which came first, the chicken or the egg? I couldn't tell. Perhaps this Entity had been there for years, deposited by his mother, messing him up with her own demons. Mothers are powerful. The ones at the party asked me about their children and whether they would succeed. I liked children and supported them unconditionally, maybe because no one had supported me. Telling mothers their children were special made me feel like I did some good in the world. Several ladies asked me about their marriages and whether they should get divorced. In those cases I read the level of unhappiness in their auras and advised them accordingly. If they were just a little unhappy, I told them there was still hope. The truth was their poor husbands just wanted to have more sex with them. Sometimes I even told them that. Then the Saras and Katies and Lisas would laugh. Some would say things like "Tell him to shave his pubes." And I would laugh too and say, "You should tell him yourself." And they would smile. It was a lot like therapy, seeing a psychic.

The two hours passed quickly. My brother was quiet. I began to wonder what all that dread was about. I was seriously reconsidering my aversion to parties. It was cozy here in the corner dining room. I had my usual dull headache after so many readings, but I didn't mind. I knew that eventually Alexa would come in. She had to get a reading. She was the birthday girl. And *her* hand I would offer to touch. I would insist on it.

Someone rapped on the thin French doors of the dining room. A feminine knock. Perhaps this was my moment. I told her to come in. It was a woman, not Alexa, and she paused in the doorway.

"I didn't sign up." She had already written her question and was holding the paper in her hand. She was pretty, like the others, perhaps a little more innocent looking, with no makeup, in a flowered dress with buttons.

"No worries. Come, sit down," I invited her. "What's your name?"

"I'm Ginny." She sat down across from me and stared, a weird smile frozen on her face. I stared back, trying to get something. She slid her paper across the table. I picked it up and opened it. Two words were scribbled there in alarming black capitals.

FUCK OFF

My brother began to mutter. Here it was. It was like a clammy fist closed around my heart, whenever they appeared. I never got used to it. Especially when they took me by surprise like this. Ginny was an Entity. I could see now that her clothing was an older style, that her skin pulsed with hunger, eyes glittering with malevolence. She knew I could see her, reveal her. I had spent my short lifetime running from these Entities. They are drawn to me, because my mind is more open, because I have the gift. In the past year I had trained with a shaman I met up in Santa Barbara and we managed to rid my apartment building of all unsavory spirits. I was finally sleeping through the night. I wished desperately that the shaman was with me now.

Ginny's face began to change, skin stretching, bones visible beneath it. Her eye sockets sunk to dark pits. She was trying to scare me. She rolled her neck, and it crackled sickeningly. Her mouth opened as if she wanted to say something, but before she could, something black and snakelike pushed out from within her, something fat and wet and too large for her mouth, with sharp white fangs that snapped out at me. I shouted and dove under the table, terrified, my brother shrieking, "You idiot!" I wanted to cover my ears. But as I huddled under the table, I came to realize, there was someone else under the table with me.

A little blond boy with big brown eyes, maybe five years old.

You.

This is the moment I first saw you. Under a table. Your arms wrapped around your knees, your fingertips tapping, tapping against one another in a gesture so similar to my own. I knew what it meant. I knew the fear you must be feeling. I knew that you must be Lucas, Alexa's child whom Renee had hissed about in my ear. And I knew one more thing: you weren't on the fucking spectrum.

My brother was still berating me. You and I watched in horror as the tablecloth slowly rolled upward and Ginny, her neck at an impossible angle, as if her head were attached at her knees, leaned toward us, smiling, her teeth still black.

"Come here, Lucas."

You shrunk into my arms, your small hand gripping mine, alive and warm and bony, a baby bird in my palm. An Entity like this could slither in and out of you with ease, your open child's mind like a revolving door. I barked in your ear with urgency, "Think about love, someone you love."

You shut your eyes tight. We both did. I thought about my brother. I knew what you were thinking because I heard you whisper.

"Mommy."

We both opened our eyes. Ginny was gone. You turned to look at me. You were so pleased, as if I had performed a magic trick. You smiled. For once in my life I felt known. You and I were the same. We recognized each other. "Are there others?" I asked. You nodded. "A lot of others?" You nodded again. "Show me."

You climbed out from under the table, and as I followed, I heard a new voice. "Lucas? What are you doing?"

It was Alexa.

I saw her face, confused and suspicious, as I emerged from under the table behind you, my face flushed red. "What's going on here?" she said, her beautiful violet aura tinged at the edges with yellow.

I tried to smile, to reassure. "I don't know how long he's been there. I just found him myself."

She kneeled before you, looking into your eyes, "Why were you hiding? Mommy was worried." You just looked at her. She spoke again, softly. "Are you afraid of the dinosaur?"

But the dinosaur was the least of your fears. Two more Entities, males, crouched up in the corners of the ceiling; the one called Ginny, her mouth and dress fouled with black slime, stood in the doorway to the living room, next to your mother, a horrific doppelganger. Beyond her two more passed by in a distant hallway. The house was teeming with Entities. Why hadn't I seen them? I understood when you slipped away from your mother and ran to your room. They followed you. It was you they wanted. A child. A gifted, powerful child with an entire lifetime ahead of him. They could live for eighty years, ninety, inside a child like you. The thought of it sickened me.

My fingers tapped uncontrollably on the shiny lacquered tabletop. To stop it I placed my fingers on Ginny's folded paper question and moved it back and forth. Alexa watched me. She glanced over at the sign-up sheet. All the names had been crossed off. She looked back at me.

"I won't be needing that extra half hour."

I forced myself to face her, and in her eyes I saw the worst vision of all . . . how she saw me. She shunned me, this powerful creature, this Violet. I could see right through her beauty to her very soul. But she only saw my patchy hair, my yellow teeth, my nervous tics, which she assumed were a response to being caught under the table with this miraculous boy, her son. How could she know we were battling Entities that were drawn to us like moths to a flame?

Why hadn't I taken precautions? Why hadn't I burned the sage? I knew better than that. My brother had warned me, but I ignored him. I had passed judgment on this house. I thought these were people who never knew misfortune, who never drew the bad card.

Alexa laid a stack of cash down on the table.

"You need to go."

She could barely look at me. My brother's voice filled my head. He tried to make me spit something mean at her, like, "Fuck you, rich bitch," but I resisted. I had to rein him in. I was afraid he would hurt her. And I had never wanted to hurt anyone less.

I stood still as she walked to the front door and opened it. A wedge of sunlight fell across the floor. Good old sunlight. I could see it made her feel better. Stronger. I passed close enough to smell her delicious perfume as I stepped outside, onto the brick porch. She was there, behind me, starting to close the door . . .

I turned back. I felt my brother's hands closing around my neck, but I had to say something. I had to. My voice came out strained and constricted.

"Mrs. Mortimer. I saw things in your house."

She stared at me. "What things?"

"Entities," I told her. "There are Entities in the house. Surrounding your son."

"Entities?" She was glowing yellow now, truly frightened.

"Energies." I tried to soften it, to keep her listening. "I can help. If you'd let me come back, with the proper tools . . ."

Almost in slow motion, an ugliness took over her face. A look of anger and cynicism. "You're trying to frighten me. Trying to make a buck, to keep me calling you, like Renee does."

"Please let me help you. Let me help your son—"

She physically recoiled. "Get out of here. Get off my property." Tears sprang to her eyes. "Fucking pervert." She slammed the door in my face.

I stood there, not moving, not leaving. You were still there, looking out a window off the living room, watching me. Then you vanished. After a moment, I trudged down the walk and let myself out the low white gate in the picket fence. My car was parked some distance away, the curbs lined with the shining vehicles of the well-to-do. As I walked I heard the distant singing of "Happy Birthday."

I got in my car and shut the door behind me, sealing myself with a thunk into silence. And then I wept. I wept for myself, and I wept at the thought that you, a perfect, beautiful child, would grow up to be like me. Why do the Normals call them psychic powers? They make films about us exploding buildings. Carrie covered in blood, a goddess of gore, burning down the high school gym and all her tormentors within it. I wish. Even when I'm angry, I have no "powers." I cannot start a fire or bend a spoon, and even if I could, I certainly wouldn't. I moved quietly through the background, afraid they'd find out. They'd have me committed and give me pills that would make me blank and simple and take away my brother, who was the only true friend I'd ever known.

He wasn't speaking now. He was punishing me. My mother told me that I didn't have a brother. That was cruel of her, to make me think I was just garden-variety crazy. Maybe she was hoping that I would "grow out of it." I knew from a very young age that she didn't like me. She was busy with work and her boyfriends. She never told me who my father was. Perhaps she didn't know. She would disappear for days at a time. She left me money for pizza and milk, but she never left a note. And when she returned she never made a fuss over me. She wasn't much for words, my mother. I discovered her lie after she died, ironically, of throat cancer.

I found his birth certificate in her old steel filing cabinet. The one with the rust spots. There was mine, Edward Jennings . . . and then behind it, there was another. Two babies had been born that day. Kyle Jennings, my older brother, lived for exactly three minutes, twenty-seven seconds. She had given birth to twins, but only one of us survived. The spirit inside my brother wanted to live. That's what all Entities want. Life in a body, even an ugly one, was so pleasurable. Kyle wasn't going to miss out on that. He must have leapt inside me while we were still in the delivery room. Kyle is the name of a strong man. A handsome man. He told me he should have lived and I should have died. Kyle said I'd be nothing without him. He said he was the brave one, I was the pantywaist. The ball-less wonder. But he was wrong. I faced the world, every day: the loneliness, the strange looks, the derision, the hurled insults from women you ache to touch. That took courage.

I started the engine. I drove around the corner and up the hill and parked on a street above the house. I got out and walked into a scrubby grove of trees, through which I could look down and see into your backyard. The guests gathered together, eating their cake with plastic forks. Tom put his arm around Alexa and kissed her, and I saw his hand travel to her ass and settle there, proprietary. He didn't deserve her. He didn't deserve you, a sensitive boy he would never understand. You were standing off to the side, away from the other children and the dreaded dinosaur bouncy. I sat in the weeds. I stayed there a long time, until the last guests trickled away, the caterers in dark pants and white shirts cleaned up their buffet stations and loaded their wares into a van that had been pulled down the driveway to the backyard. Dusk fell, and still no one had come to take away the bouncy. Alexa, dressed in shorts and a T-shirt, came out, holding your hand, leading you toward the castle. Her voice floated up, distant, on a breeze.

"See? It's just filled with air . . . like a balloon."

You were wary. There was a boxlike motor behind the castle, keeping it pumped full of air. Alexa flicked a toggle switch and the motor died with a diminishing whir. The dinosaur's long neck flopped forward, and the castle softly folded, reduced to a harmless heap of vinyl on the grass. I stood up to see you better, see your reaction. Your mother looked up, motionless, and stared. I stepped back among the trees.

I didn't want to frighten her.

My brother finally reappeared. "You don't scare anyone. You just don't want her to call the cops." I didn't argue with him. The day had taken so much out of me. I needed to sleep. "Let's go," he said. "This isn't our problem."

He was right. No one could help. You didn't stand a chance, your father a brute with no aura to speak of and your mother too frightened to see. And then it came to me. A voice, as strong as my brother's, but not his. This voice was mine. It said: "Stay."

I would wait until they had all gone to sleep, and then I would go back inside that house. I would save you. My life, so long a series of defensive postures, struggling not to be crushed like a bug, suddenly had meaning. This was supposed to happen. You could follow the chain: I know Renee, Renee knows your mother, the woman your mother hired canceled, she phoned me. I didn't like parties, but I took the party. Even at the door, I wanted to leave, but I didn't because I had seen your mother. I knew her already. My brother was wrong. This was for me. I watched the glowing lamps turn on in the house. My brother started yammering: "Whatthefuck whatthefuck?" But I ignored him.

I sat down on the cold, hard ground, settling in for the night.

I must have fallen asleep, because I awoke with a start, my head in the dirt, my body stiff, my mind disoriented. I had to brace myself against a tree to come to standing. I looked down and saw that all the lights were out in the Mortimer house. Everything was still. The witching hour, I knew, would just be starting for you. I hoped you were asleep. I hoped you wouldn't see me. I went back to my car and opened the trunk. I used the flashlight on my phone to collect the few tools I needed. Candles. A crucifix. I counted out five polished stones and I took a glass bottle with an iron stopper. I started to take the sage but realized I wouldn't need it. I didn't want to repel them. I wanted to draw them to me. I left the car keys on the front seat. I might need to make a quick getaway.

I decided to approach the house from this hill and walk down to the backyard. My dress shoes slipped and slid in the dry dirt. I had to balance myself, hanging on to scrubby bushes and tree branches as I made my way down. I would ditch the shoes before I went into the house. They would echo on the wood floors. I had no idea how I'd get inside. But people rob houses all the time. They break in and rape women. Kill their exes. I would figure out a way. As I got closer to the backyard, I found a chain-link fence at the property line. It rattled when I put my feet and hands in the little holes and scrambled up as fast as I could. I stretched one leg over and found myself clinging to the other side. I leapt down onto the grass with a thud. A dog next door began to bark. I looked at my watch. It was 1:53 a.m.

I walked around the perimeter of the house, looking for an open window, trying all the French doors. Everything was locked tight. I looked under potted plants and under the door mats. It doesn't take a psychic to know that everyone leaves a key somewhere. At the back door, an image came to me: Alexa reaching up to a ledge at the top of the door frame above me. I mirrored the movement and yes, there was the key. I slid it into the deadbolt and the door opened. I stepped inside, ready for relief, but instead I froze. An alarm panel was lit up on the wall beside the door, blinking for me to disarm it. In seconds it would blare its siren and wake everyone in the house. I started to sweat. Could I run fast enough to get to my car? The panel blinked; I remembered seeing numbers when I first looked at the house, a lifetime ago. Two sevens and two nines. I punched them in, then pressed the button for "disarm." I held my breath. The alarm turned off. I had done it. I was inside.

I took off my shoes and carried them with me as I crept in. I passed through the kitchen first, with the comforting refrigerator hum, the lit-up clock on the oven. I had a strange feeling of mischief, being where I wasn't supposed to be. I touched the counter. I wondered how long it would take them, the Entities, to show themselves. I went into the dining room, where I had spent my afternoon. I closed the slender, shuttered wooden doors that led into the living room. Setting my shoes under the table, I took out my candles and placed them on the table. The matches I brought made a shushing sound as they lit. I set the sacred rocks out. One for each of the five Entities I had encountered here. I placed them in a half circle around the candles. I set out the bottle and sat at the head of the table. I closed my eyes, opened my hands, and took a deep breath.

"I invite you. I invite you."

Nothing happened at first. Then I felt a draft blow through the room, moldy and cold. The candles sputtered and there was a creaking sound . . . the shuttered wood doors were slowly falling open. Someone was here with me. I couldn't know if the being in the room was an Entity or Alexa herself. I opened my eyes. The doors were open, but I could see no one. The bottle on the table began to shake and rattle. Above me, I heard a low bit of laughter. My eyes tilted upward. I saw her feet first, hovering. Ginny was there, near the ceiling, staring down at me, her head tilted, her grin derisive.

"What a very small bottle," she chided. I stood as she floated to the floor. We faced each other, the table between us.

"I want to help you," I said. "I want to set you free."

She scoffed. "What is free?"

In the dim throw of the light, I felt them approaching. Their energy rippled through the air. The candles blew out. I felt fear then, but it wasn't mine. It was my brother's.

"Don't, please, don't," he pleaded. But it was too late. They were here. They were surrounding me. Touching my face and my hair, as if they were a primitive tribe who had never seen another human. They stroked my skin, they moaned in pleasure, they suffocated me. Ginny entered first, prying my eyes open with her fingers, morphing into smoke and flowing into me. I opened my mouth, unable to breathe, and found myself set upon by another Entity. My body was stiff, strained. The sensations were fierce and sexual. Every cell in my body was on fire. My hair was standing on end, and my limbs were outstretched as the Entities buzzing inside me caused me to float upward. I was levitating, framed by the open double doors.

It must have been a terrifying sight.

I saw you standing in the living room, in your little pajamas, staring at me. I should have known you would awaken, that you would feel such a significant event. Then you screamed, a high-pitched wail louder than anything I had ever heard. The power of it!

Every light in the house suddenly blazed on. Every television blared out sound. The blender, the burners on the stove, the alarm pads, the toys in every part of the house, anything electrical was singing and whirring and shrieking and talking. I hit the floor with a thud, but I knew I was still carrying them all inside me. I was hyperaware of everything, even the blood in my veins. Out in the backyard, the dinosaur castle and its air-blowing motor roared to life, reinflating the monster, who grew tall, dwarfing the house. Inside was chaos. I heard your mother screaming, your father too . . . they would be coming for you. I had to get out. I grabbed up the bottle, the spirits inside me yelling and laughing, ran through the kitchen and out the back door. I paused there, hidden behind the dinosaur. I removed the crucifix from my pocket and put it around my neck. I felt the spirits inside me recoil. In one sweaty palm I held the bottle. I did what I had seen the shaman ask so many others to do when they had come to him for help.

I opened the bottle and put it to my mouth and blew. I knew I had to think of love and my mind alighted on you, your little blond head, your hand in mine when we faced the Entities.

The bottle in my palm glowed, becoming heavy. Wincing in pain at the heat of the glass, I felt them leave me. All of them, even Kyle. I could hear him screaming, threatening, begging. It was like having my insides ripped out. Tears filled my eyes. I covered the top with my palm until I could close the mouth of the bottle with the iron stopper.

And there I was, alone in my body for the first time in my life.

I heard sirens approaching. I knew I had mere moments. Still holding the bottle, I ran, around the huge barrier of the inflated dinosaur, heading for the back of the yard, to my car, to safety. As I came around the corner, I was faced with one last hurdle. Your father. Auraless Tom. Shirtless, fresh from his bed, so perfectly human and physical, no spirit to torture him, to give him any doubts.

He saw me, and I saw him, both of us holding something in our hands. He didn't wait to see what I had. He had a gun, and he raised it, without any hesitation, and fired.

Bullets ripped through my body, each one like a blast from a blowtorch. I fell backward into the grass. The bottle dropped from my hand and rolled away. I couldn't go after it. I was dying. The crime scene tape, the body on the gurney, I suddenly knew with perfect clarity that the body I had seen in the vision was my own. Tom kept firing, and the dinosaur died with me, bullets piercing the giant balloon, air bursting in whining knives of sound. The dinosaur sagged and wilted. It crumpled and I smiled, knowing it was about to be over, my short, uncomfortable life, and that I had made it count for something. In my last moment, I saw Tom, breathless, leaning over me, still holding the gun, looking down to see if I was dead. My eyes started to roll back in my head, my heart slowed, *thump, thump*, and it was then I had my last powerful, lucid thought. Not just a thought. An idea.

It took Alexa and her family about eight months to return to normal after the shooting. The police questioned them at length, first that night and also in the days that followed. Alexa told them everything she knew about Edward Jennings, which was not much. Tom was angry with her that she hadn't told him about the incident at the party, about how she found Edward with Lucas, and what Edward had said about their son. Renee Schwartz corroborated their story that Edward was an unstable personality. The detectives assigned to the case uncovered medical records that indicated Edward's mother had unsuccessfully tried to have him committed in his early twenties. The newspapers wanted to do a story about the "psycho psychic," but Tom made a few well-placed phone calls to hush it up. They had to think of Lucas. Edward's motivation had obviously been kidnapping, and they didn't ever want Lucas to know that. The police accepted her husband's explanation that when Edward's movements in the house set off the alarm system sensors, it must have triggered a power surge, but Alexa wasn't sure. She wondered if the surge had been caused by some power in Edward. She couldn't stop talking to her friends who were at the party. What was their reading like? Did Edward actually seem to know things? She trusted her own instincts, and she certainly thought there was something authentic about Edward. No matter how she tried, she could not shake what he had said about Lucas and the Entities surrounding him.

For many weeks after the shooting, she slept in Lucas's bedroom. But strangely, after a childhood plagued by nightmares, he did not have any about Edward. In fact, Lucas started sleeping through the night, a feat he had never been able to accomplish before. Alexa expected Tom to pitch a fit and insist she come back to his bed. He had warned her before they got married that he was a twice-a-week kind of guy, at the very least, and that if she couldn't guarantee that, they should split. It was a silly bargain at the time. It had made her laugh. She was very attracted to him, his masculinity, his practicality. But that guarantee had grown tiresome. It came as a surprise when Tom told her to take as much time as she needed with Lucas. Perhaps he saw the change in their son. Lucas started talking more. He looked them in the eye, and his stimming gesture disappeared.

The shooting had changed Tom as well. He'd become much gentler with Lucas. Alexa would wake up on a Saturday and find them sitting in the garden together, talking. He got Lucas a dog, and he started coming home in the afternoons for soccer. He would sometimes even put him to bed. There was nothing more attractive to a woman than a man who was a good father, and soon Alexa wanted to be with him again. Their first time after the shooting was amazing. It was like making love to a different person. He was so sensual, so into her body. There was a sweetness to their passion that had been lacking before. Right after the shooting, they had talked about moving. But she and Tom had now decided to stay. The house felt inexplicably safe to them, despite what had happened.

One night, when Alexa finished reading Lucas his bedtime story, she asked him, "Do you want the hall light on?"

Her son surprised her by saying no. She hovered, a dark shadow in the doorway, as he continued, "The bad people are gone now. Edward took them away."

Alexa felt a chill down her spine. "You remember Edward?" Her son nodded. Alexa came back and sat on the edge of his bed. "You don't have to worry about Edward, darling. He's gone forever."

And then her son did something strange. He laughed. A little giggle.

"Whatever you say, Mom."

Alexa went to look for Tom. She found him in the dining room, at the head of the table, typing on his laptop. Papers were scattered around him.

"What are you writing?"

He closed the laptop. "Something for Lucas, a little primer about life, for when he's older."

Alexa made a half smile. "Can I read it? I could use a primer."

"Nope. It's a father-son thing."

She laughed a little, then perched on a chair, glancing around the room. "This is where Edward did his readings."

Tom looked down. He didn't like talking about Edward, but she persisted. "Sometimes I think he did us a favor, in a weird way. Do you ever think that?"

Alexa watched him. Her eyes trailed to his hand. His fingers rested on the yellow paper. He was rubbing it, ever so slightly, back and forth against the table. She met her husband's eyes. They held each other's gaze for a suspended moment and then he stopped moving his hand. A clock ticked somewhere. Their hearts beat. Alexa rose. She came to him, traced a finger across his neck, and whispered in her sexy way, "Come to bed."

He smiled. "I'll be right there."

As she disappeared into the back of the house, Tom opened the computer. He hesitated and typed in one more sentence. A simple one.

Sometimes the freaks do get a happy ending.

He rose and turned out the lights. Walking down the hall, he looked into the open door at his sleeping son, illuminated by the moon. He smiled, pausing for a moment, before moving down the hall, to his bedroom and his wife.

He did not see what Lucas had found earlier that day, deep back under the bushes in the garden, covered by old dead leaves and grass. He didn't see the old blackened bottle with an iron stopper that Lucas had dug up, like buried treasure, and had placed on his bookshelf, where sometime that night it would begin to rock as if of its own volition, and fall to the ground, and break.

Novel Fifteen

STEVE FABER

The body lay on the craggy, algae-draped sea rocks like a puzzle: a jig-saw, twisted, broken, mangled. Strange, isn't it, what the mind allows us to assume and what it implores us to deny when confronted with bloody human puzzles? Assumptions and denials held hostage to our fears and desires. Strange. Yes, certain conclusions were drawn when the torturously bright police klieg lights initially blasted these rocks. One could correctly ascertain pieces of the puzzle: an arm, a leg, limbs of a human being jutting in and out of place, like a multi-needled compass pointing in different directions, pointing nowhere, pointing everywhere. A bit of the upper neck leading to an unfulfilled expec-tation, that of a head, a face. Expectations, assumptions not realized. Bright lights shining on physical chaos. Of course later, when dawn broke, when men and machines could successfully battle the undertow, moving earth and rock, a form would be revealed, that form would assume a gender, an age, and a name.

But for now, the sea owned this geometry of death.

The rhythmic tide collected and deposited this salty, bloody foam. The colors were titrating. Moving and amazing. Were it not a human body, one might think this a gallery installation. Colors deep and red, pulsating, a beautiful, kinetic work of art.

———————

Perspective. Context. One ought to know the Setting, the Routine, the Process involved in creating a Jackson Grey Novel. For at this stage in his career, the production of a novel was not simply the act of writing a book, it was an industry, an industry flush with cash, with people, with players, an industry with many moving parts. Yet a precise industry. It had to be precise, if only because the people who surrounded Jackson, the ones who worked on his behalf, the ones who read his work, expected such precision. And, given such expectations, he delivered.

He always delivered . . . and, as Jackson began to mentally construct the shape and texture of the new book, he fully intended to deliver yet again. Novel Fifteen.

These books of horror no longer had titles. Rather, they *had* titles, but they were created by other people, specifically another person. Marlene. His editor at JB & Sons Books. Book titles meant nothing to Jackson; the numbers that spelled sales and success meant everything. Those numbers were high, extraordinarily high, and were due to Jackson's mastery of a skill set: the ability to flirt, tease out an idea that led to the commencement of a novel of horror, construct said novel expeditiously, complete it, and wait. Wait for publication, tremendous sales, wait for the seductresses of television and film to call Jackson's people and make offers. Jackson didn't just write books; he had mastered a formula that translated into a career and an absolute fortune.

The Setting: Carmel-by-the-Sea, California. Beautiful, expensive estate. Jackson bought it after Novel Two, and with it came beautiful, expensive ocean views. The weather? Foggy some of the time, chilly most of the time. Sunshine, or the lack thereof, was a topic, banal as it seemed, and it seemed banal to Jackson, discussed among neighbors. Jackson loathed talking about the weather and for some reason especially loathed discussing the weather with his neighbors. Where was it written that one had to speak with one's neighbors? What was there to talk about? Only banalities.

The Routine: slip out of bed, without waking Katherine (when she was in town), his high-priced model-in-demand, live-in lover. It had been a year since Jackson's introduction to Katherine had resulted in Jenna's departure and Katherine's residence. Like an unbroken line, Katherine moved in, replaced Jenna, and did so quickly. Katherine, like Jenna, twenty years his junior, was far above his socio-sexual pay grade, far above the women with whom he could sleep, fuck, live with were it not for the fact that he was Jackson Grey. Prolific, celebrated, wealthy, famous. Jackson prided himself on the notion that he was self-aware, far from self-deluded. Knowing full well the value of his celebrity and what type of woman that celebrity commanded.

Slip out of bed at seven a.m., Monday through Friday, seven a.m. Always seven a.m. Coffee, cigarettes, quick browse of *The New York Times*, delivered daily to his gate, placed dutifully on his mahogany coffee table by his V, loyal housekeeper, keeper of his schedule, his routine, his life, and his secrets. Keeper of all the things that kept the industry of bestselling success running efficiently.

V had been with Jackson so long now (*God, nineteen years!*) this fifty-something woman, childless, with a green card, four sisters living somewhere in the States—that Jackson had forgotten V's actual name. *Victoria? Violet? Violetta?* She paid herself, signed Jackson's name, and the only time Jackson felt uneasy about this (*Was it Novel Three?*) he asked Cline, his entertainment attorney and business manager, about "the efficacy of such an arrangement," and Cline—attorney/business manager/Los Angeles–Hollywood superpower—reassured Jackson that V was to be trusted. And that was that. He trusted Cline, therefore he trusted V. After all, it was Cline who had procured V for Jackson. Something Jackson always appreciated, for Cline need not have concerned himself with Jackson's domestic issues, yet Cline went out of his way to do so. Cline felt that Jackson needed the *right* housekeeper. A perfect fit. Jackson had come to understand perfectly that is what men of power do for other men of power. They watch one another's backs. Down to the smallest detail. *Men of power. They procure housekeepers! They ensure perfect fits.*

As time passed, he was more than happy to admit that V ran his life. The idea that a housekeeper could, in fact, run someone's life was not a concession to Jackson's lack of organization, his manhood, not a concession to any failing, but rather a boast. He spoke to V kindly, gently, but he spoke *of* V as a woman he possessed, owned, paid for. Chattel.

Marlene, Jackson's editor, JB & Sons Books (since the commencement of Novel Two) was possessed of the same type of power Cline exercised. And, as well, possessed of the concern for detail that inhabits the minds of powerful people who service other powerful people.

In actuality, Jackson was forty-five years old. Marlene had made five years of Jackson's life disappear just prior to the publication of Novel Two. Jackson was to be publicly portrayed as five years younger than he was, and the people who worked for Marlene and Cline, and thus Jackson, made manifest that lie. Articles about Jackson, online musings, reviews were swept clean, people often paid off to maintain the lie. And Marlene's ability to perform this trickery, and perform it successfully, impressed Jackson. As Marlene explained, writing a bestseller, a huge bestseller, at twenty years of age, fit a particular narrative: the *twenty-year-old* writer's first novel exploding onto the scene and breaking the mold. The subsequent interviews, photos, signings, red carpets . . . money . . . fame. All quite statistically and nearly impossible at age twenty. *Thus so goddamn impressive. Make the impossible possible. Marlene had the power to do that. Looking back, why the hell hadn't Ben suggested this slight, benign falsehood?* Ben Myer, his first editor, a good guy. Garrett Books, a good operation, but again, too small. And neither Ben nor Garrett Books could distinguish ethics from reality in the competitive world Jackson inhabited. Neither the man nor the company had the shark's teeth to navigate a sea filled with other sharks. That was the reason Ben did not engage in minor conspiracies, like changing the age of his author. Jackson Grey, the wunderkind of a new brand of horror, needed power. Power to transmute his creativity, to monetize it, and more than that . . . *How did Marlene put it? The space created for such power to reside!* All these ideas of power, space, more power all emanating from one book, the explosion of success that was Novel One.

There *was* a sense of guilt as Jackson toyed with the idea of losing the people like Ben, like Garrett Books. However, when Cline and Marlene initially pitched Jackson the idea that he needed to rid himself of his old attorney/business manager, his old editor, old publishing house, they focused not on the past but on the future, bringing aboard the instruments of true power: Cline, Marlene, JB & Sons, the team that could forge a future. The pitch was perfect and simple and remained all these years later at the core of his consciousness: *Every writer has one big novel inside his brain, his gut, his soul, and some even have the courage to write it down. Get it published. But Jackson Grey wants more. He wants greatness. And what is the point of desiring greatness if Jackson*

Grey does not have powerful people circling that greatness, translating it, expanding it, making certain all the bases are covered, turning desires into realities? They spoke to him in the third person. A parlor trick of course, but an ego stroke nonetheless.

Jackson needed a Cline, he needed a Marlene. He needed pure power. He craved it.

Good ol' Ben Myer understood. And after Jackson fired his old attorney/business manager and retained Cline, Garrett Books was made to understand. Thus Cline broke the contract with Garrett; money was exchanged, as were some harsh letters from which Jackson's eyes were shielded. Was there litigation? Jackson was kept out of it. "Everyone left the table as friends," Cline reassured him. A simple transaction: Cline replacing someone, Garrett Books out of the picture, substituted by JB & Sons, the biggest, the best. Ben finished, replaced with Marlene. Guilt?

"These are transactions, Jackson, not lovers," Marlene snapped at him. Snapped . . . affectionately. Marlene could costume admonitions, dress them up, and have them appear as care.

Guilt?

Certainly no guilt now. Cline, Marlene, JB & Sons were the stuff of bestselling novels, and all that flows *from* the bestselling novel flows *to* the bestselling author. At the time, any feelings of potential regret were assuaged (as Marlene predicted) by the wholesale success of Jackson's second novel. Novel Two, a book that broke all records, by way of genre, sales, age of author, a host of other statistics, numbers all adding up to power, his present-day power. Guilt, nostalgia, romanticizing previous business arrangements? Those were the emotions that defined the amateur, the unsuccessful, the wannabe. The ones who bought his books, paid to see him appear in person and speak the nuggets of wisdom only an artist of Jackson's caliber could even contemplate. Jackson was not without emotion. He valued Cline, Marlene, JB & Sons. Of course he valued Katherine. However, the idea of . . . *meaning* had long passed. What these people meant to Jackson, he did not know. They served a purpose, and, at this point in his life, he could no longer distinguish between what a human being meant to him and the purpose that human being served. The Attorney, the Editor, the Publisher, the Girlfriend. These were the titles of the people who inhabited Jackson's life, but frankly, they were phrases, job descriptions. The people in Jackson's life were scenery. Valuable, purposeful scenery as they related to Jackson's task: gathering up all the ideas in his head, those horrifying, thrilling, grotesque, haunting ideas, putting them on a computer screen, constructing a book. The next novel. The next big, bestselling Jackson Grey Novel. That was the scenery's purpose. To service the industry of Jackson Grey.

The Process: Once out of bed, dressed, V waiting patiently to pour the freshly ground and prepared coffee into Jackson's cup, the cigarettes, the paper, the nod of appreciation to V . . . and Jackson Grey would begin slipping out of his own head and comfortably into the new novel. The words he used to describe himself, his career, the people, the ones he loved, or thought he loved, or thought he was supposed to love, the ones he worked with, lied about, lied to, that whole mess that cluttered Jackson's mind? He would bury all of that, walk into his study, lock the door . . . and commence writing. Or as Jackson portrayed it in so many interviews and speeches, "muster the courage to begin a new book." Jackson used this phrase frequently . . . in public. To the ones who paid for the nuggets of wisdom. He gave them that falsity, the "muster the courage" nugget. In reality, Jackson never thought of writing a novel as an act of courage, in fact never gave thought to his process. He simply delivered. Slipping out of his own head and easily into a new novel was Jackson's religion, born from what he felt at the time of Novel One, many years ago: to put pen to paper and create page after page required a courageous leap of faith in himself. Now, so many successes behind him, such courage was on par with that needed to slip out of bed, and the leap of faith need be accomplished only once, and Jackson accomplished it during Novel One.

The phrase "muster the courage" had become an inside joke he shared with Marlene and Marlene's assistant and associate editor, Lyla. They knew the score. Jackson had mastered the formula for creating a Jackson Grey Novel, and they admired, as many did, Jackson's mastery of that particular art. Many respected his unique signature on horror and many more desired to read the bestsellers made pure from that formula.

Jackson also understood that the way in which a Jackson Grey Novel left his mind, traveled to Marlene, and ended up in a reader's hands sounded creatively myopic to certain critics, to those who created, collected, received, and distributed opinion. Skill sets, constructions, formulas, precision, fortunes . . . words, ideas that led to success and money read like sin to the class of poseurs who waited, achingly, to judge him. And given our times, anyone with the desire to create and distribute opinion could do so; everyone could publish an opinion. *Everyone a goddamn demi-critic, with an unreadable blog. Amateurs unable to pierce even the outermost veil of literary creation and the successful sating of an eager audience. How to explain that marriage of creativity and business? How to explain they went hand in hand?* Jackson attempted to explain this on every well-paid speaking tour he booked. And he booked many. He could see in their eyes their judgment, wrapped in the unspoken words "sellout" and "hack." *Why do they even show up, pay to hear me speak? On the off chance they will lock eyes with me, on the off chance their eyes will betray their disapproval? They would kill to be me. How dare they judge? Fuck critics and their blogs, their magazines and periodicals.*

Fuck them!

Now it was about simply getting up and writing, which he simply got up and did. The Setting, the Routine, the Process . . . and the Formula. Therein lay a Jackson Grey Novel.

After the success of Novel Fourteen, reprinted in hardcover dozens of times, then to paperback, then the speeches and talks, people were, on Jackson's behalf, again flirting with film offers. That is all Jackson knew. People. Flirting with offers. After Novel Fourteen was attributed, congratulated, celebrated, and partied to absolute death, and then reattributed, recelebrated, recongratulated, and partied yet again, Jackson "mustered the courage" to begin Novel Fifteen.

He began by reviewing the contract to write Novel Fifteen, the contract Cline had drafted for both Jackson and JB & Sons, the contract Marlene reviewed, the contract Jackson had on his desk, waiting for his signature.

All of this simply . . . worked. Not by happenstance; rather by formula, by intention. The right people, doing the right things, at the right time. He read many of his peers, in print interviews, and saw them on television rehashing the same canard: creativity cannot be explained. *Such bullshit. Such delusion. With the proper Setting, Routine, and Process, with the correct Formula, creativity can easily be explained. Bolstering an audience's delusions about the writer's journey? So false. So manipulative.* In truth, and even though Jackson made a good deal of his money speaking about the production of a Jackson Grey Novel, there was no great mystery in his journey, no questions really needed to be asked, no answers were required, and the delusions? Well, for the right price, to a paying audience, Jackson indulged those delusions with a private wink and a nod.

Yes, it all worked. In its own way, it all worked.

Until Novel Fifteen.

Monday, the seventeenth of August, the first day Jackson, living in his Setting, engaged in his Routine, buried in his Process, sticking to his Formula, attempted to begin Novel Fifteen. Immediately something was off. Jackson never stared at a blank screen for more than a few minutes. Yet there he was, doing exactly that. Staring. By eleven a.m., Jackson folded his cards. It did not seem such a big deal. That day he periodically went back into his study, sat down, and tried to start over, but again, nothing. Chalking it up to a million external realities, none of which, to be frank, were palpable, Jackson anxiously awaited Tuesday. For it was on Tuesday that Novel Fifteen would certainly come. Said prediction was far off the grid. Tuesday ended up being a *practical* day for Jackson. Tormenting but practical. For, on Tuesday, plans were made. Plans for Wednesday. Jackson reckoned that if the *next* day, Wednesday, ended in disappointment, practical steps would need to be taken. If Wednesday was mimicry of Tuesday's hell, something was not only off, something was wrong and something needed to be done about it. Thus, Tuesday was about rationalization, speculation, and long odds. *Wednesday will be just fine. The past two days? An anomaly.*

Wednesday did not hold solutions. By noon on Wednesday, screen blank, "anomaly" a concept long gone, Jackson made a quick, discreet trip to Dr. Max, his internist. Dr. Max had been Jackson's doctor for years, since Jackson moved to Carmel. And the doctor was enamored of Jackson (although he claimed to have other "celebrity" patients,

Jackson doubted it). The sycophantic doctor spoke a bit too much about how the brain works, why, where, and when the synapses fire, and how they get lost, fucked up on their synaptic journey . . . until Jackson approached impatience. *I know you have to give the speech, but we both know the end game here. Take out your little pad of paper, write down whatever meds will unfuck the synapses, let's get on with it.* Finally, Dr. Max wrote a prescription for the little pink pills that were supposed to make one concentrate. The pills they give children who daydream. The idea behind this medicine was that Jackson had too much on his mind and lacked focus. *Whatever. You know nothing of me, my process, what it takes to do what I do. Just give me the script. And write it for refills.* Jackson had taken these pills before.

On Wednesday he took one of the pills, then two, then three, then God knows how many; he had forgotten exactly what his doctor had told him with regard to how this medication—more important, *when* this medication—began doing its job. He remembered, vaguely, that the doctor had given such explanations before. He remembered these words: "People think this is 'speed'; it's not." Regardless of what the pills did or were designed to do, they gave definition to his emptiness. Upon realizing that these pills *were* speed and would allow him no sleep, he called the doctor back and that transaction resulted in little white pills that would provide that sleep.

Too much sleep. Thursday was all about sleep. Yet it did not seem a wasted day to Jackson. Perhaps this was precisely what he needed. Unadulterated, uninterrupted sleep. For Friday, Novel Fifteen would appear on the screen. *God, what have I been putting myself through these past four days? I just needed sleep. Like any other human being.*

Friday, the fifth morning of Jackson's agony, Jackson realized he was utterly unable to produce a single word, not a letter, a vowel, a consonant arcing toward the construction of Novel Fifteen. So he took a shower. The third shower he had taken in as many hours. As if the shower were a baptismal ritual, something primal, an attempt to both wash off his failure and purify his existence.

However, nothing became pure, there was no redemption, for after Jackson dried himself off, got dressed, poured himself a drink, unlocked and entered his study, it was then that he first spotted The Words blinking on his computer:

BOOKS DO NOT WRITE THEMSELVES, JACKSON GREY.

The study. Jackson's study was an integral piece of the Setting, the Routine, the Process. This deep-leather, mahogany room contained a couch Jackson rarely sat on, bookshelves filled with bound, gilded books, never opened or read, a dedicated shelf with the first editions of his novels, walls lined with awards, photos, plaques: a veritable shrine to his success. Next to Jackson's computer on the large hardwood desk sat a notepad and the contract for Novel Fifteen, still unsigned, and an expensive monogrammed pen. The room was off-limits to everyone, including V (unless, of course, Jackson was inside the room and V knocked on the door to bring in tea or coffee, etc.). The room was neat, no scattered papers: just the couch, the desk, the computer, password protected, a notepad, the scent of leather and wood. Precision. All part of the Process. The study was what a writer's room should look like.

He stared at those blinking words with shock, fear, and panic. After all the accolades, the superlatives, the cash, the speaking gigs, the success that Novel Fourteen had brought, and, more to the point, after the attempted commencement of Novel Fifteen, ideas and questions that were absolutely incomprehensible to Jackson suddenly became comprehensible, possible. Everything permitted, nothing denied. Every word, gesture, act of cruelty, of contrition, of desire, of abstinence, of construction, of destruction, every act within the human realm, within Jackson Grey's realm? Comprehensible. Possible.

BOOKS DO NOT WRITE THEMSELVES, JACKSON GREY.

Ironic, Jackson thought, how seven words could send a writer like himself, of whom there were few, straight to hell.

Jackson immediately began doing something he'd sworn to himself he'd never do. He thought about his Process. He began to veer, adding and subtracting ingredients. He changed the recipe.

What diseased bastard wrote on my computer? A practical joke? That's sick. Impossible, as well. Rule that one out. No one gets in my study. Lock and key.

Break it down. Go back. Okay, yes. This did happen after Novel One. The first novel. Seven words did not appear on my computer, no. But there was a brief inability to begin Novel Two. How common is that? Quite. The huge pressure to obliterate the idea of the "one-hit wonder," as he slams into the expectations. Everybody's expectations. That turn to speculations. What that can do to a writer! Me? Got rid of people, picked up people, traveled, overcelebrated. A megaton of pressure. It's happened before. And it's happening again.

Yes, Novel Two was a headache. But Novel Twos always are! And Novel Two was a bestseller! So it is supposed to happen with a second novel. Not a fifteenth!

Yes, wait, goddamn! It did happen again with Novel Seven. After hooking up with that girl who came to the Berkeley lecture. She was living in San Francisco. Invited her to move in. She was barely twenty years old. She—Celina! Celina. A muse. That's all. Talent needs, requires, a muse. Muses. Picasso had lovers. Loved her. Nearly married her. Did I? Thank god Cline talked me out of that. Talked us both out of that! Which was smart. She was fucking with my head. I just needed a muse. Why did she not understand that? These women, these muses, they drive you, they drain you. She was an adult. Drama. Tears. Cline helped smooth things over. Gave her money. Money? Jesus, why did we give Celina my money? Nearly married—It's always about fucking money. But that was years ago.

Katherine? A completely different situation. Katherine . . . completely different. Katherine. Self-made, diffident, confident, far too confident, and she'll learn that the hard way, the way all women learn that their beauty is momentary, ephemeral. She has her own people. Doesn't need me. She wants me. Celina . . . needed me. Celina fucked up my head. We picked out a beach to get married—Oh, Christ, forget Celina. She's gone. Looked for her a few years back. How stupid that was! Living in L.A., married to an attorney. Of course. They always start with writers, these chicks, and end up with attorneys. Stability. Bullshit. Katherine doesn't have that power. Really. Katherine? Laughable. Katherine can't fuck with my head. Cline was right about me and Katherine. I own this relationship!

Who wrote those goddamned seven words on my computer?

Katherine?

V exited the kitchen and hurriedly walked into the living room, entered the space where Jackson was sitting, staring at the sea, going inside.

"She's still out. Shopping," V said.

"What?" Jackson said. *Oh, for Christ's sake, did I say Katherine's name out loud? Am I that man now? The man who cannot distinguish what he keeps and what he gives away? No. I am not that man. A mistake. Hilarious, when that happens. Too hilarious.*

Not that man.

Jackson smiled. "Oh, okay, V. Thanks." *Definitely don't want V to think, even momentarily flirt, with the idea I am that man.*

She looked at him, perplexed.

"What?" he asked, a touch too strongly for V.

"Excuse me? What?" she replied.

"You were just looking at me strangely. You know? Weird." He redefined words for V. He did this every day. Made words, sentences simpler. "Strangely" to "weird." *V's English is fine, really, but let's be honest, she lies, she pretends to understand more than she does. Peculiar after all the years she's been in the States. But fine, really. However "strangely" could be misinterpreted. "Weird?" Not precise. But simpler.*

"No, I wasn't." She smiled. That smile. That goddamn smile.

"Uh, yeah, you were." He smiled. Jackson nodded. *Yes. Definitely yes. Does she not know how well I read people? A writer reads people.*

"I'm sorry . . ."

"Oh, V! Don't be sorry. Nothing to apologize for," he said. *Get out while you can, V. We know what's going on here.*

V went back into the kitchen. She got paid far more than other men pay women who take care of their Settings, their Routines, their Processes, their Formulas. And was so for reasons long-ago, if not remembered, decided. *Like Cline said, you cannot really put a price on a woman like V, a woman who runs your life.* And she did: V ran the show, kept the place clean, the coffee coming, the meals prepared, the guests greeted, the bags packed. V was more than a housekeeper. She was chief of staff. She had power, and as such, Cline made her sign some agreement. *Nondisclosure? Something.* Could Jackson fire her? Of course. But why would he? She did her job and did it well. Yet . . . he wondered for a moment: *Can I really fire her? Or would I?* The two questions blended into one hazy question or thought, which gave him a momentary chill for no ascertainable reason. Anyway, it was of no import.

Of great import, however, was V's access to his study, to his computer. *She simply would never do that.* V was intimately involved with his life. He knew, everyone knew, that V worshipped him. His craft. He was a successful writer. And her culture respected successful writers. *Did I ever ask where she was from? Of course I did. Uruguay? Paraguay? Why was V's English not perfect? Why would I expect it to be? God, I am beginning to sound like one of those golf-course bigots in Carmel with their Pebble Beach bullshit and their non-Caucasian caddies.* His mind was racing; he was shuffling too many ideas around. The same ideas. The same questions. *Goddammit.* Yet had he not the right? Fourteen bestsellers? Then . . . nothing. And seven taunting words. Yes, he had the right to let his mind race, yet it was not healthy.

In any event, he knew for certain that V treated his craft, his success, as it should be treated. As high art.

V returned with his eight p.m. cocktail (at six p.m.), a jigger of expensive bourbon, five ice cubes, a dash of bitters, a splash of soda. Jackson forced a chuckle.

"It's so funny, I drink one or two of these at eight. Not six."

V reached for the cocktail.

"It just looked like you were done for the day," she said.

"I'm not 'done for the day,'" he said.

Jackson blocked her hand from retrieving the cocktail. He was determined to simply, casually play it off. V had power, for sure, but there were limits Jackson imposed on her power; chief among these limits was the implicit ban on second-guessing Jackson.

"Wait. You got me, V. I am done for the day. I'll drink this one now, and I'll—Jesus, I'm talking to you like you're a waitress. I'm sorry, V." *Do I always speak to this woman as if she's a waitress? My god. I should watch that.*

"It's fine, it's fine."

"It's not fine. Come on. Let's go have a smoke."

Having a cigarette with V was a ritual after six or seven hours of writing. Jackson wasn't even certain she smoked but for the end-of-day Dunhill he proffered. He motioned V to the outdoor deck.

"Let me grab my sweater," she said.

Jackson walked outside onto the deck, summer sunlight still bright. He looked at the binoculars mounted on a tripod and the telescope.

Katherine thought this all a good idea. And it probably was. A view of Point Lobos. Whale watching. All those things that one, with an expensive, spectacular view of the ocean, engages in with expensive, spectacular gear.

V walked out, bundled up, onto the deck.

"It's not that cold," he said, almost smirking. *Why does she play the victim so often? I give her everything she wants. I have given her everything she needs.*

"I'm anemic."

"Yes, I know, but . . . never mind." He didn't know. Maybe he knew at one time. Maybe he knew where she was from, maybe he knew what family she had, maybe, at one time, he knew what hardships she had to endure to get herself, her four sisters to this place. Then to pack up and move four times with him. This loyal woman who devoted her life to him. He knew the price of loyalty. He felt that. *How to repay such loyalty? Easy. Share a secret. After all, she worships me.* He offered her a cigarette and lit it. And shared himself.

"This morning, shit, this week, I just . . . didn't have it. I couldn't do it. Couldn't perform."

She looked deliberately perplexed.

"Christ!" He laughed. "That's not what I meant!"

"I know what you meant." She smiled. "Look, the best writers have an off day. Or they wouldn't be the best writers."

She did know what was wrong. Her answer leapt out too quickly. And where the fuck did she pick up that cliché? And for how long has she been hiding it, waiting to use it? Do not hate her. She is attempting to calm me. Does she hate me? Why would she? Her loyalty is compensated.

"That may be true—"

"It is true," she said.

She put her barely smoked cigarette into the tall sand-filled ashtray and began to walk inside. She turned around.

"The messenger was here. I didn't bother you. I figured you weren't ready—"

"What messenger?" he asked. "Ready for what?"

"He said he was to pick up a contract? You have to sign it."

"I know," Jackson said. *Have we done this dance before? V inserting herself in my business? Perhaps. Telling me I have to sign contracts? All right, innocuous enough.*

Yet, for a moment, Jackson went back inside himself: *Did the rules just change? Is she not the subservient and I the dominant? Or the other way around? And if so, has it always been like this? Maybe it has, this power she possesses, controlling my Routine. My Process. But I gave her this power!*

"V, this afternoon, my computer was screwed up."

V looked frightened. Jackson had opened a door he would never again be able to close.

"I would *never*—"

"I don't mean *you* did anything to my computer. Maybe you saw something or . . . Forget it."

"I didn't see anything!"

"I said forget it. Where's Katherine?"

V sighed heavily. "Shopping. Remember? She left around noon."

"Oh, I didn't know . . . or see her."

V smiled. "I know. I know you didn't." It was an odd time for V to smile. In fact, it was an odd smile. And a thought suddenly occurred to Jackson: *Maybe this woman secretly hates me. She lies for me. She has lied for me. Maybe she resents lying for me. Perhaps doing my bidding disgusts her. Perhaps she's capable of anything.*

V's potential hatreds and resentments, though a powerful thought, passed quickly through Jackson's mind. There were more profound matters on the table.

When Katherine returned three hours later, Jackson was four cocktails in; the last he poured for himself. V had prepared an uneaten meal and retired to the guest house an hour earlier, also part of the routine. Katherine set her bags down.

"Where've you been?" he asked blandly.

"Shopping," Katherine said, as if it was obvious, indicating her bags.

"It's fucking Carmel, Kat. Shops close at seven. It's nine."

"You're drunk, Jackson."

"I'm not drunk!"

"You always call me 'Kat' when you're drunk. I went shopping, met some friends for dinner—"

"You became Katherine when I introduced you to my people—"

Katherine put up with a lot; she had to. But the idea that doors were opened for her by *Jackson* truly annoyed her. She began to walk away.

"You were 'Kat' when you booked your first gig. Anyway, what friends? What dinner?"

"We're going to do this again?"

"Do what again?"

"Have a bullshit drunken argument?"

"Why don't you bring your 'friends' over? We can have a bullshit drunken argument with your 'friends' right here. And have dinner too. V cooks." A dare. A threat.

"I know what V does!"

Instinctively, Katherine looked out the window at the guest house and saw V's profile pressed heavy against the lace curtains. Katherine and V had eyes on each other for a few seconds. Then V moved away from the window. There was a pecking order, albeit insincere, in Jackson's world. V had blinked.

"So . . . your 'friends,'" Jackson said.

"Have my friends over? To see my drunk, depressed man who doesn't speak all day?"

He stared at her for a beat.

"You're fucking somebody," he said, clinically.

"My god, you are really messed up—"

"I know how this works. I know the formula here. It's how I got you."

"Got me?"

"A little over a year ago I was fucking somebody else, you were fucking somebody else, we were both speeding up the food chain, then I started—"

"You're really disgusting."

Katherine had endured his rage during the past four nights when Jackson could not deliver. Not on the literary proposition, and certainly not on any sexual proposition. She took her bags to the bedroom while he sat on the couch, ruefully shaking his head. She reentered the living room.

"Do you want me to be fucking somebody else, Jackson? Or do you want me to *tell* you I'm fucking someone else? Do you want me to *pretend* to be? Would any of that make life easier for you? More . . . definable? Justifiable?"

"Oh, please."

"Whatever makes life simpler for you, Jackson!"

"You're babbling. Don't be stupid."

She hated him at that moment, during all the moments he questioned, he challenged, he offended her intellect.

"I have a shoot tomorrow."

"Of course you do."

"I'm back Sunday."

"Uh-huh."

"Goddammit! Why are you such an asshole?" She began to storm off, then caught herself. "I was supposed to leave tomorrow. Fuck that! I don't want to be here tonight."

"Well, that's easy, Kat. Go have 'dinner' with your 'friends' again."

Moving from the couch only to pour himself another, Jackson heard Katherine on her phone, he heard bags being packed, other calls being made, doors opening, words yelled at him, a car pulling up, doors slammed.

Who cares?

Jackson got up and walked to his study. He unlocked the door and saw the computer, the screen, the keyboard, the whole setup exactly as he'd left it.

With one exception: his computer screen. Bold, the font much larger, all caps, with a rainbow of colors, blinking:

YOU'RE A WEAK, FRAGILE MAN, JACKSON
GREY. WEAK. FRAGILE. PATHETIC. YOU
OUGHT TO OWN THAT TRUTH. THAT
TRUTH WILL PROVIDE YOU COMFORT
WHEN YOU FINALLY REALIZE THE
NEXT BOOK WILL NEVER COME.
NOVEL FIFTEEN? DEAD ON ARRIVAL.

Jackson immediately called Cline.

Cline did not take client calls on his cell phone at ten p.m. In fact, Cline did not give out his cell phone number to clients. Except in the case of Jackson Grey. Anyone associated with the Jackson Grey industry took his calls and answered his e-mails, immediately, twenty-four hours a day, seven days a week.

Cline knew this call was coming, and Cline did not want it. His Friday nights were as routine and processed as Jackson's days. Leave the office at three p.m., nap, massage, poker game (thousand-dollar buy-in, a game he was studiously engaged in when the call came). Leave the table at one a.m., an after-hours spot, pick a girl, sugar-daddy that girl until early Sunday morning. Cline worked on Sunday afternoons. Years ago, Cline told Jackson, "I go dark at the end of the week. I've earned it." And years ago, Jackson did not care to know what "going dark" meant. He speculated: *Prostitutes? Drugs?* Now, years later, there were other, more serious matters at hand.

Cline took the call in an adjacent room.

"This is not a big deal, Jackson."

"It is a big deal. A big fucking deal!"

Cline was soothing. "You think it's a big deal. Trust me, it's not."

Jackson took the first deep breath he had taken in five days. This man could calm Jackson down. That is why he needed people like Cline. That was their purpose. Anyone could make a deal. Only people like Cline, people with power, only they could truly calm him down.

"So what do I do?" Jackson asked.

"Jackson, you have to change it up now and again. Too much routine. And lock it down."

"Katherine left," he blurted out. *Six? Seven drinks in?*

"I know Katherine left," Cline said. "She called me."

"Why did she call *you*? What did she say? What did *you* say?"

"Calm down. It didn't get that far, Jackson. I don't discuss my clients' business with anyone. Especially the people that my clients are sleeping with. You know that."

Jackson did know that. Or believed it. Or had to believe it.

"So . . . ?" Jackson said, begging for a nugget.

"I figured you'd call tonight—listen, Katherine *always* leaves . . . And Katherine *always* returns," Cline said, as he peeked back into a room flush with cash, his cash, sitting on a table doing exactly nothing. "Look, if you want a prima donna—I mean, if you want somebody like Katherine hanging on your shoulder, you have to take the bullshit with it. It's a whole package. You know that." Concluding each sentence with the phrase "you know that" was a low-rent trick Cline picked up years ago. And it worked. Cline enlightening the ignorant and in the process convincing the ignorant that he was already ripe with the knowledge he pursued.

"Okay, so . . . change it up?"

"Get out of that fucking house, Jackson. You're too inside your own head. And that house is where that head resides."

"Okay, but wait. The lock-it-down thing . . ."

"Let's talk 'lock it down' on Monday," Cline said hurriedly. "I'm in a game."

"A game? Fuck the game! How about now?" Jackson said.

"It's not the game, Jackson. It's the privacy. Monday I'm in my office on a secure line, in a private attorney-client setting. Which I am not in now. I'm at a poker table," Cline said. It was declarative, not an offer, not a question. And it made sense to Jackson. Everything Cline said made sense to Jackson. Other people did not need to know Jackson's business. That was true.

"Yeah, okay, Monday," Jackson said meekly.

"*I'll* call *you*," Cline said, fully aware of who called whom was a matter of power and politics and one that Cline happily conceded. "And sign that goddamn contract, Jackson. I busted my ass working the terms. Your publisher's not exactly the fucking pope when it comes to these matters."

"Yes. Okay. I know. I'll sign it."

"Good. And look, as far as that other business, your computer thing, it's just some childish prank. Some jealous asshole. In the meantime—"

"I know. Change it up."

"That's right. Have some fun. And remember, this has happened before."

This has happened before? Five, six years ago Jackson would have debated the point with Cline, with anyone. But it was true. It had happened before. Not the taunting words written on his computer . . . but the block.

As Jackson was about to disconnect the call, he heard Cline yell, ostensibly to the players at the table, "I'm all in." And one of those players laughing. "You haven't seen your cards yet, Cline!"

He heard Cline yell right back. "I said I'm all in!" and trailing off, with a sigh, "I'm all in . . ."

Jackson had no right to hear this, but it did make him smile. Cline was a player. A power player. A banger, a baller. And, as Cline looked at his phone and realized he had forgotten to disconnect, they both, perhaps simultaneously, had the same thought: Cline was getting sloppy. It was a minor thought and, by both, quickly forgotten. Cline began to charge toward the poker table, then realized there was still business left unsettled. He returned to the private room.

He dialed Marlene.

And just as Cline took Jackson's calls under these unwritten rules, so did Marlene take Cline's.

"It's one in the fucking morning, Cline."

"It's happening again," Cline said.

"Oh, Jesus," Marlene said.

"It's happening in a big way. The whore called me."

"Okay. Okay. I get it!"

She hung up. Nothing more needed to be said. Marlene found Cline to be utterly vulgar, but goddamn, she respected his talents. Cline had skills.

Jackson began packing his bag. Cline's words gave him comfort, even confidence. *Some childish prank, some jealous asshole.* He opened his wall safe and removed the Other Phone and charged it up. He packed his bag, pocketed the Other Phone, and left the house (*no need to leave V notes anymore; she knows*). It was time to change it up.

After the car rolled up, after nary a word had been exchanged between the driver and Jackson, after Jackson arrived at the Regal Hotel in San Francisco, checked into his suite under a different name (Novel Nine: he had jokingly, seemingly joking, suggested to the desk clerk that they call the room the Jackson Grey Suite. The desk clerk, the same desk clerk who'd been clerking for more than forty years, laughed. Part of Jackson's mind was serious about this, a more rational part of his mind knew it impossible. Pseudonyms and all that).

Jackson overtipped the bellman, ordered up a large pot of coffee, a bottle of his bourbon, picked up the Other Phone, and dialed a number.

The Other Phone served as an extension of a very private part of Jackson's mind. And like his mind, the Other Phone also contained ingredients. Phone numbers of Jackson's sins, his predilections, his habits. All the things he publicly and privately denied. His secrets.

"Buddy!" said Andrew. "So glad you're back in town. Head on over! I'll set it all up for you!"

"Thanks. I'm at the Regal . . ." Jackson was already dizzy.

"I know where you're at!" Andrew paused. "You okay?"

Jackson was a good poker player. No tells. Andrew's question was odd. "I'm fine," Jackson answered. "I'm always okay."

"Great. I'll send my guy to grab you."

"Why did you ask if I was okay?" Jackson asked.

"Because I care about you, buddy! Anyway, all good," Andrew yelled. There was a cacophony of noise. Andrew had clearly walked back into the Club.

Jackson hung up.

Andrew, thirty-something trust fund kid, club owner—exclusive club, members only, ten women for every man. Every wealthy man. Once when Andrew let his guard down, he referred to these rich men, well-known men, men like Jackson, as "whales." Whales were the men of money, of renown, who came to the Club, so exclusive it had no name, no address, no cameras, and lots of privacy. Ridiculous sums of money were passed around for the pleasure of being at the Club. For the pleasure of being anonymous, the pretense of anonymity, for at the Club, men did not go not to be seen, they went not to be seen by the wrong people. They went to be seen by the right people, those others of money and renown. Moreover, they went to the Club for the beautiful women, the women half their age. The women they could not procure were they not at the Club, were they not the type of man invited to the Club. They also went to the Club to do the drugs they convinced themselves were the drugs that powerful, dynamic, successful men do. Others simply didn't understand. The Club was a place of power, fame, sex, drugs, and self-delusion. After Novel Three, Jackson learned the ropes. After Novel Seven, Jackson fit right in.

Initially it was confusing when he began coming to places like this in Los Angeles, Chicago, New York, London. No lists, no ropes, no human beings allowed within twenty feet of this canopied entrance on a public street (cash properly distributed works miracles). Jackson entered a private world. He got the hang of it and was ultimately treated like a king at the Club, and, as such, ran up kingly tabs, paid monthly by Cline, from one of Jackson's accounts. Cline asked no questions at month's end, and even if he had, Jackson would be hard-pressed to provide the memories that explained the expenses. The Club experience was about diversion, not memory, meaning, or inspiration. Diversion. Were tabs not paid and cash not passed from one hand to another, the Club, and the other Clubs, would simply disappear. No phone numbers, no owners, no access. Jackson had (former) friends who were persona non grata at places like these. Men who begged Jackson to call people like Andrew, these men pleading with Jackson to get them into places, spaces he did not own. Jackson indulged these pleadings a few times. And, of course, Jackson's requests were immediately granted; however, the look in Andrew's eyes, the other Andrews, those who owned the other Clubs, their eyes, their forced smiles, hugs, and handshakes a bit too ebullient suggested that such requests were frowned upon. Jackson could read people and read them well, and further, Jackson, a businessman in his own right, well understood that should anyone attempt to change the map of another businessman's terrain, that person was on the fast track to becoming a liability. Jackson stopped indulging the requests and subsequently stopped engaging with the people who made such requests. Big fish in a small pond eat the small fish, and all that. Jackson understood that territory all too well.

Added to the transaction and the hefty tab, there was another tab: before Jackson or any other recognizable faces were allowed to reach their booth—booths stocked with magnums of champagne, a bottle girl, and many gorgeous women—he belonged to Andrew. For ten minutes Jackson was not in possession of himself.

"Hey, before you sit down, and by the way, there is major talent at your table . . ." And, on cue, Andrew would grab Jackson's arm and pull him into the main section of the Club, surreptitiously, oh-so-obviously, faux-surreptitiously, force Jackson's eyes on the very beautiful women at Jackson's table. This, of course, was the bribe. "They're big fans of your work." *Yeah. Sure they are.* "Could you do me a favor and make the rounds? Say hi to a couple of people?" This was always the moment: the ten minutes Jackson sold himself.

Prominent Author you all recognize? Meet CEO of Tech Company you all know. Fourteen Bestsellers? Meet Five Feature Films. Famous Writer? Meet Insanely Wealthy Hip-Hop Artist. Athlete with Another Woman? Meet Actress with Another Woman. Ten minutes of this nonsense. These were gentlemen's agreements. One never spoke the names of the others one met at the Club. And this nonsense kept Andrew . . . the Club . . . relevant. And, more important, kept Jackson welcome at the Club.

To the table. The girls, Katherine's age, stunning, an international demographic of stunning. The girls, properly prepped to kiss his ass. They loved his books, the film adaptations, they could hardly wait for the next book, film, whatever. False humility aside, Jackson loved this, he craved it, he needed it. This type of attention. And the alcohol served so quickly that he didn't even have a moment to question the sincerity of the compliments, the worship. The alcohol, leading to the hookup, the vials, the baggies, the powder, the visits to the restroom, and then lazily using in the open, using the girls to shield his face, the powder, all grinding toward a finale. Choosing a woman from this table to return to the Regal, a woman paid for directly by Andrew, but a woman put on Jackson's tab.

Katherine says I hate women. That's bullshit. I love women!

To the hotel. The girl, the liquor, the sheets scented with the ardor of self-loathing, of drunken, coked-out, perfume-drenched sex. Understanding, not caring that he would never know the real names of these girls; nothing was asked of him, nothing given. Everything asked of these women, everything given. Awakening to silk sheets, a sweet taste on the tongue, a sweet note on the bureau, a sweet name attached, the same sweet bullshit.

The morning after every single one of these encounters, Jackson would play with the same idea: *Must've gone dark last night.* As if it had never happened before, as if it would never happen again. Then snapping out of that odd notion, he'd order down for a large pot of coffee and begin neatly packing his bag. After which a quick call down to the concierge, making certain Andrew was sent a bottle of something very expensive with an appropriate note. A note Jackson entrusted the well-worn, well-informed concierge to conjure up.

And who had taught him how to navigate this tricky terrain?

Cline.

After Novel Three, at Jackson's insistence, Cline had caved in and taught Jackson how to curry favor, how to find the correct Club, the proper hotel, the legitimate hookups. Cline taught Jackson what to say to the right woman at the right time, where and when to do the drugs offered, never purchased. First at Cline's Clubs, meeting Cline's friends. The other kings. The other whales. Jackson, the apprentice. The darkness Jackson so earnestly avoided discussing with Cline that first year: high-end sugar babies, the cocaine Jackson swore he'd never get near, the actress with the junk problem with whom he flew to Mexico, gorgeous as she tied off and shot up on the beach. The private jet, private security, police bribes, thug threats, thug "friends," all the adventures he'd heard other men of note engaged in. Seductions, earlier in his life only dreamed of, turning into realized fantasy, creating the winner's edge Jackson believed all this hell conjured up. Cline's doing. Cline taught him the ropes, turning Jackson's curiosity into an addiction. Cline was an intensely smart man and knew that men like Jackson, men in Jackson's position, in his situation, would eventually make their own way to the Club, and do so sloppily. How many messes did Cline have to clean up? Too many. Better to teach the kid (Cline had only eight years on him, still thought of him as the kid) the difference between a club and the Club, where he could get sloppy and feel confident in the knowledge that someone else would clean up his mess.

And each time Jackson would engage in this behavior he would ask himself the same question: *Why navigate such terrain?* And even at the lowest, most self-loathing, beaten-down sense of himself, he would answer that question, and the answer remained the same. Why? *Because we are built to do this, men like us. This is our dominion, our imperative. It is a small pond, there are big fish and smaller ones, there is a food chain, we all know this, why pretend we don't? When Katherine secures (while Katherine is securing?) . . . While Katherine fucks her next homestead with Feature Film Number Five, or CEO/Tech Company, or Hippie Venture Capitalist, I am doing this. Lie to others? Fine. Lie to myself? Absolutely not.*

After Katherine moved in, that first year, Jackson abstained from engaging in this behavior . . . for a few weeks. Maybe less. Then when he returned to these outings he made the proper excuses to Katherine. *Writers conference in the Bay Area. Speech (private) in Chicago. Meeting with Marlene, the editors in New York.* Then, when it became a touch more obvious, the writer's excuse, the cliché: *I need to get away, need to get out of my head.* In the last five, six months, no excuse, proper or otherwise: *Going out of town.* Katherine stopped asking questions quite a while ago. Or if she did, Jackson forgot them. In any case, he stopped answering them.

Sunday afternoon, the Empty Ritual. forty hours after Jackson arrived at the Regal, entered the Club, made the rounds, engaged in the "introductions" nonsense, drank and snorted his way into a stupor, chose a woman, brought her back to his suite, had loveless transactional sex with her, awoke, with taste on tongue, tearing up sweet idiotic notes, ordering expensive bottles to be sent to spoiled-brat club owners, mentally assuring himself everyone's silence was paid for handsomely . . . forty hours after this had all begun, he'd pack to leave. However, this particular Sunday something felt different. Before he could reach for the phone and order up a pot of coffee, he impulsively reached for the pad of paper next to the bed, a pen, and began writing. Writing ideas for Novel Fifteen. Page after page of handwritten notes.

Unbelievable! Maybe that chick was my muse! I don't even know her name! Too hilarious! Fuck! Finally!

That Sunday night, back in Carmel, bolstered with confidence in the form of twenty-five handwritten hotel pages of (unreviewed) notes that he locked in the wall safe with the Other Phone, Jackson engaged in a well-prepared (by V) studious dinner, along with a studious, well-prepared apology designed for Katherine.

"I am so, so sorry, Katherine."

"It's okay—"

"No, it's not okay. My head's been so fucked up. My behavior's been inexcusable."

"What's wrong?"

"Okay, well, look, this is going to sound idiotic," he began. *Oh, Jesus, just get this night over with, get to the notes, the book, Novel Fifteen.* "I guess I had writer's block," he said, and before Katherine could diagnose, comment, reply, Jackson immediately stopped her. "But it's done with now."

"Done with?" she asked. She appeared not to be buying "done with," *but who cares what she buys?*

"I'm serious. Done with. Also, my computer was . . . played with."

"What do you mean, 'played with'?" she asked.

He stared into Katherine's eyes. No. Katherine wouldn't touch his computer. Why? Because Katherine couldn't care less what was on Jackson's computer. Katherine couldn't care less what Jackson wrote. Because she had read only one of Jackson's books. Novel Two. Or so she said. A woman who proclaimed, "Horror isn't my thing." *Imagine that! The woman who lives in my house with these expensive views, who uses my money when she's "in between gigs." Fuck it! Cline was right. This was the package I desired, the package I deserved. For the privilege of having a Katherine hanging on my shoulder, in my bed, in my life, pretending to adore me in public, I ceded the opportunity to have a woman in my bed, in my life who respected what I do for a living, let alone gave a fuck about it? Who cares what she respects?*

"Doesn't matter, sweetheart. Anyway, something clicked. I've got a lot of stuff on paper."

"Jackson, maybe you need to open up more," she said.

"You're right. I do need to open up more."

Open up? Oh, that's the last thing you want, honey. Trust me. Just let it go. We'll keep playing house.

This confession of vulnerability? She was obviously not buying it. Weakness did not spill out of his mouth so easily. She knew this; he knew this. But that too did not matter. The meal, the conversation, the apologia, whether or not Katherine cared? None of it mattered. All of it stumbling blocks to an eventuality. The notes Jackson took at the Regal.

Even later that night, as they lay next to each other, Jackson quickly consummated the sex he pretended to initiate, as if he had the ability to make the night pass quickly and get to his notes. The notes that would lead to the production of Novel Fifteen.

At least that was the plan. Katherine had different plans. Plans that began with a smile, then a not-so-private laugh.

"What's so funny?" Jackson asked.

Katherine, the sheets draping her body, turned around and began speaking. *To the window, to herself? To Jackson.*

"It's just funny how life works out, you know?"

"No, I don't know. What do you mean?"

"Well, you're so fucking lucky to have me, Jackson. I mean somebody like *me*." She quickly turned, gave Jackson a quick peck on the cheek, then resumed her former position.

"I know. Kat, I know I'm lucky to have you—"

"No," she interrupted. "I don't mean some greeting-card bullshit, honey."

"I don't get what you're—"

"Do you want to have that chick back here? I still have her number," Katherine asked, wide grin.

"What chick? What're you talking about?"

Katherine sat up. "'What chick'?" She laughed. "Are you serious? The one we both fucked."

Jackson cocked his head. What the hell was she . . . *Oh, Jesus. That was two months ago. Katherine was supposed to be out of town. A chick from the Club. Cline said, "Never bring back a chick from the Club." I fucked up. Didn't keep track of Katherine's schedule. Got sloppy.*

"Brittany! That's what her *name* was." Katherine laughed again. A mocking laugh.

So sloppy. I should have called V first to make certain Katherine was gone. Brought Brittany . . . Brittany? . . . back from the Club. Back to my bed. But Katherine had never left. She'd been there the whole weekend. I thought she was leaving; she said she was leaving. Was she lying then?

"I didn't dig it at first, but then I got into it," she said.

Introduced her to Katherine as a student, a student of the Jackson Grey Novel. I, her mentor. The explanation felt insipid as it was coming out of my mouth, those words. That excuse.

Katherine propped herself up. "I mean, when we . . . you . . . tied her up," Katherine giggled. "I got into it."

The woman wanted to be tied up. Way past the excuse stage. I brought a woman back, introduced her as a student I was mentoring, somehow convinced Katherine that a threesome involving bondage might be fun. God, I was a fucking idiot. I was so wasted.

"And, my god, Jackson, she sure as hell flipped your switch. No, really, it was cool to see you happy and, I don't know, loose—"

"Okay, Kat! Can we not talk about that? I apologized and—"

"You didn't have to apologize, sweetie. Like I said, I kind of really dug it. Of course"—she began to laugh again—"partying for three straight days probably helped with—"

"Enough!" Jackson yelled. "For Christ's sake! Enough!" Then, much softer, "I'm sorry. I'm sorry I yelled. I told you, my head wasn't in a good place then. And I—"

"Oh, baby, your head's never in a good place." She smiled. "That's why I'm saying you're lucky to have me."

"I'm sorry. Why . . . why's that again?"

"Because, my dear, you've isolated yourself," she said. "Because you've isolated yourself and your friends, your so-called friends ask about you . . ."

"And? They ask about me. What's your point?" he asked. He knew the answer. He felt a tinge of fear.

Katherine sat up and stared him down. "What don't you get? You're lucky to have *me*, Jackson, because I keep my mouth shut!"

Jackson tried to spit out a sentence. He couldn't.

"Yup! Mouth shut. About all of it."

"All of what?" he asked. He really did not want to know.

"Oh, forget it. It's all so silly." Katherine put her head on her pillow. "So, would you like me to call Brittany? Try it again?"

If it was blackmail, Jackson made no accusation. *Is it blackmail? Who cares? A quick call to Cline will straighten this woman out. I've seen*

Cline in action. Cline could uproot an entire family, get them to leave the country with one phone call. That's how good Cline is . . . and I have Cline. Cline is mine. Katherine? You don't have Cline. What a pity.

He mumbled something barely audible to Katherine. Barely. "Go fuck yourself."

"What was that, honey?" Katherine asked, innocently.

"I said, 'I love you, Katherine.'"

She laughed and laughed until Jackson got up, two pillows in hand, and left the room. He did so confidently. For he possessed not only the people who could make this woman go away, move out, but something far more valuable. He possessed the keys to the kingdom. The notes he took on Novel Fifteen. The Holy Grail to the next success. For Jackson knew that women like Katherine age, they age and try to correct time's toll on the body, they do so until they cannot do so anymore, until they are unwanted by men like Jackson. But men like Jackson, who were possessed of certain talents, were immune to time's toll. This notion fairly well summed up Jackson's notion of the male-female dynamic. Jackson collapsed on the den couch.

I need to sell books and speeches, which I can do in a heartbeat. I rely on no one, nor do I need to rely on anyone. That woman sells herself. And she has a shelf life.

These thoughts gave him pleasure. Sometime during the night, he believed he heard her start her car and leave.

Monday morning, Jackson changed up his routine. Awakening at 9:30 a.m., after what seemed like a night of half-hour naps, he had his coffee and cigarettes and . . . further changed it up. Changed the Process. Instead of sitting down at his computer, Jackson practically raced to the wall safe and retrieved the notes, the twenty-five handwritten epiphanous pages of hotel notes. The solution.

Jackson sat down not at his desk, where the computer resided, but rather in the deep leather chair sitting next to his carefully arranged library. Again a variation from his Setting, his Routine, his Process.

He began skimming the notes. His fix, these notes, the mainline to his brain. They confused him at first. *Wrap your head around this, try again.* Bullet points. He had forgotten he had written them in bullet points. *Ah, okay. Read them as bullet points, they're perfectly clear as bullet points.* He read them carefully. *Where's my rush? What's wrong here?* He then examined them, as if they were not notes, not bullet points, but petroglyphs, in need of decoding. They simply made no sense, these bullet points, these ciphers:

> Trees, but not
> House, not cabin, house. Large, trees. Surrounding
> Dark, not night. But dark
> Disturbance, not love. Love, but control, not freedom
> Ropes, ties, binds, sex
> Anarchy and orgasm. Orgasm and anarchy
> Neck, choke, fingers
> Blue, but not blood
> Blood, not mine
> My blood, but death, not hers
> Murder, all murder
> My murder, my orgasm, my blood

And on and on. Page upon page of handwritten detritus. Of no use. Of no point. Yet he refused to surrender to the chaos of the notes. Perhaps opening the computer, putting the notes next to the computer, perhaps it would create a synergy of sorts. A word, a sentence, something that would magnetize the handwritten notes toward Novel Fifteen, waiting to be written.

He sat in his desk chair, opened his computer, and booted it up.

A fluorescent psychedelic haze of blinking lights and letters flashed on the screen. Lights and letters, in primaries and pastels, blacks and whites, bolds and underlined. At first he could not read it, and then he could read it all too well:

> You're not Jackson, nor are you Mr. Grey. You are Jackson Grey. The *brand*. Wait. No, that's imprecise. Too generic. You despise imprecision. I apologize. Much respect, Jackson Grey. The

BRAND JACKSON GREY IS . . . WHAT? "THE KING
OF NOUVEAU HORROR"? WHAT THE FUCK DOES
THAT MEAN, JACKSON? NO WONDER YOU SHY AWAY
FROM THAT BRAND; IT'S VOID OF MEANING (AND BY
THE WAY, YOUR FALSE HUMILITY IS VOMITOUS). YOU
SHY AWAY FROM "BRAND" IN GENERAL, CORRECT?
THE IDEA DISGUSTS YOU. YET ONE CANNOT IGNORE
THE IRONY. THOSE SPEECHES YOU GIVE, THOSE
SEMINARS, THOSE PRIVATE DINNERS WITH WEALTHY
WRITERS-IN-WAITING, ACHING FOR YOUR ADVICE,
HANGING ON YOUR EVERY WORD, HEARING YOU,
JACKSON GREY, REPEAT AND REPEAT AGAIN: "BRAND-
ING IS EVERYTHING THESE DAYS. IT'S ALL ABOUT
THE BRANDING." YOU'RE THE VERY DEFINITION OF
A HYPOCRITE, JACKSON. ONE WHO PRIVATELY
DESPISES WHAT ONE PUBLICALLY PROMOTES. ALL
THIS WOULD BE FINE, YOUR HYPOCRISY, IF YOU
COULD, IN FACT, WRITE. BUT THAT'S PROVING
TROUBLESOME, ISN'T IT, JACKSON GREY? BLOODY
EYES, SLEEPLESS NIGHTS, NERVES GROUND DOWN.
BOOZE, BLOW, PILLS, WHORES, YOU'RE A BEATEN
MAN. THIS CONCERNS ME NOT, IT'S LAUGHABLE,
FRANKLY. THIS DOES, HOWEVER, <u>CONSUME</u> YOU,
CORRECT? THE TORMENT? IT CONSUMES YOU.
I UNDERSTAND, JACKSON. HONESTLY, I DO
UNDERSTAND. THE PROBLEM IS: I SIMPLY DO
NOT CARE. NOT ANYMORE. I DON'T <u>CARE</u>.

Jackson, absent any persona, pretense, utterly unworried about per-
ceptions, yelled out, like a child, for V.

V had her own routine. In any emergency regarding Jackson, she was
to call Cline. Just call Cline. As said "emergencies" were becoming
more and more frequent, so were her calls to Cline.

At some point in the day, Katherine returned. She saw Jackson lying in bed, some scattered pills on his nightstand, a tumbler half full next to those pills. For some reason he was happy to see her. Until she took in the full picture, shook her head, and mumbled, "Pathetic."

That's what he thought he heard her say. "Pathetic." Maybe not. Maybe she was better than that.

From his bed he heard phone calls being made, calls being answered. He figured some collective decision had been made to send V into his room, like a doctor, about to deliver a diagnosis.

"Mr. Cline said you have a virus on your computer. He said it's not a big deal. He said to tell you that a man is coming over to fix it."

Jackson started to interrupt. *No! No one touches my computer.* V said, "Yes. A man is coming over to fix your computer." Jackson was too weak. He nodded. He relented. *Fine, V, you run the house.*

V announced the arrival of the computer technician and, two hours later, his departure. Jackson, so completely mentally and physically exhausted that he did not engage this person, coming or going. He simply nodded to V, and he understood that she would understand that this nod, this nod of despair, meant "Let him in, let him work, let him out." Jackson had only the strength to ponder the pills on his nightstand. The pink pills, the white pills, which did what? How many to take and when to take them? The pills were not producing Novel Fifteen. Why take them at all? Why not?

That same Saturday night, emboldened with the all chemical artifice, the liquor, powders, and pills, Jackson felt fortified to make one phone call.

Jackson's direct line to Marlene was not unlike his direct line to Cline: exclusive, precious, rare. Even more so with Marlene than Cline. Even after Novel Three, Jackson had to go through Lyla, Marlene's assistant and associate editor. All of Marlene's authors had to go through Lyla; this was not a sign of disrespect, but rather a signifier of Marlene's power. After Novel Three, Jackson demanded a direct cellphone line and one was provided.

Marlene ignored the call. Her night: a huge charitable event. A charity that Marlene ran. However, Jackson kept calling and Marlene finally relented.

Jackson skipped the usual pleasantries.

"I've got a couple of problems, Marlene. I'm sorry if I caught you at a bad time—"

"I always have time for you, honey. You know that."

Is that why I had to call six times? You'd better have time for me. I make you, your company a fortune. The day you stop having time for me? The day I make other people and their companies a fortune.

"I appreciate it, Marlene," he said blandly, absent any appreciation.

Jackson went on to explain the problems, the two problems. "Cline sent a computer technician out here, and V said— Wait, Cline said he was repeating what the computer guy said."

"I don't know what *you're* saying, Jackson."

"I'm saying that somebody may have hacked my computer!" he shouted.

"Okay! So what? It happens every day!"

"Anybody in your office have a hard on about me, dislike me, a grudge?"

"Of course not, Jackson. Oh, Christ, is that what this is about?" Then softly, as one might speak to a bridge jumper: "Honey, Jackson, my dear, nobody here hacked into your computer or wrote anything on it. We run a tight ship here, sweetie. We have to." *She's doing Sweet Marlene, the phony. She's actually irritated. I know the Sweet Marlene act. How dare this bitch sound irritated?*

"Okay, fine."

"And as far as not being able to write anything for five days, I mean, five days . . . think about it. It's not that big a deal! The words will come. They always do!" Marlene began racing about her Upper East Side space looking for the right earrings, jewelry. She did not want to be late to her charity event.

Why are these people all taking this so lightly? Katherine, Cline, Marlene, V? And what will it take to jolt these people out of their frivolity and jolt them into my nightmare?

"Or maybe the words won't come, Marlene. Ever think about that? Maybe I'm just . . . done. Maybe I want to be done."

Marlene was silent for a beat.

Yes, those are jolting words.

"You're not done, Jackson. You don't want that, Jackson. The fifteenth novel! You can do that. Hey, maybe signing that contract will give you the inspiration to—"

Jackson hung up. Marlene sat on the edge of her bed. She began hunting for phone numbers. She *was* going to be late after all.

For the first time in more than a week, Jackson felt good. Other people were locked in his hell, his suffering. He took a pink pill, or was it a white pill? He took a nap, and after, when he entered his study, he did so knowing there would be new words on his computer. New words. He just simply knew it.

OH JACKSON, POOR JACKSON GREY! YOU THINK
PHONE CALLS AND TECH PEOPLE CAN FIX YOUR
PROBLEMS? YOU KNOW BETTER! YOU BELIEVE IDLE
THREATS, THE THREAT OF QUITTING WHAT YOU
STARTED NEARLY TWENTY YEARS AGO, CAN STOP
THIS NIGHTMARE? YOUR HEAD IS SEVERED
AND YOU'RE TRYING TO SEW IT BACK ON WITH
THREAD! NO, THE WORDS WILL NOT COME,
JACKSON. THEY'LL NEVER COME. NOVEL
FIFTEEN? A FANTASY. YOU NEED MORE THREAD
TO SEW YOUR HEAD ON. YOU'RE NOT IN A BIND,
JACKSON. YOU ARE A BIND.

Jackson read these words blandly, as blandly as they were written. And after the car rolled up, gathered Jackson, and dropped him off at the Regal, which led to Andrew, which led to the Club, which led him to powders, the pills he could not identify, women whose names he did not know, things he did not remember, Jackson Grey got lost, lost himself for seventy-two hours.

What he did remember, and remember vividly, is that at someone's urging (*Was it Andrew's? The Woman's? CEO of Tech Company?*) he did call Cline, he called Marlene, he told them he was done. Finished. He wanted his life back.

When Jackson returned Monday night (he stayed an extra day) absent of any memory of the past three days, lacking the desire to retrieve such memories, he entered his living room and found it occupied. Completely occupied. Sitting in or around his expensive view were Marlene, Cline, Katherine, V, and a woman, late thirties, whom he vaguely recognized as Lyla, Marlene's assistant, the associate editor.

"Oh, look, what do we have here?" Jackson smirked.

"It's not a fucking intervention," Cline said. "Don't worry."

"We need to have a chat," Marlene added.

"We had a chat, Marlene, remember? I need a break. A long break. A forever break."

Marlene looked at Cline, then Jackson.

"Jackson . . . ," she implored.

"Somebody's fucking with my computer, and frankly I don't care who it is anymore. I see it as a sign. A sign I need to get out, Marlene."

"And I need Novel Fifteen. We have a contract, Jackson."

"A contract! A contract?" Jackson looked at Cline. Cline said nothing.

"Fine! We have a contract! I didn't sign it! Tell her about unsigned contracts, Cline! Worthless. They're worthless! Cline?"

"Jackson," Cline said softly. "You really want to do this again? Just sign the contract, take some time off . . ."

Jackson glared at Cline. "You son of a bitch. Speak the fuck up! The contract!"

Katherine began softly. "Jackson. Calm down." However, Jackson could not release his glare, his visual stranglehold on Cline.

He approached Cline. "You, working your 'terms,' such bullshit! I read that contract. Yeah, I read it this time. Now I'm getting paid a third of what I got paid to write the last two books combined! What a fucking insult!"

"Well," Marlene began. "Times are tough—"

"Oh, please, Marlene! For Christ's sake! I'm not an idiot!" Then glaring back at Cline.

Cline glared back. "What do you want, Jackson? What do you expect? You're getting paid what you're worth!"

"Are you fucking kidding? My books hit the *New York Times* best-seller list at—"

"*Your* books?" Marlene snapped. She looked at Cline. "You're right. It's happening big-time. He's losing it."

V cleared her throat. "What the hell is going on here? I don't get it!"

"Of course you don't, V," Katherine said, dripping with vitriol. "You don't get paid to . . . get it."

"Listen, you bitch—" V started.

"I get paid to get it," Katherine said, plainly.

"What? You mean like a whore?" V looked pleadingly at Jackson. That say-it-isn't-so look that Jackson knew all too well.

"V! Don't! Just . . . don't . . ."

"Yeah," Katherine smirked. "Like a whore."

V stared at Jackson, pained. Jackson was suddenly somber. He remembered Novel Four. The pressure, the strain, the confusion. He'd needed release. He remembered gently pushing V to the bed. He remembered V struggling at first and then giving herself to him. He remembered it happened again, after Celina left. He remembered his desperate need for comfort. He remembered his admonition that such acts could never be discussed, and they never were. It was never discussed, it was never repeated. He paid V more than other men like Jackson paid the women who ran their industries.

Marlene looked at V. "He's a wonderful public speaker!" she said, as if that alone would bring order to chaos.

"Oh, god, yes! Fucking great! I've heard him. That's why he gets the big bucks to speak!" Cline chimed in.

"He's a writer!" V said.

Marlene stood up. "Oh, for Christ's sake! I flew out here for this shit again?"

Jackson crossed the living room toward the deck. "That's right," he said softly to himself. "I am a writer."

Marlene turned toward V. "He *was* a writer, honey!"

"And it was a hell of a book! That first book. My god," Cline said.

"It was. That's when we got him," Marlene said. "My company, Cline representing him—"

"The second book was pretty good too," Cline added.

"It was okay. Just okay. It needed fixing," Marlene answered.

"It was a hell of a fix!" Cline said, smiling.

"Can we stop this?" Jackson yelled. "I just wanted to write one book!" Then, staring at Marlene, "Then I'm stuck with a sequel you made me write!"

"Nobody made you, Jackson. And to be honest—"

Jackson interrupted. "One book! I fired everybody after that book and got all of you. And you got your sequel!"

Marlene looked at Cline and finished his thought. "We saved you!" Marlene's temper was getting the best of her. "That 'sequel,' or the thirty-something pages of it you delivered, was shit! It didn't need fixing! It didn't need rewriting! It was terrible! Just embarrassing! We didn't fix it. We wrote it!"

"And it sold like wildfire, and you got all this, Jackson! Including her—" Cline pointed to Katherine. "And all the 'hers' before her."

"It's Katherine," she said to Cline. Then, looking around, "I know," she said, staring at V. "I know I'm the whore in this picture—but it's Katherine. My name."

"Whatever. Everybody knew what he or she was doing," Cline added. "Everybody still knows what he or she is doing."

It was unclear, at least to V, if Jackson knew what he was doing.

V looked pale. "You've written fourteen books, right, Jackson? Right?"

"I don't know what I've written, V."

Cline chuckled. Marlene piped in. "Oh, Jesus, the pity party again? Really?"

Jackson sat down, head in hands.

"That first book," Marlene said. "It was just too good. Then the film."

"I wouldn't have been doing my job, I mean doing it the way it should be done, if we let it stop there," Cline added. "And, Jackson, nobody made you sign that next contract. You wanted all of this. You wanted everything. And this is how we got it for you."

"What's he talking about, Jackson?" V asked.

Jackson faced Marlene. "I told you when I met you that I needed to get a horror novel out of my head. And then write, I don't know, a book of poetry, a travel narrative, a biography."

"And I told you it doesn't work that way. Not with me, your editor, my company, your publisher, Cline, your attorney. We told you that your desires would keep you in some shithole studio apartment wasting away, unpublished, working a day job. But if you wanted us, this team, you had to play by our rules."

"You promised me a way out of this one day!" Jackson blurted.

"Well, Jackson, I guess that day hasn't come yet," Marlene said. That day would never come. They all knew it. Except Jackson. Jackson knew only numbers, the numbers that spelled success, thus Marlene naturally adjusted her position toward that, toward the numbers. "And to be honest, I don't think you can afford that day!"

"So I'm being punished for writing one great book? For being a one-hit wonder? That it, Marlene?"

"No, you're being rewarded for it, you idiot!" Marlene said.

"Look, pal," Cline said. "Do you know how many people would kill to be in your shoes? Why screw up a good thing?"

Jackson scoffed. "A good thing for who? I guess all of you."

"Jackson," Marlene began. "Just . . . sit around for another six, eight months, let's get this book out. You have a contract you need to sign, and then we can all talk about what you want to write." Marlene nodded. Cline smiled. That idea seemed to make sense to everyone. Except Jackson. And V. The place where V grew up? Well, writers were treated with dignity. Their craft a high art. She did not understand any of this. It was incomprehensible.

V picked up a book from the coffee table. She read aloud. "A Jackson Grey Novel." It happened to be Novel Five. The novel, the time period wherein Jackson became aware of his self-hate. So aware he split himself in two. And he believed in both parts. He believed that both parts of himself could function side by side. Until Novel Fifteen. Until he was unable to believe anymore.

V looked at Jackson. "You don't write these, do you, Jackson?"

The room remained silent for a moment.

"I do. In a way. I don't know," said Jackson. "In a way, I do. Right, Cline?"

"Sure, buddy. Yeah, in a way, you do."

"Oh, fuck, Cline! Don't tell him that. There are legal implications!" Marlene said, angrily.

Cline clenched his jaw. "Marlene, I'm a fucking lawyer. I know there are legal implications. But I do not have a signed executed copy of the contract for the new book. You get that, right?"

"Fine." Marlene sighed.

V kept staring at Jackson. "If you don't write these books, who does?"

"I do" came Lyla's shy voice.

Perspective. Context. One ought to know the Setting, the Routine, the Process involved in creating a Jackson Grey Novel. For at this stage in his career, a Jackson Grey Novel was an industry, an industry flush with cash, with people, an industry with many moving parts. A precise industry.

The <u>Setting</u>: Somewhere unbearably expensive, preferably by the sea. Somewhere hidden, where people did not ask a lot of questions. A place where privacy was kept.

The <u>Routine</u>: Slip out of bed, without waking the woman, the beautiful woman, whom Cline contracted privately for Jackson. New novel, new woman. Slip out of bed at seven a.m., the woman asleep, coffee, cigarettes, quick browse of *The New York Times*, delivered daily to his gate and placed dutifully on his mahogany coffee table by V, his loyal housekeeper, to whom it was made clear that visas, green cards, sisters, citizenship, all would be paid for or all would be taken away depending on how V treated Jackson's secrets. The secrets of his personal predilections. V waiting patiently to pour the coffee into Jackson's cup, Jackson adding a splash of whiskey, the cigarettes, the paper, the nod of appreciation to V . . . and Jackson would begin not by slipping out of his own head and climbing comfortably into the new novel. No, Jackson had slipped out of his own head years ago. And stayed out of his head. He'd ceased slipping into novels after the mediocrity of his attempt at Novel Two. After his booze-laden coffee, Jackson would muster the courage to take a half hour and acquaint himself with his speaking schedule. He would then muster the courage to close his study door and watch television, read cheap gossip off the Internet, and send grotesque, hateful, often shocking notes to Marlene, who long ago had stopped reading them. Lyla read some of them, and Jackson simply assumed that Lyla assembled his profanities into a Jackson Grey Novel. That usually took about six months. Marlene preferred to stretch it to eight months. Eight months made sense. Then Jackson would go on the circuit and promote that novel. When, sixteen years ago, he stopped reading the novels that bore his name and spoke in such vagaries that the last bit of connective tissue between the novel and the words he used to promote the novel dissipated, Marlene and Cline forbade him from doing interviews. They created a new Jackson Grey brand: the mysterious Jackson Grey. The author who refused all interviews about present work, or works in progress. Promotion was done in house. Expensive, well-rehearsed speeches given to audiences who opened their wallets were permitted. And that brand worked. Everyone got paid, everyone was happy.

The calculus was fairly simple. Jackson Grey would pretend to be Jackson Grey and in exchange he got the estate, the women, the house-keeper, the fame, the fortune, the Regal, the Club, the power, the powder, the pills, the booze, all of which kept him pretending he was Jackson Grey. The author of the Jackson Grey Novels. This was the deal that Jackson had made all those years ago. A deal he made when Marlene explained that nobody bought books anymore, nobody read them—specifically, nobody took a chance on spending his money to read mediocrity. He made that deal after both Marlene and Cline explained that Jackson's gift, Novel One, was indeed an anomaly. Novel Two was garbage. A solution to this problem resided in a decision: fame or obscurity. Jackson chose fame. Jackson chose power. Jackson chose to sign private contracts allowing others to write his novels. And in exchange, Jackson made manifest his fame and power. He did so by diverting his attention with expensive ocean views, with housekeepers who cooked his meals and ran his life, with private clubs, with concubines. Oh, there were promises, all those years ago, about letting him write what he wanted to write one day. However, by now, Jackson knew those promises were lies; they had been tossed off to him, just as he tossed off the nuggets to salivating audiences paying to hear him speak. Lies.

"So?" V asked. "When you get up in the morning and walk into your study for eight hours, what *do* you write?" It was a great question. It was the only question.

Jackson got up and calmly exited the living room and entered his study. He stared at his computer.

IT'S OVER, JACKSON GREY. FINISH IT.

The <u>Process</u>: Jackson's simple task. Gather up all the ideas in his head—horrific, thrilling, grotesque ideas—and put them in an e-mail, send them to Lyla. There was a time when he believed that at least sending his own thoughts gave him some sense of ownership, some bit of dominion over the next novel. His novel. The next big, bestselling Jackson Grey Novel. But that time had come and gone. Around the time of Novel Ten, these "notes" Jackson sent morphed into booze-laden, drug-addled e-mails to Lyla. They were simply pieces of violent pornography. Even Lyla, half voyeur, witness, participant in this insanity, could barely stomach the e-mails. They were too disturbing. Marlene worried they would inhibit Lyla's creativity.

Jackson's other simple task, more an imperative, a dominating impulse: gather up every ounce of self-hate, every bit of disgust, every projection of other people's thoughts, the people intimate with his process, their thoughts of derision toward him, their mockery of him, and write himself notes, self-loathing notes, hateful words and phrases he used to attack his cowardice, his sellout, sentences that extrapolated in the most base sense his self-loathing. Write them in large blinking multicolored fonts and remind himself of who he was, and who he wasn't. Torment himself day after day, year after year. Performing such a task was the only way Jackson could navigate the day with anything resembling sanity. *Lie to others? Sure. Lie to myself? Absolutely not.*

Jackson returned from his study and went back into the living room. He stared into the faces of those, all of those who held him hostage to his fame. With good intent, of course, these hostage-takers. *Good intent. At least that's what they tell me, tell themselves, these liars. There is no good intent in holding a man's dreams hostage. I can read people.*

"Here's the contract," he said. "For the new book."

Cline and Marlene looked at each other. "Okay," said Cline. "Cooler heads have prevailed. Great."

Yes, they had. And that is why the act of walking out onto the deck, up and over the railing, and jumping into his expensive views, landing forty feet below on the craggy rocks like a broken jigsaw puzzle, made perfect sense to Jackson. If one is not let free, one must escape or die trying.

Yes, Jackson Grey could read people. Unfortunately, he could not read himself.

There was nothing to read.

And if there was, Jackson Grey didn't write it.

After the police identified Jackson's body and took statements— "Clearly a sad, drug-addled man, in constant battle with depression"— after Cline paid the right people to remove the phrase "drug-addled" from any police or coroner's report, any obituary, after he and Marlene back-dated the contract, after Katherine and V were well taken care of financially, there remained a question. Marlene and Cline had briefly discussed the question privately. Lyla posed the question to Marlene but once, for she knew that asking the question again would cost her not only the promotion she had received, but her job.

"Did he really think he wrote all those books?" she asked Marlene. It was a question not to be asked. It was a question Marlene didn't answer. "Don't bring it up again, Lyla. Ever."

The truth is no one knew the truth. Except Jackson, and he was long dead. One supposes that sometimes Jackson believed he did write all those books and sometimes he knew he didn't. What he knew, what he understood, when he understood it, when he stopped understanding it? Simply unanswerable. Only one thing could be ascertained that ugly night with certainty: Jackson hated himself.

One afternoon, a few weeks after Jackson's private memorial, Cline called Marlene.

"Marlene, I had a thought," Cline said.

"Yeah?"

"When my guys did the cleanup at his house, I had them find all of those notes he wrote. I got his hard drive as well. I stashed it all in my safe."

"Oh, Christ!" Marlene said, smiling. "I know where this is going . . . and I like it!"

Cline laughed. "I knew you would. And why the hell not?"

"The Unpublished Jackson Grey Collection," she said. "You brilliant, sick son of a bitch, I fucking love it! Send the notes and the hard drive to Lyla."

"Will do. I'll be out your way next week. We can sit down and discuss strategy. You know, stretching it out over the next five, six years. The 'posthumously discovered stories'—however the fuck you want to phrase it. That's your game."

"Don't worry. I've got this."

"And Lyla?" Cline asked. "She'd have no problem with doing something like this?"

"Oh, are you kidding me? We gave that bitch a huge package. Lyla does what Lyla is told to do. She'll love this."

Cline was uncharacteristically silent.

"What?" Marlene asked.

"I've got to tell you, Mar. I looked at a couple of the pages of scrawl he wrote, I mean, he must have written it sometime in the last twelve months. It's really pure disease. Christ, he was a sick ticket."

"I know," Marlene said. "So fucked up. Years ago, I might have said I missed him."

"We gave him a good life—all right, enough. I'll have somebody scan the docs and send them," Cline said.

"Someone you trust."

"Of course," Cline said. They both hung up.

Goddamn, Marlene said to herself. *That man has skills.*

A moment later Marlene felt a wistful sense wash over her. Wistful, yet a sense leaning toward something bigger, bigger than her, bigger than Cline. She hesitated, then called Cline back.

"Yeah? What's up?"

"I was thinking about that night."

"What about it? I'm running late for a lunch."

"You know, Cline, his body that night, on the rocks, the bones, the ocean, the blood? The way it all looked?"

"What about it?"

"It kind of looked like a Picasso," she said.

"Okay."

"What he did to himself, what he did to his body, I mean, that was the first piece of art *he'd* truly created in, what? Twenty years? Know what I mean?"

Cline did know what she meant but didn't comment. They just hung up. That is how they communicated. That is how they did business. Nothing extraneous, no effluvia.

They were people of power.

The Darkish Man

NISSAR MODI

The girl wasn't especially attractive. But the darkish man didn't mind;
in fact, he preferred it. Her type was a more efficient target, lacking the
natural suspicion with which good-looking women seem to be born,
or perhaps acquire as they season. Besides, he didn't hold himself to
any particular standard of beauty. It was always something small that
got his pulse racing, a modest charm or quirk he liked to think he was
the only one to notice—a scar under the bottom lip, almost entirely
concealed under foundation, or a premature gray hair peeking out of
an otherwise luxuriant brown bob.

This one had eyes that were two different colors; in the muted half-
light of the bar, he couldn't see their exact hue but made out that one
was light and the other dark. He knew there was a technical name for
the condition, that it wasn't entirely uncommon, but he'd never seen
it before—no, he *had*, in a dog owned by a childhood neighbor—but
not in a woman, and this excited him. Less stimulating was her voice,
flat and droning, prone to proclaiming banalities as though they were
revelations. It bothered him that a girl with such unique eyes could
be so tedious. Later, maybe, she would submit to him and be silent, so
he could focus on nothing else. He liked eyes because, no matter how
skilled the actor to which they belonged, they always revealed the truth.
He had seen it in every girl who had lain beneath him, culminating in
the final moment of release, that ultimate truth laid bare in all its gasping beauty. No eyes could deny that.

They'd been talking at the edge of the bar, mostly unnoticed. This wasn't the sort of establishment with table service. It didn't even have a name, or perhaps just the simplest of ones: out front, the neon sign would intermittently flash a single word—DRINK. It was tucked away at the edge of Johnson City in an industrial area on the cusp of gentrification. He hadn't been looking for a new girl—the scent of last night's was still on him—but he'd stopped to relieve himself and, before he could even find the bathroom, noticed her. That was about thirty minutes ago. He'd downed three skunky-tasting Heinekens since then, and more than ever his bladder was screaming for relief. He leaned forward and smiled, cutting her off.

"Have you ever been choked while having sex?"

He said it just loud enough for her to hear. She stopped talking midsentence, her eyes widening, a small breath escaping from her lips. He knew he was being reckless, but he was bored and desired an outcome, any outcome. She glanced away, not wanting to seem shocked, but her expression betrayed her: it was as if she were ten years old again, being shown pornographic pictures in the schoolyard for the very first time.

"Is that your thing?" she eventually asked.

"Maybe."

She went silent, and he realized with growing excitement that she was actually considering the proposition. It was his turn to hide his shock. Talking to her had just been a whim, yet here it might actually be paying off. He waited, not moving or breathing, just studying the internal dialogue that was playing out all too visibly on her face, like an especially amateurish student film. Finally, she edged back on her barstool.

"I have to go."

For a moment, he could feel a palpable tweak of disappointment, as if a blade had nicked his insides. It swelled into a faintly throbbing anger. He smiled at her.

"If I was white you'd have done it, right?"

She flinched. He knew it would sting, having intuited that she was one of those girls embarrassed by their boorish origins, by parents who wore their prejudice as casually as a garish Kentucky Derby hat, and who would spend the rest of their lives fighting to prove how much better they were than that. Yes, he knew her type all too well, having often cajoled similar victims into leaving bars, coffee shops, and night-clubs with him, even if he knew that sometimes, deep down, they were not actually attracted to him. He didn't care. People always did things for the wrong reasons, and he saw no reason to stop them, especially when it was to his benefit.

She got to her feet and fished around in her bag for some cash. He waved her away, and she left without another word. He remained on his stool for a moment like a deposed king, posture erect, mouth slightly open, a faint aura of shame settling upon him. He scanned the room. Aside from the bartender, who was immersed in a text conversation on his phone, there was only one other customer, a bony senior with scraggly facial hair, skin drawn taut across his cheekbones as he buried his nose in his beer glass, feet tapping in frantic polyrhythm. Neither man seemed to have shown any interest in the fruitless flirtation that had just unfolded nearby.

At least now he could finally piss. He walked over to the bathroom. An off white piece of paper was taped to the door, one word scrawled in black marker: BROKEN. He hesitated, tempted to use it anyway, but worried it might draw further attention if he was caught. As it was, the bartender noticed him lingering and pointed toward the exit.

"There's one out back. Should work if you're lucky."

The skinny old man seemed to find that funny. His feet tapped even faster. The darkish man paid his bill and left five dollars on the bar, one for each beer he and the girl had consumed. It was a fair tip, neither too low nor high, and one the bartender would, he hoped, not recall.

Outside it had become night, and the temperature had fallen with the sun. He saw the bathroom, but it wasn't much more than a filthy, dilapidated outhouse. His stomach lurched at the thought of the thousands who had already marked their territory after one too many watery beers and festering hot dogs, piss sprayed carelessly across the sticky floor, dried tarry feces clinging stubbornly to the inside of the bowl. He couldn't bring himself to use it. Beyond lay a rectangular void that might have been a field. It was an option. The earth beneath his feet was cold. He pressed the toe of his boot into it and was surprised to find it yield under pressure. In the end, though, he decided to wait a little longer. He'd find a place once he was farther outside the city.

He moved toward his car. At the same time, the girl with the different-colored eyes emerged from the outhouse, wiping her hands on her jeans. Her truck was at the opposite end of the lot, and they couldn't avoid passing each other. For a moment, he thought she was going to say something more to him, but she just slinked past, those wondrous eyes cast downward, lips pursed tightly together. She was still unsettled by their encounter and would not easily forget it, which was enough to make him regret his impulsiveness. Yet he couldn't resist imagining again how wonderful it would have been to have seen those eyes gaze back at him, wide and unblinking, in a more private setting, and, in that thought, he absolved himself of all blame. He watched her get into the truck and had to stifle an impulse to follow. For a long time, he had not thought it possible to tame such instincts, but now he had come to understand that almost everything in life came down to a simple choice: to act, or not.

A few minutes later, the lights of the town were receding in his rear-view mirror. He chose the local road that wound south into what the signs called the Blue Ridge Mountains—really they were just a chain of hills, but he supposed the name's grandeur gave the region more dignity than it deserved, and perhaps impressed the tourists. There were no tourists now. It was damp and cold, with the sort of chill that gets into the bones of even the heartiest people. He turned up the heating, but it didn't help.

His eyes steadily scanned both sides of the road ahead, searching for a good place to do his business. He grinned. His father would say exactly those words whenever his bladder or bowels needed vacating. Well, Dad, I am indeed looking for a place to *do my business*. He was suddenly overcome by a fit of laughter. It was the first time he could remember feeling any fondness whatsoever toward the little tyrant.

No one quite knew where the darkish man came from; his family's bloodline was cryptic, and no one within it cared enough to trace it further than whichever wizened relatives were still alive at holidays and reunions. Swarthier than most of his kin, he came to imagine himself as a delicate quilt stitched together by artisans from the world's most exotic corners—the cappuccino tint of his skin, born of the Caribbean; Sino-Altaic eyes with almond shape and caramel shade; the wiry musculature of the desert Semite. His striking looks had been remarked on since he was a child yet even then were elusive enough to belong to an ancient era, or one many centuries into the future. His father, a more prosaic-looking being altogether, should have been proud of his role in the creation of such rare splendor. Yet the son could recall only a lingering resentment; as he played in the narrow back garden, cooed over by various sisters and nieces, he would glimpse his father at the upstairs window, staring down with expressionless eyes, and, even as a child, detected in them a murderous intent. Sometimes he wondered if the man was not his father at all. That he remained in the role of patriarch until his untimely death confirmed nothing. A more normal man might have absconded with some justification, but it would have been just like his father to stick around simply to torment this striking bastard child.

Suddenly, the darkish man noticed a speck of light appear in the hills above, like the flare of a match bursting through the dark. At first, he thought there must be a person up there, lost, stumbling through the night with just a flashlight for guidance. Then he realized it was not one light but two, and they were moving too fast to be on foot. It was a car, carefully navigating the road's dangerous switchbacks as it rolled downhill, its headlamps disappearing behind the trees, reemerging, then vanishing again, like a child excitedly flicking a light switch on and off.

It wasn't until the car was three hundred feet away that he noted the familiarity of its shape—the wide body, snub nose, and matchstick-like siren perched above the windscreen—and was stung by a sharp, sudden feeling of dread. He forced himself to remain calm. He'd passed policemen plenty of times on his recent travels and had never been pulled over. Then again, he'd not yet been this far out into the hinterlands, slinking discreetly through suspicious hamlets where a face as dark as his was either a hoodlum or the help, never to be trusted. He again cursed his impulsiveness, more emphatically this time; he should have stuck to his original plan of charting a course through more familiar territory. He tried to calculate what three beers in half an hour might do to his blood alcohol level, but as he didn't know the state of Tennessee's legal limits—if that's where he even still was—the exercise was futile. He hoped his luck would hold.

He made sure not to turn his head as the patrol car passed by. But out of the corner of his eye, he saw that there was just a single officer inside, a broad-shouldered white man in his thirties. The cop slowed down, scrutinizing him. He didn't look back. And, just like that, they were moving away from each other. He raised his eyes to the rearview mirror and watched the cop's taillights recede from view. He exhaled, and it dawned on him that he'd been holding his breath the whole time.

The road banked to the right and went into a steep incline, the darkness intensified by shrouds of towering hickories. He rounded the corner without his usual precision, and the vehicle drifted across the central divider and into the opposing lane before he righted it. He had to admit: he was rattled. It was the officer's stare that infuriated him the most, his disdain and suspicion tangible enough to cut through the thick glass and five feet of frigid air between them. He wondered what he was doing all the way out here, miles from anywhere, and with abrupt, scornful clarity, the answer presented itself, as if anyone who has ever been the Other need even ask.

He was here for *you*.

But no, that was paranoid, which was the one thing he couldn't afford to be right now. He tried to relax by again focusing on the road ahead, resuming his search for an appropriate turnoff. But he knew he wouldn't be stopping anytime soon, not until he'd put some real distance between himself and the cop. There was a dull ache now stabbing his groin, but his business would just have to wait a little longer.

Less than a minute later, headlights appeared again, this time in the rearview mirror. He sighed: the night was becoming tiresome. He wouldn't worry just yet—it might just be another civilian, someone who had a good reason to traverse a desolate mountain road late at night, even if he couldn't think of what that reason might be—but he stuck closely to the speed limit, eyes moving vigilantly between the road ahead and the mirror above. The car behind him was moving quickly. It wouldn't be long before it caught up.

It was the cop. He had made a U-turn somewhere farther down the hill and was now tearing back in pursuit. So either the girl with the different-colored eyes had phoned in their encounter, or this was just a bored good ol' boy, empowered by his starched polyester uniform, looking to unsettle the only nonwhite face he'd seen all day. He glanced at the glove compartment. The gun lay inside, loaded. It was licensed, and he'd never had cause to use it, but that wouldn't make a difference out here: its mere existence would be enough to damn him.

The cop caught up and eased off the gas. For a few minutes, they ascended the hill in leisurely procession, like neighboring families on a weekend fishing trip. Then, with grim inevitability, just as they crested the first in a chain of rolling peaks, the siren came to life. The darkish man pulled over and killed his engine; his adversary followed suit. A malignant silence descended upon them. The cop stayed in his vehicle, face shielded by the darkness, body just a silhouette of thick, square shoulders and neck, as featureless as a comic book sketch, while the flashing lights threw hellish red and blue streaks across the promontory.

Finally, the door opened. The cop stepped out onto the road and approached at a deliberate pace, footsteps crunching against the gravel. The darkish man followed what he knew to be protocol: rolling down his window, turning on the interior light, and placing his hands upon the steering wheel, fingers clearly visible. He was glad to note that his breath was even, his pulse steady: he was prepared for anything. A flashlight clicked on, and a harsh ray of light struck the side of his face. The cop appeared at the window, a solid shape emerging Cimmerian-like from the gloom; with his hairless pate, smooth, round chin, and face bathed from below in spectral orange light, he resembled an especially muscular potato. The darkish man knew it would be difficult to overpower him physically. Then again, he did have the element of surprise in his favor, and a gun.

"License and registration."

The voice was deep and even, with nary a hint of the anticipated country twang; it might have been a promising sign were it not for the grim determination in the cop's eyes, suggesting that anyone with the temerity to be stopped by him should be resigned to the murkiest of fates. The darkish man took his hands off the wheel, slowly, gingerly, as if facing a wild animal, and unlatched the glove compartment. As he fished around for the registration card, his fingers brushed the concealed barrel of the gun. For a split second he let them rest there, the very touch of the cold metal giving him reassurance. Then he handed over the documents for the cop to scrutinize.

"Is this your current address?"

"Yes, sir."

"Arizona? Long way from home."

His intonation was flat and neutral. The words, though, could mean everything. Or nothing.

"Never seen the south before. Figured it was time."

The cop held the license up to the flashlight's glare and squinted closely. The foreign-sounding surname had likely caught his attention.

"Do you know why I pulled you over?"

"No, sir."

"One of your taillights is out."

Outwardly, the darkish man appeared not to react. Inside, though, he was fuming at himself. Of all the stupid things to have overlooked! But then it struck him that the cop might be lying. After all, he had given the car a thorough inspection before he left Nashville, just a few days earlier.

"I didn't know that, sir."

"Dangerous to be driving out here in these mountains with only one taillight."

"Yes, sir. I'll see that it's fixed first thing in the morning."

For a moment, the cop was silent. The darkish man felt a flicker of hope. Maybe the man had had his fun and now had a fetching cousin to screw somewhere in the valley.

"You were driving pretty fast too. And erratically."

Another lie. This time he didn't reply. He'd learned at a young age that silence often became your sole ally against a man with a badge.

"Have you been drinking?"

He met the cop's eyes with an even gaze.

"No, sir."

"Would you be willing to submit to a Breathalyzer test?"

The gaze held.

"Yes, sir."

The cop stared at him, considering.

"Do you have a good reason that made you need to hurry?"

He had to stay cool. There had been close calls before, and he always found a way out. He grasped for inspiration.

"If you must know, I desperately needed to urinate. Still do."

"Why didn't you just go on the side of the road?"

He never blushed but now forced himself to.

"Okay . . . I'll—it's . . ."

Nor had he ever stumbled over his words. He glanced down, as if greatly embarrassed.

"Truth is, it's not just a pee I need. It's . . . the other thing. I didn't stop on the side of the road because I didn't want anyone driving by and catching me with my pants down. I was looking for a place to turn off into the woods. Probably why I was driving—as you said— *erratically*."

The cop stared at him, considering. Seconds passed, each drawn out longer than the last. By the time half a minute had gone by, it felt like time itself had been suspended, and the void of silent darkness around him was all he would ever know. Yet when the officer finally spoke again, the edginess had been drained out of his voice, like blood from a mortician's needle.

"Wait here."

The officer trudged back to the patrol car. The darkish man knew he would now run the vehicle's plates and registration information, as well as his own license; he also knew that nothing amiss would be discovered. A sudden rush of exhilaration flooded through his body, as palpable as the shocks of electricity that had been administered to him as a child. He wanted to dash outside into the night, sink to his knees naked in the scrub, and howl to the pine beetles and rattlesnakes that he was immortal, untouchable. Instead, he sat quietly in the car and waited.

Eventually, the cop returned and handed him back his license and registration card.

"I'm issuing you a verbal warning. You can go now. But drive carefully. We've had tourists go off the road before. And get that taillight fixed."

"I will. Thanks, Officer."

The cop said nothing in return but neither did he make a move to leave. His stare persisted, lips coiling in the infancy of an amused grin. The darkish man was abruptly struck by a terrible notion—that he had grossly misjudged the situation, that the cop was not going to let him go merrily on his way but instead had called for backup, and that any moment now an army of those doom-laden flashing lights would materialize out of the darkness on all sides, while helicopters would descend from the sky, roaring, like a flock of prehistoric avian beasts—and he would be cornered, with nowhere left to go except over the edge, into oblivion.

"About two miles on up . . ."

The cop was pointing ahead, deeper into the mountains.

"There's a dirt road on the left. You could take a shit that lasts a year and no one would ever see you."

His grin grew into a crooked, affable smile.

"Just watch out for spiders. They're the kind that jump."

The darkish man laughed. Whether or not the cop sensed the relief in it, he neither knew nor cared. The officer gave him a final nod, turned, and walked back to the patrol car. It was over.

He turned the key in the ignition with a hand as steady as ever and carefully pulled his vehicle back onto the road. He watched in the rearview mirror as the patrol car made a U-turn, dust rising from its tires, and drove away down the hill. Within seconds it had disappeared, this time, he believed, for good. He smiled to himself. What a friendly, helpful man the cop had shown himself to be. He almost felt guilty for having pegged him as a redneck.

He followed the winding road for two miles as directed, engaging the high beams on particularly precarious curves. His bladder now burned with diabolical intensity, but he felt serene. He should not have been able to believe his luck, but in fact he did; his narrow escape was a sign of approval, if not encouragement, from the gods themselves. He turned on the radio. A pop song he recognized was playing, and although its saccharine quality would usually have made him sick, he whistled along with the melody.

He spotted the dirt road just before the turnoff. It was barely wider than a walking trail and mostly concealed by dense, low-hanging trees, but he swung his wheel across just in time and squeezed onto it. He drove slowly. The road was littered with all manner of forest detritus— pinecones, eroded rocks, thin gullies forged in the ground by decades of spring rains—and the car trembled upon it, struts squealing in indignant protest. It was an old jalopy and wouldn't run much longer without some serious work, but it had served its purpose and, besides, he intended to abandon it at the next opportune moment.

Ten minutes later, the road petered out. He stopped the car and killed the lights. At long last, it was time to do his business. He got out and waited for his eyes to adjust to the darkness, but all he saw was black: the ends of the earth could not have been more perfectly isolated. He turned on his mobile phone's flashlight, revealing the silhouette of the treetops against the starless night and his breath emitting in frosty bursts. He chose a spot between two oaks where the earth still felt loose, unzipped, and took the longest, most sublime piss of his life, watching with fascination as the steam rose off his waste. It reminded him to hurry—the temperature was approaching freezing.

The shovel was nestled between the front and back seats. As he took it out, he again blessed his good fortune—how simple it would have been for the cop to catch a glimpse of this vital tool, both weapon and means of disposal, had the aim of his torch been less focused on the darkish man himself. As he balanced it in his hands, he was surprised anew by its heft, for he knew that when the time came he always employed it gracefully and precisely, as if it weighed nothing at all. He carried it over to the area upon which he had urinated and began to dig. It was hard work, but by now he was something of an expert.

Once the hole was deep enough, he went back to the car, put on his gloves, and opened the trunk. The interior light came alive, revealing the woman's crumpled, lifeless body, splotches of blackish blood and blond hair congealed together against the plastic sheet in which he had wrapped her. He regarded his work with quiet satisfaction, similar to the way he imagined a carpenter must feel after building an especially solid table, but under his skin he could already sense a restlessness setting in. The memory of her felt hazy, as one might vaguely recall a play or film seen many years ago, even though their encounter had occurred just the night before. The only thing he could picture clearly was the source of his initial fascination, a brown blemish on the jowl of her left cheek that could be called—depending on the generosity of the caller—either a beauty spot or a mole, and from which short, coarse hairs sprouted untamed. Aside from that, he remembered nothing, not even her name, and that upset him, as he felt it somehow diminished both of them.

Before he carried her to the hole, he peeled back the top of the plastic and shone the beam of light into her eyes. They were still wide open, a brilliant, almost translucent blue, and it wasn't so much terror that he saw in them as belated, resigned realization, befitting the shy and slightly overweight woman who arrived with the eager expectation of orgasm, and left with death. Well, he thought, the two were not really that far apart.

He buried her and refilled the hole, then tossed some cones, branches, and soil over it in a manner that seemed haphazard but ultimately looked rather natural. Not that he was overly concerned—the place was so remote that he doubted even the most intrepid of hunters would come across it. He drove out of the forest at a crawl, and it gave him time to think. He decided that he wouldn't abandon the car after all. If the cop had called in its details and it was somehow found at a later date, it would be all too easily traced back to him. While there would be no hard evidence—he had already cleaned and disinfected the trunk painstakingly, and would do so again—he did not want to give them any reason to ask questions. That damn taillight would need to be checked out, though.

He decided to head for a large city in a nearby state—Charlotte, perhaps, or Atlanta—a place where he would not stand out so much; although he would never admit that his risk taking was becoming an addiction, he felt he could be more prudent. Besides, the city was fertile ground. Legions of anonymous girls came and went every day. They arrived on buses, trains, and occasionally planes, from small towns whose names you'd have no reason to know. Girls with new identities and fresh haircuts, running away from dubious pasts and broken relationships. They were wary and uncertain and made few new friends; they were lonely and unaccounted for; they tried their luck for a few months or years before moving back home, or overdosing, or simply vanishing; they were ideal prey.

He emerged from the dirt track onto the main road, crested the last remaining hills, and began his descent toward the plain that stretched unending to the horizon. Above him, without any fuss, the clouds swallowed up the moon like vaporous predators hunting in packs, letting the night be as it always should be—at its darkest, and most glorious.

1987

ETHAN HAWKE

I remember hitching my first ride to NYC. It was fall, but it was still hot. Jake and I were sitting in the backseat of a Toyota Corolla in shorts, his sweaty leg pressed against mine. I couldn't think about anything anybody was saying. I could only feel his hairy leg. At one point, bouncing up and down the turnpike, I got a hard-on. Did that mean I was gay?

1987, one week into theater school, and already I was deep in this bout of phobia: "What if I'm a homo?" I'd go out and get drunk, make out with a couple of girls, try getting laid with some poor cleavage-revealing innocent. When I was actually drunk and actually having real sexual intercourse with them, I wasn't afraid I was gay, but the rest of the day the drumbeat of FEAR would start again. Clearly there was a big scary demon motherfucker hiding in the dark recesses of my subconscious. Something with the same rhythm and pathology I imagine inspired Evel Knievel to jump two dozen school buses with his motorcycle. Something I was not well prepared for at the tender age of seventeen.

One afternoon I tried facing my fear and in a feverish sweat bought a copy of *Honcho* magazine. My heart beat like a jackhammer but my pecker shriveled in my hand. At four in the morning I went alone to a parking lot, got on my seventeen-year-old knees, looked to heaven, and prayed for the first time in my life: "Dear God, please, if I'm gay, kill me. I can't do it. Let me die in a car accident. Let me be murdered. But please don't let me be gay . . ."

In an effort to distance myself from the show-tune-singing theater clan one night, I charged into a fraternity rush at SAE. These guys were a bunch of John Cougar Mellencamp–shouting jocks who gave out free beer. No truth or dare, no sincere artsy emotional oversharing. I started doing keg hits with some guy named Jake, and we talked about BU and how much it sucked. He mentioned that the Red Hot Chili Peppers were playing in New York City. Having just read *On the Road*, I suggested we blow off school and hitchhike to Madison Square Garden. We did.

Once in New York City we scored tickets and LSD. Jake had done it before. We dropped a tab and headed into the Garden, but after about two hours we felt nothing. Sure that we had bought fake drugs, we dropped two more tabs in case there was even a little hallucinogen on one of the others.

We were jettisoned to the far side of the moon.

I remember walking out of the concert and into the autumn midnight air of Thirty-Third Street. I saw the citizens of planet Earth walking with halos over their heads. I saw the Walk/Don't Walk signs strolling among the pedestrians. Everything was luminescent, radiant. Everyone in front of me, around me, behind me—I saw them as winged, glowing angels. I saw their skeletons inside their clothes, I saw the bones in their faces and knew we were all dying, knew that the construct of our personalities was no more significant than our outfits. I saw that being gay or straight was no more than a preference for chewing gum, or a preference for Life Savers—we were all of us involved in some massive movement in time and space. Oh my god I saw the whole world moving through the millennia and I was a lightning bug, beautiful and utterly insignificant. If I was gay, it would be a stamp of courage, a mark of bravery like a medal worn on the chest. Love and its expression needed no boundaries. I laughed. I told Jake, "Dude, you have no idea how much better I feel." He had no idea what I was talking about. He was on a different moon, but I was sure I was having an insight that would leave me changed. My shoulders aligned themselves differently. Everything—neon light, shadows, pavement, metal cars, humans, dogs—seemed to me one miracle after another. I thanked God for not answering my prayer.

At that precise moment I was punched about four times hard in the face. I made brief eye contact with the man hitting me and it was clear that his fire-white eyes were burning with something lit by crack cocaine—they were exploding out of his head. He punched me into the traffic of Broadway, into the swirling, honking cars. I didn't care. It was okay. I felt sorry for him. He couldn't hurt me. I just absorbed the beauty of the lights around me.

Then I noticed Jake. He had been beaten too and had been shoved into the street beside me. We held hands between lanes of traffic and walked to a little island where Forty-Second Street intersects with Broadway and Seventh Avenue. It was then that I saw what looked like a cat scratch across his face. Small bits of blood were seeping through his skin, forming a line that went from the hairline on the back of his head, through his ear, under his cheekbone, and up into the place where his eye met his nose.

"I think they cut you, dude," I said. He touched his face and felt the blood. Then he wiped it off, and the entire left half of his face fell free and hung down. I could see teeth where his cheek should have been. I quickly pressed my bandanna to his face to hold his cheek back in place. Suddenly, the street was filled with wolves, hyenas, and drooling dogs. Jake lit a cigarette and the smoke dribbled through the bandanna out of his cheek, ear, and eye. The smoke collected and formed the face of a hissing cat. I asked to see his cut one more time. He took down the bandanna and one small tarantula crawled out of his face.

"Am I gonna die?"

"No," I said. "It's not that bad."

"Really?"

"I promise."

"Is it going to scar?"

"Oh, yeah, definitely." I almost laughed.

He started to cry. "Fuck, what should we do?" he asked, searching my face for help. I looked through the crowd of famished dogs, saw a dirty, skinny German shepherd dressed as a police officer and approached him. The giant dog sniffed Jake and his cut. Then he gasped and got on his radio: "I got a male Caucasian, approximately eighteen years old, with his face slashed, on Forty-Fourth and Broadway."

Instantly, Jake began to convulse, sobbing while holding his face together. "Oh, fuck, I'm gonna die. I'm gonna die."

The pack of canines circling us began to grow in number.

I held Jake in my arms and looked toward the heavens. This was my fault. We raced through the city in a police car. Everything was tilted and spinning red and blue. The lights themselves seemed dizzy.

"Are you guys on drugs?" the cop asked, drooling in the front seat. I had never seen a dog drive a car before.

"No," I answered as Jake wept openly.

"Did you get a look at the guys who did this?"

"I think it might have been God."

"Did you even help your friend?" The dog stared at me from the rearview mirror.

"No."

"Why not? Some guys are beating up your buddy and you just let them?"

I sat in the back of the police car and watched the blue and red lights keep spinning into a web of arteries and veins. The siren screamed like a witch.

Inside Bellevue we sat and waited, Jake still holding my bandanna to his face. This would be one of those cool stories we could tell later, I said. We would be badasses. Girls would think we were tough. Our lives had really begun, like we wanted.

I went to the bathroom and flushed the rest of the drugs down the toilet. Salamanders chased the drugs down the drain. Briefly, the cops interrogated me. Two German shepherds. The skinny one and a new fat one who pissed on the floor by my leg. His urine spread across the tile and up the walls and dripped back down onto my head. I told them I was not high. At one point the doctors finally came out and studied Jake's face.

"Smile."

"I can't. It hurts too much," he mumbled.

"We have to see if there is any nerve damage; smile."

Jake smiled a sad pathetic crooked bleeding grin.

The doctor turned to me, intense. "Is that what his smile looks like?"

"I don't know."

"What do you mean you don't know?"

"We just met like two days ago."

The doctors left and we continued to wait. After about an hour and a half, two other young men who looked a lot like Jake and me— one guy with a bandage to his bleeding face, the other holding him— walked in and sat behind us.

"Is that what I look like?" the guy asked his friend, pointing right in Jake's face. "Am I cut as bad as him?" He almost screamed.

"Stop, stop, stop . . . ," his friend answered as he ushered his bleeding pal to their green plastic waiting room seats.

"Oh, fuck," the guy wailed. "Oh, fuck." I watched a snake slither across the floor of the hospital, climb up the guy's chair, and follow his tears into his mouth.

Jake and I sat silently, listening to them talk.

"I love you and I'm here for you," the one kept whispering, while the other mostly cried. They held each other close, the one gently caressing the other up and down the leg.

By the time Jake went into surgery, my hallucinations had subsided. It was almost dawn and there were three other young men who had been strolling Times Square seated around us with their faces slashed open. Apparently some crack-addled fool had taken a razor blade to more than seven faces in less than an hour. A typical case of gay bashing in New York City in 1987.

Walking out of Bellevue the next afternoon, Jake looked like a villain from a comic book, his face laced up like a football. He did not go back to school. He flew home to Wisconsin. I took the train back to Boston, and until now, I've never told anyone this story. Partly because homophobia is embarrassing. Partly because I still worry that razor was meant for me.

Geist

LES BOHEM

I've been staying at a hotel in Munich where many people come to commit suicide. It's a tall postwar building that rises above a flat stretch of concrete patio. A person can come into the hotel lobby and ride the elevator to the nineteenth floor, where there is a medical clinic and easy access to a balcony that has a very low railing. From there it's a quick jump back the twenty floors to the concrete patio. Quick but, I imagine, with enough time for you to think a bit on your way down. Every time I go to my room on the twenty-first floor, the elevator stops at the nineteenth floor and the doors open, but no one gets on or off.

The hotel is just across the river from the center of Munich. It's a fairly expensive hotel, and I'm staying there only because an acquaintance of mine, not even an acquaintance really, just a man I met on the train coming here, has gone out of town for a month. We got to talking on the train and he offered me the use of his place. About half of the rooms in the hotel are rented by the month as apartments and his is one of these. It's been more than two weeks since I got here and I don't have much money left. I have no idea what will happen when he comes back.

It's interesting, isn't it? The immediate bonds that you form when traveling. We found ourselves in the dining car, this man and I. He was about my age, maybe a little older, and was what I've heard French people here call *sympathique*. We fell to talking. His name was Friedrich. I told him about being asked to leave the band. Said that I'd gotten a Eurail pass, thinking that the train was as good a place to stay as anywhere else.

"If you don't mind Munich," he'd said, "I have a different idea of where you belong."

There's nothing much to do here. If the weather's good, I sit in the English Garden and watch people drink beer. If the weather is bad, I sit in the room and watch television that I don't understand, or I listen to American Armed Forces Radio. There's a DVR hooked up, but the movies that are saved are all in German. It has some sort of pay-per-view system as well, but I don't know the password. It's late April now, and most of the days are still wet and gray and I seem to spend a lot of my time in the room.

A lot of fashion models take apartments here when they come to work in Munich. Sometimes I sit in the lobby and I watch them come in and out. It's like standing in the street and looking through the display window of an expensive shop. I don't enjoy being out of money. At thirty-six, I'm far too old to find anything romantic in poverty.

There are clubs in town and maybe I could go to one, and maybe meet a girl. But the drinks are so expensive in the clubs here and usually when I go to bars, I sit staring at my drink with my thoughts ringing in my head, trying to find the words to talk to a girl across the bar who I think, in the dim lights, might have looked at me. Then, while I'm working up my nerve, she gets a text from her boyfriend, or some other guy starts talking to her, or she leaves with the bartender, who it turns out she was waiting for.

Most of the suicides happen in April and May when rapid changes in barometric pressure can cause a hot wind to blow through the city and the weather turns a snowy winter day into a clear, warm spring. They call it a Foehn wind and it is said to cause a sort of insanity. Policemen don't give tickets for traffic violations on Foehn days. There are terrible fights in the beer gardens and the Hofbräuhaus. Many people get very depressed. It's then that they come to the nineteenth floor of my hotel and jump.

In the Englischer Garten the other day, at the beer garden by the Chinesischer Turm, I met a girl. She had jumped from the hotel last spring. By some mistake she was still alive. She was a very pretty girl, as pretty as the models at the hotel, but had a scar running down the length of her face as if she had been broken and then glued back together. I imagine that is about what must have happened. She walked slowly and she had a slight limp.

It was a Foehn day. The warm wind had blown away a morning rain and it was hot now and clear. Papers and odd bits of cloth littered the streets. I walked from the hotel to the Chinesischer Turm and sat down in the sun. I'd found some change in the pocket of a coat hanging in my host's closet. I had gone through all of his clothes a few days earlier and this change was all I'd found. It was enough to buy a plate of sliced white radishes.

I was eating the radishes slowly when I saw the girl. She was standing by the children's merry-go-round watching the turning horses. There were no riders. I thought that it made a sad picture, the girl watching the empty ride turn, and I watched. After a while, she left the merry-go-round and walked toward the food stalls and my table in the sun. As she came toward me, I could see her face and the scar that cut across it.

The scar interested me. It seemed to mean something. I waited until she'd gotten her beer and was sitting down at a table, next to a large, florid-faced man wearing a traditional Bavarian suit. I couldn't offer to buy her anything and so it was easier to wait. I sat there and the thoughts started ringing in my head and I started to think that I wouldn't find the nerve to talk to her. The man in the Bavarian suit glanced at her, taking in the scar. He muttered something in a throaty, guttural German and took his beer to the far end of the table. The girl gave him a tired glance as he did this. Maybe it was that tired glance, or maybe the scar, the imperfection made it easier. I picked up my radishes and walked toward her. I was very nervous.

"Excuse me," I said. "Do you speak English?"

"Yes," she said. "A little."

"May I sit down?"

She nodded and I sat. I offered my radishes and she took some. From his new spot at the end of the table, the man in the Bavarian suit watched us with contempt. She stared at him for a moment, and the look in her eyes was of the wind: hot, harsh, and somehow out of control. The man looked away, and when the girl turned back to me, her Foehn look was gone.

"I just haven't talked much lately," I said. "And I'd like someone to talk to." It was true. I'd been by myself for so long now that when I spoke, my voice came out echoing and strange, as if a chip inside me were playing someone else's voice.

"You're an American?"

"Yes."

"It is hard for Americans here. The people are not friendly, I think."

"There are unfriendly people everywhere."

"No, but here, they are worse. If they are young, they are arrogant and wish they were in Paris. If they are old, they only think about the Russians or the war. The others are mostly stupid."

I smiled and took a radish. "My name is Paul," I said. She offered me a sip of her beer.

"You are here on a holiday, Paul, or why?"

"More like 'why.'"

"You will tell me?"

"I was on tour with a band."

"And you aren't on this tour now?"

"I was asked to leave."

"What does that mean, 'asked to leave'?"

"In my case, that I was drunk and making too many mistakes."

She looked closely at me, studied me. She saw something. Came to a conclusion. Then she said, "I think then maybe you wanted to be asked to leave."

"You may be right."

"You were not happy to be playing music? That is something that gives most people joy."

It was a lot to explain. How I'd had dreams, written songs, recorded demos, come to Europe, to England, to try to get a deal with a company there. How it hadn't gone well and I'd wound up playing in someone else's band. I had another sip of her beer and we were quiet while she waited for me to go on.

"I guess," I said finally, "that working someone else's dreams got to be more than I could stand."

That was true, but it wasn't all of it. It didn't show how it was to be with people for whom life came easily. People for whom nothing was hard and everything was fun. The ones who never had a problem talking to the girl at the end of the bar.

She watched me, and while she certainly couldn't have known all of this, she nodded, and I thought that somehow she did know.

"I will tell you about my scar," she said. "It is hard for you not to look at it."

I made a small, embarrassed laugh.

"I don't mind," she said. She looked back at the merry-go-round and then at me. "I killed myself," she said.

"But you're still here."

"Well, yes, but what I mean is that I jumped."

"Oh."

"From that hotel there." She pointed to my hotel. "It is where everyone is jumping."

"I'm staying there," I said.

She nodded. She didn't seem surprised. "Of course," she said.

"Why did you jump?" I asked her.

"It was last year in this weather. You know, the Foehn wind is blowing, eating the winter in a day. Sometimes when the wind blows, the world is opening up and you see the bottom of all things. Maybe this is like when you drink too much and make mistakes." She nodded again, and again it felt to me as if she understood the things about me that I hadn't yet shown her.

"I think that it probably is," I said, "but I've never been brave enough to jump."

"I was brave to jump."

"From the nineteenth floor?" I asked, stupidly. "Where everybody jumps?"

"You walk through the clinic that is there and out onto the balcony."

"And you didn't die."

"What?"

"That's too high up to jump."

She looked at me blankly for a moment. "I was broken," she said after a moment. "They came with an ambulance. I could hear them, but I did not care what they said. I was broken, and now I am back together. Only I am not brave to do it again."

I couldn't find anything to say, so I nodded.

"It is a sad story for your first time talking," she said.

"It's a good story and I'm glad you told me."

She ran her hand up to where the scar split her face and touched it. I ate another radish and had another sip of beer. She watched me. She smiled a little.

Next to us there was a scream and the sound of a table being turned over. We looked to see what had happened.

The large man in the Bavarian suit was on the ground. Another man was standing over him, shouting in German and waving his beer stein. A crowd had gathered. Several people tried to calm the standing man and to help the other back to his feet. The standing man's face was blood red from screaming.

The others straightened the table and chairs and said a few things and the man in the Bavarian suit got to his feet and the other man reluctantly shook his hand. They both sat back down.

"It is the wind," the girl said. "That's what it does."

The angry man's face was still red. He held tightly to his stein. The steins are made of very thick glass here and they hold a liter of beer. His was nearly full. He picked it up now and swung it with all his force into the other man's face. There was an awful spitting sound and for a moment, nothing moved. Then blood began to leak from the man's cheek and forehead. The angry man took his stein and broke it against the table. The others at the table stepped back as he dove onto the man, holding the broken stein by its handle and smashing it again and again into the other man's face, the jagged glass weapon coming away from the flesh sticky each time the man brought it back to smash it down again.

A ring of people had formed around the fighters. A policeman in the green leather suit of the motorcycle police made his way through the crowd. He drew his gun and aimed it at the man who held the broken stein. He yelled something. The man stopped, the stein held in the air, ready for another thrust. Blood dripped from it onto the dirt. There was silence. The crowd waited to see if he would drop the stein.

The wounded man lay on the ground. He groaned. The other man looked at him and spat. The wounded man's eyes were closed, but now he opened them and saw the girl. Pain and anger were replaced for a moment by some sort of recognition and by fear. He said something quietly that sounded like a prayer.

The man holding the stein followed his gaze and saw the girl. He took in her scar. Then he turned to the policeman, shrugged, and dropped the stein.

The policeman said something and the crowd began to move off. He took the man who had held the stein, the man who had been angry, by the arm and he led him away. Others in the crowd straightened up the chairs and table and waited by the hurt man. Someone ran off, I suppose to call an ambulance.

The policeman led the man past the spot where I stood with the girl. When they were almost to us, the man looked up at the girl and then at me. His face was still red from his recent fury, but in place of his scowl, there was a sad, resigned look. I felt a hand come over mine and I looked over at the girl. Her hand rested on mine now, and she was smiling at the man as the policeman led him away.

When they were gone, the girl turned to look up at me. She handed me her beer. "Finish this for me," she said. "Then, if you like, we will go."

I drank the rest of the beer quickly and we started off. As we started away from the Chinesischer Turm, we heard the ambulance siren.

We walked through the park toward the lake. We didn't say much. I was tired from the beer and the excitement. We walked around the lake and saw a few people out in little boats. The park was surprisingly empty. The wind had left litter everywhere.

"I have lived here all my life," she said, "and still I am surprised when the people disappear. I do not know where they go."

Another wind had started to blow now and the sky was filling with clouds. The first rain started just as we turned back into the park from the lake. Then it was raining hard.

I said, "We should get inside."

"I do not mind to go to the hotel," she said, and then she smiled and it was the same smile she had given the man as the policeman had led him away.

We ran back to the hotel but it was far away and we were very wet when we got there. As we came across the patio, she stopped and pointed to a spot on the concrete.

"It is here that I am landing," she said.

We went inside and took the elevator up to the room. For the first time since I had stayed there, it didn't stop on the nineteenth floor.

I unlocked the door and held it for her. She went into the room and I followed her. She shivered from the wetness. I got a towel from the bathroom and I dried her hair. When I kissed her, her mouth was just like a part of the rain.

"We should get undressed," I said. "We're very wet."

When she took her clothes off, I could see that her body was a jigsaw puzzle of scars. She didn't try at all to hide them, and, if she had wanted to, she would not have been able to do it.

We got underneath the warm comforter on the bed. There was a chill to her that I couldn't seem to rub away. Then we were making love and I forgot about the chill.

The storm outside grew loud and angry. The wind shook against the windows and then whistled off across the river.

We were careful with each other and it seemed as if we could go on moving together for a long time without anything else happening. Her eyes were open. Her caresses were simple. She hardly moved. I wanted to do something else with her but I didn't know what that was.

Then I kissed her and I moved my lips up to kiss her scar. She sighed.

I pulled myself out of her and began to follow her scars down her body with my tongue, licking every inch of the hard, shiny flesh. She began to move now, to writhe. Soon she was shaking violently. The blood came into her body and the scars stood out white against it. I thought that she would explode along those lines and collapse there on the bed as if she had dropped again to the cement below.

I kept licking. I turned her over, following the line of one scar around from behind her navel onto her back. She gave out a shrill whistling sound, a sound like a slow leak of air from an inflatable toy. She shook and trembled and seemed to rise completely off the bed, and then she collapsed, panting, onto the mattress.

We lay for a few moments. As her breath slowed, I could hear that she was crying. The storm still screamed outside. Then we slept.

We rode the elevator to the lobby together and it didn't stop on the nineteenth floor on the way down either. The storm had stopped now and she went out of the hotel and she was gone. When I looked out the hotel windows at the road, I couldn't see her among the crowd of people walking to the bus stop. I sat in the lobby for a while. I might have been hoping that she'd come back. Two models came in. They were speaking English. I looked up at them from where I was sitting. Their skin was very pale and very smooth, like cream poured gently into a saucer for a favorite cat to drink.

The next day was cold and gray and I ate some cereal that my host had in a box in his cupboard and I didn't leave the room. I could not get the girl out of my head. I looked out the window, down to the spot where she had smashed into the pavement. I watched German TV. I turned the pages of books written in a language I couldn't read.

For the first time, I found myself wondering about Friedrich. I'd gone through his clothes, but only looking for money. Now I looked around the apartment for him, for who he was, what he did, why he was the sort of person who would hand a total stranger the key to his home. There really was nothing that told me much. No family pictures, no photo of a girlfriend. There were several prints on the walls, but they were generic, no doubt put up by the staff from a selection of unobtrusive landscapes that I would find in any room in the hotel. His apartment told me nothing.

The day that followed was a little warmer and I went back to the park. I sat there all day, watching, hoping that the girl would come back. I didn't know a thing about her. Not where she lived or her phone number. I didn't even know her name. I got it into my head that I had to find her. I had no idea how I would do that. Around me, having their beers, were a few men in Bavarian shorts. But it was not a Foehn day. No one was hit with a beer stein.

I went back to the hotel. I had never talked to anyone who worked there. They knew that I was Friedrich's guest. They nodded to me when I crossed the lobby. That was all. Now I went up to the desk. A middle-aged man was on duty.

"Do you speak English?" I asked.

"Of course."

"I'm wondering if you can help me. I'm looking for a girl."

He gave me a hard look. "We don't arrange that sort of thing. There are newspapers you can find in town. There are advertisements there."

"You misunderstand. I am trying to find someone. Someone I met the other day."

"And how would I be able to help you with that?"

"She is someone who jumped from this hotel, sometime last year."

His manner grew even more officious. "We do not discuss any incidents that may or may not have happened here," he said. "I'm sure you can understand."

"This is important to me," I said. "And it's not as if everyone doesn't know that you're the suicide hotel."

He stiffened even more at that. "Was there anything else?" he said, daring me to ask another question.

I walked across the lobby, nearly tripping into one of the fashion models. She was coming across the lobby from the elevators carrying her portfolio. I left the hotel with no idea what I would do next, how I would find the girl I was thinking of now as the Foehn Girl.

"Hey," someone said behind me. I turned. It was the model I'd nearly bumped into in the lobby.

"That guy is a total dick," she said. "You wanted to know about the jumpers?"

"I'm looking for someone. A girl I met in the park. She jumped off sometime last year."

She looked surprised. "I've lived here since last year," she said. "Longer than that, really."

"You must remember then. Someone jumping who lived, that must have been even bigger news than just someone jumping."

"It would have been," she said, "if it had happened. But everybody knows that no one has ever jumped from the hotel and lived. It's a nineteen-floor jump, you know. Twenty, the way they count floors here."

I told her that I'd met this girl, spent time with her, and seen her scars. "I can show you the spot where she landed," I said.

"If that had happened, it would have been in the papers. You could look."

"I can't read German," I said.

"I can," she answered.

We went into the café there at the hotel. Her name was Lee. She was from Florida. She had her laptop with her. We went online and searched the database of the local papers, and the nationals. Each suicide was reported, but there were no stories anywhere about an unsuccessful attempt. We looked at *The Local*, the English-language paper, too. There was nothing there either.

"Did she say when this happened?" Lee asked. "I mean, she could have gotten the scars some other way. This could all be just a story she tells. More dramatic, spectacular than the truth."

"She said it was this time last year. On one of those wind days."

"A Foehn day. That could explain it. You know that wind makes people crazy."

"I saw some people acting crazy, but I don't think she was one of them."

"*Foehn Geist*," she said then, her voice playful. "A Foehn ghost. That's what we're dealing with here."

"A *Foehn Geist*?"

"Ask the gypsies in park, if you ever see any gypsies in the park. My boyfriend for the first six months I was here, Paco—he was half Romany. Gypsy. He told me all about the *Foehn Geister*. They say the wind's so strong it can blow spirits from their graves. They say they ride the wind, looking for some poor soul who's hanging by a thread. Someone they can take back with them when they go."

"Are you making this up?" I asked.

"Are you hanging by a thread?" She took a moment. "I'm not making it up, but Paco might have been." She smiled. She made her living with that smile. It was easy to see why.

She found the date when a Foehn wind had come up exactly a year ago. She cross-referenced that and found something. That smile went away and her face hardened. "Bullshit," she said angrily. I looked at her, confused. "You know what?" she said. "You're a fucking weirdo and I'm so tired of fucking weirdos. Did you think this was going to get you somewhere with me? 'Hook up with me, I talked to dead people.'"

"I don't know what you're talking about."

One year ago. A Foehn wind. There was a jumper. "Her name was Karla Engel. She was twenty-eight when she jumped."

"You found her," I said.

"You are so full of shit," Lee said.

"Just tell me," I said. "I swear I wasn't trying anything like that."

"Sure," she said. "Well, as I'm sure you already know, weirdo, Karla Engel didn't make it."

"Foehn Geist." Lee'd said that her boyfriend, Paco, had made that up. A ghost who came out on a Foehn day to suck someone back to the grave with her. Someone who was hanging by a thread. I wasn't ready to believe, based on the secondhand retelling of a gypsy legend, that I had made love to some sort of ghost. If Karla Engel had died a year ago after throwing herself from the hotel, then who had I met? Who had I been with? I wanted, I needed to know. And more than that, I wanted to see her—to see Karla, the Foehn Girl, whoever she was— again.

I saw Lee only once after that. It was in the lobby, and when she saw me she turned the other way and started talking to a group of other models and their dates, guys who laughed easily and never thought about the lives they could have been living.

Mostly, I haunted the park—I sat there every day. I ate radishes. I waited. Nothing happened. There were always the men in the Bavarian shorts. There were families. Old people. Gay couples. But there was never a beautiful girl with a long, sad scar across her face. It was the men in the shorts who gave me the idea. The man who had been hit in the face with the beer stein. He had looked at the girl with an expression of both recognition and terror. I wanted to ask him about that expression. Did he know her? Was she somehow Karla Engel? Is that what had frightened him? He had been hurt badly and they had taken him to a hospital. He might still be there, or at least someone at the hospital might be able to tell me where he was.

By now I had ordered so many radishes from the older woman who sold them at the little stand here in the park that she knew me. I went up to her window and asked if she knew any English.

"Some," she said. "I had a boyfriend who was in your army and stationed here."

"What I want to know," I said. "The man who was hurt the other day. When the man hit him in the face with the stein."

"Oh, yes," she said. "On the Foehn day?"

"Yes," I said. "I was wondering if you knew what hospital he might have been taken to. I wanted to see how he was doing."

She gave me the name of the hospital and told me where it was. I made my way there.

Everyone on the staff spoke English and it was easy enough for me to find the man. It just took a little bit of time and a little bit of explaining. I had been a witness to what happened. It had upset me greatly. I was concerned for him and wanted to see how he was doing.

"He hasn't had any visitors," a nurse who was on his floor told me. "It would be good for him to see someone. His face was badly cut and I don't think he has any family."

She led me down the hallway toward his room. For reasons I couldn't quite understand I was frightened, as if I were on my way down a hallway in a movie where there was a monster waiting behind the door. The sterile 1960s hallway with its dying fluorescent lights did nothing to help me with that feeling. The hallway was long. The fluorescents gave it no more than a dull flickering light that bounced off the municipal green walls in a way that seemed almost deliberately grim. Our footsteps echoed in a silence broken only by someone listening to an angry speech on the small speaker of an old phone.

As we neared the door to the man's room, the nurse said, "Wait here a moment," and went in ahead of me.

I heard her say something in German. As I approached, I could see her in the doorway and behind her I could see a man in a hospital bed with bandages wrapped around half of his face in a diagonal, so that only his nose and one of his eyes showed through. The bandage cut across his cheek, leaving his mouth exposed.

She smiled at me as I came in. "I told him that he had a visitor. Don't stay long, but it will be good for him to see somebody."

"Can you translate for me?" I asked. She nodded and I began to speak and she translated into German.

"Do you remember me?" I asked. "I was in the park the other day.

I was wondering how you were doing." His eyes were glassy and wet. "Also, I wanted to ask you, you seemed to know the girl I was with."

The nurse shot me an annoyed look. I was there with an ulterior motive and she did not approve. All the same, she translated.

I saw his eyes widen with recognition and then with fear. And then he raised an arm and pointed at me and tried to scream, but all he was able to manage was a low moaning sound that seemed to come from somewhere dark and far away.

The nurse looked back at him and then, hurriedly, at me. "I think it would be better if you go now," she said. "If I had known that you'd come here to upset him with your questions, I never would have brought you in. What you did was not a kindness."

For a few days after that, I didn't go back to the park. I stayed in my room. I ate cereal and watched TV that I didn't understand. Once, I heard laughter from the hallway and I wondered if it was Lee and her friends. I thought about the Foehn Girl, Karla, and about our time together. I closed my eyes and saw the way her scar divided her face. I saw myself licking that scar.

It took me three days before I turned on Friedrich's computer. It was late at night when I googled *"Foehn Geister."* It wasn't exactly on Wikipedia, but it was there. On a site about German folktales and legends: *Foehn Geister*. The wind blew them from their graves. They came to take someone back with them. Someone who was ready to go. Often, they had a confederate, someone on our side. Someone who went looking for the lost, the ones who had given up. In a footnote I read that sociologists thought that the *Geister* and their variants found among the Etruscans and other pre-Roman peoples in the parts of what is now Italy where the siroccos blow and among the native American tribes in the parts of Southern California known for the Santa Ana winds had been a primitive explanation for the otherwise inexplicable event of suicide, a thing so far out of the norm of ancient peoples that it required supernatural causality.

I'm not sure what made me do what I did next. I think it was sim-

ply that I knew and it was time to show myself that I knew. I opened
Friedrich's search history. He hadn't bothered to clear it. It was, of
course, in German, but I could recognize dates. As I scrolled back in
time, I found what I was looking for. The band that I had been on tour
with wasn't particularly famous, but they had a deal, were popular in
Europe, could fill a midsized club. Friedrich had been on their website
two days before we'd met on the train. He'd read their announcement
about me leaving the band. He'd read it and he'd gone looking for me.
Now I went deeper. I went deeper and I knew what I would find. There
hadn't been any photographs out in the apartment when I looked. But
no one keeps photos out anymore, do they? They keep images on the
hard drive. I looked and there, in his photos, I found them together.
Friedrich and Karla. They were in the park, in the English Garden.
Their arms were around each other. From all the debris around them
on the ground, I could tell that it had been a Foehn day.

The next morning, I woke up to a banging sound. I moved through
the apartment. The sound was coming from the window. An awning
had come loose and was beating against the window. What had torn it
loose was the wind. It was another Foehn day.

I dressed quickly and I went to the park. People were out, enjoying
the warmth, if not the wind. There was no bad behavior yet, but the
wind was growing stronger. Empty tables and chairs were blown over.
At one point, I moved to pick up a table close to me that had been
knocked down. I set it upright and turned to go back to my own table.
As I looked up, I saw that the other people who had been here in the
park were gone. There was no one else there. "I have lived here all my
life," she had said, "and still I am surprised when the people disappear.
I do not know where they go." I sat back down and waited in the now
empty park. The wind continued to blow. It was warmer now.

I don't know how long I had been sitting when she found me. She
sat down across the table.

"So," she said.

She looked around at the empty park. At the litter blowing and the
chairs and tables that had been turned over by the wind. There were
some people coming back now. They were far away across the park,
but I could see that they were wearing Bavarian shorts. "Do you want

to stay here until there is another fight, or can we go back to the hotel now?" The scar across her face seemed redder than I remembered it being, as if it were something new.

The wind was blowing hard as we walked back to the hotel. Newspapers blew up into our faces. Leaves and small branches. We went quickly inside. The lobby was empty. We didn't speak to each other. We just got into the elevator.

This time, when it reached the nineteenth floor, the elevator stopped. The doors opened. I could see the empty clinic facing me, and beyond it, the balcony with its low railing. The doors to the balcony were open and the wind had blown the clinic doors open wide as well. Curtains on either side of the balcony doors blew in the wind.

"Come," Karla Engel said. "It's a short walk and then you will be free."

Gentholme

SIMON KURT UNSWORTH

"Where should I be?"

The man was old, standing at the corner of the park with one hand resting on the brickwork of the low wall, running his fingers along the mortar in an action that was almost gentle, almost a caress. Channing, arms aching from the shopping he carried, stopped. The man looked at him, his face collecting shadows from the metalwork atop the wall, old railings recycled from some dismantled Victorian park and made new and good, and said again, "Where should I be?"

"I'm sorry?"

"Where am I? Where should I be?"

"Why, you're in the sparkling city of Gentholme!" said Channing, automatically falling into the singsong speech of the salespeople and parroting the advert that had been playing repeatedly in the sales office and behind all the presentations he and Miranda had attended. It had been the opposite of subliminal he had thought at the time, something that created memory and desire not by subtle, unseen pressures, but by battery and insistence. "The first city to be built this century, with homes for one hundred thousand people and road and rail commuter links to every major destination nearby, where safety and sustainability are the watchwords of the future!" Channing smiled to show the man that he was joking, but the man's expression did not change.

"Where should I be?"

Channing put his bags down, balancing them so that they didn't tip, making sure that the bottle of champagne he'd bought for him and Miranda to share that evening was safe, and went closer to the man. In the light from the streetlamps, new blue LED ones that faked a hard, brittle moonlight, the man looked weary, confused. He was wearing a long overcoat, thin and stained down its front, and his jowls were written with two or three days' growth of bristle. His shoulders were slumped within his coat, twin slopes down which Channing could imagine rainwater dripping despite the clear skies and good temperatures.

"Are you lost?" asked Channing.

"I don't know," said the man. He looked at the wall, his hand still running along its bricks. "I don't know where I should be."

"Where do you live? Can I call someone for you?"

"I was somewhere and now I'm here and I don't know where I am. Can they tell me where I should be?"

"Who?"

The man didn't answer. Instead, he raised his face to the approaching night, peering at the top of the newly black railings. He looked careworn, miserable, his hand now lifting from the brick and clasping one of the metal posts, knuckles white in the dusk. Channing looked around, wondering if the man had wandered off from family and gotten lost, but saw no one. Now the man had pushed an arm through the railings, had wrapped it around the bars as though to anchor himself, and tears were spilling down his face. Was the man from a nursing home?

Channing remembered what he had heard at one of the sales pitches. Hadn't someone asked about care for the elderly? Yes, yes, they had, and one of the young architects had answered, talking about hospitals and doctors' offices, but that wasn't it, was it? In the end, one of the older marketing men had stepped forward and spoken in smooth undulations about the second wave of sales, that the first was being aimed at young families but that there was space in the design plans already set aside for state-of-the-art long-term-care facilities.

So where had the old man, now with both arms wrapped through the metal and pressing himself up against it, come from? Channing took out his cell but saw that it had no signal; Gentholme's infrastructure was still a little patchy, despite the assurances that it would be fully functional by the time people started to move in. He walked back to his bags, stepping out into the road in the hope that he'd see people scouring the street for a lost relative, but nothing moved in Gentholme's distant spaces. He looked at his phone screen again but its signal bars were still empty. The man groaned, once, low and ragged.

"Do you want to come with me?" asked Channing, but the man ignored him. Channing reached out a hand, and now the man looked at him, flinching back, fear in his eyes.

"No," he said, a tiny froth of saliva forming at the corner of his mouth. "Where should I be?"

"I don't know," said Channing, dropping his hand. The man was obviously upset, frightened of either Channing or of the things he could see that Channing could not, of loneliness and of not finding his place. "I'll go and call someone to come and see if he can help you, okay?"

Still no signal on his phone, so Channing picked up his bags of shopping and stepped out into the road again. It wasn't late but no traffic moved on the roads and there were no public phone booths nearby; they were a lost thing now, he supposed, curios that may still exist in the streets of the older cities but not here. He glanced around but the houses here were dark, shells without life inside them yet, waiting to be filled with the playing children and smiling parents the new city's brochures had advertised. He walked several yards down the road, still looking around, and then glanced back at the park. The shadows had crept across the grass and were now wrapping themselves through the wrought-iron fenceposts and slipping down the wall to approach the sidewalk and the street beyond.

The man was gone.

Gentholme was a thing waiting to be born.

Sometimes, as Channing walked its deserted streets, he imagined that he and Miranda and the few others who had also moved in before the city was completed were the first particles of blood moving sluggishly along its concrete veins, the first movements within an embryo that would, they hoped, develop into the city of Gentholme. The more they used the shops, with their half-stocked aisles, and visited the doctor or dentist with their gleaming new equipment and bland waiting-room magazines, the more they forced its development, the nubs of its fingers and toes expanding, its limbs stretching out, its brain crenellating and creating new thoughts and memories and ideas, the closer the city would be to emerging into the world.

The disadvantage of being part of the gestation, of course, was that most of the city's limbs hadn't had time to form yet, and what there was didn't always function properly. When he got home after meeting the man, Channing hadn't known quite what to do. It didn't seem quite enough of an emergency to bother the police or health services with, although he was concerned about the man's well-being if he was wandering the streets through the night, and eventually he had tried the local government's after-hours number. His call had connected to an answering machine, so he had left a message explaining what had happened and his own contact details, but the next morning it didn't seem like enough. The image of the man's face, tears etching his cheeks and arms wrapped around the fence in a grip as tight as love itself, had invaded Channing's sleep and populated it with fractured, confusing scenes of people walking away from him and ignoring his outstretched hands as some great black sea rolled in to submerge him. *I should have done more,* he thought, as he dressed and returned to the park, walking around its perimeter. *But what?*

There was nothing outside the park except streets of empty houses, so Channing found a gate, pushed it open, and entered. Inside, he found that the park was surprisingly large, a ramble of greenery set out like the spaces Channing remembered from his childhood. It was landscaped so that its grassed lawns rose and fell in gentle slopes and its paths meandered, crossing and recrossing between copses of trees that were small and thin, their trunks still protected by plastic tubes, and sports courts enclosed by high nets and with no sign of wear on their surfaces. At the park's center, Channing found a large playground behind a waist-high metal fence, its swings and slides and jungle gyms oddly old-fashioned, and beyond this a bandstand. When he looked more closely, both the playground fence and the bandstand were adorned by small plaques that read "Equipment saved and refurbished by the Gentholme Community Trust."

He wandered around the space the entire morning, looking for the old man, but the only person he saw was a small boy standing on the far side of the playground. The child was dressed in gray shorts and a blue sweater that looked as though it had a school logo on its breast and was holding a blue balloon that floated at his shoulder at the end of a piece of twine, and he watched Channing with wary eyes.

That afternoon, Channing called the town hall again. This time, he managed to speak to a person who told him that town services were being handled by an outreach group from the neighboring town until Gentholme's infrastructure was completed, and that there was little she could do to help with the old man unless he actually presented himself to a hospital. She promised to pass on the details to the police, though, which made Channing feel a little better.

Miranda was working a long day the next day, so Channing took his lunch to the park rather than stay in the house. He ate sitting on one of the low hills, a thin scattering of trees to his back, looking down on the playground and bandstand. It was sunny, an Indian summer bathing Gentholme in tired but calm yellows and greens, the air smelling of grass and earth and dew, and Channing was happy. This move was right for him, for him and Miranda, a new start in a new town, a place they could leave their old lives behind and find something fresh. Miranda's work wasn't too far away, the new office being set up in the new city welcoming her, and Channing himself could run his business anywhere there was electricity and an Internet connection.

He chewed, enjoying the taste of his food in the fresh air, and watched as gradually people arrived in the park.

They came from all directions, some walking in across the lawns, some emerging from behind the hills, some threading their way among the new trees. They all came to the bandstand and gathered in a group in front of the structure, and although he couldn't see them clearly, Channing had the sense that they were older; it was something about the cut of their clothes, the speed of their movement, the rhythm of it. There were a surprisingly large number of them, perhaps thirty, more than he had seen together in Gentholme since that first publicity meeting. He'd seen no ads or flyers for a community concert, but that didn't mean anything. Miranda always said he walked around with his head in another world. He sat forward, expectant.

Nothing happened.

No musicians came to the bandstand; there was simply the crowd gathered, watching the empty stage. Channing looked for some kind of PA system, volume set low enough that the people by the bandstand could hear it but Channing, up on the hill, could not. He stood, brushing his clothes and sending crumbs tumbling to the ground, and started down the slope.

Closer, he saw he was right; the crowd consisted mostly of older people, although there were one or two people his own age scattered through the mass. Everyone was staring at the empty stage.

"What's happening?" he asked the nearest person, a woman in a faded floral dress and a long woolen coat, when he reached the lawn. "A concert?"

"I'm waiting," said the woman.

"Waiting? For it to begin?"

"I don't know," said the woman, still staring at the stage. "I'm waiting. I don't know what else to do."

"Does anyone else know what's happening?" asked Channing. It was warm, the sun prickling his scalp through his hair, making him logy and slow. "Surely someone must know."

"Who else is here?" said the woman.

"Well," said Channing, gesturing at the rest of the crowd. One of the other figures, a man, turned toward him and said, "Do you know why I'm here?"

"There's only me," said the woman, facing Channing. Her face was drawn and gray, the lines of her jowls heavy striations that pulled her mouth down into a shape like a smile turned in on itself.

"No," said Channing, and then the man called over to him.

"Who are you talking to? Can you please be quiet? I can't hear properly with you talking."

Channing didn't say anything. Others in the crowd had started to turn toward him, their faces catching shadows as they fell from the sun, the noise of their movement a whisper of cloth flapping and feet shuffling around. They were old, mostly, except for the ones he had spotted earlier—younger, like him, their hair less gray, their skin less lined.

"Who's there?" asked someone.

"Can you help me?" said another.

"What's happening?" asked a third, and Channing backed away. The crowd wasn't moving, not exactly, but they were leaning and twisting, as though trying to spot him through gloom rather than see him in sun. The woman nearest him said, as though no one else had spoken, "It's so confusing. I don't know where I am."

"I'm sorry," said Channing, backing farther away.

"Please," said the woman, holding a hand out, her sleeve flapping back from a wrist whose skin was wrinkled and marked with liver spots. She sounded desperate, on the verge of tears.

Behind the woman one of the younger men stepped forward, pushing past her without looking at her. "Can you tell me why things have changed? Why they aren't the way they used to be?"

Channing took another step back and then caught, on the edge of his hearing, a fragment of music coming from a place that seemed oddly distant. It was discordant, notes laid over notes, but the effect on the crowd was immediate. They turned, ignoring him, and faced back to the stage. There was still nothing to see on the wooden platform, but now one or two of the crowd started to smile, and after a moment one or two of them began to shuffle, shifting from side to side, feet and hands tapping inaudible beats against the air.

Channing turned and walked away, and the boy holding the blue balloon standing by the slide watched him go.

That night, Channing looked in the local newsletter (*The Gentholme Gazette,* a single-sheet photocopied list of events and developers' news distributed to every occupied house in the town) for information about what he might have seen in the park but found nothing. There was very little happening, if he was honest; the *Gazette* mostly consisted of lists of roads completed, roads half done, buildings growing from the earth week by week, of sales figures and reassurances that Gentholme's future was bright and secure. There was a website address at the bottom of the newsletter and, bored, Channing visited it, looking at the full list of buildings completed and sold. There were the promised doctors' offices and the hospital, pharmacists, several different denominations of church, schools, a library, ranks of shops, offices, town hall, and a dentist, most marked as "Development agreed; opening soon." He was looking for any kind of nursing home, or community facility, that might explain the presence of the old man at the park's wall or the group by the bandstand, people who seemed confused and lost, but there was nothing.

"Perhaps they were brought in on a day trip or something," said Miranda later, as they lay spooned in bed. "You know, like a day out for them? Besides, why does it matter? They weren't doing anyone any harm, were they?"

"No, it was just—" He paused, feeling for the right word. "It was just strange."

"People are strange," she said, and began to hum a song Channing couldn't immediately place. "It's the Doors," Miranda said after a moment, knowing without him telling that he'd be struggling to recognize the tune. "'People Are Strange,' and they are, aren't they? I mean, look at you and me. We up stakes and move to a brand-new town, before it's even built, I relocate my job to a new office, and why? Because we wanted a change, because we needed a fresh beginning, something new. Most people would just decorate their living room or book a vacation."

"You know why we moved here," he said, and then regretted it as Miranda stiffened against him. He waited, holding her, letting her work it through inside herself, Miranda's way, not interrupting her, not disturbing her.

"I do," she said, finally relaxing, softening back into him. He kissed the back of her neck, thinking, *People are strange.*

"I'm sorry, I know how much you wanted it. How much *we* wanted it," he said, the unspoken thing hovering around them.

"I know," she said, "and it's okay. Really. I know you're sorry, I know it's what was meant to be, I know why we came here, and I know we're happy. Mostly, though, I know you think too much about things that don't need that much thought. I know you, my love. Now let's go to sleep."

Channing, breathing in her smell, mumbled his agreement into her neck and drew an arm across her, trapping her warmth to him. In the bedroom darkness she was right, it didn't seem that important, and he let the thoughts of people with their hands stretched out to him tumble from his head and he slept and he did not dream.

Channing took to going to the park every day after that. He would eat his lunch sitting on the hill, using the quiet and the fresh air to give him space to think. He felt his mind unravel into the space about him, letting the looseness give him solutions to problems and ideas for developing his business. Sometimes the crowd returned to the bandstand, sometimes they stayed away, but he did not try to speak to them again. Usually, when they came, they stayed for an hour, but no concert ever took place and no one ever climbed onto the bandstand itself. Occasionally, he thought he heard snatches of the music again, as distant and discordant as that first time, but usually the crowd and the day around them were silent.

Each day, Channing began walking to and from the park via different routes, watching Gentholme uncurl and take its first breaths around him. One day he found a street of houses half done, façades of brickwork waiting for their smooth outer skins of plaster and paint. At the end of the street, an excavator sat motionless, front shovel and backhoe throwing shadows out, resting and weary. Another day he discovered a horseshoe street of newly minted shops, each blank and empty. Ducking under the fluttering yellow construction tape, he peered in through each glass shop front, seeing nothing but counters and bare floors. He found a set of plots, churned earth bisected this way and that with ropes anchored through metal poles, setting out the bones of the houses to come. At the development's far edge, two workmen in gleaming fluorescent coats were marking more shapes, driving a stake into the ground and threading a rope through its twisting upper loops before stretching it to the next point. Channing watched, fascinated, for several minutes as the layout took shape in front of him.

The following day, he saw the bicycle and its rider.

The man was standing in the doorway of a building that backed onto the far side of the park, a sign proudly proclaiming that it would become the Gentholme Civic Center. Its brickwork was old, reclaimed from some Victorian town hall, the space before it made from equally old flagstones, creating a public space lined with benches and gaps into which trees would presumably be planted. There were no doors in the entrance yet; it was simply a stone mouth set into the wall in which a man in cycling gear stood and watched Channing as he walked past. His bicycle was lying on its side by the curb, one wheel spinning slowly. Channing raised a hand to the man, who didn't respond but instead stepped farther back into the doorway and let himself be swallowed by the building's interior.

Had the man been crying?

Channing crossed the space in front of the building to the doorway and peered inside. Unfolding before him was a long corridor, its walls partly tiled with a delicate, swirling marble pattern. No, he realized, not a marble pattern: these were marble tiles. There was a stack of them inside the door, and they were old, Channing realized; their backs held the ghosts of old plaster, ridges and whirls of thick gray adhesive visible at the edges of the squares. Looking around, Channing saw a sign reading "A Gentholme Community Trust Project."

"Hello," Channing called, "are you okay?"

No response.

"Hello?"

The sound of footsteps, soft and gritty, receding, and another sound, a faint tinkle like water rolling over pebbles. A bell?

A bicycle bell?

"Are you okay?" he called, but received no response. Channing waited a moment and called again. There were no workmen about that he could see, no supervisor he could talk to, and he didn't want to enter the building without someone knowing; it was a building site after all, and he didn't know what work, if any, was happening inside. He called again, a last time, and decided that if the man wouldn't respond there was nothing he could do. He glanced at his watch: nearly lunch. Time to go, his gentle slope awaited him—and then there was a noise like the tearing of metal and a shriek of grinding and shattering.

He whirled about, looking back across the plaza toward the road, convinced someone had crashed into the bike, but it was still lying on the edge of the curb, undisturbed. Its wheel had stopped spinning, and in the sunlight it appeared to be leached of color, its frame and handlebars and tires reduced to a pale wash that was only slightly darker than white. Channing turned back to face into the building, wondering if something had collapsed within, half expecting to see a cloud of dust billowing down the corridor toward him, but the space was still and quiet. There was still no one else to be seen, but now there was another sound, a long, wretched wheezing.

Channing stepped into the civic center.

Beyond the pile of reclaimed tiles there was a space marked out on the floor that was clearly for a reception desk. Brackets were fixed into the concrete and white marks joined them with cryptic symbols scrawled on either side of the lines. A door beyond this was closed. The corridor ran back from the desk space, down the side of the hidden office, and it was this way Channing went; the exits to either side of the lobby were closed, neither showed signs of having been opened in the last few minutes, and the floor around them was unmarked. As he stepped from the untiled section to the tiled section, he heard another set of soft, dragging footsteps and a second bout of the ragged wheezing.

"Hello!" he shouted, his voice echoing, bouncing back at him, a hundred fractured versions of himself populating the air about him.

At the end of the short corridor, a pair of double doors stood closed. Their top halves were glass, the panes frosted and reinforced with thin black wires, the light coming through them fragmented and mazy. Channing was reaching out to push them open when something dark passed across the glass on the other side of the doors, the shape hunched and indistinct. He jerked back and then told himself he was being stupid; it was a workman or the cyclist himself, and he had only appeared distorted, his head tilted to one side and irregularly shaped, by the glass.

He pushed open the doors. There was grit in the hinges and they resisted his push for a few moments before yielding, squealing as they opened. The corridor he entered ran at right angles to the one he'd left, presumably following the rear of the center, curving slightly as it fell away from him. The wall facing Channing was filled with windows to the outside, large and without blinds or coverings, and the corridor was full of light. Motes of dust curled lazily in the air, slow, swimming in the light. The near-side walls along the corridor were broken by evenly spaced doorways, none of which currently had doors. Electrical cables sprouted from rough holes, and below each one, lying on the floor, was a lamp and a boxed long-life bulb.

What there wasn't, however, was a person, or anything to explain the shape that had passed the door.

Perhaps, thought Channing, the sound came from something in the building falling over, made worse, magnified by the space's emptiness? And the shape could have been a secondary shadow, he supposed, someone passing beyond the outer window, or even a bird, the thrown shade crossing not just that window but the panes in the doors as well? Channing went to the first open doorway and looked inside at an empty office. It was the same through the doorway after that, and the third and the fourth, and at that point he stopped looking.

Through the windows Channing watched as excavators scooped earth into piles and then rumbled over them to compress the soil down, their caterpillar treads leaving tattoo trails in the dark mud. The machines, made silent by distance and the intervening glass, were the only moving thing in Channing's vision, and he watched them for a few minutes, enjoying the way they balleted around one another, carefully shaping the earth below them into something new.

Perhaps the noise came from outside, he thought, *from the excavators. Whatever, there's nothing here, and I'm probably trespassing.* Channing went back along the corridor, taking a last look at the machines and their slow crawl of work, and then went back through the doors and found the cyclist ahead of him.

The man was standing just inside the civic center's entrance, half caught in the sun and half in shadow, and he was turning slowly around. He gazed at the floor as he turned, scuffing one foot across the tiles with a rubbery, wheezy sound.

"Hello," said Channing. "It's a nice building, isn't it? They're doing a good job, aren't they?"

"It's not fucking right," the cyclist said.

"Pardon? What's not right? The building?" *Maybe he doesn't like the way they've designed it or something,* thought Channing, walking toward the man.

"I said, it's not right. It's wrong."

Not again, thought Channing, slowing. *What is it with this damn town?* "What's wrong?"

"For god's sake, this place is wrong. It's here but not here. Not there. Where's Eleanor?"

"I'm sorry, I don't understand; who's Eleanor?" said Channing, thinking about how often he'd said something similar these last few days. "Can I help you?"

"No," the cyclist said and stepped back, farther into the shadow.

"Stay the fuck away from me. I need to find Eleanor. I'm not where I was but I'm here where I should be and I'm confused and it's not right, it's not fucking right at all."

The man was almost lost in the shadow now, the gloom creeping around the edges of him and making him seem only half there, and it was colder now, the sun not properly warming the air in the darkening lobby.

"I'm not where I was but I'm here," the man said and held one arm out in front of him, his hand reemerging into the sunlight, pointing at Channing, accusatory and shaking. The man's head suddenly snapped to one side, twisting as it did so, and he groaned, loud and breathy. His fingers spread wide, clutching at Channing, and then the darkness swelled forward or he collapsed back into it and he simply fell away to nothing. His hand lingered a moment longer, caught by the sun, and then it too disappeared and Channing was backing away on paper legs, stomach roiling, voice untethered and releasing a long drool of sound, and then he turned and he ran and ran and ran.

"I'm not sure I understand you," said the man in the sales office. "What is it you've seen again?"

Put like that, Channing thought, *I don't know. What have I seen?*

Channing was in the private part of the sales office, having been passed from the receptionist to the younger salesman to the elder, senior one. Channing remembered him from the meetings and pitches he and Miranda had attended, smooth and gray and slick yet somehow insubstantial, as though he were all front but little depth. Maybe that was all salesmen; Channing didn't know.

"You were in the park and you saw people? And in the unfinished civic center and saw a man on his bike?"

"No," said Channing, "his bike was outside."

"Ah. That's good," said the man, whose name Channing suddenly remembered was O'Keefe. "I'd hate someone to be cycling inside the building. Actually, I'm not keen on anyone being in there, bike or no, as it's not finished and it's dangerous. It's still technically a building site."

O'Keefe leaned back in his chair.

"Mr. . . . Channing, yes? You moved in several weeks ago, one of our very first residents, if I remember right?"

"Yes."

"I've worked on several new developments like this, Mr. Channing. Oh, this is easily the biggest, but I've built entire subdivisions in the past. At this stage, they're odd. They're empty, and they seem bigger than busy places because you aren't used to seeing streets without people or cars or shops without customers. Places like this, they're somehow louder and quieter at the same time. The sound *echoes*, Mr. Channing. They spook you, places like this. You've spooked yourself, Mr. Channing, but as more people move in it'll get better and you'll feel better about your new home."

"I love my new home," said Channing angrily, "but I—"

"Mr. Channing, I can't have you going around saying that strange things are happening here," said O'Keefe, his voice hardening. "Many of our properties are still unsold or the sales aren't yet completed, and buyers, both private and commercial, are skittish things. If they hear you talk about vanishing cyclists and old people in the park, they'll run. They'll run, Mr. Channing, and Gentholme will suffer, and I cannot have that. I *cannot*, Mr. Channing, do you understand?"

"Yes," said Channing. "I wasn't trying to damage things, just to understand."

"Of course," said O'Keefe, placatory now. "Perhaps you need to get involved, see more people, see if that helps? The community trust is always looking for able bodies and willing volunteers. Maybe you should go and see them?"

"Yes," said Channing. "Yes, I think I will."

Channing walked to the community trust office along streets that were, finally, beginning to show signs of life. Delivery trucks rumbled toward the shops, houses were opening their eyes, family cars were moving along the streets; Gentholme looked more like a city. O'Keefe was right, Channing realized: without residents this place had looked huge and, if not sinister, then certainly off-kilter. Was that what had happened? Had being here spooked him, touching some susceptible part of him that he hadn't known was there, making him interpret things the wrong way?

No.

He'd seen what he'd seen, the man and the crowd and the cyclist, heard the snatches of grating, discordant music, and he wanted to know a *why* and a *what* and a *how*.

The community trust office was based in a small but imposing building several streets away from the civic center. *It looks like an old pub,* thought Channing, as he approached it, and then he realized that that's exactly what it was. "This building has been created from the remains of the Old Dun Cow, a public house that stood in the village of Gentholme from 1743 until its demolition last year," read the plaque above the main door. It even had a pub sign, reading "The Gentholme Community Trust" rather than "The Old Dun Cow," swinging slightly above the door. Given that there was no breeze, Channing wondered if the swing was engineered, electrical, to help increase the impression that this was an old-fashioned pub rather than a modern office. Inside, though, the pretense of the building being aged was dropped.

Through the door was a bright open space filled with information racks and digital displays showing the development of Gentholme from a village to its current incarnation as a new city, maps outlining the green space that the government had rezoned for the development and the proposed layout of the streets and buildings. Time-lapse presentations showed the initial buildings growing like flowers, unfurling and turning to face the sun without apparent human intervention. Where the bar should have been was a row of computers, each in an individual carrel, with a large notice above them reading "Free Internet Access." There was a young man sitting behind a desk on the other side of the room who started to rise as Channing came in, but Channing waved him back down; he didn't want to talk, or to volunteer, not yet. He wanted to think and see what he could find out.

He wanted answers, or maybe to know the questions.

Channing browsed the leaflets and posters on the walls; it was probably the only public place in Gentholme he'd been that seemed complete, that didn't have gaps and spaces and unfilled lacunae. He picked up one of the leaflets and read the glossy words inside.

> Gentholme uses the most modern building and
> planning techniques to ensure a town that is as

energy efficient and safe as it is welcoming and
friendly! Public spaces have been designed using
the best elements of the past but with a modern
twist, creating a secure and comfortable environment that looks resolutely forward while retaining
an intimate knowledge of the past. Where possible, materials from other places have been used
to create Gentholme's unique personality, a careful
blending of the years that have gone and the years
to come!

The passage was in large type and surrounded by brightly lit photographs of Gentholme. Only, he saw, they weren't photographs but
rather incredibly detailed and photorealistic artists' impressions of
what Gentholme would be, digital images of the park and the commercial centers and rows of neat, attractive housing peopled with little
pixelated figures walking and shopping and lying in the sun. The rest
of the leaflet was filled with more of the same: bright exhortations
to trust in the developers' visions of the future city, promises around
low environmental impact, and grand aspirations to have a "recycled
heart."

It was on the rear of the leaflet that Channing found the phrase
that made him stop, that sent images tumbling across the inside of his
vision, dark behind the sunlight, that took his breath and clenched his
belly.

That made him really see the ghosts.

GENTHOLME: CARRYING THE PAST
INTO A BRIGHT NEW FUTURE.

Channing ran his hand along the park wall, feeling the grit of the stone
against his fingertips. It was warm from the sun and it was as though
he were brushing the flank of some huge, solid beast. When he laid his
hands flat against it and pressed down it felt as though he could feel
the heat of its life pulsing.

The boy with the blue balloon was still standing on the far side of the playground. The bright blue teardrop bobbed as Channing walked toward the boy; it jerked back and forth in a breeze that Channing couldn't feel. *How long ago was that wind blowing?* Channing thought. *How long ago, and how far away?*

The boy was dressed in a school uniform, knee-length shorts and a blue sweater. He didn't look old-fashioned, exactly, but he wasn't modern either. *He's my age,* thought Channing, *or was my age when he was given the balloon. Or I was the same age as he was when he got the balloon. Has he aged? Does he know? I don't know how this works.*

When he reached a point about twenty feet from the boy, Channing stopped and kneeled. "Hello," he said.

The boy didn't reply.

"Do you know where you are?" he asked, but still the boy remained silent. In the distance, Channing heard a snatch of the music again, or rather, he heard lots of snatches of music all overlaid, interlocked and straining against one another, strangling one another. Already, shadows were forming in the trees that lined the slope behind the boy, moving and coalescing, forming people.

Forming ghosts.

Channing held his hand out, but the boy took a step back. "I'm not allowed to talk to strangers," he said, nodding in confirmation of his own statement, balloon and head moving momentarily in time with each other.

"I just thought, with you and me being here each day, we should say hello to each other," said Channing. "You are here every day, aren't you?"

"I don't know," said the boy. "I think so, but I'm not sure."

"Where do you live?" *When do you live?*

"I don't know."

"What happened to you?" asked Channing, unable to stop himself. *I'm talking to a ghost,* he thought, *a dead child.*

"I don't know," said the boy again, head dipping and rising, dipping and rising, balloon spasming at the end of its string tether as the unfelt wind picked up. A cowlick of hair danced away from the boy's head, reaching up, and then fell across his forehead. The boy looked at Channing from behind the hair and said, "I'm lonely. I'm scared. I want my mom and dad. Do you know where they are? I want my mom."

The boy took a step toward Channing and held out his hands, string still clenched tight in one of them. Channing felt a wave of cold coming off the boy, the first real cold he'd felt since moving to Gentholme, and backed away, dropping his own hand.

"Please," said the boy, and Channing heard the people at the bandstand and the old man outside the park in his voice, heard them all begging him for something he didn't know how to give. "Please, I just want to go home and see my mom. I've been waiting for her but she doesn't come. Do you know where she is? Please?"

Channing wobbled, balance unsettled, and then fell back, legs sprawled before him. The boy took another step and it got colder still. It hadn't been cold with the man outside the park, or the crowd by the bandstand, had it? And yes, it had been cooler when he had seen the cyclist, but not cold like this, not this *bitterness*. But the boy was so young, Channing thought, so young, and he wanted his mom and to go home and it made him frigid with grief and loss and longing.

"Please," the boy said again and took another step and the air seemed to crackle with chill and then Channing was up and running and not looking back.

Channing spent the afternoon wondering what to do, trying to piece things together in his head so that they made sense. Well, made as much sense as anything that accepted the existence of ghosts could do, anyway. He walked Gentholme's streets, seeing the buildings expand, the land forming into new shapes, wondering about each person he saw. Were they real? Imaginary?

Ghosts?

Eventually, he knew he had to talk to Miranda about it. She would listen to him and tell him he was being stupid, or that he was right, or she would find the correct explanation. That was what Miranda did, she found out the right way to see things. It was why he loved her, and why he'd let her persuade him to move to Gentholme in the first place. "It'll work," she'd said after the first presentation and the tour around the various house plots, then little more than spaces marked out by plastic tape and architects' drawings. "I can see it, new and clean and healthy. It'll be good for us."

Channing went home and waited, sitting in his kitchen and looking out into the garden. They'd already planned what plants to buy and where they'd go; well, Miranda had. The garden was her realm, she'd told him, the kitchen his. She wanted a garden full of the plants she loved, so he waited, and as he waited, he imagined things growing and blooming and flowering.

"Hey," said Miranda from behind him some time later, making him jump. Channing had been so lost in his reverie that he hadn't heard her come in.

"Hey," he said back, their usual greeting. "How's your day been?"

She didn't reply but instead shook her head and turned to leave the kitchen.

"Miranda, I need to talk to you," he said, but she made a shooing motion with her hands and then left the room. He followed her, watching as she wandered around the house without settling. He waited, giving her a few minutes; sometimes this was how she was when her day had been hard, needing a period to shake off the day's pressures and to relax. "Decompressing," she called it, her decompression time. Channing made tea, brewing it strong the way she liked, and when Miranda finally returned to him, he led her into the kitchen and gently guided her to a chair. He set her drink in front of her, kissing her cheek as he did so, and then sat opposite her.

"I need to talk," he said again.

"Yes? Now? Can it wait?" Miranda replied. "I'm tired. I don't want to think."

"No," said Channing. "It's important. Please."

"If you must," said Miranda, looking around the room. "At least I'm here. At least I'm home."

Home, Channing suddenly realized. *Yes, this is home, this is our home, which we bought and made ours. It's where we belong.* He reached out and took Miranda's hand, took a deep breath, and then started speaking on the exhale.

"Miranda, it's about Gentholme. I've been walking around a lot these last few weeks, since we moved in, and I've been seeing things. No, not things, *people*, and there's something strange about them," Channing said and let the whole story out of his head and into the world. When he finished, Miranda simply looked at him, staring for so long that, eventually, Channing felt the urge to speak, to break the silence.

"Well?"

"You think there are ghosts?" she finally asked.

"Yes," he said. Miranda looked directly at him, focusing properly for the first time since her return from work. She looked around the room, through the window at the garden, and then back at him.

"Yes. It makes sense, I suppose."

"Does it?"

"Yes, my love. It does now, anyway. I was wondering but now it's clear. I understand. If they are ghosts then it's no wonder they're confused, is it? Think about it."

"You tell me I think too much," he said, smiling. Even to him, his smile felt weak and worn.

"Think," she said. "They're dead, and lost. We come to love places, we come to belong to places, even as we think those places belong to us. Those poor people are tied to the bricks and stones and tiles from the buildings of their lives, they've been tied to them for years and years possibly, and now the developers have torn them all down and are using the pieces to make Gentholme, to create a city that looks old even though it's new. Those ghosts, they've come with the pieces, they're still attached to buildings that no longer exist and that have been recycled into something new and placed somewhere new, but this isn't where they lived or died so they're confused. They've been dragged here, but they don't know where they are, they've never been here before and nothing looks the same as they're used to. That's so horrible, so awful for them. They have nowhere to belong to and no one to tell them what's happening."

"Yes!" Channing near-shouted. "Yes, that's what I thought: they've come here but they don't know where *here* is, and it's confusing them, making them feel terrible and hurt and angry."

"And there was a boy? Who wanted his mom?"

"A boy with a blue balloon," said Channing, "and a man who was lost and people waiting for music and a cyclist looking for Eleanor, whoever she is."

"A boy," repeated Miranda as a fat tear trickled from one eye. She cried for a moment, head down, shoulders hitching. "That's horrible. A boy, a child lost like that. He shouldn't be alone."

"I know," said Channing. Miranda and he couldn't have children; embryos refused to implant in the wall of Miranda's womb, instead bleeding out of her on waves of cramping and anguish. They'd had to accept it, and as neither wanted to adopt or foster, Gentholme was the new start they'd promised themselves, that they needed, the start of their childless life together. Gentholme had become their home, the place they belonged to.

"What can we do?" asked Channing, but before Miranda could answer there was a knock at the front door.

"Answer it," said Miranda, looking around again. "I'm thinking. Give me a minute, my love."

Behind the frosted upper pane of the front door two shapes moved, Gentholme's daylight behind them, turning them into little more than dark blurs. Channing, reminded uncomfortably of the crowd emerging from the trees to listen to a concert he could not properly hear, opened the door to find two policemen looking at him. Neither moved, and then one spoke Channing's name and then Miranda's name and reached out for his shoulder.

Miranda had gone from the kitchen when Channing went back in, and the back door was open, swinging gently. He left the house, not shutting the door behind him, and walked to the park. He didn't go fast; he couldn't, legs as heavy as sleep, head burning and gray. The old man wasn't outside the park, and the crowd was no longer at the bandstand, but the boy with the balloon was still there. The balloon fluttered gently as the woman kneeling on the grass in front of him enveloped the boy in her arms.

"It's okay," Channing heard Miranda say. "It's okay, I'm here now. Everything will be okay."

They were coming now, the old ghosts, the displaced ones, the lost ones, coming out of the shades and corners, gathering around as Miranda stood. She held the boy's hand tight, calling to them, drawing them in until they were clustered around her, male and female, old and young. Channing saw the cyclist, the old man, some of the people from around the bandstand and others, ones he'd not seen before, ones linked to stones and bricks he had not yet found.

Gentholme's first home-grown ghost comforted the new city's older dwellers, the boy's balloon dancing by her head, and from somewhere Channing heard music.

Donations

WILLIAM JOSELYN

(Winner of *The Blumhouse Book of Nightmares:
The Haunted City* Short Story Contest)

Jerry had lived his entire life in Detroit. The Motor City. Motown. The "D." The city of his birth, childhood, and well beyond, it was his first and last love. And so it was very difficult for him to watch it die.

Detroit's demise had been long and cancerous, a slow and painful march toward ruin. Those who didn't flee stayed to crumble and wither along with their fading metropolis. Faces once bright and vibrant turned pale and drawn; bodies once strong and agile turned slack, weak. Whatever disease ailed Detroit, it had spread to the city's residents.

Jerry did his best to get by. He had no place to go and no desire to leave. Detroit would get better, he kept telling himself as he drove his delivery truck, day after day, through his beloved, rotting city.

One night, a few weeks back, Jerry had gone down to his corner bar. Nursing his third beer of the evening, Jerry saw a slender shadow of a man holding court in a booth near the back. A handful of people sat with him, hanging on his every word. It was as if he'd been sketched into this world with a blunt piece of charcoal, drawn in thick shades of smoldering embers.

"The city is a living, breathing organism," the man said. "Therefore, it must be treated as such."

"What do you suggest?" a woman asked him.

"Surgery," the man replied. "You need to go in and cut. Excise the cancerous tissue, the tumors that eat away at the very core. I have overseen such procedures in the past, and I am willing to do so here. But the people must act. They must obey."

Jerry shook his head. Just another barroom commentator going on about how he could fix all of the city's woes. If only Jerry had a dollar for every time he heard such talk.

He ordered another drink, and the shadow man and his ideas were forgotten.

A week later, he saw the man again, on television, when the mayor broke into the regularly scheduled programming to tell the good citizens of Detroit that he was instituting a new law. A brief period of mandatory donations would begin the following day.

Jerry watched the announcement on a TV he'd salvaged from a nearby junk heap and rewired. The shadow man stood behind the mayor, a dark spectral presence who appeared an ill fit among the smug politician's standard entourage.

The picture on Jerry's rescued TV was often a blizzard of interference. Its screen a constant flurry, as if to match the snow falling outside Jerry's window.

The shadow man seemed immune to the scratchy whims of the television. He never once skipped or distorted, even as those all around him did so frequently.

Jerry turned off the TV and turned to his window. The snow was coming down in thick, cottony puffs. It had already dusted the street and ancient ruins beyond, the hills of brick and concrete and scrap that polluted his view.

Mandatory donations, Jerry thought. He wondered what more the city could possibly take from its residents. They were a ferociously loyal bunch. They alone kept the city running on fumes. But they had nothing left to give. Jerry certainly didn't.

Over the next few days, as Jerry drove his delivery truck along the cracked and buckled streets, he began to notice subtle changes here and there. Familiar things had been mysteriously altered, seemingly overnight. The alterations were small, at first, barely noticeable. A missing segment of a building's exterior piping, or an old, rusted street sign suddenly vanished without a trace. Nothing out of the ordinary. Things went missing in Detroit all the time, be they pipes, signs, cars, or even people.

But soon the adjustments to the city became more pronounced, and Jerry began to see the "mandatory donations" for what they were. Someone was taking things, ripping them away from the city as a child might tear clumps of grass from the lawn on which he sits.

Out on his standard route one morning, Jerry saw a sight so bizarre, so extraordinary, that he was forced to slam on the brakes. His truck slid on the snow- and ice-glazed road, but he quickly recovered and brought her in for a gentle curbside landing.

He climbed out of his truck and stepped into the middle of the desolate street for a better look.

The corner apartment building was missing one entire half. It looked as if a scalpel had come through overnight and sliced the structure right down the middle.

On the top floor, a young woman stood in her bisected living room, oblivious to the wind whipping her hair and the snow gathering on her carpet and furniture. She stared blankly out the opening where there had once been a wall, her eyes fixed, as though glimpsing some unseen realm.

Transfixed, Jerry suddenly noticed that the woman was missing her right arm. It ended, just past the shoulder, in a crimson-soaked bandage. Blood dripped from the wrappings and onto her snow-dusted carpet.

Jerry scrambled back to his truck and drove off. Throughout the rest of the day, he saw many more amputations, both to city and to the people who resided there. Detroit was getting picked apart by scavengers, so many bits and pieces missing, both large and small, pilfered with no discernible pattern.

He couldn't help but think of the shadow man's words in the bar, his talk of surgeries, of cutting away the cancerous tissue.

He drove down Woodward Avenue. It wasn't on his route, but he was feeling a strong urge to keep going north, out to the suburbs. As he neared 8 Mile, he came upon a cluster of vehicles blocking traffic. Drivers and passengers alike stood in the middle of the road, all in a state of shock.

Jerry brought his truck to a stop and looked past the gathering. Woodward had suffered a horrific wound. An enormous chasm sliced across the south- and northbound lanes, creating a wide-open mouth across which no one would ever cross.

Jerry played with his radio dial. There was only one station still operating in the city, but when he tuned to it, he heard the voice of the shadow man.

"Fear not, my friends," he said. "Do not panic. The changes you see all around you are the necessary measures by which we shall heal this great city. All is going according to plan. Detroit will soon begin anew."

Jerry backed up his truck and turned around. As he drove, his radio screeched with static and then the regular radio host returned in midsentence. She sounded extremely panicked as she raced through updates: ". . . no way in or out of the city. Portions of I-75 missing, Woodward, the Lodge . . ."

Jerry killed the radio and floored the gas. It would be dark soon, and he didn't want to be out on the streets come nightfall. He took a circuitous route home, for all of his familiar pathways had, in some drastic way, been modified. When he finally arrived back at his building, he was relieved to find it still standing in its entirety. He hurried to his apartment on the third floor, shut and locked and bolted the door, then took a quick inventory. Everything looked in order.

He turned on his TV. It took a few seconds to warm up, but when it did, he was able to see frantic breaking news reports from all over the city. Joe Louis Arena was gone; the upper half of the Fisher Building had been cleanly shorn from its lower half; large portions of Comerica Park were missing. The city was in chaos.

Long-neglected streets had had entire blocks carved away. The center of the Ambassador Bridge had been taken. The Detroit-Windsor Tunnel had collapsed.

But it was the people who disturbed Jerry the most, those who happened to be in view of the numerous cameras filming the city's widespread surgeries. Just like the woman with the missing arm, they had also had vital parts excised from their bodies. He saw bloodied bandages over missing limbs, gauze wrapped around heads and faces. One poor man had lost both of his eyes and was staggering about, blindly flailing his hands.

The news cut to the mayor. He was missing both of his lips, as well as one eye. His spoke like a bad ventriloquist, unable to form consonants properly as he begged the citizens of Detroit to remain calm. The shadow man stood behind him, so close he was practically sewn to the mayor's back. When the mayor finished speaking, the shadow man took over.

Jerry stared at him.

The shadow man appeared to stare back.

"These donations are important to the welfare of this great city. When all is done, Detroit will begin to heal, to regenerate, rebuild. The city will thrive again, mark my words, but you must allow us to complete our work. It is your civic duty to comply."

Jerry nodded. He understood.

Outside, the day had bled out, the city's corpse now draped in the dark cloak of night. Snow fell steadily and the metamorphosis continued. Streetlights flickered. Jerry went to the window and looked out. One by one, the lights vanished, simply plucked from existence until only blackness remained and snow falling like twinkling stars.

They were coming for him.

He had nowhere to run. By all accounts, Detroit was an island cut off from the rest of the state, the country, the world.

Jerry went to his refrigerator and grabbed a beer. With nothing to do but wait, he cracked it open and took a long, satisfying sip. Ice cold, and oh so refreshing, even on such a frigid night as this.

He sat back down in his chair by the window and watched the news reports flood in. As one reporter stood in front of the Frank Murphy Hall of Justice, the building behind her vanished.

Jerry leaned closer to the screen. Shadows peeled away from the emptiness and flowed toward the reporter like spilled ink. She dropped her microphone when they took both of her arms. She did not scream or cry. She smiled.

He reached out a hand and touched the television screen. It crackled with interference and then shut off. As Jerry sat back, the TV disappeared completely.

The walls of his apartment rattled. A few framed photos fell to the floor and shattered. Jerry calmly sipped his beer and looked down the hall to the door. It rippled, then was torn from its hinges, yanked into thick, soupy darkness.

The shadow man entered.

"I've been waiting for you," Jerry said.

"We saved you for last," the man said.

"What do I need to do?"

"Nothing, Jerry," said the shadow man. "Just sit back and relax and I'll take care of everything."

"Do what you have to do."

Jerry closed his eyes. He realized that it was all for the good of the city, his beloved Motown. He felt no pain whatsoever as the shadow man began to cut.

The Old Jail

SARAH LANGAN

"I'm possessed!" my brother Ezra shouts as he stubs out his cigarette.

"Good to see you too!" I shout back—it's a noisy autumn day in Manhattan. A construction crane packed with steel beams screams its warning like a furious dinosaur, roused after three million years of sleep.

I follow Ezra into 640 Park Avenue. He's wearing a filthy red uniform, his pale skin scabbed from too much scratching, his breath like cat shit. We round the doorman's post and head into the old-fashioned elevator. Its thick limestone shaft muffles the outside clamor.

As soon as we're in, Ezra pivots. He gets in my face, "I knew you'd come. I sent my psychic message. Listen, be warned. The demon slimed inside my ear because I love Bar-tók!"

"Is this a *Star Trek* plot?"

Ezra's eyes bulge. He shouts. "Libertine! Look at me! My eyes are **burning**. It won't let me blink!"

I'm tempted to suggest that his eyes are red because he's farting pure sulfur, and that a man who subsists on butter pickles and Beefeater Gin should expect a downside. But I've never actually enjoyed making fun of him. It's just this thing I can't help doing.

"It's got everything but my frontal lobe," he continues. "It hates higher thinking, so that's the attic where I hide. But I'm a prisoner, Grady. The only reason it's let me keep my tongue to talk is because it wants you for a host. To cast it out, I've got to call it by the name of the first human it possessed."

"So cast it out and let's grab lunch at Chipotle!"

"I don't know its name!" He flicks all ten fingers at me like an angry magician. "I don't know its name! Help me! That's why you're here, isn't it?"

"I'm here because management called. They say you punched a poodle. I'm hoping that's a euphemism. Anyway, they want me to tell you that you're fired."

Ezra's wire-tense posture slackens like someone's just unzipped him from a truss. He sighs. "Oh, the poodle . . ."

I can't help it. I laugh. Ezra watches to make sure I'm not poking fun, then joins in. "It's bad to punch dogs. I'll admit that," he says.

My brother's a paranoid schizophrenic with an IQ of 150. He wasn't ever normal, but we pretended and hoped for the best. The real trouble started when he got a job in academia. As an adjunct history professor at Bennington, he accused his department chair of activating an al-Qaeda sleeper cell with a penlight. His tenure got denied. When he moved back with my parents in Larchmont, they told him to snap out of it. A few weeks later, he greeted them at the dinner table draped in a sheet. When he lifted his arms, blood gushed down all sides: he'd driven ten-penny nails clean through both wrists.

Ezra was released from Mount Sinai's inpatient psychiatric program six months ago. He wasn't cured; we just ran out of money. Over the years, that four million dollars in hospital fees devoured my family's savings. My status in life has fallen accordingly. My kids go to public school and my clothes are off the rack. We vacation on our roof and call it Forest Hills Beach.

After my parents moved to Florida, I volunteered to be Ezra's emergency contact. Some people consider that kind of thing a burden. I don't. I love the guy. Or, I love the idea of him. That's probably more honest. Anyway, 640's management called this morning about the poodle, and also about the fact that he's been squatting in their basement. So here I am, crammed inside the closet-sized elevator of a prewar apartment building in the wealthiest part of Manhattan, talking to my wack-job twin brother about demonic possession.

"Okay. I'll bite," I say. "Demons are infectious diseases. You've come down with a bad case. That's why you're talking kind of retarded and you smell like ass."

"Yes!" he shouts, his whole body jerking, limbs shivering, delighted I might actually believe him. "Oh, yes, yes! I knew you'd un-der-stand. **God** sent you."

"Well," I say. "No."

"I'm not **alone,** either. A woman and a young boy from the sixth floor are infected too. Their names are **Margaret Brooks** and **Lucas Novo** and they speak to my demon while I sleep. I've viewed the incriminating el-e-vator security footage. You can see it for yourself." He does that magician finger-flick thing again. Think a blond David Blaine at his creepiest. "And now that you know the awful truth, you must use your writing talent for the side of good, and preach to the world!"

"Ezra, this is all compelling stuff and I'm going to think hard on it. But I've got to ask, are you snorting your meds again?"

Ezra wipes his eyes, which it's true don't blink. Then he smiles this sweet, trembling smile, and I see his future: the homeless guy you're not scared of; the old vagabond sleeping over the subway grate, whose family you decide must be useless to have left him so alone.

"Come to the base-ment," he says. "You'll be-lieve me then."

Just then, a sunbeam-skinny young woman in flamingo pink work-out clothes strides through the lobby. She seems to want to go some-place on the elevator, unwitting that its operator is insane.

I tap the century-old metal-caged lift with my knuckles. "Sorry. Technical difficulties."

She looks from me to Ezra. We're identical, but I'm clean-cut. A button-down polo, buzzed-short hair, married, two kids, a mortgage and migraines. I keep a reporter's notebook in my pocket because I like writing more than typing. "Ever see *The Patty Duke Show*?" I ask. I'm an utter clown around beautiful women.

She shrugs, and I realize that no one born after 1980 has seen *The Patty Duke Show*. We're so goddamned old. "Can you guys do your plumbing or whatever later?" she asks in this screeching, high-pitched whine. "I need to go to my apartment."

"It's a private matter. We're just—"

Propping her hands on bony hips, she gets nasty. "See this building?

This is my house. I come here to relax. One of you needs to take me to my apartment. That's what I pay you for!"

"But—" I start.

"Right now!" she shrills.

"Go eat some poor people," I tell her.

The woman glares at my chest, then Ezra's. She finds his name tag and presumably memorizes it. I notice, then, that she's emitting that same eau de cat shit as Ezra. Stranger still, what I'd thought was gloss on her lips is glistening blood. It crawls down the sides of her mouth, vampiric. She spins, her white-blond ponytail whipping, and jogs for the stairs.

"Let's get you checked into Sinai before she calls the cops on both of us," I say.

He looks at me with puppy eyes. "What about my proof? It's in the base-ment."

"Make it quick."

A funny thing happens as we descend. There isn't enough light to see past the elevator's metal bars, so I tell myself it's shadow play as an inky thing swims out from behind my brother's irises. It blooms, swallowing the whites of his sclera, until his eyes are black as giant marbles.

"Ezra?"

Clink! We land in the basement. He swings open the gate door. It's not as well kept down here. The paint is peeling. A ceiling bulb splashes chiaroscuro radiance against pink cinder block.

"So, what's the magic surprise?" I ask.

Ezra heads into the long hallway without answering. His arms, legs, and neck move jerkily and out of sync. I watch him from behind, and the only comparison I can draw is that he's like a puppet with a giant hand crammed inside him, tearing his very fabric wherever it needs extra space.

"Hey! Ezra!"

He rams his bony shoulder against the last door on the left. I catch up and see that someone has penciled eyes all along its archway. They're true sized, all differently proportioned, all intricate. I get the feeling they're watching me.

"Trapped souls. Trip-trap!" he says as he walks inside.

I follow. It's a boiler room. Scribbled in black Sharpie on the dingy white walls are thousands of inscrutable hieroglyphs. Scattered among these hieroglyphs is one sentence of English, written again and again: *Ezra is Dead*.

"Ezra? I'm a little freaked out right now."

"You see?" Ezra asks in this hollow, echoless voice that I can only describe as a digital approximation of sound. I'm so goddamned scared. He opens the third locker from a row alongside the door. A four-foot pile of glinting white and red hunks cascades out.

I point. "Is that a human femur?"

Ezra charges. His legs jerk underneath him like a dog on ice. I don't see the switchblade, but I know enough to raise my hand. He stabs clean through my palm. It's not painful. All I feel are cold blue sparks.

He keeps swinging, his aim terrible but wide and manic enough to harm. I'm nicked between the ribs, then again in the shoulder. I clench my good hand and spring.

It's a straight blow under his chin. The kind of punch that ought to bring a man down. But he grins like it's nothing, black eyes glued to mine. He works his mouth, jaw clenching. I don't understand what's happening until he spits. A wet mound drops. It's his tongue.

"Hey! Don't!" I rush toward him.

It's a trap. He gets a leg behind me and swipes. I hit the floor. He straddles me, driving the blade down with both hands. I knee his balls and roll. Steel plinks against cement.

"Ezra!" I shout like we're still fifteen. "Truce! Jesus, truce!"

The knife cuts the air. I'm grunting, or he is, or both of us. I turn the blade around and slide it easy as grease into the depression between his clavicles.

The thing—my brother—reels, blood gushing. **"Uhhhhh!"** he grunts, slapping against the boiler and walls, leaving giant moth-shaped stains like there's an animal inside him that's trying to fly away. **"Uhhhhh!"**

It takes a while before I'm able to catch and hold him still. "I've got you," I say. "Calm down so I can help." As I watch, his black eyes recede to blue. He smiles like the goofy kid he used to be, sweet and nervous and hiding his madness like a set of soiled sheets. He drives the blade deeper into his own throat, slicing left to right.

"It's the story of the century," I tell Tom White, my publisher, over the phone. "I want a three-part series."

"We don't do long form anymore. You know that," Tom answers.

It's been a month since my brother's suicide. The events immediately following remain a blur. Eyes watched. An inky thing slithered. Police came. My hand was stitched and bandaged. A southern woman in a black suit shined a flashlight in my eyes.

"You're blinkin' like a pro," she told me.

"Well," I said.

She handed me a card:

Anna Beth Cassavetes
Interglot
(212) 555-0341

"Keep this whole shebang on the down low and give me a shout if y'all have any symptoms," she instructed.

"Symptoms?" I asked. "Are you a doctor or a detective?"

She winked one of those perfectly skilled winks that only talk show hosts can manage. "If you gotta ask, you don't need to know!" Then she left with three other guys, also in black suits.

Ezra's body was cremated without my family's permission by a funeral director I didn't hire. His obituary, which I did not write, attributed his death to a tragic accident caused by his mental condition.

I called Ms. Cassavetes repeatedly, asking whether Ezra had murdered those bodies in his locker, and what her capacity was in the investigation. She never got back to me. But I've been a reporter for almost twenty years, and I've got friends. The beat cops at the Twenty-Sixth Precinct tracked down his sealed files. Turns out, that boiler room locker contained the dismembered remains of three recently missing homeless men. Though they've been identified as former residents of the East Side Shelter, no one has informed their families.

"I've just read the autopsy reports," I tell my boss. "Ezra didn't act alone. Three separate bite diameters were found on the bodies."

"Let's hold off," Tom answers. "One of our board members lives at Six Forty Park. You know how these rich guys hate scandal."

I wait. We both know the unspoken: I could take this story someplace else. "Okay, all right, yeah yeah. If I get a hallelujah from the top, it goes in the metro section. Two parts, five thousand words."

"Metro? You're kidding."

"How do I know you'll crack it without raining a libel suit on the whole company?" Tom asks. "Give me something airtight. If you can manage that, I'll make it page one."

"Done," I say. "Just give me two weeks. I'll turn in the Red Hook teamsters' article today and I can work on the Astor family for the style section concurrent."

"Concurrent?" Tom asks.

"Contemporaneously."

Tom chuckles. He's dumber and happier than I am. He's divorced too, and sees his kids every other weekend. It's like he climbed into a time machine and traveled back to 1980. "Aren't you a thesaurus?" he asks.

"Yes," I agree. "Because I'm a writer."

"One week," Tom says.

I'm about to argue this point when my brood starts squawking. "I waaant it! Sharing is caaaaring!" four-year-old Lisa shrills.

I'm calling from a two-bedroom apartment in Forest Hills, Queens. By this stage in my life, I'd expected a classic six in Manhattan. But my one and only publishing deal happened ten years ago, and the book in question, about mafia ties to the Ground Zero clean-up crew in Staten Island, sold less than five hundred copies. In case you don't know, five hundred copies is abysmal. I'm the Walter Mondale of true crime reporting.

"Help me! Daaaaddy! It's still my turn!" six-year-old Elaine screams so loud you'd think the little one was dousing her with lye. They're in their bedroom, where I've bribed them with rug-ruining Play-Doh so long as they stay quiet for the duration of this call.

"Daaaaddy!" they both shout.

"Who is that? Your kids? Why aren't they in school?" Tom asks.

"It's Columbus Day. I've got to hang up."

I burst into the girls' cramped bedroom. All the toys are on the floor, along with the *Frozen* bed sheets and pillows. They've made a nest. My bare foot lands on a Playmobil policeman.

"Goddamn you!" I mutter as I hop to a naked twin mattress to inspect the damage.

"Bad!" nervous Elaine shouts at the offending Playmobil cop.

"You're all bad," I snap.

Little Lisa hurls herself against the nest floor. She's naked except for a homemade Batman utility belt, her chubby bottom pricked with dimples. "I hate bad!" she mumbles through a pillow.

Elaine slaps her own face hard enough to leave a mark. "Bad! Bad! Bad!"

Then they're both bawling, literally scream-crying, which they turn into a competition to be loudest. "Bad! Bad! Bad! OOOOOOhhhh! Daaaaddy!"

"Calm down!" I yell. "Shut up!"

Rookie mistake. My fury fuels their hysteria. "Ooooooh!" they scream, even louder. The neighbors down below start banging. What do they use to reach the ceiling? A broom?

"You're not bad! I'm just depressed!" I shout.

Curious, Elaine stops screaming. Like always, Lisa follows. My nervous system flowers in gratitude. "What's depressed?" Elaine asks.

"Frustrated. Stymied. Horribly unhappy. I need to finish some calls and then I'll take you to the park."

Recovering so quickly that I wonder if she's been playing me for a sap, Elaine leaps from the floor, grinning wide. "And get pink donuts?"

"No."

"ICE CREAM?" Lisa shrieks, her Weeble-wobble-shaped body shivering with crazy joy.

"I'll take you to the park and that's it and you'll like it and you'll say *thank you*!"

"Thank you!" Elaine says.

"You're a bad guy and I won't say thank you, never! Never!" says Lisa.

"Hug your bad guy!" I tell her.

Elaine dives into my arms. "Dad," she moans, blissed out and star-struck with love. She's always needed extra affection and never been able to ask for it. "Daddy-dad-dadda. Googy-ga-gagga."

Giggling, Lisa follows. Group hug. "My rug rats," I say. "I'm over the moon for you."

They climb my shoulders and flop around, shoving their naked bottoms in my face, bouncing on the bed. Everybody's laughing, even me.

Moments like this are great. For lots of people, they're what life is all about. But for me, they're also pretty fucking oppressive.

After we put the kids to bed that night, Daisy and I split a bottle of Chimay. I'm horny, so I try to get things started by rubbing her feet with my good hand. "I hate my job," she says. "I miss the kids. I even miss you."

"Don't go overboard."

"It's true," she says. "I miss you."

I press my thumb inside her plantar fascia until she purrs. "This story might be the thing. I watched the elevator footage today. It's bizarre. This old woman and this ten-year-old kid from the building really do seem to think they're possessed. I can't imagine I won't get more features if I crack this story."

"I hope so," she says. "I'd love to quit the bank."

"Yeah." I listen for blame in her voice but can't find it.

She took the job so we could stop struggling, but it meant giving up on her novel about star-crossed werewolf teenagers in lust. When I read the first chapter, I told her I liked it. This was a lie. It's crap. Then again, I'm having a hard time supporting other people's dreams lately. Probably it's because my book agent dropped me and I haven't had sex in more than three months. For a while, I jerked off in the shower. Now I just dry fantasize about pliant women with kooky senses of humor and large libidos—young Daisys, basically.

"How about another Chimay in the bath? I'll suck your toes . . . ," I say. "Dais?" She's already asleep, her cheek mushed up against the side of the gray Ikea couch.

I press record. "Can you state your name?" I ask.

Margaret Brooks's mouth is her most prominent feature. It juts, horselike. She's a Hungarian immigrant turned 1950s pinup girl who married rich, raised two kids, and has reached the grand age of ninety-three. From the looks of her morphine-brown IV drip, she won't see ninety-four.

"I have many **names,**" Margaret wheezes from her antique wooden wheelchair.

The receiving salon of this classic seven is decorated in 1940s post-war boom: vintage *New Yorker* covers in brass frames; a silver tea service; a Tiffany lamp; a *Playbill* signed by Maria Callas; geometric furniture built to last. Bartók is playing on a restored phonograph—an eerie string piece. There's not a speck of dust or grime, as if the entire room is sprayed daily with a fire hose and then oven baked.

"Would you mind itemizing those names?"

"Pshaw! You're not interested in us! You only like pret-ty young things," Margaret rasps. "The younger the better."

"I'm the father of girls. That's not a funny joke to me," I say.

"**Huhssss,**" Margaret laugh-wheezes, slapping her scarecrow knees. "**Huhssss!**"

"What's so funny?"

She bares her giant horse teeth. They're way too big for her face. "Eat my cock!"

Margaret's granddaughter Minnie, who's been on the couch playing iPhone Zombie Tetris since answering the door, looks up at last. "I just love kids. I wish I had 'em. Cutie little babies! But the clock is ticking, you know? I'm gonna be thirty-five."

I nod. She's at least forty.

"Still," Minnie says as she reaches across the couch to hand her red-eyed grandmother a bottle of Visine, "you should know I'd definitely make a good step-mommy. I'm super nice and I'm okay with not being the most loved."

"Well, you never know. Mr. Right could be waiting for you right now, on a park bench outside Hooters," I say. Then I summon a photo of Ezra on my phone. "Do you recognize this man?"

Margaret flashes a teasing grin. "It's **you**."

"It's my brother, the former elevator operator of this building."

"Sure **looks** like you!" Minnie chimes as she snaps the phone out of my hand.

"He stabbed himself in the basement of this building," I say.

"Ezra Wright," Margaret says, leaning forward, her voice low with the import of a secret. My heart races because I think I'm going to learn something. "I knew him . . . Bad brea-th! **Huhsssss! Huhsssss!**"

Minnie, meanwhile, squirrels my phone down the front of her electric blue Lycra jog tights.

"I noticed that you and Ezra rode the elevator together, sometimes all night. What did you talk about?" I ask.

"The pigs," Margaret says.

"Pigs?"

Margaret points to her head with a liver-spotted finger. "They're cunny pink on the inside too."

I turn to Minnie. "Can I have my phone?"

She sticks out her tongue and squirms it around like a snail loose from its shell. "Can I have your number?"

I ought to be polite for the sake of the story, but this is gross. "My brother died, lady. They found three bodies in the basement of your building and nobody gives a damn. Give me my phone!"

Minnie's mouth makes a lip-gloss-greasy O. She peels the phone from her pants and chucks it at my head.

I catch it. "Thank you from the rock bottom of my heart."

"I hate you!" Minnie cries as she runs into the kitchen. Her giant backside shakes unevenly, as if her ass cheeks are fighting.

Margaret bursts into donkey-bray laughter.

I look out the window, wishing it were open. There's a view of the Park Avenue Armory outside. Guys in hard hats walk the roof, clawing back hundred-year-old slates so they can tier its hulking interior with condos. "We both know you're not really possessed," I say. "You just want to clear your conscience before you die. That's why you agreed to this interview. So clear it."

Margaret's laughter slows. She rubs the tape over her IV needle, which is yellow with age. It can't have been changed in days.

"I've seen the footage. I know you and some kid—Lucas Novo—were in the basement with my brother around the time those homeless men disappeared down there. The autopsy reports show an adult set of gums with a two-and-a-half-inch diameter. Not teeth; gums. I'd say you're wearing your husband's dentures today—that you don't actually have teeth. Funny coincidence, isn't it?"

Margaret tongues the roof of her mouth. *Click!* Her giant dentures unlock. Bright red blood trickles out the sides of her mouth, where the edges have bitten her skin. She uses her index finger and thumb to put them back so she can talk. "You've got some dark secrets yourself," she says. "So don't cast stones."

Minnie's back. She's drying her eyes with a cherry-embroidered handkerchief. I try to smile like I'm happy to see her. "When did this possession begin?" I call to the doorway where she's standing.

"About three months ago, Gray-Grady."

"What was she like before?"

Minnie frowns, and I can see that she's pretty like her grandmother used to be. A Lauren Bacall–type gone to seed. Her eyes are sleepy lidded; her heart-shaped face clean and symmetrical. "The devil didn't change her. Gawd, she probably changed the devil. Did you know my grampa died 'cause she fed him old meat? Scrombrotoxin, the lawyers called it."

"I read that," I say. "Why do you think she was acquitted of his murder?"

Minnie laughs a worldly, bitter laugh. "My mom and uncle died of stomach cancer—a whole lifetime of bad food she made them eat. You could call that murder too. But if you sent everybody to jail for killing the people they're supposed to love, the streets would be pretty empty.

"Anyway, here's what you need to know," she went on. "Bad people are easy to possess—that's why, when the demons excaped, they went to my grandma first. It's the nice guys the devil has to work on, you know? Your brother was real nice."

"Was he?" I ask.

Minnie grins. "You-know. You-know," she sing-songs.

I check the time. This interview began nine minutes ago. I'm screamingly uncomfortable. "A polite suggestion: you both need psychiatrists. Now, Minnie, on the phone you mentioned that your grandmother writes runes. They're these pre-Christian letters that look like knobby sticks. My brother Sharpied your boiler room with them. May I see Margaret's?"

Margaret yanks out her dentures. Her whole face sags as if sucked inside the vacuum of her mouth. "Ignore the idiot! I'll phfow you!" She spins down the hall, morphine IV skating along behind. There's a glue trap stuck to one of her wheels, so the sound goes *roll-scat! roll-scat!*

Minnie and I scurry after. *Roll-scat! roll-scat!* We pass doors on the left and right, all closed. Margaret throws open the last door at the very end, then signals for Minnie to help her turn around and head back. The stink brings water to my eyes and I'm reminded of the boiler room. I feel for a light. My fingers come back gritty.

"Clappy-clap, Grady-Gray!" Minnie calls.

I clap. The grit on my hands dusts the dark.

"You have to clap twice, fast, you silly billy!"

I clap twice, fast. The hall and bedroom lights flick on.

"My god," I say. I wipe my shit-crummy fingers against my khakis and gag. The runes cover most of the walls and the ceiling just over Margaret's king-sized bed. Like Ezra's, they're written backward as a means of cursing their reader with bad luck. Unlike Ezra's, they're written in excrement.

I search the room. It's gross. Hand over mouth (and then spitting, because I've forgotten that my hand is filthy), I open the closet last. Along the doorjamb, she's drawn a row of shit eyes:

One of them looks especially familiar. It looks like it belongs to Ezra. To me. Something slithers. I look at that eye for a long time.

When I come back out, the den where we've been conducting the interview is dark. My stitched hand aches, alternately burning and numb under its gauze bandage.

"Hello?" I call.

Scrape! Margaret crouches beside her wooden chair, knees wide to reveal girdle-tight medical support socks and a thatch of gray pubic hair. I don't know what she's doing at first; I only get that same feeling I had with Ezra in the basement—that's she not a person. That something hard and unknown has shoved itself inside her skin. Then I realize—she's carving the floor with a human tooth.

I panic and get turned around. Minnie's in the kitchen, drinking iced tea straight from a plastic gallon-sized Lipton's jug. Her mouth encircles the entire thing, tongue lunging in and out, fellating it.

When she sees me, she puts down the jug and squares her shoulders. "Silas Burns, you dirty girl killer! Nice to see you. But where are my manners? May I offer you some cold tea?"

"Who's Silas Burns?"

"Nobody! I didn't say anything, you crazy! Shut up and have some tea!"

"Oh. Well. No, thank you. I'll be taking my leave now."

She swipes crumbs from the top of her jog bra. "Did you know? It's super-hard for them to find that perfect kind of fit—somebody nice and smart and I guess the word for it is "ambitious"—somebody like you or Dan Khan, that they can live in for a long time. It ought to be a partnership. Like in your case, you'd get famous, and in return they'd get good press. Or for me, I'd fuck anybody they wanted. And I'd get babies." She laughs and looks out the window behind me, her expression far away. "Little itty-bitty babies that loved me no matter what."

"You can't live like this," I say.

Daintily and for show, Minnie dabs her mouth with her sleeve. "Isn't it just awful, Grady-Gray? I weeaaally need your help."

That's when I notice that the counters are blanketed with bagged foods—Pirate's Booty, Cheetos, Pringles, frozen burritos, jelly beans, coffee cakes, donuts, soda bread—all picked over and riddled with finger holes and saliva-darkened teeth impressions.

"There are services for people like you," I say.

Minnie's fingers glisten slimy yellow with Entenmann's coffee cake. "You got me all wet," she giggles, because she's so punny.

I get the feeling she's referring to something specific. That's when I realize with a nightmarish kind of horror that my pipes are raw. I've recently ejaculated. But where? When?

She comes toward me. I walk backward into the guest salon where the old lady squats. Margaret's free hand has crawled up, rubbing between her legs. The exit is just to the side and through the servant's hall. But they've shut all the doors and it's gotten so dark. Everything feels closed in and wrong.

"Grady?" she asks.

Did I sleep with this awful woman—Minnie Brooks? Have I cheated on my wife?

"I couldn't connect with people the way I wanted after my brother had his nervous breakdown. I shut down as a kind of penance for being the one who didn't get sick. Now that he's dead, I feel like he took a piece of me with him. I'm bereft. I'd like it to be the other way around. I'd like to carry his memory with me instead, do you understand? I want to be whole," I say, as if these harpies will understand and take pity. "Can't you tell me what happened to him?"

Margaret smears the blood from her cut-up mouth to decorate her drawing—a circle of stick figures with giant sex organs: dicks and holes. Squiggling snakes connect one organ to the next.

Minnie follows me to the door. I'm walking backward, she's going forward. It's a long-distance waltz. "Does Daisy give good head, Baby-Grady?"

I get a flash of something impossible: I'm bent over Minnie's pliant body. We're on Margaret's shit-crusted bed. Bartók plays. Did that happen?

I turn the knob behind me. Unlocked. A breeze of clean air rushes against the back of my neck. My god, it's a relief. I'd almost forgotten the outside world existed.

"Oh, Grady. Fuck me, baby, one more time!" Minnie whispers.

I'm out the door, running down the stairs. Margaret's echoless laughter follows me. **"Husss! Husss!"**

"Noooo!" Minnie shouts. "Come back! He raped me! RAPE!"

The next night, when the rest of my family is in bed, my phone rings. I've been transcribing Margaret and Minnie Brooks' interview. The time I spent in Margaret's bedroom fills nearly two unaccountable hours. There aren't any words, just hissing and grunts. Some of those grunts sound like they belong to me.

I remind myself to name-search Anna Beth Cassavetes, the doctor/cop with the Interglot business card, who still hasn't called me back. As I transcribe, I add two people to my list: Silas Burns, the name Minnie Brooks called me in her kitchen, and Dan Khan, the man she claimed was happily possessed.

"Hello?" I ask.

"Grady?" It's in keeping with Tom White's character to call at nine p.m., like the entire world exists to please him. "I read what you sent. It's a joke. Who cares about a couple of methed-up *Grey Gardens* bitches? You've gotta get more witnesses—Lucas Novo for one. And you need the cops to comment on your evidence."

Lucas Novo is the ten-year-old who rode the elevator down to the basement with Margaret and my brother. The footage of him is freakish. He howls at the camera. What's more, the autopsy reports show 1.5-inch diameter bites taken from all three bodies—in other words, a kid-sized mouth. But Lucas's parents are a power couple. She directs global warming documentaries; he funds them as the vice president for oil at Goldman Sachs.

"Novo's parents sent a cease and desist," I say.

"Break into their apartment. Find out if he's got a shrink and hack the records. Anything! Just get the job done."

"You said you don't want legal trouble!"

A muffled, feminine voice comes through on the line. "Hold on," Tom says. I wish I wasn't curious, but I can't help but listen. Is it the ex-wife, the new girlfriend, the twenty-something *New Technology* reporter with the long blond hair?

Words I pick up: *gold, my mom, her lingerie, you prick.*

Nine minutes, eighteen seconds later, Tom's back on the phone. He doesn't even check to make sure I'm still there. "Forget liabilities.

Upstairs turned around on this. They want the story. Your job's at stake. You've gotta hit this full tilt."

"I need parental consent for anything from Novo. He's a minor," I say.

"You think Nigel Jaquiss worried about the slammer?" Tom asks. Jaquiss is the guy who won the 2005 Pulitzer over me. I grind my teeth just thinking about him. "You're sitting on a gold mine—a ten-year-old rich kid murdered and ate three deadbeats from the off-ramp. People in black suits covered it up. Give me proof. Bing-bang-boom, home run! There's your story, Grady. Your book deal too."

I look into the phone, wishing Tom's dick syphilitic so that it might fall off inside the next woman he beds. "You're right," I say. "This is my last shot."

"So?" Tom asks.

"I'll do it."

Once I get off the phone, I call Novo's mother and ask if I can interview her for a piece in the *Times* on global warming. We want to photograph her house and her family. I give her Tom White's name, and she agrees. We're to meet at her apartment next week.

After that, I look up the cop/doctor, Anna Beth Cassavetes. There's no record of her name, which either means it's a fake or she's had her identity scrubbed. The only agency that can pull that off is the U.S. Defense Department. Then I look up Interglot. It's from a Dutch word meaning "jail." The closest instance is also the most likely: Interglot is the name for the offices located in the six basement floors of the Park Avenue Armory.

I look up the armory, which is right across the street from 640 Park. Turns out, it's been owned by the city since it was built one hundred and thirty-five years ago. Budget cuts forced the sale of its upper levels to a real estate titan named Martin Fuller. The city kept the Interglot. A story in the Manhattan construction blog *Demolition* notes that three months ago, Fuller's company accidentally broke through the Interglot's four-foot concrete ceiling. The entire block was evacuated. I scroll through comments and photos until I find something familiar: a crowd of officials in black suits, drinking Starbucks near the hole. I've seen all of them before, in the basement after Ezra died. The woman shielding her pretty blues from the summer sun is Anna Beth Cassavetes.

I call Anna Beth Cassavetes again. It's late and I don't expect an answer, so I'm surprised when I get her secretary. "Are the recent murders at Six Forty Park Avenue related to your building? Did something happen during the construction accident?" I ask.

"Uh?" she says. "Can you hold?"

"Ms. Cassavetes promised she'd let me inspect the Interglot to make sure it's up to code," I lie.

"Code? We just renovated all the cells. Houdini couldn't break out this time."

"So it really is a jail?" I ask.

"Oh," she says, her voice suddenly nervous.

"Who do they hold there? What secret is so great you'd have to clear a city block for it? What did Ms. Cassavetes mean when she told me to call if I had symptoms?" I ask.

Anna Beth Cassavetes's secretary hangs up.

Aloud I inspect the phone and ponder, "What the hell?"

After all that, I'm simultaneously burned out and wired. I'd love to shake Daisy awake and coax her into sex, but I know I'll make zero progress. She works twelve-hour days and is perpetually exhausted. So I check on the girls, who aren't sleeping like they're supposed to but watching Kevin Bacon get stabbed from under a bed in the movie *Friday the Thirteenth*. Little Lisa thinks it's funny. Elaine is crying. To muffle her squeals, she's jammed both her thumbs into her mouth.

"Why are you watching this?" I ask as I turn the thing off.

They both seemed shocked by the possibility that they have a choice in the matter. "This is bad!" I say. "At least, if you're going to sneak, make it a cartoon!" After that, I spend forty minutes answering questions about bad guys, and whether there really are psycho killers with hockey masks at sleepaway camps. Then I read "Three Billy Goats Gruff," a perennial favorite.

"I'll protect you like the biggest billy goat," I tell them.

By the time they fall back asleep, I've lost two hours of work on a deadline too tight to make, and I'm pissed. As I leave, I notice that Elaine has taped a strange drawing over her bed. It's one of her typical triangle-skirted pink princesses, only the princess in question has been bisected by a curved red smear.

Weird.

Back at my desk, I look up the name Minnie Brooks called me: Silas Burns. There's only one on record. I find him through LexisNexis.

Silas was a lecturing mathematician from Quebec City who invented the continuum hypothesis. When he set down roots in Evanston, Illinois, in 1893, little black girls like Elaine and Lisa went missing by the half dozen. With the Great Panic back east, there weren't resources to investigate. Then, in 1895, a six-year-old escaped Silas's root cellar by chewing through her rope restraints and climbing out his coal chute. The milkman heard her moans and drove her away from Burns's property.

This girl wasn't like the rest. She was white. The police got a court order. They found the bodies of twenty-six children, all shallowly buried in his root cellar, all partially eaten. Silas confessed to strangling while raping them, so that he might eat their souls and in that way grow stronger. He claimed to be possessed by a demon he'd met while researching his theories. The demon needed a body. He'd needed the courage to commit the heinous acts he'd always dreamed about. They were the perfect team.

He kept himself busy while awaiting trial by drawing eighty-four sets of eyes along his jail cell's archway. He claimed these came from the souls he'd eaten. When locals set his house on fire, they found the remains of a dozen more young girls, all horribly mutilated. He was sentenced to death by hanging with no audience, at a secret location in Manhattan called the Interglot.

The Interglot?

When I finish reading, I wonder if I've gone crazy like my brother. Obsessive pattern recognition is an early symptom of schizophrenia. I rub my eyes, stretch my legs. Search Silas Burns's name all over again, on a different engine. The first image that pops up is a drawing from the inside of his cellar. The walls are marked by runes identical to Ezra's. One English sentence is sprinkled throughout: *Silas is dead.*

And then, in the very middle, I find something new:

Fucking kyl those litel grrls.

Something inside me squirms. It's like eggs breaking along my face, the yolks falling back behind my eyes. My hand hurts. Everything goes dark.

When I look up, I'm holding a red crayon.

It's dawn now, that wonder hour when I feel most like a stranger in my own home. I check on the girls, then crawl into bed with Daisy. In that moment, it's as if I have a special sense of smell for the female body, and I'm repulsed.

Not that I want them all dead. Of course not.

"Dad!" Lisa calls as she climbs into bed with me three hours later. We've been feeding her too much. She's fat. But we're doing a lot wrong with these kids. Daisy's so fucking lazy.

"Is today a school day?" Elaine asks as she enters the room. She's more polite then her little sister. Then again, she's fragile. You'd think we fed her milk from a barbed wire teat when she was born. She leans against my side of the bed, gazing unblinkingly into my half-open eyes.

Daisy's got a conference at the data center in New Jersey, so it's just the three of us this fine Saturday morning. I sit up. "Clothes," I say. "I'm timing you little bastards."

They scamper from the room like it's the best game in the world. They're back in a blink, wearing fresh footie pajamas under tutus and pink shawls. They've both got watery red eyes from lack of sleep, meaning I should expect double the usual meltdowns. "Two minutes flat," I tell them.

We three stagger into the kitchen. I pour cereal. Then I set up my laptop to stream classic cartoons. It's a weekend tradition. I stare out the window, pretending the best of my life isn't over; they eat Honey Smacks.

Four hours of television later, they get cabin fever. Lisa pinches Elaine, who slaps her face. It's got something to do with a broken pink princess wand. Then they're rolling around the den, bawling, screaming, etc. Someone bangs from the apartment below. It's our bad luck to live over booze hounds with hair-trigger tempers.

I bundle them up and we head to Central Park. On the N train, people stare. "You can't do that," an old black woman tells me, pointing at Elaine's footy pajamas. "That's for bedtime!"

I'm used to this. Old black women all over New York City feel it's their obligation to advise parents on child rearing. Because my daughters are black and I'm white, I'm particularly targeted, as they seem to think I might be a child molester.

I take out my reporter's notebook. "Let me write that down. Pajamas are for sleeping and not for subway rides. Sage advice."

The woman turns to her obese friend. They're sharing a super-sized bag of half-eaten movie popcorn, sitting in the handicapped section while the girls and I stand. "Got no sense," she says.

"No business with those girls," the other woman agrees.

The girls pay zero attention. They're used to this nonsense, just like they're used to being told that blond-haired, blue-eyed people are prettier, and that they come from slaves. Neither of these is true, and I resent all these shitheads we're surrounded by, who feel it's their moral obligation to educate my daughters in victimhood.

We get off at Columbus Circle and our first stop is the hot dog stand. Then the Ramble, where we watch turtles stack on top of one another in the man-made pond, the weird things. By now, the girls' hands have turned red from cold. Lisa's moaning from discomfort. Elaine's threatening to hit her for it. I'm wishing I'd brought scarves and gloves.

From the boulder upon which we sit, we can see the entire East Side: the Metropolitan Museum, the Pierre, the Frick, the Park Avenue Armory. "I always thought we'd live in Manhattan," I tell them. "I wanted you girls to go to a proper school with proper friends."

"We're proper," Elaine says. "I can do capoeira and real ballet."

"And mommy too. Mommy's proper," Lisa adds.

"Do you love us?" Elaine asks, just at the moment when I'm wondering how my career might have progressed without them. It's like she's psychic sometimes.

"I think so," I say.

"You'll never hurt us?"

I feel a rush of fury. My hurt hand stings. "What a terrible thing to think. Why would you ask that?"

"I don't know," Elaine says.

"What are you talking about? Do I know what you're talking about?" Lisa asks.

I want to shove Elaine off the rock and break her in two. Then slaughter her sister. I want to make them disappear. They're mine, so I have that right.

"Of course I love you. I'd never hurt you."

"Really?" Elaine asks.

"Yes," I say.

She starts to cry, so I take her in my arms. She's so sensitive. Just like me. "Promise?" she asks, her brown eyes digging straight into mine, holding me.

"I promise," I say.

Then comes Lisa, who has no idea what's happening but wants to be part of the hug. They're both on my lap. I rub their hands to warm them up, and they kind of purr in gratitude. "Oh my daddy, oh my dadd-a, oh my da-da-, do-be do!" Elaine sings to the tune of "Darling Clementine." "Poopy rabbit, poppa-pooh-pooh, pee-pee-pee, and shoop-dee-doop!" Lisa answers.

Right then, I feel what I've told them. It shivers through me like electricity. "You're everything," I tell them, because they are. "Every goddamned thing."

When we get home, I find Daisy waiting with a huge home-cooked dinner: chicken cordon bleu, baked potatoes, greens, and pumpkin pie. We eat a hot meal for the first time in weeks, sitting at the round kitchen table like normal people.

At bedtime, I notice that there are now a dozen bisected princesses taped over their beds. "Creepy," I say, pointing at the topmost picture, in which a stick figure's been cut open from the waist down, her legs bleeding. Or is it just red trousers over a triangle dress?

"You're crazy!" Daisy answers.

We're exhausted by the time we shut the kids' door, so I'm surprised when Daisy leads me to our bedroom. She hasn't bathed. It's a musky, familiar scent that I used to like but lately seems too human. We make routine love: hands on genitals, quick here, quick there, half clothed. I'm so angry with her. I don't even remember why.

But we keep going. After a while, we loosen up. She lets her belly go slack and so do I. It's playful. To keep from waking our nosy children, she bites my shoulder. Then we lay there. It's the first time we've both sweated in years. I remember then what I've forgotten. I married her because I loved her and could imagine no one else.

"Thank you," I say.

"It's been too long if you have to thank me."

"Yes," I say, still high. "It's my favorite thing."

"I don't always feel as good about myself," she says. "I don't look how I used to. I mean, in high school I was prom queen runner-up. I wish you'd seen me then."

"You're beautiful," I tell her.

"Have you seen my ass? I'm turning into my mother."

"Don't be vain. I like your mother."

"Grady?"

"What?"

"Are you having an affair?"

I laugh, but I'm not amused. "So that's what this is about."

"Are you?"

"No."

"Then why have you been such a weirdo?"

I almost roll over and say nothing. Keep it bottled, so that in my dreams tonight, I'll scream at her. But she's looking at me, her face flushed and frightened. I remind myself that when people ask these kinds of questions, it's because they give a damn. "It's Ezra," I tell her. "He killed those men. He wasn't alone, but still. It's not how I want to remember him . . . I have a theory that it was toxic exposure from a nearby jail—this place called the Interglot—but I can't get the EPA or the Department of Health to investigate. They say they need proof. I can't even get Adult Services to check on these crazy women I interviewed." I look at the ceiling, which is low and cheap. "I feel like the world's run by invisible monsters. I can't navigate it. Everything I do is bound to fail."

"I hear you," she says. "I really do."

"You do?"

"Of course. Look who you're talking to."

"That's my problem with this story! Jesus, with all my stories lately—no one'll talk to me! The people who are supposed to help, they say it's not their job. The cops, social services, environmental services, wrongful-death lawyers—none of them cares! I mean, who cremated Ezra? Not me; I didn't sign any paperwork. Not my parents. So, who did it? And why?"

She presses her bare bottom so it's against my hips. Her warm skin is a salve. "Have you tried a private investigator?"

"There's no money for that." I'm furious. Shaking. "How are we supposed to raise girls in this kind of world?"

"Like people have always done."

I sigh. "I miss Ezra."

"I know," she says. "You're going to be okay, Grady. You'll get through this."

"Thanks," I say, and it occurs to me for the first time that I'm still grieving.

After that, we talk about meaningless things, laughing softly so the kids don't wake. She wants a vacation in the Poconos, so she can take a bath in a champagne glass. I tell her she's gotten tackier with time.

We have sex again. It's better the second time because we're both aroused.

I fall asleep feeling lucky and less angry. I might even be smiling.

First thing Monday morning, I head for my next interview. It's at the armory construction site. A guy in a hard hat takes me up an outdoor elevator. We rise above floor after floor of steel beams until we're at the top, an airy penthouse. The street-side wall isn't there. Everything's open. You could fall right out.

The guy in the hard hat rides back down, leaving me in the penthouse in the clouds. I find a sixty-something-year-old man in a high-backed leather chair. Smoke wafts all around him. "Mr. Fuller?"

He signals for me to take the matching couch, then blows a smoke ring from his Marlboro Red. The gesture is vaguely sexual. **"I'm Dan Khan. I run things."**

The name rings a bell I can't place.

"Sorry. This was supposed to be with Mr. Fuller. What's your capacity?" I ask. "For my article."

He pulls a long drag. His smoke crackles. Another ring. **"Chairman** of the board," he says. **"Fuller's just the president."** Khan's wool suit is perfectly tailored, his six-foot frame tall and fit. I, on the other hand, could pass for homeless. My bandage is bleeding and I haven't shaved yet this week.

"I don't want to squand-er your time, so I'll get right to the point," I say. "No one at the In-ter-glot will take my calls, and I wanted to ask you about the axdent that broke its ceiling."

Dan smiles. His teeth are perfect. **"Of course."**

"Have there been any murders at this site? Complaints of demonic po-ssession?"

Dan puffs out a wide ring. This one hits my chest. **"That's rich,"** he says. I'm about to get up and tell him to blow someplace else, but I realize with stark horror that I can't stand because I've got an erection.

My hands go south and my smile comes fast and forced. I can't calm down. It's like a swollen blister. What's wrong with me? "Well. Ahem. Okay, then. Three people in Six Forty Park Avenue thought they were possessed by demons. I was wondering if you'd had anything like that over here. I believe the symptoms are related to your company's accidental break into the Interglot."

Dan leans forward. He's sitting a lot higher than me. **"Buddy, I agreed to this because I'll scratch your back if you scratch mine. You've gotta be a fucking cracker to think I'd tell you if my staff was demonically possessed. This company's worth three billion. Here's my deal: I've got headaches with the city—they don't want us here, but they can't afford the upkeep. They're trying to Indian give."**

Smoke-ring fragments cling to my arms and legs, wriggling. Does he do this with all his reporters, or am I special? "What do you want me too doo about it?"

"I want you to write a pretty fluff piece about all the happy taxpaying billionaires who're going to live here."

"I don't rite fluff pieces."

"No shit, Sherlock! Look at you," he says. **"You're one of those assholes who thinks he's too special to sell out. So now you can't rub two nickels together and you wish you could do it all over again. Great American fucking tragedy. Am I right?"**

"Well," I say. Something slithers. My stitches have all popped and my bandage is gone. I'm bleeding on his pretty couch and my dick is stiff as a rock.

"**Kid,**" Dan says. He's got the most beautiful black eyes. They're like aggie marbles. "**I've done my homework. I've got an interest in you and that could work out for both of us. This is your last shot at the big top. If you're smart, you'll take it.**"

My blood's soaking his couch, but I'll turn it around. I'll do my job better than I've ever done it before, and he'll forgive my mess. "Why doo yoo nede good press?" I ask. "You've got the deed."

Dan grins. "**Well, like all the girls say, there's lawful possession, and there's consensual possession. But why am I telling you? You don't have the salt.**"

"Give me a chance," I say.

Dan laughs heartily. If I worked for him, I'd be rich and loved and I'd never have to ride the subway again. I'm in love with him, I decide. I'd have his babies if he wanted. Tiny little worm babies.

"**The city lost the space because it filled out some forms wrong, kiddo. We slipped in and nabbed it. Typical red-tape bureau-cracy. The right hand and the left hand and nobody's washing anything.**"

"What about the lower flors? The In-ter-glot? Have you bene there? I have reeson to believe it's a secret jail. I suspect they experimented with psychotropic drugs on the prisoners and now they're trying to cover it up."

Dan waves his hand. "**Who knows with these public titty douches? Listen, they played the poor card and blackballed us for building condos, but nobody's mentioned how much taxpayer money they dropped on this place. And what for? Listen, water levels are rising. We gotta build fifty-foot sea walls all around this chintzy island. Who's gonna pay for that? New York doesn't need working stiffs. It needs taxpaying billionaires!**"

"Oh." Then I get it. I understand. "You plan to acquire the In-ter-glot, and you want my article to pro-pel you toward that goal. I'm to eviscerate the current owners and enginder a popular uproar."

"**The boy can read tea leaves,**" he says, still smoking and exhaling rings. They wriggle all over me, fondling me like gauzy snakes. Am I stroking myself? Why, yes! Oh, god, yes! I am!

"So? Can you horse-trade?"

"I'll do it," I say. "I'll do the best job in the world."

Dan smiles wide. Instead of a tongue, he's got a stump. How's he been talking? Then, I understand. Something else lives in there. It's moist and black and it kisses me.

It happens. I come.

The lights flicker. A pig squeals. My hand opens. Everything blurs. I'm dreaming, and in my dream, a rat bites the strings off a violin. I sink down beneath this floor, and the next, and the next, to the bottom of the armory—the Interglot. I'm trapped in a tiny jail cell lined with funhouse mirrors. The man in the mirrors looks like Ezra: "Get thee to an exorcist!" he shouts.

I wake with a snap, looking back at Dan, who's dripping Visine into his eyes. There are about forty stubbed-out cigarettes in the ashtray; when last I looked, there were two.

"How long have I **be-en** here?" I ask. Words feel funny on my tongue. My skin feels funny on my body.

Dan grins. I get a flash of something—I'm screaming in an impossibly small space, but the scream is wrong. It's the sound of a pig.

"Sorry?" I ask.

"I was just saying how glad I am we met!" Dan announces as he stands and walks me out. **"Now, you write what we talked about, and you'll see, the world will pay you back a thousandfold. Fuck that bitchy little Pulitzer. You'll get a Nobel."**

"Oh . . . What did I say I'd **write**?"

He reaches across me to open the elevator gate. In a glimpse, I can see that he wants to shove me off the ledge, to my death. He's shaking from the temptation of it. But the guy in the hard hat is waiting, so instead he leans in, his eyes utterly black.

"Take good care of those littel little girls."

"I cracked it. There's a tox-on leeking from the lower levels of the arm-o-ry. They've been experimenting with prisoners and chemical weapons. It infected **Margaret Brooks,** and she manipulated the hallucinations of the weeker personalities under her control," I tell Tom

White from my cell phone as I walk across the East Side to the 6 train. "This guy Dan Khan was exposed, too. He's crazy. Anyone near the Interglot too long goes nuts. I've got a touch of it myself."

"Get the hell outta here!" Tom laughs. "I got your article this afternoon. Different direction than we talked about, but it works. Front page, buddy. I love you, you joker. I knew you had it in you." I hear close, loud moaning and realize he's rubbing a girl out.

"Really?" I ask.

"See you tomorrow!" Tom answers, and hangs up.

I load my e-mails and get on the train. It takes two hours to get home because of the transit slowdown. I use the time to read the file I sent to Tom White. Around the time I was sitting with Dan Khan, I apparently wrote and delivered a twenty-thousand-word, three-part series on the battle over the Park Avenue Armory. It's a gorgeous piece of propaganda. I'll have convinced anyone reading it that the armory, including the Interglot, belongs in the hands of the Fuller Corporation. I had no idea I could write this well.

I'm digesting all this as I debark in Queens. A text arrives, telling me that my bank account in Switzerland has been activated. Its first deposit of two million dollars, from the Fuller Corporation, has arrived.

I call Tom White back and tell him he needs to pull my story. It's corrupt. Someone paid me.

He laughs. "Kid, I already kicked it to the top. They love it. And not for nuthin, but who do ya think's paying *me*?" All the while, a woman groans. Still? Is he fucking her or killing her?

I look at my phone. Make sure it's plugged in and I'm really talking to someone. I'm not totally out of my mind. Yes, it's plugged in. "Fuck you. I'm going to the *Post*," I tell him as I hang up.

When I get home, I write about everything that's happened, from the moment I met Ezra at 640 Park until now. The result is too fantastical, even for a rag like the *Post*, so I rewrite it to cover just the things I can prove: three homeless men were found dead and eaten in 640 Park Avenue's boiler room. I can't get police corroboration or comment, but I don't need it. The autopsy, interviews, and photos of runes are enough to indicate that some crazy people live there, and they did some really bad things. I send it to my contact at the *Post*.

When the front door opens and my family arrives home, I'm surprised by the dark. The only signs I've been sitting at my desk for eight hours without moving are my sore hips and the urine I've just released all over my khakis.

Someone has drawn an eye on the palm side of my bandage. It looks like Ezra's eye. Like my eye:

We wake that night when Daisy punches us dead in the chest. It takes us a second to figure out that we're in our bedroom, that it's night, that we're not having a heart attack.

Daisy leaps out of bed. The air smells like her adrenaline. "What the hell, Grady?" Her voice is rags and broken glass.

"Did yoo **hit me?**" we ask.

She peels the neck of her flannel nightgown and angles her left shoulder. Finger-shaped impressions look like they've been branded into her flesh.

"Who did that to yoo?"

She's panting, her face flushed, her polyester nightgown dog ugly. "Listen! I get it. You want more sex. But what the hell? You mount me in the middle of the night and start strangling? Since when are you an animal?"

We notice that the stapler on our nightstand is a perfect blunt object. We could murder her and eat her remains. It would be cleanest. Kindest. Why lead her on?

She follows our gaze, and it's like she's reading our mind. "I think you're having a nervous breakdown," she says. "I don't want to force you into this. But one of us has to call Sinai."

Her thick hair is braided in pigtails so it won't tangle in her sleep. It's glossy and was one of the first things we noticed about her fifteen years ago. "I have vi-lence," we say.

She comes back to bed and sits on the corner nearest us. We giggle on the inside, frown on the outside. She's so dumb. "I wish you weren't so unhappy," she rasps, still holding her throat.

"I'm not un-happy. I'm **dee-lyted.**"

She plants her palms on her knees. Eczema has rosed her finger creases. We'll wait until she looks at us, so she sees it coming.

"Well, I am. I'm unhappy." She looks up, her eyes red, and we forget we're supposed to murder her and rape our children to death. Her expression is scarier than anything Grady's ever seen.

"Yoo don't luve me anymore?" Grady asks.

Her eyes skate over the bare walls, the cracked ceiling, the chintz bedspread. "I feel like the last grown-up in the world." Then she's crying. Tears drip-drop down her nose like snot. "Why do you bother living here? We both know you want to leave."

"That's not troo," Grady says. I say. I'm Grady, aren't I?

"Huh! Huh!" she bawls. Her entire stomach cramps as she gasps for air. "Huh! Huh! I mean, I get it, you resent us. But you've got to stop scaring them. Those drawings you hung over their beds are disgusting!"

"I didn't do them. **E-lane** did."

"I saw you tape them up! I thought it was a joke between you and the girls, but come on. It's not funny. It's sick."

I'm holding her, and I'm crying too. I'm Grady, her husband, and it kills me that she's so sad. It's my job to make her happy, and I keep screwing up.

"Huh! Huh!" she gasps. "You think you're the only one." Her lips draw tight and her brow creases in ugly mockery. "I'm so sad for you that you're not rich and famous. Huh! Huh! I'm so sure it's all our fault. Like I don't have dreams. Like I don't feel trapped. You're so arrogant!"

"It's not that," I tell her. "I'm a-shamed. I hate witnesses."

"What does that mean?" she barks, pure fury. A neighbor bangs and she bangs back with both fists. "Go back to Manhattan, asshole!" Then she turns to me. "Witnesses? What?"

"I'm . . ." I can't say it. It's too hard. But then she stands, and I have the strangest notion that once she leaves the room in that ugly night-gown, she's taking our children and she's not coming back. "I'm a fail-ure!" I bark. "I hate myself. I always have."

"And me?" she asks. "The girls?"

I can't answer. I should, but I can't. "There's something wrong with me," I say instead. "It's a toxicological exposure. The same thing that killed Ezra."

As she looks at me, sees me, her spite recedes. In its place is softness; compassion.

I lay my hand on her throat. It's as if someone set fire to her skin. "That must smart."

She cries more softly now. "How do I make up for hurting you like this?" I ask. "Is this something that can be forgiven?"

She keeps crying and I wish she'd answer. There's this hole in my heart that not even the slithering thing can fill. But at least she's next to me, and we're talking about something besides the children and our jobs and what groceries we can't do without.

"Let me show you something," I say. Then I give her the articles I've written. We stay up most of the night going over my research. It's only then, talking to her, working with her, that I realize I've been lonely too. What a strange thing marriage can be. You can stand next to the person you love for so long that she becomes invisible.

After dropping the kids at school the next morning, Daisy calls in sick to work and we head to the clinic on Ascan Avenue. We tell the on-call doctor I've been having vivid dreams and hallucinations from a potential toxicological exposure. *Also,* I whisper to one of the nurses, *I tried to strangle her. But it's not like it sounds. I don't remember it.*

The staff runs full toxicological panels and neurologic CTs. They release me five hours later with a tube of Visine, saying that whatever the problem, I'm not in imminent danger, though I do have a porous amygdala—my eyes don't blink as often, nor do my pupils react quickly enough to light. They tell me that if it gets worse, we should come back. I find myself wishing I had better health insurance, because I've just been told that I have holes in my brain, and I'm still getting released.

Good news arrives when the senior editor at the *Post* rings my cell. "Classified autopsy reports? A cover-up in a glitzy building? Hot diggety! How can I poach you from the *Times*?"

I quote double my salary and ask for benefits too. Why not? What's crazier, he takes me up on it. I'm suddenly an employee of the *New York Post*. The editor's one condition: I've got to get a comment from

Lucas Novo's family. This is opportune, since I'm supposed to meet them in two hours.

When I get off the phone, Daisy gives me an open-lipped kiss of congratulations. She's genuinely happy for me, and for just a second, I remember that we're on the same team.

"You know," I tell her, "I especially like that the teenaged girls in your novel aren't damsels in distress. Also, your historical details are pitch-perfect. Mustard gas! I feel as if I'm really inside a mobile hospital on the western front."

She beams. And I mean *beams*. She's a laser of joy bopping inside a chunky blue sweater and high-waisted mom jeans. "Really? You like it? Because I thought you didn't."

"I love it," I tell her. "I'm so proud of you."

She grins wide as a cat. "I love you."

I want to answer in kind, but something holds me back. What if this mutual goodwill cascades and I wind up telling her about the giant fucking snake in my mouth?

She frowns. "Oh, Grady. Get over yourself."

We split up. She heads to Metropolitan Avenue to pick the girls up from school. I take the subway to Manhattan for my final interview. I wave to her and watch her get smaller, and somehow, I know that Grady Wright will probably never see her again.

On my way to 640 Park Avenue, I pass the armory. There's this tiny steel door at the bottom of a set of stairs. You can hardly see it beneath all the construction. A posted sign reads:

Interglot
Reduced Hours Due to Government Slowdown

At 640, I make it past the doorman without any problems. It's like I'm invisible. The new elevator guy is at least eighty years old. He stinks horribly, his breath a rat's caked nest. That same skinny woman as before joins us on the second floor. She stinks too, and her lips are missing. She's chewed them clean off.

As we ride, everything closes in. The space is too tight. I can't breathe. A wriggling slug unfolds inside me. Its arms extend in every direction, as if it's a plow packing the loose snow of my organs tighter and tighter.

"Are we dy-ing?" I ask.

"**Hssss!**" workout shrew answers.

Two young men in business suits board on four. A family with teen-aged kids boards on five. Slug-widthed serpents slither out from the teenaged kids' mouths like second tongues.

"Are we **bio-log-ic-al** weapons? Will we **die** of cancer?" I ask. No one answers.

"**Last stop!**" the operator calls at six. "**Everyone off!**"

All ten of us head in the same direction. The kid holding the door open at the end of the hall has sandy brown hair and a freckled nose. It's Lucas Novo. He's standing beside his parents, both of whose eyes are gouged out. Tentacles flick from their empty sockets like upended hermit crabs.

We go in. Lucas shuts the door behind me.

The apartment is enormous, with vaulted twelve-foot ceilings and marble floors. On the mantel are photos of Novo's parents tucked between famous actors and lesser-known but far more powerful poli-ticians, like John Blankfein, the head of the World Bank.

We converge around an oak dining table, where the fading sun-set casts fractured rainbows through the crystal chandelier. I squeeze between two businessmen to see what's for dinner: a gutted horse, still saddled. Its leather etching reads: Preakness, 2016.

The people around the table—the inhumans—begin to feed. Giant black slug-snakes slither in and out of their mouths, lapping.

I decide this isn't happening. I'm not here, even as Minnie Brooks sneaks up and drops a rubber monster mask over my head. The eye holes don't line up and I can't see anything but low-down pricks of light. I can't move. I can't speak.

The squirming thing fills my voids. It presses against the wound in my hand, and my chest, and my throat, until the real me retreats. I'm banished to a dark place with a window so tiny that I have to squint to see outside. Someone else is driving me.

My driver takes me closer to the table. I'm standing over the horse. I think I'm eating it.

"**Grrls!**" a voice says. And then they're all chanting with what words they're still able to speak: "**Kill the girls! Keel huh grrls! Kuh-th-grls! Kuh-th-grs! Kuh! Kuh! Kuhhh!**"

My voice joins, only it's dead and without echo: "**Kill the girls!**"

The next thing I know, I'm on the subway to Queens, my mouth wet with horse blood.

We're standing in our daughters' bedroom. Someone is shouting. Another is banging. Then comes a scream. It's Grady, trying to break from his attic.

"Yes. Obviously it's an emergency!" Daisy says into her cell phone. She's cornered against the window, the girls behind her. Her left eye is swollen shut like she just got sucker punched. "He outweighs me by thirty pounds! Please, hurry."

We come closer.

She drops the phone. "The police are on their way," she says, like this isn't an outer borough, like budget cuts haven't castrated the entire emergency system. Like we don't have all the time in the world.

The girls' bare knees edge out from behind their mother, giving the impression of a disfigured, feminine beast. Daisy smiles a fake, placating smile and steps forward. "Now, Gra—"

We bash the side of her face with a Swingline stapler. She falls nose first into the nest of pillows on the floor. Like blades of grass missed by a great and terrible mower, the girls stand unmoving at her sides.

"Trip-trap, trip-trap!" we shout. "Gobble-gobble!"

A thick black tentacle bursts through Grady's broken hand. It wiggles and giggles, and we laugh too. "Come grls!" we say.

Elaine does as told. We take her into our slithering arms and squeeze.

Neighbors bang on all sides. "Shut up!" a man shouts from below. "Keep those kids quiet!" Daisy moans on the floor and starts crawling. We step on her back. Inside us, Grady rages.

We don't do these things because it pleases us to harm. We do them because nothing has ever pleased us.

"**Trip-trap!**" we scream at little Lisa. "**Come kiss us or we'll break your sister's neck!**"

Lisa won't budge. We swing a tentacle arm and pull her in while she kicks. Now we have them both. We giggle. We cry too. Because it's so sad and funny and ugly.

"Daaaddy!" Elaine shrieks. "Let go!"

We shove them both to the floor, our knees dug into their small bellies as we bind the bigger one's hands to her feet with a pair of rainbow tights. She's doesn't fight us. She's too scared. She's weak Elaine.

We move on to Lisa. She wriggles free and bites our tentacle.

It's red-hot pain. We slap our wet arm against her face. Her small skull hits the floor. She stops moving.

Grady rages. He's watching through his tiny window, trying to get out and drive. We decide it's time. He's ready. He wants this too. We unfurl, filling all the spaces, even the attic where we've locked him. There's nowhere left for him to live, except as part of us.

"Help me, Daddy," Elaine calls from the floor.

Grady hears. Through his tiny window, he sees his girls on the floor. He courses through us, a burning behind our black eyes, then our chest, our legs, and at last, he breaks through, into our true body. He's doesn't dissolve like the others before him. He's stronger than we thought and he's everywhere as he raises our arm and bites down, into our black flesh.

"**Hssss!**" we scream. His teeth come out, all eight, and ride us like shark fins. It hurts. We retreat from that hurt, pulling our tentacles back inside, shrinking our skin from his holes like a salted slug.

While we're gone, the fucker gets control and starts driving.

"Avert your eyes, ladies," Grady says as he steps over his family's bodies. Then he opens their bedroom window and jumps.

Grady breaks a leg, the dumb shit.

We're disappointed. We can't absorb Grady, but he can't keep us out, either. It's a loss like his brother. We'll need a new host. By the time the police show up, we've regained control. He's back in his attic.

Two men strap us into a straitjacket and carry us in a stretcher down the block. Pedestrians gawk. We stick Grady's stumpy, ragged tongue out at them. When we get to the armory, a woman—Anna

Beth Cassavetes—ushers us down the steps and inside the old jail we've inhabited for the last hundred and fifty years.

A pneumatic glass door opens with a fresh-sounding pop. Jailers in white lab coats wait on the other side. Cassavetes shines a light inside our open mouth. "He's not fused!" she shouts.

They move with great speed. We're shoved in a wheelchair and rolled through a long corridor that opens up to barred jail cells with soundproof glass inlays. The floors are dirt and broken clay.

We pass the first cell. Margaret Books has lost her dentures and eaten the outsides of her mouth. Her face is a bloody star. After that is Minnie, who slams herself against the glass, her belly pregnant with slithering tumors. We keep going, past Lucas Novo and his dinner party. They howl and hoot and fling their excrement. The skinny workout woman from the elevator looks down at us, her expression no different.

We know her. We know all of them, and all their memories. Like your God, we are one.

We go down one more level. We're out of the prison and in a medical lab with bright lights. Orderlies strap us onto a bed.

"It's deep," says a woman in white. She flicks our cheek with her index finger, the rude thing. "Do you know its name?"

"We have many names!" we say.

Grady's family enters with Cassavetes. They surround us, hot breathed and hurt but still standing. Grady shouts from his attic, but no one can hear. *Don't look at me!* he cries. *You're safe. Run away!*

"Listen closely, Grady. You need to say the name of your demon. Do you know it, or am I gonna have to run through the whole list of escaped convicts with you?" Cassavetes asks. Then, to the family, "He's gonna need your help."

"Mares eat souls and does eat souls," we say. **"Wouldn't you?"**

"Silas Burns," Daisy says. "That's the name from his notes."

One of the men in white whistles. "Silas? That's a bad one."

"Can you say that, darlin'?" Cassavetes asks. "It's two little words, and I know you can do it, 'cause you still got your tongue."

Silas Burns! Grady shouts from his attic. But he's not driving. We push him farther away until his has no window. He's locked in total darkness. We burst his puppet edges. His nose, eyes, and ass are bleeding. We will not be evicted from this body. Never again will we live in a pig.

"Say its name!" Daisy cries. She's bent over us, her head pressed against our chest, crying. "Oh, for the love of god, say it!"

"Trip-trap!"

"Forget it," one of them says.

"Y'all, I'm so sorry for your loss," Anna Beth Cassavetes answers. "Lock him up."

Daisy blocks the bed's front corner wheel with her foot. She shoves hard on our forehead so we can't lunge or bite, then gets in our face. "You want it out. I know you." Her image is distorted. Her eyes are too small, her nose too wide. It's not a human way of looking at people, but like perceiving through a funhouse mirror. "You love me."

"Say it, Daddy," Elaine cries. "Say it!" Lisa chimes. "Say it! Say it! Say it!" says Daisy. And then all three shout, "Say its name!"

Grady tears at the black but there's no way out. He's so far away he can't hear.

"Say it!" Grady's family keeps crying.

In the attic, their voices take on a new property. They become a light: *Say it! Say his name!* The light shines under the locked door, which is how Grady finds the handle. He twists. Pulls. The family knows, with a gut-level intuition, that he hears and needs them. They keep chanting: "Say it! Say it!" The room brightens like dawn. All is illuminated.

It occurs to him (to me, I'm Grady!) that when people die, they see this light and mistake it for God, when it's actually just the last glimmer of the people they love, calling them back.

"I can't do this without you, Grady," Daisy says.

I shoulder the door. It won't open. But I can't give up, because I know what will happen to them once I'm gone. I was broken when Ezra got sick, and a part of me never recovered. It left a space for this terrible thing to grow. If I leave my family, they'll be broken too. I will not surrender them to an indifferent world populated by invisible monsters.

"Come back, Daddy," Elaine says.

"Silas Burns," I whisper. "You're not welcome here."

The door swings open. I say it again. My tongue moves with the words. "Silas Burns, I cast you out!"

I'm in a hospital room, surrounded by people in white coats. A woman yanks the edge of the slug from my mouth. With the help of the guy standing next to her, she gets enough slack to wrap the slithering thing around a cylinder, then brings down a thin, metal bar that locks into place. Three people turn a lever that twists the cylinder. They pull the slug from me, inch by inch. My jaw unhinges. The demon is the width of a liter-sized bottle of Coke. By the time they finish, they've pulled out nineteen feet of slack. It shrieks, this terrible, high-pitched birdcall, as it shrinks in the atmosphere to the size of a garter snake.

A door opens. In comes a screaming pig. They feed the snake to the pig.

And then I'm empty. It's almost as lonely as losing a twin. Everything goes black.

I'm able to walk out of the hospital room on crutches. I'm led past another wing, full of pigs locked in separate cells. Then I'm deposited into a packed waiting room with linked chairs. Some people are alone, some with friends. I spot a guy in a business suit from Lucas Novo's party. His lips are stitched back onto his face, and he's scrolling through e-mails on his cell phone.

In the corner, I see Daisy and the girls. I get to them as fast as my crutches will take me. I can't help it, I'm crying. "Girls," I say.

Daisy stands. I drop the crutches and take her in my arms. She stiffens. I hold her until she goes soft. She cries into my shoulder.

"Please don't send me away," I say.

After a while, we sit. The girls won't look at me. I don't want to scare them, so I wait. Minutes pass. Lisa scoots from her chair and touches my stitched hand. "A monster lives in you," she says.

"It did. It's gone."

She climbs over the chair, into my lap. "Gone?"

"Gone. Never coming back."

Lisa closes her eyes and almost immediately falls asleep.

There's Elaine left, yet. I wait a half hour, then hand Lisa to Daisy and kneel before Elaine's chair. "I'll spend the rest of my life making this up to you and your sister and your mother," I promise.

She looks at her hands.

I sit back down. She stays in that chair, watching the Shake Weight infomercial on the wall-mounted television for another twenty minutes. I'm about ready to beg all over again, when she comes back and stands in front of me. I don't want to scare her off, so I don't speak directly to her.

"Whatever you want, I'll do," I tell them all.

Lisa wakes. We all hold hands. Soon, the girls cry. They recount what happened from their small perspectives. Daisy and I listen and try to hold them in such a way that they don't see we're crying too.

After a few hours, Anna Beth Cassavetes calls us into a bustling office. There's only room for two chairs, so the girls sit while we stand. Everything's cheap and fluorescent, like a discount store's corporate office. "I'm your caseworker," she tells us. "That was a serious infection. But I see here that y'all have clean bills of health."

"That's what you said last time. Why didn't you ever call me back?" I ask.

"The city's overrun," she tells me. "I didn't have the manpower."

I expect an explanation. Instead she walks us to the dimly lit exit, just below the armory construction. "Y'all are free to go!"

By the time we get back to Queens, it's dawn the next day. My newspaper article in support of the Interglot's buyout is on the welcome mat. Next to that, a headline announces the gruesome murder of three hookers by the paper's publisher, Tom White. He claims he doesn't remember what happened, that something possessed him.

The two million dollars is gone from my account.

We spend the morning cleaning the kids, the house, ourselves. After that, the four of us play Go Fish, walk the neighborhood, get souvlakis, and come home again. I've got a message waiting from the editor at the *New York Post*. He says several occupants of 640 Park Avenue have been arrested for murder. My story's going to scoop every other outlet in town. He wants to know what I've got next.

I still remember the demons' collective memories. I know where the escaped ones are hiding. Their corruption is what I'll report on. Because it's everywhere.

But for now, we rest on the couch as a family, each fitted together under a warm blanket, like perfect jigsaw pieces. I turn to Daisy and tell her, "I'm the luckiest man alive."

The Words

SCOTT STEWART

It wasn't until their fifth session that Dr. Beth Harper first heard Toby Rheva speak. As far as she knew, the boy hadn't said a word to anyone in the six weeks since the murders, leading Beth to determine he suffered from progressive mutism brought on by acute traumatic stress disorder. He had been, quite literally, scared silent.

Toby's case, and the particulars of how he came to be in her care, were among the most disturbing Beth had encountered in her sixteen years treating child trauma survivors. The Padesky Murders were shocking as much for their casual brutality as for how quickly the public nodded and moved on, numbed by the twenty-four-hour news cycle's unyielding stream of similar atrocities. The story was all too familiar. Jerry Padesky shot his wife and two children to death before killing himself. Twelve-year-old Toby and one of the dead children, a nine-year-old girl named Sara Brobeck, were under the foster care of the Padeskys, a detail not originally found in the news reports but later revealed to Beth by Toby's caseworker.

Married fourteen years to Anne Padesky, Jerry Padesky had no criminal record, no history of psychiatric issues, and no chemical dependencies to explain why he went to the basement of his Langston Street row house that uncharacteristically warm March night and loaded his father's hand-me-down Savage 99 rifle. He then climbed the stairs to the second floor, passed through his bedroom to the bathroom where his wife stood brushing her teeth, and shot her in the face.

The force of the blast knocked Anne Padesky into the bathtub, where the police found her and fragments of her teeth approximately twenty minutes later.

What happened next is less clear. Neighbors reported hearing that initial gunshot at five after eleven, at which time they called 911. Over the following thirteen minutes, Jerry Padesky lined up his ten-year-old son, John, and foster daughter, Sara, in the upstairs hallway, where he shot them at point-blank range, then carefully placed them in their beds, as if they were sleeping. Finally, he went downstairs to the living room, where he sat in his favorite chair and put the rifle in his mouth.

The police didn't know how Toby escaped Jerry Padesky's deadly march through the house. Given where he was found, they could only assume the child was sneaking a late-night snack when he heard the shot that killed his foster mother. According to the crime-scene report, the police were in the house an astonishing forty minutes before they discovered Toby. Officer Ramirez was standing in the living room near Jerry Padesky's body when he heard a faint whimper coming from the kitchen.

"At first I thought it was a family dog or something," Ramirez later recounted. "The place was such a horror show, we had no idea what we'd find. I've seen some pretty fucked-up things, but this? Nothing like this. Anyway, we entered the kitchen, and for a moment we didn't hear shit, so I started thinking my ears were playing tricks. Nerves can do that to you. But then we heard it again, all of us this time—a child crying—and nobody breathed. We found the boy under the sink, wedged between the disposal motor and cans of roach spray, bone white and shivering, like some kind of animal waiting for the slaughter. I don't know who was more scared, him or me.

"We couldn't get the kid to talk. Not a word. Needed a neighbor to identify him. He had this look in his eyes like he'd seen the devil himself. Can't get it outta my mind, that look. Only other time I saw something like it was in Kabul. We'd be clearing a house of mujahid-een, most of 'em in body bags, and sometimes we'd find their kids hiding, pale as ghosts, piss running down their legs from the fear. Toby Rheva looked at us like that."

———

A social worker brought Toby to Beth's office twice a week. At the first session, they were accompanied by a homicide detective named Alice Ganza, a fireplug of a woman, small and tough. "No one's been able to get through to him," Ganza told Beth, nodding to the dark-haired boy with the haunted eyes sitting in her waiting room. "I'm hoping you can." Then she added, "It's not just to help him cope with what happened."

"I don't understand," Beth said. "You know Padesky did it. What else is there?"

Ganza shifted her weight, as if unsure how much she wanted to share. "You're right. Officially, the case is closed," she said. "But I *knew* Jerry Padesky. We weren't close but I knew him well enough. His boy John was friends with my son." Beth went still. She was no longer talking to a cop. She was talking to a mother. "People close to these kinds of killers always say they had no idea so-and-so was capable of such a thing, and I never buy it," Ganza continued. "I've been working homicide for twenty years and there are always signs. No matter how out of character the act may seem at first, if you dig deep enough, you will find some overlooked detail that whispers in your ear, *This one's a monster.* But with Jerry?" She shook her head. "I've gone over it six ways from Sunday, and I still can't find a damn thing that convinces me the man I knew was capable of killing his own family. Something *happened* to Jerry Padesky, Dr. Harper. Something that changed him. And that boy is the only person alive who might know what it is."

There was a troubled silence before Beth spoke. "I'll do what I can," she said, "but my first responsibility is to Toby, and I won't force a child to relive a trauma he's suppressing before he's ready."

Ganza gave Beth a hard look, as if she'd been reserving judgment about the kind of person Beth was and had finally come to an unpleasant conclusion.

"Of course," she said, handing Beth her card. "Call me if anything comes up."

Four sessions had passed since Beth began treating the silent boy. Despite her efforts to draw Toby out by encouraging him to play and express himself, he remained verbally unresponsive, and she decided to take a new approach.

"Your teacher, Ms. Barnes, told me you're good at art," she said to him.

Toby stared into his lap and shrugged in a way that suggested he didn't disagree with the statement. Beth placed a sheet of blank paper on the coffee table in front of him along with a basket of colored pencils.

"I was wondering if you would draw something for me?" Toby eyed the paper with rising interest and shrugged again. Beth smiled, taking that as a yes. "Okay, I'd like you to draw a picture of a tree, a house, and a person. Can you do that?"

After a moment, Toby slid forward on the couch and peered into the basket of colored pencils. Choosing a green pencil, he began to draw. Line by line, color by color, the images formed with care and precision. First the tree, then the house, and finally, the person. Occasionally, he glanced up at Beth, looking for approval. She was careful to smile and nod her assent for him to continue. When he finished, Toby sat back on the couch as if to say, *Now what?*

"May I look at it?" she said, rotating the drawing to her. What she saw caused her smile to waver. It wasn't what he had drawn that disturbed her so much but rather what he *hadn't*. "This is very good, Toby," she said in a measured tone. "Ms. Barnes was right about how talented you are. Can I ask you some questions about your drawing?" She pointed to the house with its rectangle base, triangle roof, and four squares for windows.

"Where is the door?" Toby offered his now familiar shrug. "Well, then how do people get in or out?" she pressed. His eyes shifted between her and the house as if the idea never occurred to him. Sensing him start to close down, she moved on to his drawing of the person, which was little more than a stick figure with a large circular head, black dot eyes, and a jagged mop of brown hair like Toby's own. In this image too something important was missing.

"You didn't draw a mouth," Beth said. Toby stared at the face of the figure, fear crossing his expression. "How does he talk?"

He looked up from the drawing, his dark eyes drilling into her.

"He doesn't," the boy said in voice that was high and clear.

Beth's breath caught in her throat, as if all the air had been drained from the room. She should have felt a sense of breakthrough and professional accomplishment at hearing him finally speak, but something about his voice, its lingering prepubescent register mismatched with his older boy's countenance, cut through her like a hot knife. She pictured herself standing on the edge of a precipice while across from her, on the other side, was Toby Rheva, her patient, a traumatized boy, beckoning her forward.

Beth's father was a minister at the Grace Baptist Church in Fairchance, a small borough on the outskirts of Fayette County, Pennsylvania, where she grew up. Her mother died when Beth was three, and her father chose God and a fifth of bourbon over remarrying, leaving her an only child in an otherwise empty house. During the summers, when she was off from school, Beth's father would pack her into his rusting Ford F-150 and drive south from Fairchance into West Virginia, stopping to preach in towns even smaller than theirs with names like Monongah, Granville, and Salem. She would watch him from the back of the pews, thick sweat slicking his forehead, his hollow voice settling over the parishioners like a gray fog.

> "In the beginning was the Word, and the Word
> was with God, and the Word was God."

On their long rides home, her father, flush with the pride of being heard, would tell Beth how it was their duty to spread the Gospel, to share the Word of God with as many people who would listen and, even more important, with those who would not. Beth loved these hours alone with him, the rise and fall of his speech, the comforting glow of his attention.

Not all their road trips south went so well. Sometimes no one would show up to hear him speak, and Beth's father, a stubborn man if ever there was one, would preach to an empty hall. On these occasions, Beth would sit close to the pulpit, careful to hang on his every word, hoping he would feel it was enough that *she* heard him. Afterward, they would drive the hundreds of miles home in silence, her father's heavy-lidded eyes fixed on the dark road ahead, a cigarette dangling from his lips and an open bottle of Jim Beam on the seat. Beth could sense the quiet storm of anger building in his mind with each passing mile. She longed to speak to him, to fill the silence with the sound of familiar voices, but she knew this would only make him angrier. He withheld his voice as punishment for her sins. *She* was the reason why no one came to hear him preach. It was the only reason that made sense to her.

As the years passed, her father's silence grew until Beth became lost in its inescapable shadow. He preached less and drank more. He no longer took her on his summer trips south, leaving her to be cared for by old Ed and Mary Clancy, members of their congregation and the closest either of them had to family.

"Your daddy loves you, Beth," Mary Clancy said, helping her onto the porch, suitcase in hand, as she watched her father's truck disappear down the road. "Even if he can't always find the words to express it."

When news came of her father's death in a road accident one summer when she was fifteen, Beth reacted as he would have, not with sound and fury or cries of anguish, but with silence.

At home that night after her session with Toby, Beth watched her husband, Alan, help their eight-year-old daughter, Rose, with her spelling. Rose sat on the living room floor, her worksheets spread around her, chewing the end of her pencil, staring expectantly up at Alan as he read aloud sentences for her to write down. *"She could not see the coat that hung behind the door."* Rose pitched her head up, eyes narrowing, spelling the words in her mind before committing them to her worksheet. A moment later, she looked up at her father again, ready for more. *"Do not show her the small mirror that broke."* Beth frowned at Alan.

"That's really what it says?" she asked.

He turned the study guide to her with a smirk.

"That's not even the weirdest one," he said. "How about, *'Soon the boy will tell you about the bear?'* "

Beth laughed.

"Whatever happened to those lists of like-sounding words to spell? Lock. Smock. Clock."

He smiled at her. "Care. Dare. Stare."

Rose lifted her gaze from her worksheet to watch her parents, unsure of what kind of game they were playing.

"I have news," Beth said to Alan in bed that night. "The new boy I'm treating, I got him to talk."

"That's fantastic, honey," he said, putting his hand on hers. "You should feel proud."

She nodded with a half smile, comforted that he knew her well enough to sense she felt something less than pride. He went back to his book, and then, realizing he'd forgotten something, looked up at her again.

"Did he tell you what happened?"

"No," she said. "But he will."

Toby's opening up was like the easing of a tightly knotted fist. He was never going to be a verbose child, but she soon had him talking freely about the food in the state-run home he was currently living in—bland—or a cartoon he liked on television—*Star Wars Rebels*. After a time, it seemed he would talk about anything—anything, that is, but the Padeskys. Whenever she asked him questions about them, Toby would fall silent again, abruptly ending what had otherwise been a productive session.

"We're making good progress, but it's going to take time," Beth told Detective Ganza during one of her follow-up calls. Beth sensed the only reason the city was paying for Toby to see her instead of some wet-behind-the-ears grad student was because of Ganza's continued interest. As soon as the detective had the information she wanted, or believed no new information would be forthcoming, Beth's sessions with Toby would end. Despite Beth's professional reluctance to push her patients, the reality of this time pressure weighed on her.

"I'm sure you'll do your best," Detective Ganza said after a long silence.

Her "best" was a variation on a novel therapeutic technique used to treat post-traumatic stress disorder called eye movement desensitization and reprocessing. EMDR involved encouraging the patient to talk about the traumatic event while pulsing a light in his peripheral vision. The light disrupts the body's physical stress response often felt when recounting a traumatic memory, allowing for gradual desensitization and recovery, or so the theory went.

At their next session, Beth dimmed the lights in her office and told Toby they were going to play a game wherein he was to describe as vividly as possible whatever she asked him. They had already played a number of "games," and Toby had responded positively to each of them. She started with the innocuous, asking him to describe things she knew he enjoyed talking about: the *Star Wars Rebels* TV show, the latest Jay-Z album, an old gray cat he cared for at the Home. All the while, she held a penlight near his right temple, just on the edge of his peripheral vision, and clicked it on and off as he spoke. *Click on. Click off. Click on.*

When she sensed he was ready to proceed, she eased him into a more difficult subject.

"Describe your room at the Padeskys." *Click on. Click off. Click on.* At first Toby looked at her, unsure, like a child standing at the edge of a pool, staring at a parent, arms outstretched, who's telling him to jump. Beth was afraid Toby would fold in on himself, as he had done many times before, ending this experiment in failure, but then, after a swollen silence, he spoke.

"It was okay, I guess. Kinda small. I shared it with John."

Beth was so surprised by his response that she forgot to operate the penlight. She regained her composure and shifted the light from Toby's right temple to his left.

"Tell me about living with the Padeskys." *Click on. Click off. Click on.* This time, Toby's response came more easily. He told her that he missed Mrs. Padesky's meat loaf and that Mr. Padesky could make him laugh with his funny faces. He most enjoyed Sundays, when the entire family would watch football in the living room and Mr. Padesky would shout at the television.

As the words began to flow from Toby, Beth couldn't help but feel she was experiencing one of those moments she'd only dreamed of as a therapist. How many times had she imagined herself like Judd Hirsch in *Ordinary People,* the heroic therapist helping a desperate and suicidal patient face his most traumatic memories and be miraculously healed? All through the power of talk. So hypnotic was her reverie that it took her a moment to realize that Toby's recollections had taken a disturbing turn.

He was talking now about Sara, the other foster child who came to live with the Padeskys only a few months before Jerry Padesky put her to sleep for the last time. She was quiet and scared, Toby said. All he knew about her was that her mother had died in a car accident and that Sara had been in the car when it happened. At first, she didn't say much to anyone and stayed in her room most of the time, but eventually, little by little, she began to talk to Mr. Padesky. She felt safe with him.

Then, one night, a week before the murders, Toby overheard Mr. Padesky arguing with his wife. He sounded different, somehow. He kept talking about Sara's mom and the car accident until Mrs. Padesky told him to stop because he was scaring her. He said he needed Sara to tell him what happened.

Beth lowered the penlight, the elation of moments before replaced by a jolt of confusion and fear, the self-reflexivity of the boy's story making her think of a snake biting its tail. She felt as if she'd wandered halfway down a road she no longer wished to be on, but she knew she couldn't stop now.

"Did he?" she asked, forcing herself to raise the penlight again. "Get Sara to talk about the accident, I mean?" *Click on. Click off. Click on.*

Toby nodded, his eyes locked on hers. "Yeah, and that's when he started telling us about the Mouth."

"The Mouth?" she said, her throat dry, her voice barely above a whisper.

"The one inside his head," the boy replied. "He said it talked to him. Told him to do things."

So there it is, Beth thought. The whispering detail that Ganza failed to find had at last revealed itself. Despite Jerry Padesky having no history of psychiatric issues, he'd been hearing voices, a textbook paranoid schizophrenic, and tragically no one noticed. It made perfect sense, she thought, given what he had done.

But Toby wasn't finished talking, and what he said next made no sense at all.

"Mr. Padesky said the Mouth spoke to Sara's mother too."

Beth was quiet at dinner that evening, and Alan took care of Rose so she could go to bed early. At first Beth's dreams were untroubled, but as the night wore on, an image surfaced out of the recesses of her subconscious. She saw a mouth, disembodied, floating in darkness, its lips a flaccid gray with skin cracked, but the teeth? Oh, the teeth were fine, ramrod straight and glistening white.

"I'm sure you'll do your best," the Mouth said in Detective Ganza's voice. *Do your best. Do your best. Do your best!*

"Honey?" she heard Alan say. "Who are you talking to?"

Beth was awake now, standing in the kitchen near the dim light of the stove. She looked up to see Alan leaning against the doorway, rubbing the sleep from his eyes.

"You okay?" he asked.

She nodded quickly, trying to hide her disorientation. That's when she realized he was staring at the kitchen knife in her hand.

The days passed and the Mouth increased its hold over Beth, until thinking of It became like an unconscious tic or mannerism, a part of her she couldn't control.

Sometimes the Mouth looked like her father's, with his reed-thin lips set against those small, tobacco-stained teeth. When It spoke, she heard *his* voice:

"In the beginning was the Word, and the Word was with God, and the Word was God."

Other times the Mouth was Alan's:

"Lock! Smock! Clock! Soon the boy will tell you about the bear!"

She tried everything to silence It. Talking with patients. Turning up the volume of the television. Increasing her daily dose of Lexapro. Nothing worked. Its voice was always there just below the surface, inhabiting her.

Detective Ganza had given Beth the case files on the Padesky murders in the hope that some kernel in them would help her draw out Toby. She hadn't looked at the files since their first session, finding little of therapeutic value. Now she returned to them, a question gnawing at her, searching for information, not about Toby, but about the other foster child, Sara Brobeck. As Toby told her, Sara had been under the Padeskys' care a shorter time than Toby, arriving only a few months before the murders, after having been bounced from foster home to foster home for more than a year. Beth could find no explanation for why none of the prior placements had stuck, other than a single cryptic comment on one of the transfer forms calling her behavior "antisocial and uncommunicative, likely due to acute traumatic stress disorder." Beth stared at the diagnosis. It wasn't unusual for children in the foster care system to be afflicted by similar disorders—after all, if their lives were easy, they wouldn't be in the system in the first place. But the parallels between Sara and Toby's cases troubled her. It was almost as if the trauma had been passed from one child to the other. She looked through the case files again, searching for details about the car accident that killed Sara's mother, but there were none.

Detective Ganza sounded surprised to hear Beth's voice when she called her a few minutes later.

"How's Toby?" Ganza asked.

"We're making good progress."

"Is there something I can help you with, Doctor?"

"I hope so," Beth said. "In our last session, Toby mentioned something about the other foster child, Sara Brobeck, appearing traumatized by the accident with her mother, but I couldn't find any information about the accident in the files."

"There isn't much to know," Ganza said. "Sara was wearing a safety belt in the backseat and survived when her mother drove off the highway late one night and collided with a lamppost. It was assumed she must have fallen asleep at the wheel."

"Why assume that?" Beth heard herself say. She had the sudden sensation of coming unmoored from her own body.

"Because she never used the brakes," Ganza replied. "There were no skid marks on the road."

Beth's pulse exploded in her ears with a deafening thrum. She felt sick, a pit opening up in her stomach. *Mr. Padesky said the Mouth spoke to Sara's mother too,* she heard Toby say, and Beth pictured herself sitting next to nine-year-old Sara Brobeck, strapped into the backseat of her mother's car. *Hold on, darling,* her mother said with a smile, unbuckling her safety belt and pressing the accelerator to the floor. *It'll be over in a minute.* Beth squeezed her eyes shut, struggling to will away the horror in her mind, but when she reopened her eyes, she was in the car again. *Hold on, darling,* she heard a voice say, but now it wasn't Sara Brobeck's mother behind the wheel. It was Beth's father. He smiled back at her, unbuckling his seat belt. *It'll be over in a minute.*

"What's this about, Doctor?" Ganza asked. "Has Toby said anything about the case?"

"No," Beth replied after she found her voice. "But I should have something for you soon."

Beth sat across from Toby and for the first time since the start of their sessions together, *she* was the one who was afraid to speak.

"Are we going to play that game again?" he asked.

"Do you want to?" she replied, hoping against hope he would say no. Never in her life had she longed more for all the voices in the world to stop talking, but for a reason she could not fathom, she felt compelled to continue.

"Yes," he said. "I have something else I want to tell you."

"What is it?" she asked. The penlight felt like a weight in her hand. *Click on. Click off. Click on.*

"He made me watch."

There was a deadly silence as Beth's voice strangled itself in her throat.

"He made me watch it all," Toby said. "When he killed them and when he killed himself."

Beth felt the room tilting beneath her and all she could do to stop

herself from falling was to hang on, desperate and clawing. *Lock!*
Smock! Clock!

"Why?" she asked, her eyes stinging, tears welling up. It was a condi-
tioned response, but she already knew the answer—an answer Detective Ganza would never be able to reconcile.

"Because the Mouth told him to. Just like It told Sara's mother. Just
like it's telling you."

As he said those words, Beth no longer saw Toby Rheva's face.
Instead she saw an enormous mouth, lips stretched wide in a sickening
grin. Then the Mouth opened, baring Its hideously sharp teeth, revealing an abyss where a throat should have been. Beth felt the floor's ver-
tiginous tilt grow steeper until it became a cliff's edge she no longer
had the strength to cling to. She was plunging now, tumbling, end over
end, into the gaping maw of the insidious thing that had taken hold
of Jerry Padesky and Sara Brobeck's mother and her own father before
them as It continued on in a great generational line of parents and
children, stretching all the way back to the age of Abraham.

The monster watched her husband sleep, the faintness of his breath,
the gentle rise and fall of his chest. Even when she ran the knife
across the fragile white of his throat, his sleep went on unbroken. The
sedative she'd put in his dinner made sure of that. After it was done
and the wet choking sound subsided, the monster that was once Dr.
Beth Harper turned to see her daughter shivering in the corner of the
room. "When your mommy's finished, you'll go and hide like we told
you, okay?" The child nodded with an obedience born of fear, and the
monster smiled with satisfaction. Then she raised the knife to her own
throat, and the Mouth Inside Her Head sang her to sleep.

The girl sat silently, feet dangling off the chair, staring at the laces of her
pink Keds. Someone had wrapped a blanket around her even though
she wasn't cold.

"Rose?" Detective Ganza said, kneeling down in front of her. "Can you tell me what happened?"

After a long moment, Rose Harper looked up at the woman whose face was serious but kind. She knew she had to talk to her, to describe every horror locked inside her mind. Sooner or later, she'd have to tell this woman what her mother had done to her father and then to herself. *Speak,* the Mouth whispered to Rose.

But she wouldn't say the words.

Dreamland

MICHAEL OLSON

At first it seems almost the same as her lovely first dream.

We're in the same fantastical seascape filled with a whirling ballet of sparkling bream, swooping giant mantas, and flamboyant parrot fish. A pod of dolphins cavorts nearby as we swim toward the wreckage of an ancient, sunken city.

Gradually we notice differences. The shore is far away now. The beams of moonlight don't quite penetrate all the way. We're gliding deeper into the ocean as though pulled by a riptide. The marine life begins to change in a way that's hard to put your finger on. A huge, serpentine oarfish ripples along the sea floor. We see the glowing lures of toothy anglers. A school of iridescent jellyfish. The octopi here are much larger.

We follow the sinuous oarfish, but a dolphin dances right in front of us, butting us with his snout. He's insistent, and we pause as he swims a tight circle, as if he wants us to turn around.

We pass by him. And this time, none of the dolphins follow as we descend toward an ornate colonnaded temple shattered by a dark fissure tearing violently into its foundation. The oarfish disappears into it, and we trail behind.

Down here it's still beautiful, but in an eerie, haunted way. The darkness cut only by veins of phosphorescent crystal reaching through the chasm's rock walls. Below we see the architectural skeleton of some fossilized leviathan. Just as we're swimming toward a strange anemone crawling from its eye socket—

The scene jerks hard downward into the ravine.

Our hand flails at the rock in front of us, but we're yanked down again. Bubbles pour into view like our heretofore magic breath has been squeezed from our lungs.

Then another great heave. Our fingernails tear as we claw for purchase on the rocks. And then the last remnant of light we can see far above us is obscured with curling tendrils of dark liquid.

Blood.

There's another sharp movement you can't quite make out in the confusing dark whorls.

Then black.

That was when Cassie bolted awake so fast she slammed her head against the underside of the MRI.

Jerking upright after a scary dream is one of those things you see all the time in movies, but it rarely ever happens in real life. Though when you fall asleep in the coffinlike cylinder of a million-dollar brain monitor, I guess you're more liable to bump your head when you wake suddenly.

That's not to say bad dreams are at all rare. The famous dream researcher Dr. Antti Revonsuo has proposed that the very purpose of dreams is "threat simulation." That we're rehearsing encounters with predators to prepare our minds, should one actually come to pass. Which explains an odd attribute of dreams: we tend to think of them as pleasant interludes, weird and disquieting at worst, excepting a very occasional night terror like Cassie's. But when you actually wake people from a dream and ask them about it, you find that nearly all of them are unpleasant. The most common emotion associated with dreams? Anxiety. Most of our dreams are nightmares in one way or another.

But Cassie's nightmare is special: we recorded it.

She's one of my "Somnonauts" here at Dreamland—what we call the brand-new South Texas Sleep Research Center, a gleaming four-story complex just west of UT.

The Land of Nod has finally started getting the research attention it deserves, given that poor sleep kills more people than cancer. Thus the forty billion dollars we spend every year on sleep aids.

I was the first researcher to move into Dreamland. Contractors are still working on my floor, and the place is nearly empty. Everything bright and pristine, with that new-building smell.

My Somnonauts are all volunteers with chronic insomnia who signed up for a twelve-week "presearch" study on techniques to promote better sleep health. Yes, they're confined to the facility, but they get $1,500 a week, free room and board, and (the key incentive for most) *time* to pursue whatever unfinished project has been haunting them. They're almost all struggling writers.

The project demands very detailed pictures of my subjects' unconscious brains, so I've trained them to sleep in the barrel of an MRI machine. No easy feat for insomniacs. They're just now starting to get the hang of it.

That was why William Tynes showed up at my door.

I'd been disciplining my balky computer when I looked up to see him standing there just inside my office. A face from my distant past.

Though I'd last seen him twelve years ago, Bill seemed to have aged twenty-five, as if his body was in a hurry to honestly reflect his wizard's brain. He had a patchy beard and long sandy hair hanging in a limp ponytail. Large amber eyes that always looked so *tired*, like he could never find enough fuel to light that incandescent mind.

A slightly embarrassed smile, then, "Hey, Glo." Like we'd just had coffee last week.

I met Bill in graduate school at Rice University. One day, he sat down across from me at Fondren Library and said, "What's up Glo? Hey, I was thinking . . . We need to figure out *sleep*."

Then, unprompted, he detailed a program of neurological research he'd mapped out. Vast in scope, breathtaking in its ambition. I sat there spellbound for more than an hour until I finally asked, "Bill, why are you telling all this to *me*?"

He blinked, surprised at the interruption, then said, "We're going to work together. I mean, sure, I can think up all this stuff. But you can actually *do* it."

Over an amazing couple of months, we did work together. Until he unaccountably disappeared. I tracked down his mother in Little Rock, who said, "I can't tell you where he is, but he ain't dead, if that's what you're worried about. Anyway, you're better off. You shouldn't depend on that boy."

And I heard nothing from him until the day he came back into my life a dozen years later.

"Bill . . . What a surprise." I examined him for any trace of what had made him vanish. Once fulsome and free, his smile now seemed wary, as though dark years had taught him not to tempt fate with any expression of joy.

"Sorry . . . I just need to talk to you."

I waved him in, and he sat and stared at me for a moment. "I've been over with Baynes writing the algorithms for MindDraw," he finally said. "And I thought we might look at dreams."

That made me smile. Dr. Robert Baynes was an undistinguished researcher at UT's Institute for Neuroscience who'd suddenly shot to the pinnacle of our field due to his breakthrough work on brain imaging. Not just recording images of brain activity, though that was certainly part of it, but actually *taking images* from the brain. You think of a cat, an apple, a pipe, and bang! There it is on the screen in front of you.

He wasn't the first to pursue this work. Kamitani attempted it back in 2005. Jack Gallant at Berkeley made some beautiful reconstructions in 2011, but Baynes's stuff was on another level. They'd found one test subject who was so good with the system, he could instantly reel off hi-res digital photos of anything he could imagine. The papers Baynes now published at an unheard-of clip were revolutionizing our understanding of how the brain processes visual information.

I'd often wondered, admittedly with a little pang of jealousy, how that mediocre intellect was making such great strides. Turns out he had William Tynes.

And now William Tynes wanted *me*. Again.

"I hear you've got some residentials trained to sleep in an MRI," he said.

That was the genesis of Project DreamCatcher. Was there a tingle of apprehension at letting Tynes's project hitch a ride on mine? Not really. I had a lot of "middle insomniacs"—people who can't sleep through the night—and I wanted nothing more than a clear window into what their brains were doing to shake them awake.

Beyond that, you just don't often get the chance to work with someone like Bill. If we got results, there was no telling where the collaboration could take me. And he was that rare creature almost totally innocent of normal human motivations like pride, greed, and envy. He had only a voracious need to understand his subject. To my mind, the perfect partner.

Since Tynes's MindDraw system already worked for conscious subjects, we thought that by adapting it for sleeping brains, we could vastly improve on the flickering abstractions of earlier attempts and really bring our dreams into the waking world.

As the architect of the whole thing, Tynes had to prove he could get our DreamCatcher to work for other people. Once we created a primitive prototype, we tried to test it on me, but I knew it wouldn't work. I'm more than a little claustrophobic and, though I could tolerate lying inside an MRI machine long enough to learn MindDraw, I'd never managed to fall asleep in one. When we approached my band of Somnos with the notion, it looked like a no-go.

You want to record my dreams? Um, no thanks.

I understood. Who knows what we might see?

They glanced at one another uneasily. Everyone except Cassie. She looked right at us and said, "I'll do it. I never remember my dreams. And I want to know what's going on in there."

We planned to give her the full three-day training course on MindDraw in the hopes that her brain would retain those image-making skills when she fell asleep. But Tynes came in that first evening, looking disheveled, with darker-than-usual bags under his eyes. He said, "Fuck it. Let's just hook her up to DreamCatcher tonight."

Cassie snuggled into the thin cot as best she could. She smiled at me, but I could tell she was nervous. I popped in the special earbuds that gave her the UnderTone, another one of Tynes's innovations. Mind-Draw demands a kind of focused visualization that takes practice. Our brains can be lazy, and the images they produce tend toward chaos without careful attention. The MindDraw group found it incredibly helpful to give their subjects feedback regarding how well the system could interpret their brain activity as it tried to draw a picture from the data. Too much visual feedback distracted people from what they were trying to imagine, so the team introduced subliminal audio, using a fancy music-generation program.

Amplified and slowed way down, the UnderTone sounded like a tinkling fairy melody when you were resonating well with the machine. Atonal discord when your mental data stream was unclear. For reasons not fully understood, most people's brains automatically adjusted to seek the "pleasant" music. Which made the UnderTone like a sheep-dog herding the relevant parts of your brain, keeping them moving together in the right direction so the software could understand where they're going.

I hit the button to send Cassie into the tube of the MRI machine. She gave me another faltering smile before her head disappeared.

"Sweet dreams, Cassie," I said.

It took her almost two hours to fall asleep.

But once she did, what emerged from her mind that night was gorgeous beyond compare: a seascape of such surpassing beauty, it was bewildering. Great columns of flowering kelp. Filigreed arches of coral. All lit by bright rays of moonlight lancing through the water. She swam among glittering helices of fish dancing together as if to welcome her. Eventually she discovered the ruins.

In the morning, when we showed Cassie the video, her eyes filled the moment it started. I could tell she *recognized* it, *knew* it was from deep inside her. Pure wonder on her face, like a woman handed the ultrasound of her first child.

When it finished, she wiped her eyes and whispered, "It's beautiful . . . isn't it?"

That same afternoon, Marco Ilgunas came by my office. An enormous Lithuanian, he used to work the door at Tension, an unbearably au fait after-hours club off Sixth Street. At our first get-acquainted meeting, he told me he came to Dreamland to give himself time to work on his screenplay. I said, "Let me guess, it's about a heroic bouncer defending Austin's minor celebrities from the unwashed hordes."

Marco looked away almost bashfully. "Nah, man. It's about elves." Then he flashed the warm, mirthful smile that made everyone here love him.

Weeks later, standing there in my doorway, he led with that same smile and said, "I want to go next." Cassie must have shown him her dream.

Of course *now* the others wanted in. We started training them on MindDraw that day. You can't see something like Cassie's beguiling undersea idyll, spun from nothing more than a night's sleep— something it would take an animation studio a year and millions to produce—and not wonder, Can I do that too? Do I have that inside me? And all you have to do to find out is fall asleep. Who knows what you'll have when you wake up? Maybe nothing, but that first dream of Cassie's was a work of art.

Her nightmare was one too.

There in Lab A-4.107, Cassie keeps watching the dead black of the last frame for a moment before turning to me. She seems perplexed. Like she missed something she expected to find. She's still shaking like a drying drunk despite the thick flannel pajamas she wears against the lab's merciless air-conditioning.

"I guess that was it . . . though . . ." She folds her arms around herself, trying to stop her delicate, avian frame from trembling. Technically we're never supposed to touch our subjects, but her gesture evokes my daughter, Maya, so I can't resist embracing her.

"I can see how that frightened you," I say. She disengages, staring again at the monitor.

"I mean, yeah, it's sort of spooky, but . . ." I tilt my head, asking her to continue. She says, "There was just a sensation. Or like a *presence* . . . I've never felt anything like it." She shivers again.

"I'm happy to stay up with you until you feel like you can get back to sleep."

I silently curse as my phone chimes, and Cassie looks away from me. It's Maya, of course:

Good night Mommy. I love you!!!

I have to tamp down a spike of irritation. She *knows* she's not supposed to disturb me at work. But then I think, *What's wrong with you? You're mad that your daughter texted to say she loves you? Okay, let's try to focus.*

Cassie's edging toward the door. "No way I'm going back to sleep tonight, but I'll be fine. You should go home to your daughter." On her way back to her room, I hear her cough a couple times, like she's trying to clear something from her throat.

I text Tynes.

Cassie had a nightmare.

In the ensuing silence, I wonder what made me bother him with that information in the middle of the night. It just seems like he'd want to know. One thing I'm sure of, he'll be up. My phone chimes:

Send it to me.

That's a little strange. The files are huge, and sending one via e-mail would surely be frowned upon from a privacy perspective. He can look at it all he wants tomorrow—

My phone chimes again:

Right now.

So I send it.

Then I head home to Maya.

My daughter always gets up early. She doesn't wake me, but sits and draws until I rise to throw something together for breakfast. So I wasn't surprised to see her kneeling on her chair, bent over the kitchen table, when I shuffled in to start the coffee. But this morning, I can tell from the rise and fall of her chest that she's crying silently.

My *amour fou* with Maya's father, Joaquin, a musician, lasted until just after the moment she came into being. Somehow he knew before I did and vanished like he'd been a figment of my imagination. Of course that put pre-Maya in grave danger. I'd just gotten my doctorate and a pretty good postdoc fellowship at UT. People like me don't have children out of wedlock. Everyone I knew was secretly horrified when I broke the news. I still remember Dr. Wilson, my fellowship sponsor, saying, "Well . . . that's wonderful." His eyes already turning inward to riffle his list of applicants to replace me.

I tell myself that her name, taken from the Buddhist teaching about the illusory nature of what we call "reality," had nothing to do with my feelings about her father. I should have thought of something else, but it's such a pretty name, and she responded to it like she already knew it was hers.

Maya's the reason I'm where I am today. I've got a *fairly* good tenure-track faculty appointment. My research on sleep-cycle disruptions is *interesting* but not groundbreaking. I'm *well respected* in the field but not celebrated. At conferences people don't flock to the podium after I give a talk. Since high school, I've been the smartest person in *most* rooms, but not one of the real stars. I work very, very hard.

But now Maya always comes first.

Which isn't *really* a sacrifice. She's a precocious, happy, wonderful little girl—though not *this* morning.

I rush over and take her in my arms. She buries her face in my hair. "Sweetie! What's wrong?"

Maya wipes her nose and says, "Look." She points to the picture she was working on. "It's ruined."

Indeed, the graceful unicorn she'd been crafting over days had come out great, except for an unfortunate jerk of her colored pencil that made a thick line neatly bisecting his eye. It had gouged into the paper, and there'd be no way to erase it.

Maya suffers from a condition they call "essential tremor." Her hands shake when what she's doing requires fine motor control. It gets worse when she's stressed. To compensate, she's developed a lovely crosshatched style that *almost* makes an asset of her limitation.

"He looks great to me. I'm sure we can fix it."

"No, we can't, Mom." She sobs. "This always happens. I can never draw *anything* right. I don't even know why I keep trying." The heartbreak in those last words is about more than I can bear, but then she queers my sympathy, pushing it too far: "I can't go to school today. Everyone is going to laugh at me."

Maya is always trying to get out of class, even though she knows I can't ask our nanny, Rosalind, to stay with her on short notice. She wants *me* to stay home today, as though I can constantly place my career at the whim of a nine-year-old. Particularly irritating about this little demand is that we've been engaged in a long-running battle of wills over the emotional energy she invests in her drawing. I just want to spare her the pain of inevitable disappointment. The harrowing loss of dreams coming undone.

I've been subtly suggesting that she find a different creative outlet. One that, given her tremors, makes fewer demands on—

That's when I have the idea.

"How'd you like to take the day off and come to work with your mom?"

Maya and I spend a little while looking for Tynes. He lives very much alone and had seemed particularly pleased to see her the last time I brought her in. For her part, Maya liked his twinkly wryness. "William the Wizard" she called him. But Tynes hasn't come in to work.

I load the MindDraw program on our DreamCatcher machine and

start Maya with the training module. She's a natural. By the end of the day, she beams with delight as her best effort glides off the printer. A majestic unicorn of far nobler bloodline than the mutilated hack now grazing in our kitchen wastebasket. She names him Gyllandynion.

I try to make a portrait of her, but it doesn't turn out nearly as well. Maya's brows knit as she compares my crabbed and blurry image to her masterpiece. She's too polite to say anything, but I'm thrilled to see her private glee that hers is so much better.

Nothing like watching your child find something amazing in the world. Especially if she realizes that what Mommy does every day isn't always the tedious grind that she suspects, but actually can be kind of magical.

Back at home, Maya hesitates when I invite her to hang Gyllandynion up in her room. When I insist, she takes the thumbtack from me and solemnly gives him pride of place over her bed.

At seven, my phone wakes me with a text alert from the server I use to store all the sleep data from the wrist monitors my Somnonauts wear 24/7. With insomniacs, you're going to get someone who pulls the occasional all-nighter. Staying up a second night is far rarer. My database tells me that Cassie hasn't been asleep since she had her nightmare two days ago.

She takes a long time to answer when I knock and doesn't invite me in. She won't quite look me in the eye.

"Cassie, is everything all right?"

She stares at the floor. "Doesn't seem that way, does it?"

"No. What's wrong?"

She turns around and wanders away from the door. "I'm just . . . afraid."

I follow her in. "Of what?"

"Of sleeping. I can't explain it. Just feels like something terrible's going to happen."

"It'll be terrible if you *don't* sleep. Look"—I reach into my coat pocket and pull out an Ambien sample—"why don't you take one of these?"

She regards the tablet suspiciously. "I thought we were 'learning strategies to promote *non*medicated sleep.'"

"Sometimes we need a little help getting back on track."

Cassie turns away from me and gazes, I'd have to say *longingly*, out the window. "I don't want—" She turns back to me. "You know what I want? To get the fuck out of here."

I'm not easily shocked, but those words coming out of her mouth throw me. I clear my throat. "Listen, Cassie, you're exhausted. Why don't we discuss this after you've had eight good hours and you're feeling more like yourself?"

I press the pill on her again. She looks at it like I want her to eat a scorpion. I have to take her hand and place the tablet in it. "Honey, you just need some rest. Everything will look different then. I'll be here when you wake up, and we can talk about it."

"I'm not sleeping in that machine." She puts the pill on her tongue and dry-swallows. "Dr. Dennings, will you check on me? Make sure I'm okay?"

Leaving Cassie's room, I feel like I could use a sedative myself. I want to talk this over with Bill, but he still isn't in the empty office he's appropriated. Isn't answering his cell. I walk a couple blocks over to the anonymous complex off Guadalupe Street that he shares with a bunch of graduate students twenty years his junior.

After knocking for a long time, in sheer frustration I try the knob, something I never do. The unlocked door creaks open. That's disturbing.

But there's Bill hunched at a twenty-dollar folding table under which he's stashed about sixty grand worth of high-powered workstations. He clearly hasn't been to sleep in two days either.

Tynes has the annoying tendency common to alpha geeks and supervillains of not turning to greet someone when they enter the room. An affectation I guess is meant to say "The work is more important than you." I forgive him, because he's studying Cassie's nightmare.

"What's going on, Bill?"

"There's the problem." He points to an on-screen image he's poring over. Then taps it with his too-long fingernail three times, hard, like he's trying to pin it in place.

I step up behind him for a close look. But that only confuses me.

At first it's just an undifferentiated blob of swirling gray on gray, like the kind of storm clouds that spawn tornadoes. But after staring at it for a couple of seconds, features emerge. If those two darker regions were eyes . . . then I can make out a slightly angular face. Those wedges high on either side could be ears . . . or maybe the peaks of what? A crown? Then below an oversized gash of a mouth stretched into a macabre grin. "Maw" would probably be a better word, given the hideous jumble of teeth. Black iron nails and jagged shards of obsidian. I guess you could say fangs.

I force myself to look away. "You found it . . . ?"

"In Cassie's nightmare."

"I don't remember seeing anything like that."

He finally tears his eyes from the screen. "You didn't. It's in the data."

"What?"

"This image is *encoded* in the data DreamCatcher recorded and then rendered into her dream. Took me forever to find the right set of filters, but it's there the whole way through." On another monitor Tynes pulls up Cassie's nightmare, and as he scrolls to the start, the insidious face in the main window mostly disappears, then gradually coheres in the middle of the dream. Near the end, it seems almost to press against the screen. Stretching it. Like the face is trying to push through an invisible membrane.

It's deeply unsettling. I ask, "You're saying she was dreaming two things at once?"

"Not exactly. I doubt she was ever aware of Mr. Smoke here—"

He's already got a nickname for that thing?

"—but the dream she had was carrying him along with it . . ."

I ponder for a minute how your mind could embed a hidden parasitic image into a dream. "She can do that kind of math . . . in her sleep?"

"Not like we have a real understanding of what goes on in the old noodle." He flicks his temple. Then frowns. "For the life of me, I don't know how her brain could produce a multimodal signal like this. It would be a thousand times harder than, say, singing two notes at the same time. Only a few people in the world can do that, and they have to train their own vocal cords for years. This is . . ." He whistles.

"Bill, are you sure you're not—"

"Torturing the data? Conjuring ghosts? Check it out yourself. See what *you* think."

"I think I'm worried about my group. Cassie hasn't been back to sleep since she had that dream . . . and Marco never went to bed last night either. Losing that much rest can be dangerous."

"I know."

"What do you think this is?"

"I'm not sure. Maybe a deep process in the brain we don't even know about is tuned to respond to signals like this one. And it turns on an acute stress response. We're constantly finding new mental phenomena that are . . . schizogenic. So—"

"So your machine transmitted some kind of *dream disease* to my subjects?" I freeze for an instant as a blade of panic cuts into me.

Maya used that machine.

No . . . We only tried the MindDraw software that day. Not our new dream-reading code. Neither of us ever went to sleep hooked to the machine.

Bill says carefully, "I'm sure we'll find a better way to characterize what's happened, but—"

"We need to figure out what to *do*."

"We need to study it."

"We need to *help her*."

Bill tells me he has some ideas, but I have to leave him there staring at that baleful face while I race back to the lab.

Because it looks like Cassie is melting down.

Her sleep tracker says she'd been in REM for a minute and twenty-three seconds before she shot awake. Since then, any short period of immobility indicating that she's falling asleep is immediately followed by a burst of frenzied movement. She's fighting the Ambien.

Her door's cracked, so I don't knock. She jumps like a scalded cat when I barge in.

"I thought we agreed you'd try to sleep."

I notice first her guilty eyes, then the way her fists are balled, like a child trying to conceal something in each one. "Cassie. What are you doing?"

"Nothing."

A moment passes as I wonder how hard I can push her. I'm about to try another tack when I see the drop of blood trickle out from her left palm.

I lunge over and grab both her wrists. "Open them."

She finally breaks, deflating with a helpless sigh. Both hands slowly unclench, and she looks at them with horror. In one she's squeezing the blade to a penknife. The other is covered with a hundred small cuts in an intricate starburst pattern.

"Cassie! What is this?"

"It's . . . the pain. It's the only way to keep Him away."

"Keep *who* away?"

She looks at me, I guess figuring what will happen when she says something totally crazy to me. Then her eyes narrow and her mouth opens with surprise.

"Wait . . . You know, don't you? You *know* who! . . . What are you *doing* to us?"

Her accusation rattles me. What I learned from Tynes was so bizarre I haven't really processed all the implications. Cassie brings them home:

You've infected your subjects with something that you don't even begin to understand.

Telling her that isn't going to help. I need some time to think, so I deflect. "I know you've had a nightmare, and now you're so afraid to sleep, you're hurting yourself. And we can't have that, can we?"

"You think I want to do this? Dr. Dennings, what's happening to me?"

"You need rest; I'm going to give you some lorazepam. That'll put you down and help with your . . . anxiety. You won't have any dreams, or none that you can remember anyway. Tomorrow morning I'll take you over to my colleague Dr. Hendricks in neurology, and he can run some tests. But I'm sure a good night of sleep is really all you need."

Without waiting for a response, I go down the hall to the supply closet my clinical partner Mark Hendricks keeps stocked with all sorts of tranquilizers and hypnotics. I'm obviously not supposed to have access, but I found an extra key taped to the floor of the cabinet when it was installed. Cassie doesn't protest when I slide the spoon into her mouth. She seems, in a very profound sense, exhausted. After swallowing, she collapses onto her bed. I scan her desk for more sharp objects. From behind me, her voice is almost a whimper:

"Will you please leave the light on?"

Late that evening, Tynes lifts his fancy earphones off and looks at me with the ghost of a smile. "I found it." He hands the headset to me. "Here. Listen."

I subdue a little spike of worry. I don't really want any contact with our system now. It feels toxic. But I got my group into this. It's my responsibility.

What he plays for me is a cousin of the fairy music you get when system and dreamer are in sync. But this is different. It's darker, minor key, mysterious. More Bartók than Bach . . . Thirty seconds in, I think, *I like it. It's seductive.*

I rip the phones off my head.

"It's all subliminal," he says, "but that 'track' is playing at a different frequency than the main UnderTone. It creates its own feedback loop, and that must be what puts Mr. Smoke into the dream data."

Something feels off about that explanation, but I can't put my finger on it. This dark thing infects your head through a tune you can't even really hear? On the other hand, that music came from *somewhere.* And for now it's what we have.

"You can look for His encoded signal in their dream data, right? Then rewrite the UnderTone generator so when you see Him appear, you stop it from playing His music. Anytime you see something from the brain that might be encouraging His sounds—inviting Him in— you make the UnderTone play the unpleasant music. You code the system to do the opposite of what it's doing now. Tell their brains *not* to let Him in. Maybe a new version could even train them to automatically suppress the patterns that He attaches himself to."

Tynes looks at me for a long time. I can see him rolling the idea around in his mind. Training the UnderTone, our faithful sheepdog, to bark and warn the brain away from this dangerous ravine we've discovered.

Finally he replies, "Why didn't I think of that?" I can't tell if he's being ironic. But the next thing he says is "Go home to Maya. I'll get to work on it."

Fatigue from the acute stress of the day washes over me. But I'm still jittery, on edge, feeling cracks forming in the ground beneath me. I need to see my daughter.

So I go home.

There's a note from my nanny, Rosalind, that says she found Maya reading under her blanket with a flashlight well past bedtime. When I sneak into her room, I get a little tingle of joy to find her slumbering peacefully. She doesn't move a muscle when I kiss her forehead.

That night *I* wasn't so lucky.

The darkness enveloping me is total. But in a dreadful way beyond my comprehension, wisps of the dark cohere, and though there's no light, I can SEE Him. Churning in the blackness. His horns shifting and deforming. His flickering grin. And those teeth. It feels like He's nothing but teeth.

I can't move at all, but I'm not physically restrained. Just paralyzed. And yet I'm being held in place. I need to move, to fight. An animal panic wells within me. But I remain trapped, pinioned. I can feel Him somehow pressing. Not down upon me, but INTO me. Inside me. The weak membrane between Him and me stretching. So close to bursting.

Then it breaks, and I finally really feel Him. A front of searing pain followed by an even more horrifying numb. A stench unlike any I've ever known. This is what it's like to rot.

I beg. I plead with Him to kill me. Every horror I've ever imagined is nothing compared to this. The sickening hurt, the filth. How can anything so terrible exist?

That's when He starts whispering, and somehow this is worse. It's no language ever known to man, but what's left of my debased body responds like a tuning fork. He's showing me how it'll be now that I'm His.

But suddenly a reddish glow flashes into the blackness. Something touches me, and I know it's not Him. I can still feel Him pressing and pressing, but that sensation slowly localizes in my head. Like He's receding there. Or getting pushed.

It touches me again, this time on my chest, like a doctor vainly inspecting my corpse for signs of life. I grab at it . . .

And she yanks me awake.

But no, that's not right. I've just slipped into another nightmare, because there's my daughter standing in front of me, a scream frozen in her throat.

She's covered in blood.

Grilled cheese at 4:30 a.m. Maya contentedly munching away. My heart rate starting to return to normal. Shedding the scary palpitations and double beats, but the core of the horror remains.

You're infected just like the others.

How? Was just seeing Tynes's image of Mr. Smoke enough? Listening to his UnderTone? And if I have it, what about Maya?

I try to keep my voice steady. "So it wasn't a bad dream?"

"No, I told you. I just woke up, and there was something wet on my face. And when I saw it was blood I got scared, but it was just my nose—like happened last winter—but it didn't stop. I came down to get you, but you wouldn't wake up and . . . you were making noises . . ."

She has a bloody nose tonight. And this is what? Just a coincidence?

"Mommy had a nightmare. I didn't mean to scare you."

"I know."

Maya drops a crust on her plate and starts on the other half. After a sip of milk, she says, faux casually, "You asked, 'What did He do to you?' Who were you talking about?"

I unclench my teeth. "No one, darling. Sometimes when you wake someone from the middle of a dream, they can be . . . confused. Not quite all there yet."

She searches me with those blue eyes for a long time. Her sandwich forgotten. It makes me think, *She knows something.*

But she says only, "I'm not really sleepy anymore. Can we read a story?"

It's only two hours until she'd be up anyway, and I sure as hell won't go back to bed.

My phone is full of alerts telling me none of the Somnonauts slept last night either.

Once Maya disappears through the stark white doors of her school, a fog of unease descends upon me. I've never been so tired, but it's more than that. Some kind of psychic residue from my nightmare clings to me. I feel . . . *soiled*.

To say nothing of my dread at what I'll find when I return to my lab.

Walking under the lovely row of huge plane trees out front, the place seems peaceful enough. Then the door opens, seemingly of its own accord. I stop dead until I make out Tynes standing there in the gloom. I guess he's been watching for my arrival.

As I step into the stairwell, he says, "After you left, I rewrote Dream-Catcher's UnderTone code. Still early, but I think it's going to work."

Pure relief floods into me when I hear those words, but it quickly recedes, leaving more questions. The worst of which is: *Wait . . . how do you know?*

But I don't need to ask him. The answer's obvious.

He tried it on himself last night.

I look at Tynes with new eyes, the root of all this coming into focus.

His aged features, his tired face, and all the strange bulges and lumps in his baggy clothes. I grab his arm and clock the way he winces. I pull up the sleeve of his sweater to find an odd brass bracelet around his wrist with the head of a thick screw sticking out. The sharp end pressing into his flesh. There's another one on his forearm, and I imagine a line of these devices going all the way up his arm.

Mr. Smoke came from him.

As he rolls back his cuff, he says, "They're a kind of cilice I adapted from a Dominican design."

"How long has He . . . been inside you?"

A shadow passes over his face. "Hard to say. The dreams began when my MindDraw engine really started working, but He got strong only after I dozed off during a session . . . Of course that's why I came to you. I wanted . . ."

"A record of your nightmares. So you could see Him while you're awake. Study Him. Try to understand what was happening to you. Maybe start on a treatment."

"I . . . I never imagined He could infect other people."

"But He has. All of us now." His eyes ask the question: *Even you?* I nod. "And I never even went under in DreamCatcher. How is that possible?"

Bill thinks about it. Haltingly, he says, "When you run MindDraw on the machine here . . . it uses the same recognition engine as Dream-Catcher. So the data's been tuned by . . . the bad dreams."

"You mean contaminated. By Him." I think for a minute. "But look how fast my group is falling apart, and you've been able to live with Him for a while . . ."

"Yeah. I think he comes in a lot stronger when you're asleep and your brain is almost defenseless. When I tried DreamCatcher, He got a lot worse. But by then, I was already pretty good at holding Him at bay. Your people had no tolerance, and they got a real concentrated . . . exposure."

He notices my fists clenching, and his voice rises with urgency. "I tried the new code I wrote last night, and He didn't come for me. I actually slept, and it's hard to explain, but I don't feel Him *pressing* anymore."

I wish I didn't know exactly what he means.

He continues, "As if the new software made me . . . smoke-free. Maybe it's like you said: suppressing Him even once has an immunizing effect on your brain. Like a vaccine."

I try to sift my welter of emotions. This man knew he was sick, and in his desperation, he brought his illness to Dreamland. Without telling me about it. It makes me want to bash his head into the wall. But after last night's dream, I'm a little desperate now too. Enough to demand a session with his new software right away. I'm so tired I feel like I could actually pass out in the machine. But how could I ever trust him to—

The piercing sound rips that thought apart: a woman's scream.

Coming from the floor above. My floor.

I race up the stairs ahead of Tynes. Running down the hall, I hear them before I get around the corner. Cassie's pleading, a sharp edge of hysteria in her voice. "No. Stop it. It's what He wants!"

Marco's baritone: "Shut up. It keeps Him away."

"No! You don't understand. It keeps Him *satisfied*. Please! You have to starve Him, or else—"

"GET THE FUCK AWAY FROM ME!"

I round the corner to see Cassie grasping Marco's right arm, using all her weight to pull his hand toward her. In that hand he's holding a bread knife, which he's been using to saw his left index finger into fine slices like he's cutting pepperoni for a charcuterie plate. The table is a lake of blood.

Marco lashes out. His first stroke opens her scalp from ear to eyebrow. Cassie screams and falls to the floor. Marco plunges the knife into her back. Yanks it loose with a squelchy kissing sound.

I yell, "Marco!"

He turns and stares at me, his kindly features twisted into a mask of rage. He steps toward me, lifting the knife.

All I can think is: *Who is this person?*

I point at the half mirror of the room's large window and shout, "Marco Ilgunas! Look at yourself!"

I have no idea what he sees in his reflection, but Marco screeches and wrenches away from the window, stumbling over Cassie and slamming the back of his head so hard into the opposite wall that it punches through the plaster.

The blow seems to wake him up. He drops the knife as poor Cassie scuttles away from him in terror. His face collapses into a sob. Tynes arrives behind me.

"I . . . I didn't mean it. I just . . . She was—" His eyes catch the window again, and he lunges for the door, knocking me out of the way and spilling Tynes to the floor.

I check Cassie's wound as she cries uncontrollably. It's high on her shoulder, so no organs, and it's not bleeding hard enough to be arterial.

Tynes gets up and stares at the blood and slivers of finger on the table. I snap at him. "Take her down the street to emergency." I run into the hall to deal with Marco.

From Dr. Hendricks's supply cabinet, I fill a syringe with a big dose of propofol, the stuff that killed Michael Jackson. Once Marco's down, we'll have to get him over to the psych ward. A voice inside me resists the plan, proposing that this disaster can still be contained. But it's too late for that. Things are spiraling out of control. Cassie could have been killed.

Rounding the corner to the dormitory section, I see Teresa, another of my Somnos, coming down the hall in her nightie, pacing through a layer of thick white smoke gathering on the floor. She smiles like she's won the lottery and doesn't seem to even see me, clearly in a sleep-deprived trance. A problem for later.

Where's all this smoke coming from?

At first I think Marco set a fire, but then I see the mist's source: our deep freeze in which we store dry ice for packing blood samples is open and boiling a cloud of CO_2 onto the floor. I shut it and approach Marco's room.

He's sitting on his bed weeping. Holding his bleeding left hand.

I stop at the door, but he can feel my presence. He says, "I didn't want to hurt anyone else. But He made me . . . Doctor, what's happening to me?"

I creep forward to avoid spooking him. "Marco, this isn't your fault. We know something's wrong, and we're going to fix it. We just need to work together."

"You have no idea what to do, do you?"

"We're going to find a way—"

"I do. I know exactly what has to happen. He thinks He's in control, but He's not. He'll go away if we just stop dreaming."

As I close on him, I carefully reach into my pocket and take the syringe in my right hand, hiding it against my leg. Marco's not looking at me. He's examining his hands joined in a bloody knot in front of him.

He continues, "But it's hard, right? How do you keep someone from dreaming?" He cocks his head as if still pondering the question. "I asked myself over and over. But I'm so *tired,* you know? All this *pressure* building up in here." He pokes a bloody finger into his forehead.

I'm near enough now, thinking, *Jab it through his shirt into the meat of his shoulder. Then get the hell out of here.*

But I freeze, realizing that won't work. Propofol needs a vein. I might as well stab him with a toothpick for all the good it'll do.

He turns and levels a sick grin at me. "Then I figured it out."

Marco slams a fat cylindrical thing into his mouth. He looks like he's doing something silly to amuse a toddler. The object has a white cap and translucent curves, but it takes me a second to realize what it is: one of the little airplane bottles of water we leave in the break room. But there's something strange about this one. Inside it's full of white, eddying . . . smoke.

What the fuck?

My mind goes so quickly to this strange demon haunting us that a crucial instant passes before the obvious explanation seeps in: it's CO_2. Marco stuck a chunk of dry ice from the deep freeze into the water bottle.

Why would he do that? Is he trying to symbolically consume—

Then I get it.

He made a bomb.

Just as I reach for the bottle, Marco's head explodes.

I lose a little time. Here I am, ears ringing, my left hand numb, wiping blood out of my eyes. Gobbets of flesh dangle from my hair. My fingers pass over something hard embedded in my forehead. A piece of plastic? I pull it out and look: a tooth.

You and Tynes have killed someone . . . He's dead. He's dead. He's dead . . . And soon you will be too.

In the mirror, my blood-drenched face seems to flicker.

I stumble back over to his bed, just to make sure. The blast tore his face into several loose flaps of skin, the two on either side spreading to make a wide bloody chasm. Part of his scalp peeled up in jagged shreds. In that mess of gore and shattered bone I can't help but see it: a rough outline of Him.

You're going crazy.

Then: *What the hell am I supposed to do now?*

I pull out my phone to call 911, but stop. The screen shows four missed calls from Rosalind. A series of texts, the last one reading:

Emergency. Pls call now. Maya n trouble.

It's too much. I can't handle any more. I just stare at my phone like a drooling zombie.

This is your daughter. Get it together.

Marco is past all help. He can wait. I call Rosalind.

"Dr. Dennings, thank god!"

"What happened?"

"Maya . . . on the field trip today? She . . . she *stabbed* her teacher."

"What? That's not possible."

But of course it is . . . And that means now He's inside my Maya too.

"I . . . It's true. She did. With scissors. I was taking a video for you . . ."

"Send it to me."

Rosalind pauses. "I don't think you want—"

"I need to see what happened!"

"Okay, I'll send it."

"Where's Maya now?"

"With me. I'm driving her to the hospital. She started shaking . . . and saying things . . . I can't understand her. They called nine-one-one for Mrs. Laird. Said the *police* were coming. But I couldn't just *wait* there. She was having a seizure. I didn't know what else to do! So I—"

"You did the right thing. Bring her to me. I'll take her over."

I hang up. Thirty seconds later, a new text comes from Rosalind. I open the attached video link, and no nightmare has ever been worse.

At the Balcones Children's Craft Center, Maya stands at a kid's easel totally absorbed in her painting. But she's not having fun. Her face is pale and blank. Her eyes glazed over. I can't see the surface, but it looks like she's finger painting. Something she hasn't done since she was four. There's a drop of dark paint trailing down her arm, and I realize she's not using paint. Mrs. Laird comes over to admire the work with a big patronizing smile that I watch sour into dismay, then disgust. She takes Maya by the shoulders, saying something like, "Honey, are you okay?" Maya tries to turn back to her painting, but Mrs. Laird holds her in place. Maya *shakes*. The camera starts coming forward, Rosalind realizing something's wrong. I watch Maya's little hand snake into the pocket of her apron, and then, nearly too fast to make out, she strikes Mrs. Laird in the neck. The woman topples back onto her ass, and I can just discern the orange handles of a pair of craft scissors sprouting from the side of her windpipe. The camera falls to the ground.

It can't be real. My child. My baby girl.

A braying sob of grief and terror erupts from my throat. But Maya needs me. I can't give in to despair.

Take a deep breath. Get through this.

I know you will.

It feels like *someone else* whispers those words to me. Almost as if Marco's mangled corpse spoke them. Him, I guess.

I stumble out of the room. I want to scream for help, but something tells me that will only bring further disaster. The police would shut down the entire floor.

Can't allow that, can we?

I close Marco's door and lock it with my master key.

Then I run for the stairs.

Tynes is just coming through the door as I arrive. He looks like hell. A traumatized vacancy in his eyes, as if he's going into shock. There's a big patch of hair missing on the side of his scalp that bleeds down his hairline behind his ear. His lower lip is bloody too. Cassie must have attacked him. But whatever happened, I need him now.

"Bill, set up DreamCatcher with your new program. I'm going to get Maya."

"Maya?"

"We've infected my daughter with this . . . *thing*. Now we're going to get it out. Whatever it takes."

I step past him and down the stairs. Behind me I hear, "Glo . . . I don't know if—"

"Goddammit, Bill! I need your help. *Maya* needs you."

As I sprint to the ground floor, I hear something like wailing behind me.

He's coming apart . . . But fuck him. I'll do it myself if I have to.

I wait through six minutes of agony before Rosalind's blue Civic zips around the driveway. I open the rear door before she even gets it stopped. Maya's lying on the backseat, shaking and whispering nonsense. Her pixie hair standing up in spikes from the blood in it. As her empty gaze alights on me, she wipes her bleeding hand from ear to ear, making a grisly crimson curve on her face. Then she twitches like something's stabbed her deep inside.

I drag her out and carry her across my arms. She feels so light, I wonder crazily if she's somehow been hollowed out. Rosalind calls after me. "Where are you going?"

"I'm going to give her an MRI. It'll save time. I'll see you at the emergency room."

She stares at me as I run with my daughter toward Dreamland.

The door opens on an empty room, all the DreamCatcher's monitors still dark.

Fucking Tynes. He picks NOW to pull another disappearing act?

I run with Cassie back into the hall, wondering where the fuck he is. There's a trail of blood droplets leading right to his office. The drops turn to spatters, which turn to puddles and smears. By the time I get to his door, I can make out his footprints.

Inside, there he is, clutching the armrests of his office chair, facing away, contemplating the stupid phrenology poster up behind his desk. He doesn't turn when I enter.

He's still doing this shit at a time like this?

"Tynes! Goddammit, will you fucking look at me?"

He slowly swivels his chair, and the sight of him slams me back against the doorjamb. Not him . . . HIM.

Tynes has yanked all the hair out of his head in meaty clumps but for two spikes atop the bloody remains of his scalp. Worse, *he's chewed through his own cheeks,* the whole middle of his face gone to expose all his teeth and gums, flaps of skin hanging loose to make one giant gruesome grin. His eyes are lit with madness.

Maya swivels her head toward him. Her arm rises as though . . . *she's reaching out to him.*

"Oh, Bill, what have you done to yourself?" He frowns, confused by my question. I ask, "Is . . . is He . . . ?"

A weird spasm runs through him. "No . . . I'm still fighting."

"Bill, look at your face. You're *turning into Him*."

He rotates his head disturbingly far around to check his reflection in the poster's glass. He frowns as though he can't see what I'm talking about. Then he whips back around to strafe me with his hungry eyes. "You're not looking so great yourself."

I take a step toward the door.

Bill rises from his chair, his hands out like he's soothing a rabid animal. But his fingers are flexing into claws.

I take another step back.

"Gloria. I know what you're trying to do," he says, urgency making his voice waver. "Please think for a minute."

"I don't even know who I'm talking to right now."

Maya shivers in my arms. Tynes gets around the edge of his desk.

"Look at me, Gloria . . . your old friend Bill." He tilts his head, then shakes it as if dismissing some internal argument. He says, "For Maya's sake. I . . . I just can't let you do it."

He doesn't want me to try to save my daughter? *Now,* after bringing this fiend into our life, he's worried about what might happen?

That thing is NOT your "old friend Bill." Of course He doesn't want you to cure Maya. And . . . and . . . he keeps calling you "Gloria." Bill always called you "Glo."

We stand locked there for a final second.

Tynes lunges for me right as I turn and bolt out the door, but slipping in the blood, he crashes to the floor.

Alone I would have made it, but with Maya squirming in my arms, he catches me just outside our lab. She flies from my grasp as we go sprawling down on the cold linoleum. Tynes grabs my belt and lurches on top of me, his mouth dripping blood into mine. I get my knee between us and kick out with all my strength. Emaciated Tynes goes flying off and slams into the base of an AV cart packed with gear for the nearby visualization facility. The impact topples a fifty-inch LED monitor onto him, which lands with a sickening thud.

I crawl to my feet and haul Maya into A-4.107. I turn to slam the frosted glass door, but it *won't close.*

Even pressing as hard as I can, the latch won't engage. Then I look down and see why: four now-crushed fingers wedged in near the floor. Through the tiny crack, I see Tynes's left eye rolling to white. His curdled voice: "Gloria. Stop."

"Bill, let go of the door."

"No. I can't let you do this to Maya."

He wants your daughter.

That alien voice inside me again. I almost lose it right there. Just fall down and surrender.

But no, you will never give her up.

I brace my foot against the door's base to keep it from opening. I say to him, "I fucking warned you, Bill."

Then I hurl all my weight against it. Once . . . twice. Again. Again.

Outside, Tynes shrieks as the door finally snaps closed, the sharp edge of the glass cleaving through his fingers.

He howls.

I turn to see my little girl staring at the fingers lying on the floor like bloody slugs. I pick her up and throw her onto the DreamCatcher's platform. Then I realize how hopeless this is. She has to be asleep.

Do what you must.

That voice again. I can't bear it anymore. My hands flap down to my sides in impotent despair.

And my right one finds the propofol syringe I'd meant for Marco.

Maya doesn't flinch when I jab it into the vein in her elbow and press down the plunger. Her eyes beam the purest terror at me for an instant before she collapses onto the bed.

Outside, Bill is screaming, "No! No! No! . . . I won't do that. I . . . I have to try to—" His words dissolve into a gurgling cry. He slams his head against the glass, leaving a spatter of blood.

I frantically wake up the DreamCatcher's computers.

Outside, Tynes goes quiet, and despite myself, I offer him a prayer of thanks for the smooth build file he's made of his new Mr. Smoke–fighting DreamCatcher code. It installs perfectly, and in two minutes, the system dings that it's ready to go. I hook up Maya to the vital-signs monitor and put in the UnderTone earbuds. Right away, the EEG tells me she's plummeting toward REM. I hit the button to send her into the MRI.

The door breaks.

But it doesn't shatter. The glass has heavy-duty lamination on both sides, which keeps the shards together and inhibits the cracks spider-webbing out from the point of impact. Behind it, Tynes's shadowy form winds up for another blow with a sledgehammer. He must have found the workers' local tool stash.

He smashes shards to powder, and the plastic coating bulges. It'll never hold.

Do I call the police?

Not yet; they'll pull Maya out. And you won't get another chance. They'll destroy the DreamCatcher when all this comes to light.

Maya's descent into REM is inhumanly fast. Mr. Smoke *wants* her dreaming. But this time He's got a surprise in store. The first image from her dream flickers to life.

It's Him.

But not via some mathematically encoded trick. He's right there in the main signal. The demonic face *grins* at me. Maya's UnderTone becomes a tortured shriek. Her body spasms once but then goes utterly limp.

Tynes's third blow snaps the outer laminate. He drops the hammer and tears at the hole, even using the stumps of his left fingers to rip stuck shards out of the way. His face presses against the inside layer. His gaping mouth seeming to gnaw at the glass, his transformation into Mr. Smoke now complete.

The Mr. Smoke on the DreamCatcher's screen is faring less well. Fractals of static stab in from the edges, breaking up His evil visage. The whole image clouding. Then He snaps back into focus, but the UnderTone screams loud again, and the screen twitches and blurs and smashes Him into a thousand swirls of chaos. He's breaking up.

Please let the door hold. Just a little more.

Tynes claws savagely at the broken glass. The laminate gives until it seems it must break, but it doesn't. Tynes picks up the hammer and bashes at it again. He throws his body into it.

It holds.

With a scream of frustration, Tynes stalks back into the hall.

Maya's UnderTone screech now harmonizes with a new alarm squealing its distress. Maya's vitals have crashed.

My daughter is dying.

But Mr. Smoke is almost gone. I can barely discern the outline of him in the fizzing static of the screen. "Hold on, Maya. Just hold on."

I've never prayed in my life. I don't even know who I'm asking, but I say, "Please just let her live."

Are you sure that's what you want?

I pound my head, trying to jar loose that infernal hiss. A dim rumbling sound starts outside. A faint vibration in my feet.

Now there's an earthquake? . . . Stop it. You're going crazy.

The dulcet ping of Tynes's program hitting some kind of success threshold. The horrific siren of Maya's pulse flatlining. I slap the release button on the MRI bed. Then . . .

A massive gray block explodes through the door, knocking me clear across the room into the wall. The last thing I see is a white appliance flying off the top of the cart Tynes has rammed through the glass. It slams into my face.

Wake up now, Gloria, I'm not finished with you yet.

A crushing pain in my head wrenches my eyes open. They clench shut again before I can process what they've seen:

Tynes straddling Maya on the MRI bed. His hands clutching at her chest as he leans over, biting her face.

My head jerks up, and I look again.

No, that isn't it . . . He's KISSING her. His charnel house of a mouth over hers, bubbles of blood forming around his teeth. What is he DOING? Does he think he can breathe more of his sickness into my daughter?

I rise like a marionette getting all its strings yanked at once, ripping free of the cord tangled around my shoulder. I throw myself on Tynes and hurl him off the platform. He shouts, "No!" as we slam to the ground.

I find that my arm has popped snugly under his chin. As if of its own accord, my right hand finds my left biceps, my left hand the back of his head. I squeeze with all the fear and hate and despair now boiling inside me, and the choke slots into place like a dream. It feels perfect. Pure and true.

He hurt my daughter and now I have him, and he will never be able to harm her again.

Tynes's feet beat against the floor, and I wrap my legs around him and squeeze with those too.

Yes, finish it.

"Go to Him, you motherfucker," I whisper.

Tynes gives up so easily. It feels like only a few seconds until he's still.

As I push him off me, his head lolls to the side and I get a final view of that hideous grin. I take Maya in my arms and find her pulse. It flutters faintly, but then there's a stronger beat. Then another . . .

I stare at the DreamCatcher's final image and see no sign of Him. The tide of relief staggers me.

I survey the shattered ruin of our lab. My daughter will live, and maybe she's even saved . . . but what am I supposed to do now?

Run.

Two people are dead, and who knows what'll happen to the other Somnos? There is no way I can explain this. They'll think I'm crazy. They'll take away Maya and lock me up. And what if she's not cured? Who's going to help her?

Run.

Upload the new DreamCatcher code to your private repo. You'll find a way to get access to an MRI. You're going to need it for yourself.

I run with my daughter out of Dreamland forever.

The parking lot of a cheap motel. ATM card maxed for the day. I'm looking at my broken nose, both eyes starting to blacken. The long gash along my eyebrow. *Don't go in there. They'll call an ambulance. They'll call the police.*

The asshole manning the desk takes my cash and asks if I want him to "check on me" later.

You're a junkie who just got rolled. He won't call anyone.

As night falls out the window of this comically disgusting motel room surrounded by fat, tatted gangsters hanging around the parking lot, I feel the slightest respite. My head swims, and I so badly want to collapse onto that sticky polyester bedspread and . . .

But no. I don't want that at all. And my daughter has blood all over her. I dampen a washcloth in the sink.

We can clean ourselves up, but the problem's on the inside, isn't it? What will you do if Tynes's cure didn't work?

Look at what happened to him. His new DreamCatcher didn't help. It made him worse. He didn't feel Mr. Smoke pressing on him today because He had already taken over. Tynes tore out all his hair and *ate* his own cheeks. He made himself *into* Mr. Smoke. He's been fighting his demon for months, and then one night after his "treatment," he's all the way gone.

Maya stirs as I wipe her face. Her eyes flutter open, and I almost think she's about to smile at me. But then she recoils.

I try to calm her. "Honey, it's okay . . . It's okay. You don't have to worry about that man. You're safe. He will never try to hurt you again."

She stares at me. "But . . . but, Mommy . . . I think he wanted to *help*."

Something flickers in my mind. Tynes screaming at me, "Look at *me*, Gloria . . . your old friend Bill!" It wasn't him, it was Him.

Though is that right? He wasn't ALL gone. He was still fighting. Using the pain to keep Him away. Why else would he yank his hair out . . . and CHEW THROUGH his own cheeks?

The memory returns: Tynes up on the MRI bed, straddling my daughter, air hissing out from between his teeth. The way he clawed at Maya's chest . . .

He wasn't really CLAWING . . . more like he was PRESSING. Like trying to . . . Like he was giving her . . .

It hits me. A blow to the temple.

CPR.

He was trying to save her life. You gave her a propofol dose sized for a two-hundred-pound man. No wonder her vitals crashed. And the cart he smashed through the door? That was the first-aid trolley we're required to keep on hand for our residents. The plastic thing that hit you? Think. You pulled a cord from around your shoulder and you felt something on the end of it. A paddle . . . It was a defibrillator.

Bill was trying to save your daughter's life.

And you strangled him.

Maya murmurs, "Mommy, what happened to him?"

"He got very sick, sweetie." My mind is a crackling blaze of panic. Screaming over and over, *What have you done? What have you done?*

Get a grip. Tynes was a monster. He attacked you and Maya. He was trying to stop you from treating her.

You do what you have to.

She says, "No . . . I mean—"

I can't have this conversation right now. "Here, honey, let me clean up your hair." She trembles as I sit her in front of the mirror and try to tease out the brown clots. She grabs a crusty strand and regards it, rubbing the dark granules with her thumb.

Good. She's trying to help.

But then with a sharp jerk, she yanks it out.

"Maya, no!"

That's when I see it. In her once immaculate blue eyes: little ripples. Swirls. Smoke.

He's still inside her.

I look away, knowing she'll catch the horror on my face. It takes everything I have to stifle a cry of grief. Our cure didn't work. And He still has my beautiful baby girl.

But you knew that, right?

I notice Maya studying my face intently in the mirror. She says, "I *have* to . . . the Man is still here. And He won't go away. What does He want, Mommy?"

What does this evil thing want?

All of it.

The words are out of my mouth before I can really make sense of them. "He wants to take over. He wants to hurt anyone who tries to stop Him. He wants us all for Himself."

Maya nods. I take a shuddering breath. "But that's not going to happen. We're going to keep fighting."

Maya yanks out another lock of hair. I wrap my arms around her and grab both wrists. Maybe a little too roughly. She struggles against me. "I *am* fighting. Why are you telling me not to?"

"You don't have to hurt yourself."

"Yes, you do! It's *how* you fight Him." She twists hard in my arms, but I hold firm. Maya abruptly goes slack and slumps into my embrace. "But *you're* not," she says.

"Not what, sweetie?"

"You're not fighting Him . . . Why aren't you?"

"Listen to me. I *swear* to you, honey. I will never let Him have us. I won't rest until we figure out a way to get rid of Him."

She closes her eyes. "You can push Him back when you're awake. But when you're asleep He's too *strong*. When you're dreaming He's always there . . . and it feels like you'll never keep Him out."

She's right. My eyes overflow as I face the truth: our only chance to reverse this sickness, to drive Him away, died with Tynes. I squeezed the life out of our only real hope back in Dreamland.

Alone, I'll never be able to fix the new DreamCatcher code. I don't have what Tynes had, and no amount of determination, no amount of hard work, will ever change that. Mr. Smoke is with us now. He'll warp and scour my daughter's mind until her life is a festering hell. Until she begs to die. He'll get stronger and stronger every night.

Every time she dreams.

I let go of her hands and just gaze into the shifting mist in her eyes. She pulls out another strand of hair.

Maybe I can't destroy Him. But there's nothing in this world I won't do to protect my daughter. To spare her this terror and pain. Nothing.

My hands fall to her shoulders, on either side of her fragile little neck.

But how do you keep someone from dreaming?

Meat Maker

MARK NEVELDINE

A young lawman woke up fully dressed in Phoenix. He stepped over Jack Daniel, who was lying down, feeling empty. The lawman felt empty too. He stepped outside, then stepped into his vehicle. It was noon. His shift started five hours ago, exactly at seven a.m. Late, yes, but a first for him. The good lawman had perfect attendance at the PPD and tardy was never on his list of attributes. The Phoenix chief of police would go as far as to say that this specific officer of the law was the best he had. Well liked too. Always remembered a name after he shook a hand—even if the name required seven or eight words to get the point across.

But right now, sitting in his boiling-hot car, he can't remember a thing.

I can't hear anything. I'm fucking deaf.

Three hundred and sixty-one days ago, the lawman arrived to his post forty-five minutes early to get his paperwork done. He was more concerned with doing "real" police work when the clock hit seven: catching criminals, pulling speeders, and serving citizens. As he was parking his personal vehicle he noticed a commotion in the alleyway. Quick to service, he ran over and stopped an armed mugger from attacking a pregnant woman, who was kind enough to relieve her morning sickness into a trash can. Just before the criminal could stick her belly with a four-inch blade, the lawman struck the pathetic human in the throat and had him in a wrist-breaker and cuffed. Two months later, the proud mother named her baby boy after the heroic lawman. But a hero's name is never important, only his deeds.

On this morning, at this moment, the dazed lawman started driving. Fast. Boot to the pedal, metal. Hold on.

Why can't I remember what he told me? I gotta drive.

His car finds a middle-aged couple, biking. Janet and Danny Marlin. Two peas in a pod. High school sweethearts who made their money in shady real estate deals. Supposedly, last December, Janet sold a rat-infested home to a blind man from Gallup, New Mexico. When he complained about all of the scurrying she told him that the house might be haunted, but there were certainly no disclosures for that sort of thing. Suddenly, the lawman's car plows into the real estate agents. SMACK! CRUNCH, CRUNCH. Blood and body parts slide off the front of the car.

Just drive.

A woman holding her smart technology looks out of her second-story window and doesn't understand why there's a bike in the tree, dripping blood. Halloween is four months away. *Must be the pot smokers. Or some failed excuse for modern art.* Then she looks at a bloodied cop car racing away. Our lawman turns on his flashers and cruiser-mounted cameras. There are three of them: grille-cam, back-up-cam, internal-cam. Standard issue. You've probably seen them, definitely been on them. All used to help in the pursuit of justice. However, justice is not exactly what he's serving today.

His cruiser makes a sharp turn and rips down an alley . . . two homeless bodies, sons of two unconnected drunks, stir against the brick wall. One takes a swig of cheap malt, the other picks his chapped nose while rambling incoherencies. The car quickly leans in to the malnourished bodies, scraping skin, guts, bones, and brain matter against the already burnt-red wall. A bloodshot eyeball erupts from one of the skulls. The bottle of malt, however, goes unharmed, ready for another hand to wash it down. The cruiser slams into a steel trash can, which flips up over the car.

The black-and-white (and red) cruiser blasts through the puddled alley. Ninety-degree right turn. Ninety-eight degrees outside. SMACK, SMACK. Two unidentified Phoenix hipsters, just leaving a poetry slam, become more unidentifiable.

RED AND BLUE LIGHTS. The young lawman is being chased by his brethren. He checks the rearview.

Friends.

The lawman smiles for the first time. Other police vehicles fall in line behind him. He drives even faster now, leading the men in blue on his quest for an answer. His weary eyes grow strong again and his knuckles crack as he grips the wheel. This march will finish strong and he has his comrades on his side.

The lawman thinks about his best friend.

Good times, BBQs, chasing girls, hangovers, and hunting trips.

They took one hunting trip where the then-aspiring lawman dropped an eight-pointer from 325 yards—a record distance for either of them. His best friend took a doe on the last night of the trip because he didn't see "any horns." Besides, a doe tasted better unless they were making venison jerky, in which case it hardly fuckin' mattered. The lawman joked once or twice that his best friend always took the doe, while he always found a perfect buck. It made sense that the lawman would follow the gun, and his best friend would dive into hydroponics. CRUNCHHH! More bodies and blood fly, bits and pieces hitting the windshield. Simply randoms. No backstory, barely a front story. A ligament hangs over the lens of the rear camera. The lawman checks his digital monitors, habit. A tibia or some leg bone swings off of the ligament.

People are disgusting.

BOOM. BOOM. BOOM. The lawman's vehicle takes a hit. Counts three of them from the vibrations. He calculates, then executes a strong maneuver left like an F-16 dodging a heat-seeking missile. The cops pull triggers. Stamped metal whizzes through the air. Making meat seems to warrant an open-fire policy. Our lawman dodges the swarm of kill-stones and cuts across the opposing lane of traffic and through the corner gas station. Chaos and collateral damage halt the chasing cruisers. He skirts through more oncoming traffic and then finds an on-ramp leading to the freeway.

The sun sneaks out from behind the shrooming clouds and blasts into the windshield, cutting through the thick red blood. The lawman unfolds his aviator sunglasses, also standard issue, and puts them on. He has a moment of regret. One moment. It's over.

He off-ramps.

Suddenly, and crunchingly loud, another human body hits. It looks a lot like his aunt Shelly, except for the fresh gashes and contortionist ability. His aunt Shelly hasn't stretched a day in her life, and he realizes it couldn't be her. The lawman closes his eyes and tries to remember what he was told last night. His crow's-feet grip tightly, working to extract the information with their horrible little claws, but the vault won't budge an inch.

Come on! What did he say?

His eyes snap open and up ahead is cute little Jenny Walker, spelling bee champ 2009–13, walking her well-groomed pug. The last word she spelled, competitively, was "crepuscular." It was on a blog about some vampire and werewolf movie that she first came across the word when she was eleven. She could never forget the abs on the lead actor or the eleven-letter word. Jenny was addicted more to the letters in a word than to the word itself. She didn't understand the purpose of misspelling a word. "What an affliction," she told her fifth-grade teacher after one of her classmates spelled "burial" wrong. Little Jenny appears camera left on the edge of the grille-cam . . . the camera veers over and suddenly eats up the spelling bee. A piece of dog hair annoyingly hangs over the grille-cam.

Dogs. D. O. G. S. Dogs.

The cop car does a celebratory three-sixty, then peels left down a major road riddled with terrified faces and middle-weight children. Time slows for the lawman. He remembers the first time falling in love. It was on this very street, Central Avenue. A miniskirt was involved. It was long before he understood the term "easy access." Nevertheless, he was in love for a week, until the Xbox was released in 2001, and from that very moment, he never saw nor thought about Mini again. Grille-cam reminds the young lawman of Xbox quite a bit. The pixel-perfect resolution, control in his own hands. It was, and still is, electrifying. His engine roars down the busy street.

Faces smash into the lens, one after the other . . . almost funny, as if the fools were jumping headfirst into the car. SMACK, SMACK,

SMACK, SMACK, SMACK, SMACK, SMACK, CRUNCH, CRUNCH, BOOM, SMACK, SMACK, SMACK, SMACK, BOOM, BOOM.

The bulletproof windshield starts to show signs of weakness. A .44-caliber head attached to a four-hundred-pound body finally makes a decent spiderweb on the passenger side. The car bounces over human speed bumps and then digs into another lemming as the lawman adjusts his mirror. He drives the body hard left through a fence that immediately wrinkles around the car, then just as quickly flies off. A kidney and some intestines twist back and forth on the hood. The kidney rolls off, and the long, stringy, small intestine stretches over the fender to the ground, leaving a lengthy trail of gut . . . and we see it's still attached to a stomach . . . and farther up to an esophagus and tongue.

We're dealing with things that very few volunteer firemen could handle. The lawman stares at the healthy pink tongue.

Tell me, again.

Throat/tongue fly off the side of the car as it burns right.

Let me just watch you say it.

Acceleration. A construction worker pouring sixty yards of concrete for a fast-food chain gets beheaded . . . but fortunately for his skull, his faithful yellow helmet stays put. SMACK, SMACK, CRUNCH, BOOM, SMACK . . . a flock of not-so-faithful yellow lids go flying—heads and body parts captured on all of the cameras. Any freeze-frame could be directed by a Wachowski sibling. Anyhow, those heads were building a new McDonald's, because, well, we need another one. The kaleidoscope of colors is beautiful. It reminds the lawman of the vintage wallpaper in his fiancée's bathroom. One color doesn't sit well with him.

What organ is green? That's her favorite color . . .

The cameras are completely obscured by blood and tissue. The innards drip off now that the car is in reverse. SMACK, CRUNCH, SMACK, SMACK. The lawman remembers how he used to reverse the Evinrude motor on his fishing boat to get the weeds off the propeller. This is sort of like that. Unathletic bodies, currently residing at the Dunkin' Donuts, do backflips over the car and land on the hood. Parkour is apparently not an option at this speed. Pathetic, really. The lawman looks to the right.

Maybe I should call him.

Suddenly, he jacks the car into forward. GLUNK, GLUNK, BOOM, BOOM, CRUNCH. Bodies barely slow the car. The cruiser targets Wrett's Body Shop, but he's not stopping for repairs. One second later, he's blasting through wrenches, drills, sheet metal, blowtorches, and the hands attached to them. Mike Fernandez had just earned his auto-mechanic's license last week, and his wife, Julia, retrieved the embossed certificate from the mailbox this morning with a giant smile.

Tomorrow she'll receive another certificate from the county morgue and will attempt to recover benefits from their mediocre insurance company to cover living costs for her and the three kids.

It's almost pitch-black inside the garage. Bodies and blood cover the lenses. BLACK. BLACK. BLACK. EXPLOSION! The lawman breaks into the light and the car jumps across the street with a hint of a fishtail. A portly older woman, Ms. Greene, never married for obvious reasons, stands in front of a stone building. KERRUNCH. A perfect spray of blood as the car pins the old woman against the gray—now red—building wall. Soon Ms. Greene will finally look her color. Livor mortis, rigor mortis, algor mortis, eventually green at some stage of mortis.

It's so quiet right now. I can't hear a thing. What did he say?

Engine revs and the car jolts backward, one-eighties, and blasts off down the empty road. Fast. Wind attacks the car. Tissue, bone, ligament, and debris slide free from the roller coaster, then even the individual cells, plasma, and platelets disappear. The camera lenses crystal-clear. That's a verb. The car jumps over a railroad track and the road becomes more rural. The lawman must be going 150 miles an hour, but his speedometer only goes up to 85. I'm not sure why that is. It's very deceptive. The lawman is moving so fast now that he can barely read the road signs through the motion blur. Roads and inter-sections pass like a dream. An old cemetery passes on the left.

Get more stones.

SMACK. Feathers slap the window. A barn swallow—an annoying little bird with mathematical precision. Must have been the runt.

The car gets angry and turns into a field. Grazing cattle unknow-ingly prepare their steaks. BOOOOM. The hits are devastating; these fuckers are big. The car takes a beating. Cattle are getting branded left and right. It sounds like waves crashing into breakers. Blood, guts, and a head or two land on the car. A slab of rib eye lands on the hood. Up ahead, swine mingling with the beef. The lawman has a tangential yet quite insightful thought.

He heads straight for the pigs. BOOOOSH! Hot dogs.

When we met we had hot dogs at T.G.I. Friday's. I proposed to her there last year. Why am I so fuzzy? We're getting married soon, aren't we?

The car still manages to pay its bill at the steakhouse and then heads for the farmhouse. A farmer uses his hand, brow level, to look at the law-enforcement vehicle tearing toward him. SMACK! Farmer Brown takes an early retirement. His organs will not be donated to science. Mrs. Brown rushes toward the man-of-many-pieces and she gets crumpled under the car. "Crumpled" and "run over" are sort of different. FYI. Oh, important point, apparently the dog is faithful too, or maybe just hungry to eat some of the human tartar. CRUNCH! Second dog of the day.

The cruiser narrowly misses a tree and finds itself safely back on the road. Now the car is blasting toward the upper part of a lower-middle-class neighborhood. A group of kids are playing hooky around an aboveground pool. The car targets the group, then suddenly veers off and skid-parks in front of a white-and-beige double-wide. This is the home/office of his best friend. Attached to the back porch is a small greenhouse filled with hydroponics. There's a Phoenix medical license displayed in the square window. Respectable cannabis leaves gently waving inside. The cruiser shakes a bit as if someone is getting out. The car door closes. Our hero—correction, my hero—walks up the stairs of the home/office and enters.

Best friends need to talk more.

From outside everything sounds calm. Then a pleading. Quiet. A minor rumble. Quiet. The clanging of silverware. Quiet. Human efforts. Quiet. *Click*—the shitty screen door opens. *Clack*—it closes.

The young lawman exits with a severed head. It's wearing sunglasses and a baseball hat. It's handsome, at least for a guy in sunglasses and a baseball hat with no body.

He said something, but everything's silent again.

He attempts to make the head a hood ornament. It's a fail. He drops it on the ground, gets back into the car, and runs it over. CRUNCH.

I want to see her but something has changed, and I'm not feeling very well.

The car blasts off straight into the group of kids at the aboveground pool. This time he doesn't veer off but splashes through a red tidal wave that overtakes him and caves in the cracked windshield. The lawman punches it out of the way and notices he has company. A piece of a kid in the backseat.

The car safely reaches legal pavement.

The patrol cameras are once again clean. It may be a fresh start, and the road now becomes suburban. A very sloppy father-and-son basketball game is in progress, SMACK, SMACK, and now it's not . . . a father-and-son funeral will be scheduled for next Saturday, ruining an absurdly incredible playoff game on NBC at the Johnson home. The car takes out the hoop and screams across the lawn. An insurance adjuster in the opposite driveway is getting into his car, KERRRUNCH! He is now half in and half out of his car. Literally. He will not qualify for an adjustment.

Breathe. Breathe. She always wanted me to take yoga.

An arm flies through the open windshield and takes a passenger seat. More company. Okay with it. A meter reader runs behind a liquor store with healthy discount stickers and finds safety. A telephone worker is not so lucky and phones his mom from heaven. Don't worry, he had rollover minutes.

The car cruises down the street and slams into a fire hydrant. The water sprays through the windshield, and the lawman rubs his wet head.

I'm starting to remember.

The tax-fed police cameras find five dudes drinking in the back of a moving pickup truck. BAM! The truck tumbles into a ditch, and the five dudes crumple bones and scream like girls, as far as pitch goes. The patrol car roller-coasters up and out of the ditch, new limbs growing from the grille.

The car is speeding down the opposite lane. Johnny McAllister, born with a degenerative spine condition and told he would never walk, strolls across the yard. He joins his mother, Carrie, who carries rods for today's fishing trip, and whose stomach was bloated from her pancake breakfast. Their morning hug will hold for eternity as the car mows them off the lawn. Spine and pancakes battered in the truest sense and jammed into the space between the bumper and the radiator.

I need to know what he said and why my fiancée was involved. Can somebody tell me? I'm not asking you for that much.

Acceleration.

Then I need to go to her.

The lawman takes a hard right and heads across a high-school football field. No one's playing. The team sucks this year anyway. Paul Murphy, the star quarterback, transferred to Dover Prep because his grades blew. The lawman's best friend and licensed medical marijuana grower also happened to be the assistant football coach. The headless coach wanted to make himself feel better the day Paul quit, so he decided to buy a car way above his pay grade. This left him in an all-too-familiar position, and he had to take out a loan.

The loan officer happened to be a very pretty twenty-seven-year-old blonde named Rosie. Coachless was crazy surprised that the young lawman's girlfriend was his ticket to a new ride. Rosie was equally elated to see Coachless and loved his choice of the deep-green BMW convertible. Coachless happened to be carrying some medical cones (joints, for those of you who don't have a medical condition). Rosie had a horrible penchant for oral habits. He and Rosie's shared cigarette break turned from oral to anal within minutes. In the midst of a great high and sensual bliss, Rosie whispered, "I like to break the law."

BAM! A surprise PIT move from a police SUV behind the lawman tears off his bumper and the various human remains curled inside it. The young lawman quickly corrects and voices his only word of the day:

"Oh."

He wakes up, snapped out of his insanity for a moment, and his ears start to pop. No longer is he above the flawed innocents; he is one of them. Another police cruiser positions for a PIT move, but the lawman aggressively shark-tails his cruiser and launches it over the curb and into a McDonald's. Build one, break one.

More cop cars descend on the lawman, and he's trapped on every side. BOOM, BOOM, BOOM. BOOM. BOOM. BOOM BOOM. Bullets connecting on metal, rubber tires, back windows, and mirrors. The lawman's rims tear through the hot pavement. He zigs where they zag. Sparks explode as he rips through the sidewalk, crossing into a full parking lot. Cops hold fire—too much collateral. Our hero severs a couple's feet with his black steel interceptor rims. Toe fungus immediately chopped from their list of problems and personal hygiene regimen. He guides his sparkler back onto the boulevard.

BOOM BOOM BOOM. The lawmen resume. Our lawman is leaking. Split clavicle, powderized coracoid process. He battles through and hard-rights. Rims grip perfectly as the chasing cruisers overshoot and slam into one another. He reaches into his glove compartment and grabs his Glock, .40 caliber. Checks it. Loaded. Thumbs off the safety.

More black-and-whites, cherry-tops, unmarkeds, and a SWAT van join the party. The lawman cuts across the divider, narrowly missing a UPS truck, and somehow breaks through the web of officers. He sticks the gun in his mouth. Tastes the cold metal. It's nice. He squeezes the grip . . . fingers the trigger . . . then . . . he bites down on the barrel and removes his hand from the gun. He chomps hard. Jaw clenches, red face. His teeth start to crack on the steel—central incisors, lateral incisors, canines, chipping, breaking. He pulls the gun out and rubs the cold metal on his face. Doesn't last long. He stares at the internal camera, which stares back at him.

He points the gun at the tiny thing and pulls the trigger— SMACKKK!

Suddenly a metro train comes out of nowhere, launching his cruiser sky high. Reports will say that the conductor was inebriated, seventeen people were killed, and another forty-eight were injured, including the lawman's fiancée, Rosie, who was going to stay with her mother for a couple of weeks to sort out her perverted constitution. The hospital will have to do for now.

Barely alive, still spinning midair, the lawman's last thoughts:
I feel a little better . . .
Last contraction of heart. Brainwaves draw to a close. End of life. Black. Black. Black. Black. Black . . .

Eyes

GEORGE GALLO

Boredom is an awful thing. It's the deadening of everything you do and experience. It devalues all that you once loved. Your wife, your work, friends, movies, food, long walks on the beach, sunsets, cigars, booze, laughter, you name it. It all just blends into one gray, lifeless, unamusing void. Once you're on the boredom express, it's impossible to get off. Days turn into months, months turn into years, and you rattle along bored by everything around you until you realize that there is absolutely nothing out there that can shake you into taking an interest in life again. That's where I found myself. I was one of those poor assholes commuting to and from New York City, heading to a job that meant nothing and back home to a place I was indifferent to. I read somewhere once that boredom was nothing more than repressed anger. Maybe that's true. It would certainly fit the bill, considering what happened.

I'd seen the homeless guy before. He was tall, thin, and dark with his features hidden under a hoodie, but I could feel him staring at me as I passed above him on the train. I'd be at my usual window seat looking down from the elevated tracks and he'd be there, as always, by his fiery trash can below. Since the first time our eyes locked we'd wait for each other, same time every day, to continue our stare-off. Neither one of us blinking. Neither one of us backing down. His stare was like nothing I'd ever experienced. It told me that I was the total embodiment of everything he had ever hated. It became a sick game for me, and I'm sure for him too. It was something to look forward to in our boring, monotonous lives. Some guys at the office had golf, others had women on the side, others jumped off bridges with bungee cords. I had my homeless guy who wanted to rip my face off and eat my heart while it was still beating.

And then I got bored with him too. One ice-cold afternoon as the train approached, he raised his head through the flames of his garbage can, his arms hanging at his sides as always, and I realized just how much I hated him. He was the mirror to the stupidity and redundancy of my own life. My dissatisfaction with everything. My home in the suburbs that I couldn't afford. My wife, Victoria, whose words I could hear before they left her mouth. My inability to get her pregnant. My suspicions that she was cheating. My idiot boss. My need for booze and pills just to fall asleep. For one final time, I locked eyes with the hulking scarecrow. I stared him down as I'd done at least a hundred times before, and then I changed the rules. I smiled and flipped him the bird. His reaction was intense. His gaze bore right through my skull. And then he was gone.

My house in Mamaroneck is just a few blocks from the train station. I have to admit that I like hearing the train from my bedroom. It's one of those things that I can count on. Every half hour the train rolls in and at night I lie in bed counting them, some nights two or three, before I fall asleep.

I walked up to my house with a little pep in my step. Sure, it was bite-ass cold and Victoria was waiting inside with bullshit about some co-worker who was trying to destroy her. I was just happy that I finally let that homeless creep know I'd had it and that the game was off. As ridiculous as it sounds, I felt pretty damn manly about it.

Victoria didn't even bother to say hello and asked me if I'd been drinking. I told her no, but she didn't believe me. She goose-stepped over like the damned Gestapo to smell my breath. I told her that I didn't need to be boozed up in order to be happy, but she wasn't buying it. It was my fault that she wasn't pregnant and that I wasn't taking her fertilization seriously by ingesting alcohol. We used to fuck like rabbits, in cars, on the floor of her parents' house, in the park. Anywhere and everywhere it hit us. Now she wanted to be fertilized. *Fertilized.* I couldn't think of anything less sexual than that. She was a woman, not a goddamn garden. Then she sounded off about the same predictable subjects and I followed my normal pattern of not listening. Adrenaline was coursing through my body. I couldn't wait until morning so I could board the commuter train and see the reaction on my homeless guy's face.

I counted trains until about two a.m., when I finally dozed off. That homeless son of a bitch was in my dreams, living in some awful place that reminded me of hell. The air was filled with the perfume of rat shit, sweat, and urine. His face was as unclear to me in my dreams as it was in reality. I kept walking down strange corridors where he was always up ahead, but he would turn a corner before I could get a good look at him. *If I could only see him more clearly,* I thought. *Get a better look at his face. See his eyes up close.*

The morning was clear and upbeat. I practically ran to the station and got on board the train. When I got to our spot in the Bronx, the homeless guy wasn't there. Just his trash can. I was deeply disappointed. In short order the train got sucked into one of the tunnels that led to Grand Central and another boring day of work.

I made calls, talked to clients, and did my best to make a few sales. Packer, my co-worker and the closest thing I had to a friend at the office, was jacked up about going to Vegas in a few days to make a presentation. He gave me the hard sell of how much fun we'd have. Packer saw himself as a kind of cowboy, although the next horse he would see would be his first. Under different circumstances I might have gone, but something told me that I should stay in town. Packer called me a pussy for declining his invite and assured me it would be his most memorable trip ever so he could rub it in my face.

I went to a lunch meeting uptown on the West Side for the new Volvo account and afterward decided to walk back to work. At first all I had was a feeling. It was nothing that I could pinpoint, but I had the increasing suspicion that I was being followed. As I walked through Central Park, passing everyone from students on field trips to old hippies singing Beatles songs, I kept looking back to see if someone was behind me. Every time I looked I saw no one. My thoughts began to run amok. There was no way the homeless guy could be on my trail. Or could he? Could he have somehow followed me to work? *No. That is nuts.*

Was I actually *enjoying* this?

Back in the office I anxiously awaited the evening so I could get on the train and see my homeless friend.

Finally, I was in my normal seat on the commuter train heading home. I counted the seconds as buildings, bridges, and pedestrians zipped past. I looked down at our spot and once again he wasn't there. He wasn't anywhere. I got out of my seat and scanned the opposite direction, hoping I could catch a glimpse of him. Again, nothing. No bum, just city streets and life as usual. Deflated, I went back to my seat and casually glanced into the next car. My blood ran cold. My heart rate doubled. There in the next car, looking back at me through the grimy doorway window, was my homeless guy. I could tell that he was staring me down from under his hoodie. He had angular features and a goatee of sorts that seemed to drip oil. I couldn't make out his eyes. They were hidden in the deep recesses of his shadowy sockets. He didn't budge or flinch. He didn't even appear to be breathing. He just stood there staring at me from those black sockets for what felt like an eternity.

The train slowed, the doors hissed open, and I jumped off quickly in the town of Larchmont. I moved with a group of people, hoping I'd lose him in the crowd. He was nowhere to be found as I headed down Main Street. My excitement evaporated as I realized how far I'd gotten from the train station. It was still a couple miles to Mamaroneck. I grew up in this area and knew plenty of shortcuts. I kept looking over my shoulder to make sure the homeless guy wasn't around.

At Spring Street I decided to cut through the woods to the Flats, which would put me near the Mamaroneck train station. My feet crunching through autumn leaves made a racket. When I stopped, I could still hear the sounds of leaves rustling behind me. It wasn't the homeless guy. It couldn't be. There was no way he'd followed me. I picked up the pace and in no time I was in a full-tilt sprint. I'd forgotten that there was a creek zigzagging through the woods. We'd had a lot of rain lately, and the creek was moving fast. I took a deep breath.

At least I'm not bored.

I tossed my briefcase over to the other side and then did my best to feel my way across the wet rocks in the dark. If I found a rock that felt sturdy enough to hold me I'd climb on top. This worked brilliantly a few times until I fell on my ass. The ice-cold water did a fine job of helping me get to my feet and to the other side.

I had to search pile after pile of leaves for my briefcase until I found it with my left foot and tripped forward. My shoulder caught the side of a maple tree and it tore through my clothing and skinned me. I became overwhelmed with nostalgia. The pain of skinning myself was something I hadn't experienced since I was a child. I picked up my briefcase and weaved through the trees, trying to find my way out of there.

I heard something behind me. Someone or something was crossing the stream. I was struck with the most bizarre thought, and I chuckled because it seemed like the most logical and simple of solutions.

There's no way I could do it.

I took a few steps and then ducked behind an enormous maple tree. I bent over and felt around in the dark for a large rock. I found a real beauty: smooth, cold, and very heavy. I picked it up and smelled the raw earth that clung to the bottom. I held the rock close to my chest and my quickly beating heart.

Who's gonna know? Just do it. Do it, do it, do it. Just kill the son of a bitch. Crush his miserable fucking skull.

The wind blew, the trees creaked, critters crept about, but no homeless guy ever showed up. Eventually I dropped the rock, picked up my briefcase, and moved through the woods once again. Then I started to run. I was running as much from my thoughts as I was from him. I found myself running as fast as I could. The cold autumn air hurt my lungs. I had been only a moment away from murdering someone. *No, that's not possible. That isn't me. I'm a nice, normal, civilized guy who lives in the suburbs. Get a grip.*

Something else was going on inside me. Something bizarre and totally unexplainable. It made me tremble with delight. It was fireworks and butterflies. The adrenaline rush was intoxicating.

I stopped running, caught my breath, and listened. After a long silence I heard the sounds of footsteps rustling through the leaves once again. I could feel him gaining on me.

There were the lights of homes up ahead. I ran and slammed right into a fence and hit the wet leaves hard. I hoisted myself over the fence, landed in the backyard, and hauled ass down to the street.

Luckily I saw a taxi, which I flagged down and took straight home.

My plan was to avoid Victoria and change out of my torn and muddy clothes, but she, ever the cop, headed me off at the bathroom. I told her that I tripped on the way home. She didn't buy it at first, but I told her a story about falling that had her laughing to the point of pissing me off. A story where I acted like a clumsy fool was totally believable.

Victoria continued droning on and on, and, oddly, she was more interesting than usual. I seemed more in tune with things. The sounds outside. The taste of my food. It was as if all of my senses were heightened. Animals must feel this way, their very survival depending on their ability to stay alert. I grappled with the notion of telling Victoria the truth about all that had happened, but I decided to keep it my dark little secret.

Later Victoria got some wild hair up her ass and wanted to go out. She, of course, didn't realize that I'd had enough excitement for one evening. I told her that there was no way I was going out, but she just wasn't hearing it, and we were in the car and heading to Rye Playland to ride the Dragon Coaster, one of the last great wooden roller coasters on the East Coast.

Rye Playland smelled like popcorn and cotton candy, and best of all there was the scent of the old, salty pier. I'd come here since I was a kid, and just the combination of all these aromas brought back memories of a much happier time. Victoria was like a little kid, and it was good to see her this way.

We got on the Dragon Coaster and began that wonderful, terrifying climb. Suddenly, I could have sworn I saw that tall, hooded figure watching us. Victoria screamed with joy and I did my best to join in, although I couldn't shake the notion that we were being stalked. The roller coaster hit all the turns I'd come to know by heart and we were eventually swallowed up by that big, old, smiling dragon. We spun around in the dark and out the back, where the ride quickly came to a stop.

Back in the park by the big clock, I thought I saw him again, but at second glance he was gone. Victoria asked me several times if I was all right. Even though I told her I was, she didn't quite believe me.

We stopped at the shooting gallery, where Victoria wanted me to win her some stupid prize. I didn't like guns all that much and Victoria knew that. It was at times like these that I felt she was testing my manhood.

I was heading to an empty spot at the counter when a gravelly voice called out that I was cutting. I turned and saw a hulking, tattooed biker type flanked by two equally tattooed blond biker chicks. I did my best to apologize, but Victoria stepped forward and informed them that we were first. Victoria was testing me. I knew that there was no way this could end well, so I said nothing. Victoria then moved over to the gun and took her position to fire. The biker dude protested again and threatened to bust me a new hole, whatever that meant.

Before I could respond, I saw him. Saw him for sure, watching us. Tall and hooded. Standing still while everyone else around him moved. I hooked Victoria under the arm and pulled her away. She was like a two-year-old, insisting that she didn't want to go. I looked her in the eye and made it clear that it was time for us to leave. We headed off, moving through the crowds toward the parking lot. I stole glances behind me as we walked. I couldn't see the homeless figure anywhere, but I knew he was somewhere in the crowd.

Victoria wanted to know why I hadn't stuck up for her. She insisted that she wanted to see me act tougher once in a while.

What would you like me to do? Kill him? Cut his throat? Cut out his fucking eyes? Would that make you happy?

She had no idea how close I had come to murder earlier that evening. If I had told her, she would have laughed in my face. What she said next was particularly disturbing.

I let people walk all over me.

There was a kind of finality to it. It was as if this had been brewing in her for a long time and it had finally surfaced. As concerned as I was about rescuing my manhood, I was even more worried that he was out there in the crowd, stalking us.

There was a white stuffed bunny rabbit back at the shooting range that Victoria wanted me to win for her. I laughed, saying I'd buy her one. Then she snapped. The bunny would have been a prize, a victory, a triumph, a way to remember the evening. Then she went off on a diatribe about how keepsakes and souvenirs were important because they reminded you of things that happened in your life. I checked out and stopped listening when she started talking about astronauts collecting moon rocks. I didn't think it would have done me any good to inform her that it wasn't the same as collecting seashells.

Then she took me by the hand and pulled me toward the Olde Mill. A few minutes later we climbed aboard one of those rickety old wooden boats and went up an equally rickety ramp, which dumped us into a torrent of water, sending us off into the tunnel of love. Victoria wanted to make out with me, to be ravished. She was switching gears so quickly it was difficult to keep up. One minute I'm some ball-less creep who won't defend her from bikers, the next I'm some Viking rolling into town to rape her. Her craziness was exciting seven or eight years ago. Now her unpredictability was the thing that made her the most predictable.

I gave her a lackluster kiss, but her lips convinced me to give her more. This would be one of many battles she would win that night. We were soon making out passionately.

We lurched forward in the darkness as if we hit something and Victoria giggled. I leaned in to her and was about to tell her everything when she actually surprised me. She wanted to have sex right then and there in the boat.

Before I could answer her, we were illuminated by the beam of a flashlight. A large, hulking figure stood over us. I leapt up and grabbed the flashlight from his hands and was about to throttle him with it when I heard the squawk of a walkie-talkie. I turned the flashlight around and discovered that I had grabbed on to a ride attendant. I apologized profusely as he unhooked the boat and shoved us on into the dark. I did my best to catch my breath. Victoria couldn't stop laughing.

My mind reeled as I drove home. Should I tell Victoria? Should I go to the police? This was the most exciting thing that had happened to me in a very long time, and I was reluctant to let it go.

As I got ready for bed I couldn't find my iPhone. I had no luck locating it anywhere in the house. I didn't remember using it after I left the office. Did it fall out of my pocket on the Dragon Coaster or on the Olde Mill? A chilling thought crossed my mind. I had dropped it in the woods. I prayed it was at the bottom of the stream as opposed to being alongside the fence I ran into where it could easily fall into his hands.

I was about to slip into a deep sleep when the landline rang just after three a.m. Victoria jumped awake, convinced something bad might have happened to her mother. I picked up the phone and listened. No one said anything. There was only silence, followed by the sound of the wind and then a passing train. A moment later, I heard a train pass just a few blocks away. Victoria asked who was on the phone. The caller broke out into a blood-curdling scream. It sounded almost like gargling. The cacophony ended as the voice fell to a calculated whisper.

"Your wife is very pretty," the caller said and hung up.

Victoria asked who the caller was. I told her it was someone from the amusement park who had found my phone. She got pissed that they would call so late and within minutes was back asleep. But not me. I couldn't sleep now. I knew that fucking lunatic was out there and that he had my phone.

The next morning I could feel his presence as I walked to the train station. Victoria had left ahead of me and gone to work, so I felt that she would be okay. It wasn't her he was after anyway. It was me.

I got on the train, hoping I would see him. I went car to car, checking every last seat to make sure he wasn't on board. As we came up on 125th Street, I thought about getting off, heading north and finding him. *Reconciliation,* I thought. *That's how I'll end this.* Maybe money would do the trick. I'll tell him I'm sorry. I stepped forward as the doors hissed open. I wondered if he could even comprehend the notion of forgiveness. He was the personification of evil—or was this just my upper-middle-class fear of the homeless manifesting some way? He could certainly be psychotic. Trying to reason with him might just make it worse.

In Grand Central Terminal I could swear he was on the upper level looking down on me. I took the escalator up and looked around. I found a homeless guy there with his hand out, seated with his back against the wall. He stunk of his own piss and vomit. I handed him some money, hoping I could leverage my guilt with the universe. He refused to take the money and laughed a horrible throaty cackle. Then he told me that I was dead, I was dead and didn't know it. I put the money back in my wallet and headed to the office.

At lunch, I told Packer about everything that had been going on over the last few days as he gulped down beer after beer. I ended by saying that I was thinking of going to the cops. He convinced me that this was a bad idea and that there was nothing the cops could do. I would come off like an idiot trying to explain it all. Last, he gave me his patented hard sell that he could straighten all of this out if I invited him over for dinner. There was nothing he could do, but I agreed.

We stopped and had drinks at a bar in Grand Central and then got on the train. When the doors opened at 125th Street, Packer leapt up and took off down the platform. I yelled after him to get back on the train, but he took the stairs down to street level. I had to follow him just to make sure he didn't get himself killed.

I felt very alone and vulnerable. It was a loud place. Lots of riffraff, and I felt like a target. I finally caught up to Packer. We walked for several more blocks and over a bridge into the Bronx. I took him to the spot where I had first seen the object of what had become my nightmare. Packer laughed and looked at me when he saw the trash can. He admonished me for being frightened of some homeless idiot and called me a pussy. Then he yelled out into the evening that we weren't afraid of him and kicked over the trash can. There was a shopping cart a few feet away. It was filled with the necessities one would have to use to live on the street. There were plastic bags, old dirty blankets, cans, and for some reason, a teddy bear. Packer took the cart and wheeled it away. Against my wishes he pushed it down a set of stairs that led to God knows where. After shouting some more obscenities at whatever phantom might be listening, he turned and headed back to the train station. If this was Packer's idea of fixing the situation, it was far from helpful. I caught up with him and said that what we were doing was wrong. Some sense of civility took over in me and I said that the homeless guy was a person too. Packer laughed in my face and said that some people just didn't count.

At dinner, Packer drank a lot more than usual. He had twice as much steak as Victoria and I put together. Then, after smoking several of Victoria's cigarettes, he grunted something about her being very beautiful, followed by his need to go home immediately. He was leaving for Vegas the following day to do his presentation.

A little later, I drove him back to his apartment in Brooklyn Heights. It was raining hard: a cold, mean, nasty rain that punished everything around us. I let him off and watched him as he stumbled toward his building. The doorman took over from there, letting Packer inside, used to this behavior.

As I took the Bruckner Expressway through the Bronx, I wondered where the homeless guy would go to stay dry in this kind of weather. I couldn't imagine him in a shelter, grateful that someone had given him a roof over his head and a bowl of hot soup. How the hell does someone get so far off track? Was he always crazy, or did it happen incrementally until one day he just gave in to madness? Then I wondered about myself and the way I was behaving. I was being threatened and doing very little about it. I thought for a moment that I would take the exit, go to his neighborhood, and end this, whatever that meant. But no, I was civilized. I kept driving. I wondered if being civilized was just an excuse for being cowardly. I couldn't shake what Packer said to me. *Some people just don't count.*

When I got home I walked into the bedroom and found Victoria lying there naked and asleep. She looked amazing lit by the light coming through the bathroom door. *She did this on purpose.* I was sick and tired of asking permission for sex with my wife. She wasn't about to get fertilized, or we weren't about to make love, or any other bullshit. We were going to fuck and that's that. I rolled her over. She moaned and whispered something unintelligible as I entered her. She seemed to be going along with the program until she finally awakened. Then her eyes went wide and she looked at me in an indescribable way. Then she started to fight me. She cursed. She flailed. She did everything she could to get out from under me, but I just wasn't going to stop. *We used to have rough sex all the time,* I told myself. *So what?* She tried to cry out but I covered her mouth. Then she bit my hand. Hard. I didn't let up until I was done. Afterward she rolled over on her side, silent. I waited for her to say something, anything, but it never happened.

I went to the kitchen and had some orange juice. I sat in the dark for a while. The longer I was there, the more guilty I felt. I knew that if I woke her and apologized it would only make things worse.

I was awakened in bed around three a.m. The phone was ringing again. On the other end all I could hear was grunting and what sounded like someone beating watermelons with a baseball bat. Then, after a long silence, that same voice whispered to me as it did before. It was oddly calm and even more oddly articulate. "I'll bet your wife has a pretty cunt." Victoria, having been awakened, called me every name in the book. She told me that what I had done to her was horrible and that I needed to go see a psychiatrist. Then she ordered me to sleep on the sofa.

The next day at work my boss informed me that Packer had not showed up in Vegas.

I left work early and cabbed it to Packer's apartment. I had a key to his place, having had to crash there a few times when we worked through the weekend. The apartment looked immaculate, except that the faucet to the kitchen sink was dripping. I turned it off and I noticed some fruit flies buzzing around the drain. I hit the garbage disposal button and what I saw made my mouth fill with vomit. Blood, hair, and chunks of flesh bubbled out of the drain and began to form a sticky, disgusting pool. My legs gave way as I heaved my guts out. The pulpy remnants of what I assumed was Packer spilled off the sides of the sink and spread across the floor toward me.

I don't remember calling the cops or what I said, but a short time later I was surrounded by detectives in Packer's living room, telling them all I knew. After questioning me from every angle, they said I could go but that they'd be in touch.

When I got home I saw my cell phone on the table. Victoria picked up right away that I was surprised to see it. *Jesus,* I thought. *The homeless guy has been inside our house.* I did my best to play it off and suggested that we get a hotel room for a few days. I told her that I wanted to make up to her for what I had done the night before. She wasn't buying it and kept on pressing me. Finally, I told her the truth. Every last horrible detail. I expected her to yell and scream. None of that happened. All she did was quietly grab a few odds and ends and leave. I couldn't blame her and didn't try to stop her. She took our car and was gone in no time.

A little later I picked up my cell phone to call her, but my photos came up instead. Shots of the yard. Shots of the house. A great one of Victoria laughing as we watched TV. As I continued to scroll, I came across some new ones I didn't take. Victoria shopping. Me on the street in New York near my office. Me and Packer in the Bronx dumping the shopping cart. Victoria and me as we slept in our bed. Packer beaten to a bloody pulp. Packer gutted and chopped up into several pieces. Then more of Victoria. Her meeting some guy for lunch. Laughing with him. The two of them kissing in his car.

Hours later I was still sitting on the sofa. I was shattered but not all that surprised. Victoria had been slipping away for months. Somehow it all paled next to seeing my friend Packer chopped to little bits and pieces. Then my iPhone buzzed. I hoped that it was her and that she had come to her senses. I wanted to know who the guy was and how long all of this had been going on so that I could punish myself with all the gory details. But truth be told, I was relieved. I'd been living under a cloud of lies for too long. I had thrown off a switch in my brain. I was just marking time day after day doing everything in my power to not look at what was clearly in front of me.

But instead of a text from Victoria, there were photos. Victoria was naked and tied to a pipe in a concrete room with dirty water on the floor. A text followed.

"Not only pretty, but tasty."

Something welled up in me that I didn't know existed. It was a wonderful feeling of joy and complete excitement. I felt that a great weight had been lifted from my shoulders and that I was about to indulge in something that I had kept at bay for nearly as long as I'd lived. I was *really* going to kill someone, and I had no sense of anxiety or guilt. Someone who didn't deserve to live. Someone no one would miss. Someone who didn't count.

I went into the kitchen and collected several knives, the largest being our carving knife, which I sharpened to perfection. Then I went to the neighbor's house and told him that I had a family emergency and I needed his car.

I drove to the Bronx. The night was alive and the air crystal clear. I listened to jazz as I drove south and into the wretched bowels of his neighborhood. I parked the car a few blocks from the train station and got out with a sense of power. I was amazed at the clear, cold smells of concrete and steel. The moon was bright, and I moved joyously and without a shred of fear. I was using senses I didn't know I had. I went where I could feel his presence.

I found an entranceway to the storm drains where all the waste from Manhattan washed out into the river. I walked into the cavern and was instantly hit with the smells of rat shit, sweat, and urine, just like in my dream.

There was a whole world down here that existed apart from the city streets above. Bums out of Dante's *Inferno* were huddled in groups. Some of them were asleep, others gathered around fires. The deeper into this stinkhole I traveled, the more I felt the desire to rescue Victoria. Not because I dreamed of some happier future for both of us, but merely for an odd, pulsating, egocentric desire to liberate the primal male that beat in my heart, which had been denied for way too long.

I could feel eyes watching me. No one was going to stop me as I continued downward. Not one. Not a single one. Then I heard Victoria sobbing, pleading for someone to help her. She was calling out my name. I was still the one she counted on in her moment of terror and weakness. I took solace in that. She had married me for a reason.

I found her tied to the pipe just like in the picture. She couldn't believe her eyes when I appeared.

"Martin?" she called out. "Martin?"

It was as if I were hearing my name for the first time. I untied her and wrapped her up in my coat. She broke down, but I told her to be still.

"Where is he?" I asked.

"I don't know," she said. "Let's just get out of here."

I could feel him close by. This wasn't about her. This was all about me.

Victoria shrieked and I turned and we finally came face-to-face. It was the first time that we were separated by only a few feet.

He was so much larger than me. He had a long face, almost too long for his body. In the dark I couldn't tell where his head ended and his hoodie began. His breath smelled like garbage. His teeth went every which way. He held an aluminum bat and smiled. Then he took a swing at me.

I could have ducked but chose not to. I let him hit me square in the jaw. I felt my jaw break and saw stars. Considering the blow, I recovered quickly and allowed myself to relish this new feeling of pain. It was wonderful. I was alive. Fucking alive. My mouth filled up with warm blood and it sent tingles of joy throughout my body. He swung again and this time I ducked. He overreached and lost his balance. I took the opportunity to stick him with my carving knife. It was a lovely deep plunge just below his ribs. He was surprised that I'd stuck him so quickly. He flailed at me, but I only drove the knife in more deeply. As he screamed, I grabbed a steak knife from my back pocket and stuck him through the neck. Blood sprayed in my eyes and mouth. Then he smiled. I couldn't believe it. He smiled as his life was leaving him, and he fell to the wet concrete with a nasty thud.

Victoria cried out, but I sure as hell wasn't through yet. While he was still breathing I placed my knee on his throat and cut out his fucking eyes. Victoria was right. Keepsakes and souvenirs do help us remember. She was nothing short of a fucking genius.

Afterward, I led Victoria out of the sewers and back to the street above. The pain in my jaw was overwhelming, but I was still enjoying it. The sun was just beginning to crest as we reached the car. The streets were empty except for a few bums. One attempted to give me some attitude, but I stared him down in a way that told him it was in his best interest to move on.

I put my wife in the car. She said nothing. I reached into my pocket. His eyes were still warm. They felt good. Alive. Like victory.

Then I heard a rumbling sound. It was the sound of the commuter train I took to work every morning. I looked up to see the faces of the passengers on board. *That's what they are,* I thought. *Just passengers. Not one of them at the controls.* They all looked so pathetic to me. One guy in particular. He had an owlish face and glasses.

He looked down at me and our eyes locked. My contempt for him and his stupid pointless life was beyond description.

We didn't unlock our eyes.

Fuck him, I thought. *Fuck him.*

Procedure

JAMES DEMONACO

1

The nightmare is always the same. The mile-long midnight parade moves down Broadway, hulking and wending its way toward some indeterminate destination. The parade floats are black and shapeless, just heaping mounds of papier-mâché, bulbous black tumors hovering above this endless New York street. Twelve-foot-tall black-robed and hooded figures pull these monstrosities along with ropes, like pallbearers hauling megacoffins.

These carriers are not only faceless but also soulless.

This I know—in my dream I know this.

I am the only person in this night parade—I am the only soul. I stand atop a mountainous float, carefully balancing on the dark-papered amorphous street mass—slowly moving along—ushered by the empty hoods. What did I do to deserve this soulless tribute in this, my city—my city that I love to hate?

Then I hear it. A cacophony of cries and screams as wails of mindless agony rise all around me. So many. So many. I am overwhelmed, spinning, trying to locate the source of this collective cry of despair, pain, and fear. I find it in the city's skyscrapers, each reaching high into the sky dome of night, like fingers outstretched and groping futilely for heaven's aid. The buildings' windows open simultaneously, revealing hundreds of sinewy hooded figures. Their rotting hands grip people—

people I recognize. The last time I saw them they were dead—victims of NYC's psychosis. Infants imploded inside microwaves by cracked-out parents. Children eviscerated by pederasts. Teens cut down by bullets in gangland shoot-outs. Women pummeled to pulp by piss-drunk husbands. Merchants murdered for pocket change.

New Yorkers I couldn't save—all alive again.

The soulless hang the innocent victims out of windows, high above the city, above the midnight parade, above me. I reach up to them but there are too many and they're too far—and their cries for help are deafening. I can't take it. I can't reach them. I can't help them. Make it stop.

The soulless oblige me. They reveal knives.

They slice open each citizen's chest simultaneously. The rhythmic, incessant stabbing begins as it always does—each of the soulless jackhammering the bloody chest with its respective blade, knife-fucking lacerated flesh. Over and over and over. The killers are moaning now, titillated by the spewing blood rush that rains down over the parade, staining the city streets, pouring over me like Satan's benedictions.

Once again, I couldn't save them. I am awash with their blood. Their screams have stopped.

Mine have just begun.

2

I've worked the late shift at the Two-Seven on Forty-Fifth, Midtown, for twenty years and the journey is always the same. I lumber down Broadway—awake now—under its neon sensory signage blast urging me to buy this shit, buy that shit, buy all the shit. The rain of blood from my dreams is invisible to everyone but me. It's always there—as are the screams of those innocent citizens. The nightmare parade is ever present—awake, asleep, unconscious—whenever and wherever I am. It's barely dulled by the drugs running roughshod through my system 24/7—a futile attempt to create a wall between me and those victims, those infinite cries, their flowing blood. These dead New Yorkers are fucking strong, fighting through whatever I imbibe—begging for my help. I can't hide from them. Instead, I just run. I pop another Vicodin and barrel onward. It's all I can do. I keep running.

The precinct is packed with the late-shift zombie squad—the pill poppers, drunk skunks, psycho po-po, the flotsam of the force, placed here in the center of the shit to deal with the nastiest the city has to offer. We barely speak—mirrors of one another's pain—tormented by all we've seen in NYC's witching and bitching hours.

I am the only broad—but gender doesn't matter here. It once did, when I was a newbie with tits that stood tall and a face that wasn't a map of places no one would want to visit. Against popular feminist opinion, I liked it better when they glanced my way and ogled my ass. Now I'm just another one of these damaged dicks with two ex-husbands, no children, a lot of acquaintances (no friends), and tired eyes that have seen unforgettable misery. We all share a similar story. We're all just sifting through the detritus of our shattered psyches. We have nothing to offer one another. No solace. We leave one another alone.

My decrepit captain, who could sweat in Antarctica, grumbles at me from across the cramped room.

"There's a new file on your desk."

"Fuck you."

"I understand."

The file lies precariously on top of my shit. I don't have time for this. I'm backlogged with twenty-five open homicide cases, some going back eight years. Before I raise holy hell and tear clammy Cap a new asshole, I glance inside. Morbid curiosity drives me, nothing else. It's another body. Surprise surprise. *How were you violated, John Doe?* I riffle through the dossier and see it. This is not a new case.

It's the same as the others. The fifth one in three weeks.

3

The white-robed and bespectacled coroner stands next to the body, describing in great detail how John Doe departed our earthly sphere. For a moment I wonder how many victims of NYC have lain upon this shiny table, how many gallons of blood were disgorged here? How many hearts honeycombed by hollow points were tossed nonchalantly into the garbage bin to my left?

The coroner drones on excitedly and I pay little attention, as it's the same cause of death as the last four Does. This John is in his thirties, good-looking, in tip-top shape, with strong shoulders, tight abs, and a nice husky cock.

I can't help but look. The coroner waits for me to peer back at him.

"Isn't that something?" he says with a probing smirk, raising his eyebrows toward the exposed dead genitals. I toss him a look that conveys my venom—*I'll snap your fucking neck if you don't look away from me.* He gets the point and continues his medical musings.

I refocus on the victim's chest, which bears the same foot-long crudely stitched incision as the four others who were on this table recently. Infected, swollen, oozing multicolored pus and bile. It's as if JD went in for a heart bypass at the world's worst hospital, with the world's most incompetent doc, had his skin scalpeled with a rusty steak knife, his breastbone rent asunder with a chainsaw, and was then stitched back up by handicapped kids using Pixy Stix and a ball of yarn.

Like the others, the cause of death was sepsis, a fatal blood poisoning stemming from his filthy, man-made chest cleft. The quack "surgeon" who performed this procedure must have worn gloves he recently used to scrub a subway toilet.

The coroner proceeds to open John up and finds nothing that can tell me why his chest was opened and crudely closed. Once again, there are no signs of organ harvesting, nothing out of place.

There's a serial killer loose in NYC.

It's my case. I have no leads.

4

The nightmare continues, always the same. The midnight me parade. The soulless hooded hosts. The NYC citizen victim choir crying for my help. The blood flood. I combat its corrosive effects with more Vicodin. Weed. A hit of whiskey. Occasional porn and thoughts of John Doe's pretty prick lead to attempts at masturbation, but I am uninspired and can't lose myself enough to achieve release. Orgasm eludes me as it has for several years now. My evenings often end with Google searches of my ex-husbands and their current fat-assed wives, before finally I throw myself a pity party attended by the children I aborted. I named them Raymond and Darlene. I cut them loose from this world so they wouldn't be subject to its unavoidable misery. I don't regret sparing them the pain of this existence. It was the most maternal thing I could've done.

This daily routine of dope and distractions keeps the helpless victims at bay behind that frosty wall. Nothing blocks them completely. They are always there. I keep running.

Two more bodies land on my desk. This killer works fast and efficiently. He's got a hearty appetite for whatever sick shit it is that he desperately desires. My mind races with theories—speculative, not one backed by any hard evidence. There could be more than one killer. It could be a woman. There were no signs of struggle . . . *Do the vics know their killer?*

The most recent John was a Wall Street broker and had a mild sex addiction. (Doesn't everyone?) We do some interviews with cohorts and colleagues. Once again, all leads to nothing.

The routine continues. The nightmare, the waking dream. The dulling agents that don't dull shit. Helpless New Yorkers hot on my ass, chasing me through thick and dark. They're wearing me down. I can't outrun them much longer. Where can I hide?

Then—a break.

5

She convulses spasmodically, her eyes rolled back in that clichéd found-footage-film possessed-by-a-demon way, bucking violently against arm and leg restraints.

She won't stop. She emits high-pitched squeals that seem to come from the depths of her soul. Her pain is infinite, incomprehensible. Sedation isn't working, not even a constant morphine drip. Something inside keeps her perpetually conscious and howling like a plump pig awaiting execution at a red-state slaughterhouse.

The doctors are baffled. I am baffled. I want her to stop screaming.

I need her to stop screaming. This is too much pain, too continuous and bottomless. The mere thought of it makes people weep openly around her.

She will not relent.

I was called here because this Jane Doe bears the same crudely stitched incision on her chest. It too was infected. Three days ago, someone dropped her off anonymously in front of the hospital and drove off abruptly.

She is the first living victim of this serial crime. She hasn't stopped convulsing in these demented paroxysms since she was brought in. Doctors have her on heavy antibiotics to fight the sepsis, with pads around her arms, legs, and head to prevent further damage from the convulsions and uncontrollable spasms.

The screeching wails don't subside. They peak and valley, dipping to low-wattage moans, then crescendo to a fever pitch, echoing through the hospital halls in waves.

She can't speak. The doctors attempt to communicate, but Jane's lost inside her infinite suffering, unreachable. What can cause such continuous pain and fear? How could this level of pain be sustained for so long, unabated? Is she caught in some timeless expanse of tortured existence from which she can't escape?

Jane keeps screaming. They gag her so as not to wake the other sicklies.

I pop Vicodin and watch her day and night. I can't leave. I can't take my eyes off this woman. She has become a spectacle. People come to see her thrash and rock and howl and moan. She's become famous within these walls and without. Priests want to perform exorcisms. I tell them to fuck off. Whoever did this is of our sick little Earth, not born on some otherworldly plane. Don't explain this shit away with nonsense.

The priests don't like my candor. Fuck 'em.

We cordon off her area, to keep the curious at bay. I have a front-row seat. Jane's screams wash over me like sheets of rain. I can't communicate with her so I fancy myself the Rosetta stone of wails, entering into them and trying to understand. Perhaps there are Morse code–like meanings in the ebb and flow of her screeches. Perhaps she's trying to tell us something in the varying ululations of agony. Something that would allow us to help her. I listen intently, trying to decode caterwauls. I find nothing. I have one fleeting insight on the fourth day of yelling. Just before I doze off, her moans valley out and a subtle whimper is emitted from her raw throat. It sounds like ecstasy.

Blood pours from her mouth on the fifth day. Her larynx has ruptured, spurting ruddy pus. Her vocal cords severely damaged from overuse and abuse, Jane continues screaming, but her voice box no longer yields sound. Her mouth agape, silent wails escaping her insides. She appears like a tortured silent film star, under whose face the word PAIN! would be etched in the celluloid matte.

These new muted screams seem louder than anything before.

I can't bring myself to leave. I am obsessed with her and her unrelenting pain. (Did the other victims experience this much pain before dying?) I stare at her for hours on end. Her ever-changing, twisted grimace, her contorted bruised, bucking body. I barely sleep in the white corridor, barely eat in the cafeteria. I can't leave her. I've been up for days with nothing but Vicodin and nicotine in my system. I don't want to miss anything. Late one night, I glimpse a harried nurse telling a doctor that Jane's not only sweating profusely but also excreting urine and feces uncontrollably.

"And there's an expulsion of fluid by the paraurethral ducts through and around her urethra."

The doctor stares at the nurse, utterly baffled.

"As if experiencing orgasm?" he replies.

The nurse pauses, her expression betraying deep confusion and shock, as if she's been contemplating this detail for some time. She then nods very slowly. The doctor evaluates this information as best he can.

"Her body is releasing everything—I wouldn't be surprised if she began bleeding out from every orifice. None of this makes any sense . . ."

I remain right outside her door, unable to abandon her. I catch a glimpse of myself in a nearby window, a ghostly cop apparition. I am a mirror image of Jane's sallow visage. Maybe that's what I want. Doctors become concerned with my health. I tell them to fuck off.

On the seventh day, the silent screaming and spasms cease and Jane falls into an unconscious state. I stand anxiously at the threshold of her room, waiting. The pain seems to have ended. I weep silently for her as she's been freed from whatever chains bound her. Her fever falls as the antibiotics work their magic. She suddenly seems serene, placid to the point of beatitude.

I'm jealous of her.

That night, I get light-headed from lack of sleep and food and all the other basic needs of human existence and I fall hard on the tiled hospital floor, passing out while staring at Jane, Jane of the Once Infinite Pain. It is the first time I've left her since this all began.

I wake up the next morning with an intravenous drip in my arm. My overworked and sweat-lathered captain hovers over me like a sick, bloated heavenly host, waiting to escort me up to some slightly better place. He informs me that in my absence Jane has regained consciousness. I move quickly and yank the intravenous needle out of my arm. Captain grabs my hand and stops me.

"I questioned her for three hours. She won't get her voice back for weeks, so she wrote everything down. Her name is Evelyn Harchee. A nurse at Lenox Hill Hospital. She says she doesn't remember anything."

"What?"

"Nothing. She doesn't know who cut her fucking chest open. Who dropped her off here. Or what's happened this last week. No memory of the screaming, the convulsing, nothing." He rolls his eyes. "She acted surprised."

"You don't believe her?"

"Maybe. Maybe not. I pushed her: *Someone almost killed you.* She held firm: *I don't remember anything.*"

He furrows his brow. He wants me to ask what's on his mind.

"Something's bothering you."

"Her fucking chest was cut wide open. She should be more shocked. Doctors say it's the morphine. I'm not sure."

"Let me talk to her." (I need to.)

He holds my wrist. "No."

I'm going to bite his fucking plump, moist head clean off.

"I want you to take sick leave. Get healthy. You're pushing too hard on this one."

I stare daggers at him.

"Are you fucking kidding me?"

He nods, acquiescing immediately in the face of resistance. He, like many others on this job, has given up the fight.

"Here's what's gonna happen. By the time Ms. Harchee's released, I'll be more than one hundred percent. I'm gonna follow her around, see what's up once she falls back into her routine. Your rotten old gut is telling you that she's hiding something. I trust your gut. She hasn't seen me yet. I could trail her, get close, see what she's not telling us."

He nods, liking my plan, or just too tired to disagree.

"Good. Let's hope you find something quick. Another body turned up this morning. Same chest incision. People want answers."

6

Evelyn Harchee lives alone, like me, on the Lower East Side. It's been several months since she was victimized, and she's back at work traveling uptown via the D train, carrying a used paperback (always a bio of some long-forgotten film star). She works the late shift as an emergency room nurse at one of the busiest hospitals in Manhattan. She's seen the shit and then some; her hands are regularly bathed in the bloody guts of the same victims I see on these dirty streets. Her mother and father are both deceased, both taken out by that cunt they call cancer. Her alcoholic yet sentimental brother lives in Michigan. She was an A student in nursing school and has since been a good citizen who pays her taxes on time and never jumps a turnstile.

Maybe Evelyn really doesn't remember anything. She keeps her head in the sand and plows ahead. Maybe she's another victim of Manhattan's midnight marauders, preying on the innocent. Maybe she's just one of the lucky ones who came out the other side still kicking.

Maybe there is nothing to find here. But I have to make sure. I have nothing else.

One thing about Evelyn gives me pause. Whether or not she remembers what happened, she carries the evidence of extreme trauma on her chest—a foot-long jagged scar, a constant reminder of the mysterious desecration of her body and soul—yet she doesn't exhibit any other signs of someone who's been violated: no jumpiness, no fear of what's around the corner or what's coming in her nightmares.

This draws me in for a closer examination.

We're sitting next to each other in Cafe Gitane on Jane Street, replete with rough stucco walls, mosaic tiles, and woven kilim rugs in a futile attempt to evoke some kind of Moroccan vibe (or so I surmise). I guess that's what hipsters deem cool nowadays, who the fuck knows? She's sipping a double espresso and reading a book on Jean Harlow. I did some research on Harlow the last few nights and quickly strike up a conversation about *The Beast of the City*, one of her forgotten films. Evelyn's intrigued that I've heard of it. I continue spouting some Google-learned nonsense about Harlow that really gets Evelyn jazzed up, and soon we're sitting at the same table, sipping and shooting the shit.

I say I'm a social worker in the city, assisting the forgotten folk of the five boroughs. It cuts through and snares Evelyn like a fishhook. We're kindred spirits now. I don't feel guilty about lying. I'm undercover, trying to save some fucking lives here.

We start meeting once a week to discuss Harlow and Garbo, as well as the people caught in this city's crossfire. We tell each other stories of the ones we could never forget. The heartbreakers and soultakers.

"I remember every single victim's name."

Her words resonate, reaching my damaged core. I am not lying, no longer undercover, when I respond.

"Same here. I remember every name. The date of every death. How they all died. Everything about them. They're my only family now."

Evelyn reaches out and touches my hand. Tears rise from human contact. I shudder, scared by my own emotion.

We continue meeting, more than once a week now. After several months of spilling our lonely, destroyed guts, Evelyn Harchee becomes a confidante, someone I can tell about the midnight parade and the blood rain that stains both my sleeping and waking worlds. She's no longer a lead, no longer someone who could provide answers. I've found nothing in her life that requires deeper investigation. She's a New York woman with a warrior's heart who wakes up every day alone in this sick city; a survivor of some mysterious evil, who, against my shitty judgment, has become a friend. I crossed a line here and I know it. Fuck the line. I leap over it. I need Evelyn. She admits she too has tried everything from Vicodin to Valium to keep the victims' cries for help as muted as she can.

One day I ask her, "You don't seem nearly as stressed as I do. How do you deal with it? The ones you can't help."

She stares hard at me, lost in a tugging thought. She has the need to say something but is unsure how. Finally, she smirks.

"I masturbate—a lot."

We hold a look and I am overcome by a vicious wave of envy. I open my mouth to explore her revelation, but Evelyn quickly laughs it off and goes into a bullshit diatribe about relieving stress with yuppie yoga and yerba maté tea. I zone out and so does she.

My thoughts linger on her original answer. My envy wanes, and a new thought emerges: Evelyn Harchee is hiding something. She has a secret.

7

The bodies are piling up in random locations all over the city: alleys, rooftops, dumpsters. Each one bloated and destroyed from the sepsis stemming from that man-made, infected rift, target center in their chest. The consensus opinion is that this can't be the work of one person. There is something else going on in my city, some greater evil, a murderous movement, a vast epidemic of death that has no origin or name—just the signature of some larger apparatus at work. There is never a lead, only an infected body left behind. We are not battling a lone evil entity, we are at war with something massive and coordinated, singular in its intent: death without detection. Rumors run rampant. Some saying that a gateway to hell has opened, releasing demon soldiers bent on extracting our souls through this filthy incision. I wish I had a better theory. I keep asking myself one question over and over:

What does this powerful group need from us, the weary citizens of NYC, who have no defense against them?

My late-night talks with Evelyn are no longer enough to keep my dreams at bay. The innocent horde is catching up with me, gaining on me. I'm running through the muck of a perpetually hazy existence, my mind fogged out by Vicodins. Desperate for a crack in the case, I break into Evelyn's apartment while she's working—violating her just like the unknown evil—hoping my instinct that she has a secret was correct.

I search everywhere. Every closet. Under beds. In each drawer. I rifle through all of Evelyn's personal accoutrements. I find nothing that speaks to the case, just the stuff, the shit, the things one accumulates over years on this planet—knickknacks, books, photos, et cetera, fucking et cetera. Nothing raises my eyebrows until I find a box under her bed full of sex toys, dildos of varying sizes, vibrators of varying textures, and other paraphernalia that I cannot easily identify. Rubbery nubbins peppered with spiked prongs, stainless-steel speculum-like spreaders, drainage tube contraptions that resemble excised bladders. I am not shocked; it's the size of the stash that draws me in. There are three large bins, each filled to the brim. I stare at it all, analyzing the various instruments of penetration and oscillation. Is this her secret? John Doe had a mild sex addiction; are these clues? Or maybe I am merely curious and envious of my friend's voracious self-pleasuring appetite. I conjure images of Evelyn using the tools intimately, lubricating and inserting steel and rubber into her misty vaginal gulley. I am trespassing. I am titillated. I immediately feel great shame and guilt. I force myself to fight against my own yearnings, against the opening chasms of desire. I need to refocus and find the police angle here, yet I can't see how this applies to my job. I must leave now. I see my own treachery and deception. I am overwhelmed and sickened by my subterfuge. I have deceived a friend, ogled her inner life, and I am tantalized.

I have also proven to myself and everyone else that I am inept and have no game against this grand evil at play in our city. The pressure is mounting. My knees are buckling under the weight of the city. New York demands answers. I have none.

The eleventh corpse is a sixteen-year-old woman (girl) named Theresa Lam. She is the youngest victim yet. She immediately joins the midnight crying choir, yearning for my help, hell-bent on my demise. I am sprinting now under the bright blazing signs of Broadway. Sweat gathers heavy on my brow as my lungs expand and constrict like a bellows. I have never run this fast. It's a dash to the finish: tired feet pounding the proverbial pavement, but the innocents are overtaking me. I want to help them but I can't. I have no help to give. I've let them down. LEAVE ME THE FUCK ALONE! The Vicodin are doing shit, nada, but I still swallow them like sour fucking Jelly Bellys.

I knock hard on Evelyn's door at three in the morning and fall into her arms, weeping. She holds me tight, comforting me as best she can, which is not enough this time.

I have lost the race. She sees defeat on my face. It's an expression she's seen before in her own mirror. She leans in close to me, whispering, "I can help you."

Something about how she said that makes me fight through the milky fog, trying to see her.

"You have to trust me. Complete trust. No questions. Can you do that?"

8

I'm blindfolded in the back of a van, sitting next to Evelyn, eyes also curtained. We are not being held against our will. We are here voluntarily, and the blindfolds are a precaution. Evelyn explains that the procedure we are about to witness is illegal and has led to several deaths around the city. She has no idea that I am the leading investigator of these deaths. Yet I haven't told anyone where I am going. I can't take any chances that we could be discovered. I am going down this bunny hole alone, hoping for answers, hoping to stop the pain, the immeasurable fucking pain.

Before we left she unbuttoned her shirt and unveiled the scar on her chest as if I had never seen it before. It's still healing, raw red and ragged. Yet Evelyn displays no shame. She caresses it in a way that sends a chill up my spine. She's fond of it, petting it as one would a purring, long-haired movie-villain lap cat. She explains that something was done to her—"on the inside"—that changed her very existence and made life bearable. She is taking me to witness this procedure.

She wants me to know that what I am about to see will be disturbing, but she can tell me from firsthand experience that it is the most beautiful thing that can happen to a person. She is of the enlightened.

"The great risk is worth the infinite reward . . ."

I can't see through the blindfold but my eyes are wide. We drive on. My mind on overdrive. Were my instincts only half right? Evelyn has a secret. But she's not speaking of some unfathomable evil perpetrating crimes that generate infinite pain and fear and death.

She speaks only of epiphany, revelation.

Where is she taking me?

9

I don't know where I am. I believe I am underground, the air bearing the sweet earthy stink of the subterranean. A male voice rises in the darkness, telling us to remove our blindfolds. The voice is warm, inviting. I do so and see a tall man standing in front of me wearing a ski mask. We are inside a small white room with chipped paint and exposed pipes. He hands us our own ski masks and instructs us to put them on. Evelyn nods. "It's okay. Don't be afraid." We put on our masks. We are faceless now. We are led down another corridor toward a door. The door is opened. We are led inside another room.

This room is much larger. The size of a gymnasium. There's a small stage in the center of it, on which a makeshift operating room has been assembled, replete with a bed, medical machinery, and a table laden with surgical tools (scalpel, suction, buzz saw, etc.). A small movie screen hangs next to the operating table, displaying nothing.

Ringing this stage are chairs filled with several dozen men and women wearing ski masks. Evelyn and I are seated in the back of this audience.

Powerful lights on high stands are set in the corners of this expansive room, lending bright white light, creating a shadowless interior. There is nothing that can't be seen under this hot fluorescence. There is no mystery here. Only our faces go unseen.

My heart pounds at jackhammer speed. Evelyn clutches my hand. "You'll be fine."

Another door opens. Four people enter and step up on the stage. Three of them wear surgical gowns and rubber gloves. The fourth, a very thin man, wears a hospital robe. Their faces are concealed by ski masks, like us. The slight man in the hospital robe takes center stage and addresses us, the enshrouded crowd.

"I am here voluntarily. I understand the risks of the procedure. No one is forcing me to do this."

He removes his robe, dropping it to the floor. He is nude, his genitals adangle. He lies on the table. I am shaking. I peer at Evelyn, who glows with anticipation. She is licking her lips with a moist tongue.

Two of the people wearing surgical gowns secure the nude patient to the bed with ropes and chains and straps. They are prepping needles, whispering to him, giving him injections and manipulating medical equipment around him. They are performing the duties of surgical nurses.

On stage, the third person, her long white-gray hair protruding from under her black mask, approaches the medical-instrument table and examines the buzz saw. She holds herself with authority. She is the leader of this small surgical troupe. I can only assume she's the surgeon.

The crowd around me is hauntingly quiet, and the silence of the arena is broken only by the clatter of medical equipment and the soft whispers of the nurses prepping the slender patient. Finally, after securing him to the bed, one of the nurses nods to the female surgeon. They are ready. The masked surgeon picks up the buzz saw and addresses the audience.

"We have all heard the stories of infection and subsequent death after the procedure. Not at this facility. We are not charlatans who act impetuously, using old, unsanitary equipment, or hacks who don't know what they're doing. We take proper precautions. Our equipment is clean and we've never had any fatalities. Yes, the risk is there—but the reward is unfathomable. Let us begin . . ."

I don't know what's happening, but I am trembling. Evelyn continues to clutch my hand.

"What's going on, Evelyn?"

She doesn't respond, eyes forward and riveted on the stage. What unfolds next is a series of concussive, mind-shattering images and sounds that shake the foundations of my existence. Surrounded by masked figures and intense phosphorescent coronas of light, I stare unblinking at the makeshift operating room. An image appears on the movie screen. It is an extremely close shot of the patient's bare chest, a live feed of the procedure for all to see.

On stage, the patient is hooked up to life-support systems, a gas mask administers some anesthetic, thrusting him into unconsciousness. The magisterial surgeon slices his center open with a scalpel, then takes the buzz saw to his exposed, bloodied chest plate. Spinning steel blades cut through hard bone, earsplitting grinding sounds resonate and throb in my brain—sounds I'll never forget, images I'll never shake, displayed in all their explicitly ensanguined details on the screen.

Something is happening to the crowd around me. Masked audience members begin to undulate; a collective sexual arousal unfolds inside this mysterious space. I can smell it as they undress (including Evelyn, who unbuttons her blouse and jeans), revealing ruby red scars on their chests. They grope at themselves and at one another—the air reeking with the marked crowd's sexual perspiration.

The surgeon proceeds to fold back skin and bone, exposing the patient's viscera.

"What are they doing to him?" I am growing frantic. "What's happening, Evelyn? What is going on?"

Evelyn finally speaks; moans and groans surround and accentuate each whispered breathy word, her hands having found their way down into her pants.

"They found something—doctors, somewhere, found it—inside of us—deep inside—in our chests, beneath our hearts—on the aorta—a muscle—a tissue—cartilage—I don't know what it's called. They discovered that this small area was an erogenous zone—the most powerful on or inside of us—by far. Hidden until now. It is so sensitive that it can bring sexual satisfaction we never knew existed. You can't believe what it feels like. Oh my god. You don't know. You won't believe. You need to understand. So hard to explain. It lasts for days. Days and days of the most intense, unimaginable cumming, over and over. This spot, this divine spot, can be accessed only through surgery—like this, like what's about to happen, and like I had, here. The procedure."

She grabs my hand, placing it inside her shirt, on her raised scar. Her heart is beating out of her chest. Her scar squirms under my hand like a tense, scared snake in a wrangler's sack—or perhaps I am imagining it. Perhaps it is just her heaving chest that makes it worm.

"It is the greatest pleasure—and once this spot is awakened—it never sleeps again—all future stimulation—fucking, licking, touching, sucking—gives you pleasure that lasts for days. You only need one procedure—it's my escape, I get lost, I never want to be found. It is what you need . . ."

I am speechless. Overwhelmed. Scared. This is not at all what I thought it was. I was so wrong. Evelyn and I look back on stage, at the screen. We watch as the surgeon's hands enter the open chest cavity. My mind is on overdrive, trying to assess—this is the patient's newly discovered sexual orifice, being penetrated by sinewy, latexed fingers—as the surgeon, his lover, will soon administer the arousing rhythm to his aortic pleasure spot.

People howl all around me. On the screen, the surgeon's gloved and bloodied hands are gliding past the beating, veiny heart, searching for the concealed erogenous zone.

She announces, "I've found it."

There's a collective gasp from the audience and a surge of manic activity. Masked, scarred people fondle one another, administering oral sex voraciously. The surgeon's hands penetrate deeper into this man's open chest cavity—his life source just millimeters from her fingers. She is massaging the thick-walled underbelly of the aorta—rhythmically, quickly, with sensual care and focused energy—when the slender patient suddenly bucks furiously on the table—consciousness crashing through the anesthetic. He awakens in a frenzied burst—wide eyes rolling back in his head, he emits a scream that I once perceived as pain. Now that I know what it is, I see its source: it's pleasure—immeasurable pleasure.

I was so fucking wrong.

My eyes are taking inventory of everything now—a sensory overload of medical equipment, blood, flesh, bone, the throbbing human heart, the surgeon fingering the aorta and moaning over the open wound. A rampage of smells and flesh and light all around me rises and the orchestra of sexual wails deafens me. The audience orgy reaches a fever pitch, mounds of nude bodies writhing as sexual union commences. The room has become a concertina of unveiled pudenda spilling mucosa that baptizes lips and fingers. On stage, the patient howls in abounding arousal. His sharp tongue darts from spit-glistened lips like a reptile's, trying to lick something, anything.

It's all happening fast now.

Everything is exposed here, in this arena. The human body is on display in all its manifestations—the exterior and interior. There are no longer barriers, as skin and bone have been unsealed, revealing the mucus-membraned penetralia in all its glory and ugliness—all its mysteries unveiled on that screen and under these bright lights. There is no distinction between the repulsive and the seductive here—dripping blood, sawed bone, exposed cartilage and rubbery tendon, mingling with the curvature and contours of breasts, hips, bare skin, and moistening genitalia.

I jump up, eyes lanced by light, mind blown to pieces. I am running, falling over chairs, but no one pays attention. I push through doors and sprint up stairs until I find an exit. Empty warehouses surround me and I am still running, my underwear and jeans soaked through; I have never run faster. I am escaping.

I must call this in. I could stop the murders right here and now. I could crack this fucking case wide open.

But I am lost inside these screams, these screams of pleasure. I still hear them echoing through my mind and reverberating like aftershocks in the asphalt.

They envelop me wholly.

I am gone.

10

There are two new files on my desk. Two dead bodies, chests riddled with sepsis, have been found in the last forty-eight hours. I pretend to read the files. It's been a week since I witnessed the procedure. I can think of nothing else now.

I have told no one.

The midnight choir still sings and beckons, the victims still give chase.

I sit unmoving, incapacitated by everything and everyone.

11

I lie here—hands bound, legs restrained, hooked up to rudimentary machines that barely hold my life, these tubes, these things. I can see my insides—my ventricles, my pulmonary veins, my new aortic genitalia. Places we should never lay our eyes on—our innermost secrets—exposed for all to see. I am naked.

I am bucking and screaming like a freak banshee in a sea of pure pleasure, deep below the surface of my once torturous existence, here transformed into bliss. They were right. They were right. They were so right. I want to stay, untouched by anyone or anything. Let me stay. Let me stay here. Let me stay here forever, cumming over and over and over again.

There is only chaos around me. A flurry of furious movement. The orgiastic audience runs wild as a slew of cops give chase. I was followed here. My brethren sensed I was hiding something. Like me, once, they were only partially right. My arthritic captain hovers over me, dumbfounded. His shock is not that he can see me wholly in and out. His shock is that I am howling incomprehensibly and convulsing spasmodically as if possessed by a rabid demon seeking escape from my soul. He still believes, as I did, that I am moaning in fear, in pain.

He has no idea.

I may die from this procedure. Infection will most likely take hold deep inside me and tear me to shreds. But I simply don't give a fuck. About. Anything. Anyone. Anymore. The midnight parade's been canceled. The citizen choir is muted, no longer crying for my help. For the first time in forever, I am not being chased.

I scream. I scream. I scream because it feels so fucking good.

Permissions Acknowledgments

About the Contributors

LES BOHEM has written *A Nightmare on Elm Street Part 5*, *The Horror Show*, *Twenty Bucks*, *Daylight*, *Dante's Peak*, *The Alamo*, *Kid*, *Nowhere to Run*, *The Darkest Hour*, and the miniseries *Taken*, which he wrote and executive-produced with Steven Spielberg, and for which he won an Emmy Award. He's had songs recorded by Emmylou Harris, Randy Travis, Freddy Fender, Steve Gillette, Johnette Napolitano (of Concrete Blonde), and Alvin (of the Chipmunks).

C. ROBERT CARGILL is the cowriter of the *Sinister* films, and the author of the books *Dreams and Shadows* and *Queen of the Dark Things*. He wrote for *Ain't It Cool News* for nearly a decade under the pseudonym Massawyrm, served as a staff writer for Film.com and Hollywood.com, and appeared as the animated character Carlyle on Spill.com. He lives and works in Austin, Texas.

JAMES DEMONACO is the writer/director of the feature films *Staten Island, New York*, *The Purge*, and *The Purge: Anarchy*. He also wrote the films *The Negotiator* and *Assault on Precinct 13*, as well as created and executive-produced the cable TV miniseries *The Kill Point* starring John Leguizamo. DeMonaco lives in both Staten Island and Manhattan with his wife and daughter. He is an avid New York Yankees fan.

CHRISTOPHER DENHAM is the writer/director of *Home Movie* (IFC Films) and *Preservation* (The Orchard) and several Off-Broadway plays. As an actor, his film credits include *Argo, Sound of My Voice, Shutter Island, The Bay, Charlie Wilson's War, Forgetting the Girl*, and WGN America's critically acclaimed television series *Manhattan*. He lives in New York.

SCOTT DERRICKSON is a screenwriter and director known for *The Exorcism of Emily Rose, Sinister, Deliver Us from Evil*, and Marvel Studios' upcoming *Doctor Strange*. He lives in Los Angeles.

STEVE FABER is an American film and television writer/producer whose credits include *Wedding Crashers* and *We're the Millers*. He has written and produced many television projects (including *Married with Children*) as well as numerous pilots at various studios. In addition to a great deal of public speaking on matters regarding entertainment, politics, and culture, he also contributes to *The Huffington Post* with his acclaimed political blog titled *Washingwood*. He does not frighten easily.

GEORGE GALLO is a veteran Hollywood screenwriter and director, writing such classics as *Midnight Run* and *Bad Boys*. He is also a renowned artist, painting in the style of the American Impressionists, and is coauthor of the book *Impressionist Painting for the Landscape*. His work hangs in public and private collections around the world.

ETHAN HAWKE is an accomplished actor, screenwriter, film director, theater director, and novelist. He has appeared in more than forty films, including *Dead Poets Society, Before Sunrise, Before Sunset, Before Midnight, Reality Bites, Gattaca, Training Day*, and *Boyhood*. His numerous stage credits include, as an actor: *The Coast of Utopia, Henry IV, The Winter's Tale, The Cherry Orchard, Hurlyburly, Macbeth*, and *Blood from a Stone* (2011 Obie Award winner); and as a director: *Things We Want, A Lie of the Mind*, and *Clive*. He has written two novels, *The Hottest State* and *Ash Wednesday*, the former of which he adapted and directed for film. He has also been nominated for a Tony Award, Academy Awards for both acting and writing, and Drama Desk Awards for both acting and directing.

WILLIAM JOSELYN has had a lifelong love of dark tales. He lives, dreams, and writes in Michigan.

SARAH LANGAN is the author of the novels *The Keeper*, *This Missing*, and *Audrey's Door*. She's at work on her fourth novel, *The Clinic*, and lives in Brooklyn with her husband, J. T. Petty, and their two daughters. She thinks twins are walking metaphors. Particular thanks to first readers Lee Thomas, the hubby, Robert Bloom, and Nick Simonds.

NISSAR MODI was born and raised in London, England, and moved to the United States to attend film school at the University of Southern California. He wrote the screenplay to the film adaptation of Robert O'Brien's classic novel *Z for Zachariah*, which will be released in 2015 by Lionsgate/Roadside Attractions.

MARK NEVELDINE was born in Watertown, New York. After graduating from Hobart College, he worked as an actor, writer, and director in New York City. Neveldine hit the feature scene when he and Brian Taylor wrote, directed, and camera-operated *Crank*, starring Jason Statham. He went on to write and direct *Crank: High Voltage*, *Gamer*, *Ghost Rider 2*, and *The Vatican Tapes*. He lives with his wife and two children in the middle of nowhere.

MICHAEL OLSON is the author of the novel *Strange Flesh*. Before that he was a professor at NYU studying virtual environments. He now lives in Los Angeles and is working on several projects for TV and film.

ELI ROTH is an award-winning filmmaker and actor whose works include *Cabin Fever*, *Hostel*, *The Green Inferno*, and *Knock Knock*. In front of the camera Roth is best known for his portrayal of Donny Donowitz, "The Bear Jew," in Quentin Tarantino's *Inglourious Basterds*. He lives in Los Angeles with his wife, Lorenza, and their dog, Monkey.

JEREMY SLATER is a screenwriter residing in Burbank, California. His credits include Relativity's *The Lazarus Effect* and Fox's new update of *Fantastic Four*. He is currently adapting *Fables* and *Death Note* for Warner Bros.

DANA STEVENS's screenwriting credits include *Safe Haven, City of Angels, For Love of the Game, Blink,* and *Life or Something Like It.* In television, she was the creator and executive producer of *Reckless,* a sexy legal drama currently available on Netflix, and *What About Brian,* an ABC series produced by J. J. Abrams.

SCOTT STEWART is a writer, director, and producer whose credits include the feature films *Dark Skies, Legion,* and *Priest* and the television series *Dominion* and *Defiance.* In a prior life, Stewart was an accomplished visual effects artist with credits including *Ironman, Hellboy, Pirates of the Caribbean: Dead Man's Chest, Blade Runner: The Final Cut,* and *Sin City.* He lives in Los Angeles.

SIMON KURT UNSWORTH is the author of *The Devil's Detective.* He is the author of many short stories, including the collection *Quiet Houses.* He was born in Manchester and now lives in a farmhouse in Cumbria with his wife, the writer Rosie Seymour, in the United Kingdom.